The Wonder of You

Center Point
Large Print

Also by Susan May Warren and available from Center Point Large Print:

The Shadow of Your Smile

The Deep Haven Novels
My Foolish Heart
You Don't Know Me

The Christiansen Family Novels
Take a Chance on Me
It Had to Be You
When I Fall in Love
Always on My Mind

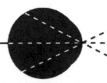

This Large Print Book carries the Seal of Approval of N.A.V.H.

The Wonder
of You

A Christiansen Family Novel

SUSAN MAY WARREN

CENTER POINT LARGE PRINT
THORNDIKE, MAINE

This Center Point Large Print edition
is published in the year 2015 by arrangement with
Tyndale House Publishers, Inc.

Scripture taken from the Holy Bible,
New International Version,® NIV.® Copyright © 1973,
1978, 1984, 2011 by Biblica, Inc.® Used by permission.
All rights reserved worldwide.

The Wonder of You is a work of fiction. Where real people,
events, establishments, organizations, or locales appear,
they are used fictitiously. All other elements of the novel
are drawn from the author's imagination.

The text of this Large Print edition is unabridged.
In other aspects, this book may vary from the original edition.
Printed in the United States of America on permanent paper.
Set in 16-point Times New Roman type.

ISBN: 978-1-62899-689-0

Library of Congress Cataloging-in-Publication Data

Warren, Susan May, 1966–
The wonder of you : a Christiansen family novel / Susan May Warren.
— Center Point Large Print edition.
pages cm
Summary: "Mortified after her semester abroad is cut short, Amelia
Christiansen returns to Deep Haven, certain she isn't brave enough for
the adventures she's dreamed of. The last thing she expects is for the
man who broke her heart to cross the Atlantic and beg forgiveness"—
Provided by publisher.
ISBN 978-1-62899-689-0 (library binding : alk. paper)
1. Large type books. I. Title.
PS3623.A865W66 2015b
813'.6—dc23

2015020458

For Your glory, Lord

Acknowledgments

I'M ALWAYS AMAZED and grateful for the team of people the Lord surrounds me with as I write a novel. I'm deeply grateful to so many in helping me craft this story. In particular, I need to thank the following people:

My writing partner, Rachel Hauck, for her ability to help me sort out the real story from the clutter of ideas in my mind.

The amazing David Warren, who is one of the best story crafters I know. Thank you for your brutal honesty, your brainstorming skills, and the fact that you won't let me write unrealistic men. Thank you for helping me keep it real.

Sarah Erredge, for helping me grasp Amelia—from her photography skills to her experience in Prague to thinking through the man who would capture her heart: the hometown boy or the exotic foreigner. We all know which one you chose!

My lumberjack-tastic sons Peter and Noah Warren, who wear flannel like nobody's business and make being bearded woodsmen from the north cool.

Andrew Warren, my own exotic prince who swept me up and took me back to foreign lands. Here's to more adventures!

Steve Laube, my fabulous agent and friend,

who always has the right word at the right time.

Karen Watson and Stephanie Broene, who work so hard to help me get it right. Thank you!

Sarah Mason, my talented editor. You bring your A game every time, and I'm so grateful.

The Lord of my life, who calls me to be brave and walk into the unknown, amazing future. I am always awed by the wonder of You.

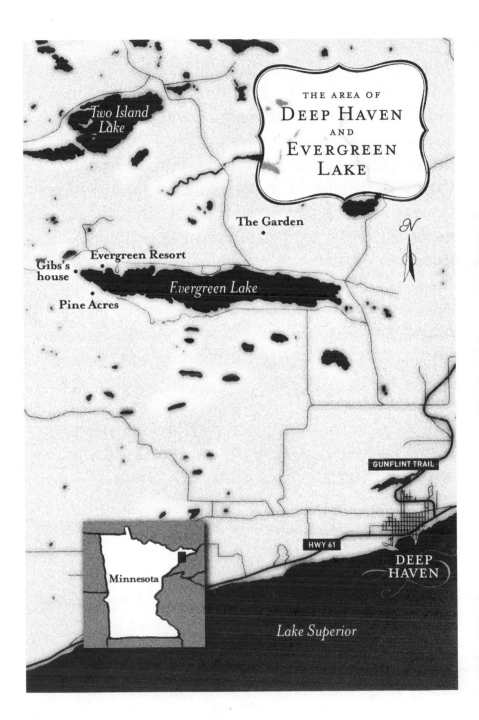

THE AREA OF
DEEP HAVEN
AND
EVERGREEN
LAKE

Two Island Lake

The Garden

N

Evergreen Resort

Gibs's house

Evergreen Lake

Pine Acres

GUNFLINT TRAIL

HWY 61

DEEP HAVEN

Minnesota

Lake Superior

My dearest Amelia,

I suspect, should you ever read this, it might be on the back of an elephant, while venturing through the jungles of India. Or perhaps in a dugout canoe, paddling down the Amazon. Or even, most likely, while capturing the sunrise over the grasslands of some African country.

For I know God has great plans for you, my beautiful youngest, the one who has always looked beyond the horizon. And inside you is the courage to reach for that horizon. You, more than any of the others, possess an independent spirit to drive you out of the family embrace and into the world. I have no doubt that comes from your father, who always nursed an adventure-seeking spirit. I hope it is also because of your confidence in our love for you, the surety that you can always come home. But I pray this independent spirit quickens inside enough to push you past your own limited vision to see the one God has for you.

I know the challenge of the youngest is always to discover her own voice in the chorus. Yes, Amelia, you are the culmination of all the wonderful traits I see in your siblings—Darek's courage, Eden's loyalty,

Grace's resourcefulness, Casper's thirst for treasure, and Owen's singular, focused passion. You are my cherry on top of the sundae.

And yet you are also so much more. You are also unique in the vision God has given you to see the world through His lens. You are beautiful and patient, giving and kind, and the one who helps us see ourselves the way God does—unique and cherished, despite our blemishes. This gift is precious and desperately needed in our world.

Amelia, you help us see others.

I pray that God will also help you see yourself.

It is so easy to get trapped inside the picture we create for ourselves. As the youngest, you've been sheltered, over-protected, and constantly advised. If they could, your siblings would arrange for your future, leaving nothing to chance.

Your challenge is to look past the view others choose for you, look past even your own limited perspective, and see the view your heavenly Father has chosen for you. Lay hold of the vision and don't let go. Do not settle for the expected, the known, only because you can't see past today's focal point to all God has for you.

There is more left to discover of Amelia

Christiansen, and it will be, to use your word, epic. Break free of your own expectations and see what vista awaits.

Know that you carry my heart with you wherever you go and that I will always be here, waiting to welcome you home, my brilliant, beautiful daughter.

Your mother

Chapter 1

THE DANGER OF LIVING in a big family was that to do anything of notice, a person had to go big or go home.

Amelia had leaped, hoping to grab ahold of her dreams, show every one of her five siblings that she was just as amazing as the rest of them.

The whole thing wouldn't have been so epically tragic if Amelia hadn't harbored such high hopes.

A year in Prague, chasing her vision of becoming a professional photographer.

Go big . . . or go home.

Amelia moved to take a wider-angle shot of the couple. Sabine, her lush brown hair up in a loopy, messy bun, was caught inside the embrace of her groom, Kirby Hueston, swaying to the Blue Monkeys' version of "(I've Had) The Time of My Life." The song lured couples onto the tiled dance floor, under the twinkling lights strewn from the faux pine trees that framed the reception and pool area of the Mad Moose Motel.

A rock-edged garden area brimming with early blooming violets and irises, combined with the aroma of potted hydrangeas on the tables and the heady smell of the roses twining up the wedding arch, managed to conjure the necessary magic for a north-shore-in-early-May wedding despite the chlorinated air. More, tonight the heavens were cooperating, the stars sprinkling the glass canopy with hopes of tomorrow, the moon a perfect halo of divine approval.

The viewfinder framed a life Amelia Christiansen knew she should want. But after the crash and burn in Prague, and her hightail back to the one-sled-dog town of Deep Haven, Minnesota, she wasn't sure *what* she'd describe as her own personal happily ever after.

Adventure? True love?

Maybe just a good reason to get out of bed in the morning. One that didn't include big brother Darek's list of housekeeping to-dos at the Evergreen Resort, thank you.

At least she'd landed a gig, albeit free, taking pictures at her friend Sabine's wedding.

She adjusted the focus on her Canon EOS Rebel, taking a number of burst shots as Kirby twirled Sabine out and back in. She checked the shots, increased the shutter speed, and climbed on a chair, just in case one of the dancers decided to cut into her frame.

"For crying out loud, Amelia, you act like you're stalking Sasquatch. It's a wedding, not a show on Animal Planet." The voice came from behind her, a husky, familiar tenor that could still send ripples through her entire body.

She held out her hand, not taking her eye from

the viewfinder, and pinched her fingers together. "Zip it, Seth. I'm working."

"You're not working—you're not even the official photographer."

She glanced at him. "One does not need to be paid to do a good job. Sabine asked me to take photos, and one of these is going to be—oh, shoot!"

Kirby swung his bride down into a dip as the song ended. And it would have been exactly the breathtaking shot she'd waited for—Sabine's head thrown back, her dark hair trickling over Kirby's arms, a smile playing on her lips: the intoxicating surrender of a woman in love.

"I missed it." Amelia snapped one last smooch between Kirby and Sabine before climbing off the chair, Seth's hand at her elbow.

"I've no doubt you have about three thousand good shots from tonight. Now, please put the camera down and dance with your boyfriend."

He smiled at the word, and Amelia didn't have the heart to contradict him. Later she'd remind him that she hadn't agreed to officially date again. Just because she'd failed in her first post–high school launch attempt didn't mean she'd returned to pick up where they left off.

Except Seth's voice could still elicit the sweet tingle of heat inside her, just like it did when he used to find her after a victorious football game, his blond hair wet from his shower, smelling of Axe and turning her world just a little smoky.

He'd always slicked up well off the field also, tonight wearing a white dress shirt, open at the neck, the fabric tight against his frame, honed by hours of cutting wood at his father's lumber mill. He wore a pair of black dress pants, slim at his waist, creased to a fine edge as if he might be trying to prove something.

His hair brushed his shoulders, begging to be tangled with her fingers, and his brown eyes fixed on her so long it should stop her heart in her chest.

It occurred to her that maybe God had returned her to Deep Haven after a semester abroad because she never should have left.

Seth's voice turned soft as his hand closed on the camera and urged it out of her grip. "Please put the camera down, and let's dance."

On the dance floor, Kyle Hueston, drummer for the Blue Monkeys, took the mic. He'd shucked off his gray vest, wore his black shirt rolled up at the forearms, and beamed at Kirby and Sabine, then the audience. "You might not know it, but my little bro is an Elvis junkie. Kirbs, this one's for you and your girl."

Behind Kyle, his wife, Emma, strummed the introductory chords.

His low baritone began, " 'Wise men say only fools rush in . . .' "

Amelia wanted to wince at the way the lyrics

18

rubbed along her conscience, hitting her choices from the past year and, most recently, the blowup at the Christiansen family home. But Seth seemed to not notice as he unwound the camera strap from her neck. "I've been waiting all night to have you to myself," he said.

"Seth—"

He set the camera on a folding chair and took her hand. "It'll be there when you get back."

She couldn't exactly protest with the town watching. Besides, Deep Haven expected them to dance. Probably thought they'd be next.

A thought Seth confirmed as he took her into his arms. "Maybe we should start thinking about our own wedding playlist."

Oh. Boy.

He wrapped one big linebacker hand behind her; the other he held out for her to grasp.

"Since when did you learn how to do more than sway?" she said as she took it.

"I may not be as fancy as that jerk from Europe, but I am house-trained."

Yep, clearly something to prove. She couldn't be sure where he'd gotten his information about her recent unexpected guest, but someone—maybe even a traitor from the house of Christiansen—had spilled her secrets, probably in an attempt to keep her from repeating her mistakes. She'd hunt down her brothers and pry out the truth at the next family campfire.

Now she met Seth's eyes and recognized hurt behind the veneer of redneck bravado. "Roark is gone, and he's not coming back."

There, she said it out loud.

Despite the echo of Roark's words, rising up to haunt her. *We belong together! Please forgive me.*

"Mr. James Bond had better not show his face in Deep Haven again," Seth said, "or he'll get a taste of what—"

"Seth, stop." She pressed her hand against his lips.

He made a face. "Sorry. You're right."

Amelia leaned into him, winding her arm around his shoulder, laying her head on his chest. The familiarity of being in his broad, safe embrace caught her up, spoke to her. Maybe she needed this, needed Seth. The boy she'd shared her first kiss with. Shared dreams and unraveled her fears with as they lounged under the stars on a beach blanket of stones, the great Lake Superior lapping at their feet.

Always, until she left for Prague, those dreams had included each other.

"Amelia! There you are!" The voice was too high, too loud, to be sober—and of course it belonged to Vivien Calhoun. "Hey, Seth," she said, then took Amelia's hand. "C'mon, I got something to show you!"

"Viv, we're dancing here," Seth said, a growl in the back of his throat.

"Oh, whatever, Seth—deal. C'mon, Ames." Vivien tugged her across the dance floor, leaving the hint of something stronger than wine in her wake. Amelia threw an I'll-be-right-back glance over her shoulder to Seth.

Or maybe she wouldn't because Vivie pulled her across the reception area—Amelia breaking free long enough to grab her camera—then through the lobby and outside to the parking lot, where the sky shimmered with starlight, the night air sweet with the buds of spring. "What?"

"You'll see!" Vivie wore her sable hair long and loose in waves, and if possible, she'd lost even more weight since jetting off to an NYC film school, her body rail-thin in a light-blue baby doll dress, her legs as long as the Empire State Building in wedge platform sandals.

She looked like the movie star she longed to become.

At least one of Amelia's high school friends had reached for her dreams—and not fallen on her face.

Except Sabine, the bride, *also* had her dreams safely in her grip, finally tying the knot with the boy she'd loved since sixth grade, even if he didn't figure it out until last summer.

Vivie wove her way through a tangle of cars, then out onto the long drive of the motel, where more cars edged the grass. "Look what I'm driving!"

She pointed, even as Amelia stopped, shot her a look. "No, really?"

"That's right, bay-bee, a vintage, 1967, cherry-red convertible Mustang." Vivien slid onto the hood and posed like she might be Bettie Page. "And it's all mine. Sorta."

Amelia ran her hand across the hood, glanced at Ree Zimmerman, sitting in the passenger seat. "Sorta?"

Ree, an aspiring journalist, wedged in freelance hours at the Deep Haven paper between helping her parents with the twenty-four-room Mad Moose Motel. Tonight her short blonde hair was held back with a gold headband, and she wore a faded jean jacket over her lime-green dress. She'd pulled off her sandals, now held them in her grip, dangling out the window. Amelia should have grabbed her sweater to put over her own coral swing dress.

"How long have you known about this?" she said to Ree.

"Just now. She pulled up, and . . . I thought I'd better come along quietly." Ree made a face. "Get in the driver's seat. I grabbed the keys." She dangled them from her hand.

"Hey, those are mine!" Vivien said, sliding off the hood and leaning over to swipe them. She missed, and Amelia opened the driver's door, pulled down the front seat.

"Get in, Vivie. We'll pretend it's red carpet night."

Vivien climbed in, sitting high on the back as if she were Miss Minnesota. "So? It's a wicked ride, right?"

Amelia got behind the wheel, ran her hand over the red leather seat, the shiny red steering wheel, the polished chrome radio knobs. "Is it really yours?"

"It is for now. My new boyfriend let me borrow it."

"Your *boyfriend* let you borrow his vintage Mustang?" Ree said. "Sheesh, Viv, who is this guy?" She shot a look at Amelia.

Amelia could read the question on her face. *What did he get in return?*

Or maybe she just heard it inside. Amelia had managed all of two e-mails to Vivien since hopping the pond to Prague and back. She simply couldn't face her own failures against the shiny victories of her girlfriends. But maybe she shouldn't count Vivie's new role as a victory.

"Just a producer friend." Vivien said it like they all inhabited that world. "But . . ." She slid down onto the backseat. "Let's talk about Rrrrrroark." She enunciated the name with a long roll of her *r*'s. "Dahling, a Brit? Was he royal?"

Just when Amelia thought she'd shaken off the specter of her mistakes for the evening. "How about we talk about something—"

"Oh no, honey," Ree, the betrayer, said. "We want all the juicy details. I didn't even know

Putnam County Library

there was a scandal until a couple weeks ago, after the dustup with your brothers."

"It wasn't a scandal—" Amelia started.

"Not true," Vivie said. "Everyone's talking about the hot souvenir Amelia Christiansen brought back from her trip to Prague."

"He wasn't—"

"Hot?" Ree turned to Vivie. "For the record, he could melt a girl from fifty feet. Tall—he's probably six two—with dark curly hair and blue eyes brimming with mystery. Very MI6, superspy with a nice stack of muscles."

"Ree!"

"He went swimming. I looked. Shoot me. But oh, the shoulders! I'm sorry, but Seth is all brawn. This one is . . . chiseled."

"Stop."

"And did I mention the accent? He was all 'fancy' this and 'rubbish' that, with a few *blimey*s and *chips* and *horses for courses* thrown in. I'd work the front desk just in hopes he'd come down and ask for more towels."

"He stayed here?" Vivien said, leaning forward between the seats.

"Where else was he going to stay?" Ree said. "My parents offered him a room half-off after the Christiansens practically tarred and feathered him and rode him off their property on a rail."

"Oh, we did not," Amelia said.

Well, they sorta had. Or her brothers had. Got in

24

his face, yelling—Casper just might have hit him had her father not intervened. And more yelling outside in the driveway before he finally drove away.

The memory elicited a groan that made Amelia bury her face in her hands.

"How bad was it really, Ames?" Vivie said.

Amelia leaned back, stared at the stars overhead. More Elvis—"Love Me Tender"—drifted out from the reception. Maybe Seth was on his way to rescue her.

What she really wanted to do, though, was put the car in gear and drive away, flee the humiliation—not to mention her future, the one she saw before her like handwriting on the wall.

Not quite the life she'd dreamed of when she jetted off to Europe last fall.

"Start with where you two met. Was it romantic?"

The Charles Bridge at sunset, turning the Vltava River to deep crimson; the sky mottled with tufts of light purple, maroon, and burnt orange.

The smell of roasted pork and cinnamon trdelník*, the taste of adventure rich and full as she caught the laughter of nearby lovebirds tossing wishes from the bridge.*

"It was Prague. Everything in Prague is romantic."

Ree glanced at Vivie. "And this is why I want to escape Deep Haven and see the world. I'd like to meet a handsome man in some exotic location."

"What, you don't think covering the doings of the city council for the *Deep Haven Herald* is exotic enough?" Vivie said.

Ree ignored her. "What did he say—first thing—when he met you?"

"That wishes come true if you touch the cross of St. John of Nepomuk."

The voice, low, sharp with accent, belonged to a man dressed in a pair of crisp jeans, a gray printed T-shirt, and a blue cardigan—open in the wind—that only accentuated the mottled blue of his eyes. He wore a messenger bag over his shoulder, held a camera . . .

"Oh, Amelia . . ." Vivien rested her head on the seat, sighing. "What happened?"

What happened? Was it possible to look at someone and just . . . know? To see your own future in his eyes? Probably not. Amelia blamed the magic, the adventure, of Prague.

"He . . ." *Made me feel brave. Smart. Beautiful. . . . Foolish.*

"I heard he was older than you. Hmmm," Vivie said.

"Five years, but it didn't seem that way. He was just another photography student in my group. Then, by the time I found out, it didn't matter. I met him first on the Charles Bridge, then in Old Town Square; then we started working on assignments together. Anyway, of course he was charming, and I read way too much into it."

"Oh no." This from Ree.

"It was after we'd spent Christmas together on the same trip to Italy, Switzerland, and France that I thought we were . . . Well, I thought I loved him. Then, one day, after we got back to Prague, I was walking to class and saw him on the Charles Bridge, in the arms of another woman."

"Jerk!" Ree again.

"We had a big fight. I was so angry, I refused to talk to him, even after he claimed they were just friends. And then he left the country. Vanished. No explanation, nothing. And I realized I had read way more into the relationship than he had. In fact . . . that's when I put it together. He didn't have a job. He spent money like he didn't care where it came from, and he knew food, art, wine, and—"

"Women! Oh, Ames, you fell for a European playboy!" Vivie said, clamping her hand over her mouth, eyes wide. "Girl, I didn't know you had it in you!"

Amelia winced but didn't contradict her. Yes, that was the worst part—feeling like just another conquest by a man she thought she could love. Not that it went that far, but the realization horrified her.

Humiliated her.

"No wonder your father dragged you home," Ree said.

"He didn't exactly drag me home. He and Mom

came to visit for Valentine's Day, and by then Prague had lost its luster." Or rather, her bravado had vanished and left behind a girl she didn't know. Afraid. Unseated.

"And two months later, Roark has the nerve to show up at your house and ask your forgiveness?" Ree said. "Okay, your brothers are heroes in my book for chasing him away."

"Wow, you dated a European playboy." Vivie seemed caught on some version of Roark that Amelia knew needed amending. "Did you kiss him?"

"Once. On New Year's Eve."

"That's it? A New Year's Eve kiss?"

Even Ree shook her head.

"See, maybe we weren't even dating. Maybe I just made it up in my head. Maybe I overreacted to the whole thing. And now I feel even more foolish. Thankfully, it's over. He's gone, and I can just . . . start again." Except, three months after returning home, she still struggled to get her footing. She'd forfeited the rest of her one-year photography course by fleeing home—too late, sadly, to enroll in another program. And maybe she didn't even want to.

Maybe this simply proved she wasn't the adventurer she hoped to be.

"But wait—Roark came all the way over here. Faced your *family*. Playboy or not, that sounds contrite to me," Vivien said. "Even romantic.

Apparently you made more of an impact on him than you thought. Please tell me you forgave him."

Amelia leaned back, lost herself in the swirl of stars. So much light against the darkness. So many what-ifs.

Like, what if she had forgiven him? What if she had believed him when he said he hadn't meant to hurt her? What if she'd held on to her courage, stayed in Prague?

She might be having a summer of adventure in Italy instead of sitting in a parked Mustang, trapped between a Prius and a Chevy Silverado.

"How was she supposed to forgive him with a wall of Christiansen brothers standing there, glaring at him?" Ree said.

"I'd do just about anything to have even one of the Christiansen brothers glance in my general direction," Vivie said. "But that's a dream that'll never happen. So—did they really run him off the property?"

Amelia sighed, remembering Casper's disbelief, then Darek's suggestion that Roark leave. Not to mention the sudden hovering of her brother-in-law, Jace, and her sister Grace's fiancé, Max. As if they'd adopted the family role to meddle in her life.

"It wouldn't have been so bad, maybe, if Casper hadn't spilled to the family just how much he hurt me, adding in a few of his own suggestions about Roark being a European playboy. Roark didn't contradict them, and my dad asked him to leave, and he . . . he just stood there. As if he wasn't leaving."

"Oh, it's so *West Side Story*!" Ree said.

"No, it was scary! It got very silent, and my father took one of those deep breaths, and then he made the face."

"The one he made when he found us playing spin the bottle in the basement with Seth and the guys?" Ree said.

"Mmm-hmm."

"Oh, I remember that face," Vivien said. "No wonder Roark ran."

"That's the thing—he didn't exactly run. My brothers pushed him out into the yard, and even after he drove away, he stuck around, calling—"

"And you never talked to him?" Vivie shook her head.

Amelia closed her eyes, and suddenly the sight of Roark, dressed in his oxford and suit coat, every inch the dashing European hero, except for the contrite expression, shuffled through her mind. "I . . . should have. I wanted to . . . but . . ."

"But he'd already humiliated you once. You didn't want to give him the chance again," Vivien said, the sound of experience in her tone.

"Something like that." More, it had to do with the fact that she couldn't bear to repeat her mistakes, lead with her foolish heart. Disappoint herself again.

"So, after a week, he finally checked out," Ree finished for her.

The thought turned Amelia's throat raw all over again.

"Oh, Ames," Vivien said, wrapping a hand over Amelia's shoulder. "Are you okay?"

She brushed her cheek, found it moist. Took a breath. "Yeah. It's more than the fact that he hurt me. We're from different worlds, and I see that clearly now. I'm a small-town girl from Deep Haven. And maybe that's all I'll ever be. Maybe this is the life I'm supposed to have. Besides, it's not like he's going to jet over here, settle down in one of the cabins, and become a lumberjack. Even if he isn't some kind of rich playboy, he clearly has a big life—a European life—and we don't belong together. Not really, despite the fairy tale I bought into last year."

The question of who she belonged with went unasked. Already answered.

Because the *who* suddenly appeared, ambling down the driveway, his hands tucked into his pockets, a casual mass of muscle that could probably wrestle down a moose. Seth Turnquist, high school sweetheart, defensive end for the Deep Haven Huskies, and the man most likely to meet the approval of the Christiansen mob.

"So what are you going to do now? Stay in Deep Haven? Go to college?"

31

"I don't know, okay? I always thought I was . . . well, the adventurer of the family. I think maybe I ventured too far." Amelia turned to Ree. "I've got an interview at the paper, so maybe I can get on as a freelance photographer. Maybe get more wedding gigs and senior photos. I'm pretty good at capturing the lives of others."

It was her own that seemed, over the past few months, out of focus.

It wasn't just her colossal embarrassment with Roark. It was that she no longer trusted her own instincts.

"I'll put in a good word with Lou at the *Herald*," Ree said.

Seth edged up to the car. Whistled. "Hot wheels, Viv."

Vivie was probably grinning at him from the backseat, flirting. Seth leaned down, caught Amelia's eyes, and lowered his voice into something soft, husky. "They're getting ready to throw the bouquet, and I thought you might want to be there to, you know, catch it."

"Of course."

He grinned, slow and sweet, and it syruped through her, into her pores. Then he popped a kiss on her lips, just like old times.

It wouldn't be a tragedy for her to end up living happily ever after with Seth Turnquist.

He backed up, opened her door, winked at Ree, and narrowed an eye at Vivie.

"What?" Vivie exclaimed, but Seth ignored her and took Amelia's hand.

"It's a beautiful night," he said, lifting her hand to kiss it. Then he tucked it under his arm, pulling her close, his body warm, strong. Solid.

She didn't need instincts to figure out that she had a happy ending waiting for her, right here.

Time to stop looking back and start living the rest of her life.

"You've had some crazy ideas in your life, Roark, but this time you are certifiably off your trolley."

Ethan Barlowe folded his arms, creasing his Alexander Amosu wool suit, and sat on the settee in the living room, watching as Roark St. John finished signing the last of the stock transfer agreements and real estate contracts.

"Instead of selling the place, how about we just rent it out? *Please.*"

Outside the open window, pigeons cooed, perched on the metal railing that overlooked the four-story drop to the street. A sweet, jasmine-laced breeze fluttered the chiffon drapes. The Eiffel Tower rose to dissect the cityscape just across the river.

Roark would miss the view of it at night, the cascading lights on the hour, the memories he'd shared with Francesca. But the place wasn't his—

not really—and never had been. Time to let go. "No. Sell it, Ethan. And transfer the cash and the shares into my account."

"This is it, you know. The last of your father's equity in the company. The walkabout is over. You'll be officially broke if you don't take over the company as your grandfather instructed." Ethan shook his head. "Billions to broke in a day. This girl better be worth it."

"I'm hardly broke. Keep your horses in check. I plan to take the helm, and then yes, I'll inherit the family stocks."

"Good, because I was starting to think *if* more than *when* you take over. Two years is a long time to grieve." Ethan got up, took the file off the table. "I know you loved Francesca. And blamed yourself—"

Roark held up his hand. "Enough. I can't fix that mistake. But this—this I have the power to fix. I promise I'll be back by July's quarterly board meeting."

"That's what you said last July. You offered your so-called scouting report, as if you were seriously looking for future locations, sold more stocks, and took off again. I got that, then. But now—be serious, Roark. This girl dumped you. I know that bruised your massive ego, but it happens to the best of us." He shook his head again. "There's no such thing as true love, mate. I promise you that."

But, see, that was the problem. There was. He'd found it, finally, in Amelia.

Roark had never been the type of guy to believe in love at first sight. It wasn't until after she'd left the country that he'd figured out how to put feelings into words, but yes, something different and real and terrifying had happened the day Amelia Christiansen wandered into his viewfinder on the Charles Bridge in Prague.

God had finally called a truce, perhaps. Because right there, the urge to keep moving, to not settle too long in one place, died a quick and long-overdue death.

Amelia Christiansen was his best—and last—hope to leave behind the man he ran from. And to start being the man he saw in her eyes.

Honest. Responsible. Honorable.

The man he longed to be. Not the guy with so much carnage in his wake, but a fellow traveler, a little lost, hoping to find the one person to bring him home.

"Women want too much from us. Not just our hearts, but our wallets. Our very souls." Ethan opened his satchel, slipped the file in. "The worst part is, you already tried to apologize."

"I did it poorly. I went in thinking I could throw out an apology, hand her flowers and some jewelry, and she'd fall into my arms."

"You didn't even do anything wrong!" Ethan flung the satchel's shoulder strap over himself.

"I kept secrets. I lied to her—made her think I was someone else."

"You had no choice."

"I had every choice. I was a coward." He stuck his hands in his pockets, walked over to the window, leaned against the frame as he stared at the tower. "Just like I have been all my life."

Behind him, Ethan sighed. "I know you have demons, mate, but you're hardly a coward."

But Ethan didn't see the rest, the man afraid to face the way he'd disappointed God. Or the fact that God kept reminding Roark he couldn't outrun His wrath.

With Amelia, it had all dropped away. The fear, the regret—as if being with her made him new. Or better.

A man worthy of winning back the woman he loved.

"Didn't her family practically throw you out? What makes you think they'll be all, 'Glad you popped by! Come in for a spot of tea'?"

Roark smiled at that. "I have an in with the family—a local who claims to know their bark is worse than their bite. And a job."

Ethan raised an eyebrow.

"I'm working in a coffeehouse."

Ethan put his hand on the door latch. "I know you like to live on the edge, fast and loose, without a plan. But this might take more finesse than you think. In the case that you don't come back, though, I want the keys to the Fiorano."

"Don't be coy. I know you already have a set. Just keep it clean."

Ethan smiled. "You really *don't* have even a smidgen of a plan, do you?"

"Just one. Win her back, then tell her the truth. Beyond that, I'm following my heart, hoping it's enough."

"You might consider going at that backward. Secrets first, then love."

Roark sighed. "But in that case, how will I know it's real?"

A pulse of camaraderie passed between them. Then Roark took a breath. "I'll be back in two months. With the woman I love."

Chapter 2

WAGING WAR FOR Amelia's heart in the picturesque town of Deep Haven had its benefits. Like the view of the harbor from Roark's efficiency-apartment window, with the pristine blue lake washing the shore, the cry of gulls to awaken him. The fragrant, bushy pine trees standing sentry around the north shore hamlet. He'd rented it two weeks ago, just before leaving town, as security against his courage tucking tail and fleeing.

He pulled up to the tiny coffee shop with the

second-story apartment accessible via outside stairs, parked the used Ford Focus he'd picked up in Minneapolis, and got out.

Jensen Atwood stood in the lot—Roark's inside man, his compatriot in battle. Rusty, Jensen's collie, ran up and pressed his nose into Roark's leg.

"Hey, Rusty," Roark said, bending down to rub the animal behind the ears.

"The British are coming," Jensen said, ambling over to clasp his hand. "One light or two?"

Roark found a smile. The grime and fatigue of the past three days of traveling from Paris, finding a car in Minneapolis, buying meager supplies, and driving five hours north had scoured away his good humor.

"Let's get you unloaded."

Roark popped the boot, where he'd stashed a crate of kitchen utensils, some linens, and his suitcase.

"The life of a vagabond, I see," Jensen said. "Well, cheer up, old chap. Deep Haven is a splendid place to put down roots."

Roark didn't correct him; his Good Samaritan didn't need to know that he had no plans to stay. That this was a two-way trip to amend his mistakes and return a champion.

Finally.

However, he did owe Jensen the credit for knocking him out of his doldrums after the miserable row with Amelia's family last month.

If it weren't for his run-in with Jensen on his second mournful day in town licking his wounds, Roark might have thrown it in and would now be setting up his station in his uncle's sleek offices in Brussels.

Jensen, it seemed, knew a little about being judged prematurely and awaiting acquittal. And he'd been the strategist behind Roark's return to Deep Haven to win the hand of the fair maiden Amelia. Now he seemed to also be his stalwart companion, a brother in arms.

"Roark. Hello, Roark?" Jensen said.

Roark came to himself. "Sorry, I was off with the fairies."

Jensen raised an eyebrow.

"Perhaps you'd say, off in thought."

"Right. Maybe keep the fairies thing to yourself. Still, I'll bet you're thinking about what you might say the first time Darek Christiansen sees you hanging around Deep Haven. I know this was sort of my idea, but I've had two weeks to think about it, and maybe . . ."

"I should leg it out of here?" Roark led the way up the stairs, inserting the key into the door, swinging it open.

"Righto," Jensen said as he dropped the box of utensils on the table. "But before you do, Peter Pan, my wife, Claire, says that you have to come up to the house for dinner. You can unpack your suitcase and these wobbly boxes in your spacious new pad when you get back."

Jensen was no doubt eyeing Roark's one-room flat, with the living room cluster of a faded red sofa and brown rocker facing the electric wood-stove, and the L-shaped kitchen that housed a four-burner unit, a tiny refrigerator, and a wooden table.

Roark set his suitcase on the bare, gray-striped mattress of the single bed and stared out the picture window to the foamy wash of Lake Superior along the rocky shoreline. The sun hovered low, the day holding fast to a feeble strip of fire along the horizon. The rich aroma of brewed coffee wheedled up the stairs from the downstairs eatery, a coffee emporium aptly named Java Cup.

His new employer and landlord.

Of all the places he thought he'd end up, here, learning to brew a cup of American espresso, seemed the last. But he'd made worse choices over the years, right?

"Listen, I once lived on a sailboat for three months in quarters the size of a shilling, so this is indeed spacious." Roark smiled as he took a leather jacket from his suitcase and pulled it on over his T-shirt, twisted a scarf around his neck, and added a tweed cap.

"All you need is an Aston Martin," Jensen said. "If you want to lay low, lose the cap for a tuque and throw on a sweatshirt."

Roark frowned and made to pull off his hat.

"It's fine. We'll soon be under the cover of darkness. Let's go."

Roark followed Jensen outside, where the collie waited in the bed of his truck. He opened the tailgate and the dog jumped out, then into the cab, where he climbed on the seat.

"Rusty, get down."

"I've got it sorted." Roark climbed in, and the dog settled across his lap, paws over the seat's edge. He ran his fingers into the fur around the back of the dog's ear and rubbed. "How old is he?"

"Not sure. He's a shelter dog. Just needed a good home. Some love."

Didn't they all?

Roark said nothing as they drove through the town. He had already gotten his bearings on his first runabout two weeks ago—met the locals, tried to devise a plan. And convince himself that he wasn't completely barmy for hanging out where he wasn't wanted. He hadn't settled on a verdict.

"You'll like Claire. By the way, she lived in Eastern Europe as a kid. Her parents are still missionaries in Bosnia."

Roark bit back a noise that would betray the sudden churning of memories.

"We run the resort across the lake from the Christiansens'," Jensen said as they climbed the

41

hill out of town. "If you look behind you, you can see the lights ringing the harbor. It's beautiful."

Roark obliged and indeed, twilight fell around the hamlet, red-and-yellow lights like diamonds against the velvet swaddle.

The kind of place where he might have decided to settle down if he didn't have obligations.

They turned toward Evergreen Lake, silvery now with a fingertip of moonlight parting the middle. Houses sheltered in towering pine remained dark, yet well-groomed, and when Jensen stopped at a security gate and keyed in a code, Roark realized he'd entered resort property.

Jensen drove into the complex, heading toward a three-story, timber-sided lake home.

"Blimey."

Jensen laughed. "It's not mine—we're renting from my father. I work as the caretaker of the community. But it's a nice view." He parked inside a lit garage, and Rusty climbed out, wagging his tail as he ran up the stairs to the house.

"It's just you here? No concierge?"

"I am the concierge. And the maintenance man. And the housekeeper—when needed—and the front desk receptionist and the general manager." He hit the garage fob to close the door. "Mostly these are private homes, but sometimes the owners rent them out. I'm on duty to make sure the guests are treated right."

He opened the door, and the rich redolence of

tomatoes and beef stewing on the stove could make Roark weep. He hadn't had a home-cooked dinner in . . . Well, he couldn't actually put a finger on it. Perhaps a decade.

"Hey, honey, this is Roark," Jensen said, walking over to a petite brunette who wore her hair in two pigtails. She sported a pregnant belly that appeared ready to pop any moment.

"The infamous Roark," she said, pulling off an oven mitt to shake his hand.

"Infamous?" he said.

"You have no idea." She winked, then turned to her husband. "Hey, handsome," she said to Jensen and lifted her face for a kiss.

Roark looked away and wandered past the leather sofa, the trestle table set for dinner, to the wide picture window that overlooked Evergreen Lake. His gaze found the glittering lodge on the opposite shore. Evergreen Resort. Amelia's home. When the investigator he'd hired to track Amelia down mentioned that her family owned a cottage in the woods, he'd pictured something quaint with a garden perhaps. But the Christiansen lodge, made of peeled logs, exuded the stately aura of history, a landmark hewn from the lush landscape of the north. The land held a wildness reminiscent of the places he'd visited as a child in Russia.

Maybe that's why it called to him. Or maybe he simply heard Amelia's voice lingering in his memory. Stories about fishing with her brothers or swimming in Evergreen Lake, hiking back trails in search of grouse, pheasant, eagle, and beaver. Tracking down the perfect photo. Behind her words, he'd seen the pieces of her—adventurous, brave, breathtaking—and they'd captivated him.

She had the courage he longed for. That drew him, perhaps, the most.

Now, thanks to the moonlight, he could easily trace the scrub trees along the shore, the smattering of newly rebuilt cabins, the wasteland of devastated forest beyond the lodge. The wreckage stopped just west of the lake, at the tip.

"It's from the forest fire," Jensen said, coming up beside him and handing him a cold root beer in a glass. "Almost two years ago. Darek and I dug a fire line with his bulldozer and stopped it just along our property."

Roark pointed to the lodge with his free hand. "Nice view of the Christiansen place."

"Four generations it's been in their family," Jensen said. "Lodge, cabins, and outfitters."

Roark took a sip, studying the cabins, wondering what they rented for, then dismissing the question. He wasn't in that business anymore. Or yet.

"Suppertime," Claire said, setting a Caesar salad on the table. She went to the stove, grabbed her hot pads.

"Oh, let me get that," Roark said, setting down

his drink and fast walking to the stove. He put on the hot pads and grabbed the pot.

Claire untied her apron, grinning.

"Thanks for that. I was just about to help her," Jensen said. "I'm watching you, 007."

007? His frown at Jensen elicited a laugh.

"It's what they called you in town. 'Bond. James Bond'—that sort of thing. You raised a few eyebrows with your appearance. And subsequent disappearance."

"I had to attend to things at home." He threw his leg over the bench on one side of the kitchen table.

"Home being . . . ?" Claire said as Jensen pulled out the end chair for her. He sat opposite Roark.

"Brussels. Oh, this smells delicious."

"My grandfather's recipe—old shoe soup, he calls it, but it's really just beef stew." She sat and held out her hands. Jensen took one.

Roark hesitated only a moment before he took the other.

Claire bowed her head.

Oh.

Roark bowed his too. It just seemed right.

When she finished, Claire reached for the first bowl to dish the stew up, but Jensen grabbed it away. "I got this."

"You're a good influence, Roark."

"Please," Jensen said but handed him a filled bowl of stew.

"Okay, Roark," Claire said, buttering a piece of crusty bread from a basket in the middle of the table. "Jensen says you've landed a job at the Java Cup."

He took a sip of the stew, the flavor of thyme settling into his bones. "I've rented a flat above the shop. I start Monday."

"You should take the weekend to see the sights. Go up to Cutaway Creek, hike the falls. It's cresting with the spring runoff—gorgeous," Jensen said.

Roark nodded, reached for the bread.

"And then what?" Claire said. "Jensen told me what you're up to, and I have to say . . . I'm not sure you have my vote."

"Give the man a chance, Claire," Jensen said, taking his own bowl.

"I'm all for true love, but I'm trying to figure out why a guy who stepped out on Amelia thinks he deserves a second chance."

Oh. "It wasn't quite as she suspected, but I know I hurt her." And if that didn't take him right back to the beginning, stymied by a truth he loathed to tell.

He swallowed, dove into his stew.

Claire raised an eyebrow. "I'm giving you mercy here. Amelia is the Christiansens' guarded child. The youngest. She not only grew up with three brothers, but she's as stubborn as they are. So tell me, Roark St. John, why is Amelia so important that you'd hop a plane and camp out in Deep Haven to win her back?"

He could start, perhaps, with the way they met, how the sight of her waiting for the sunset to paint the perfect version of the sky upon the Vltava before she captured it with her camera had rendered him breathless.

He could talk about how Amelia laughed at his insistence she make a wish and hoped that yes, she'd return. How he had wrangled his way into the same photography tour group and how the city took on new brilliance when they explored Týn Church and Old Town Square together.

How, when he discovered her age, he'd planned to ease out of her life, until she made it okay. By then, perhaps she'd suspected his feelings—even before he did.

The weekends they spent traveling to nearby villages, then on to Germany and even into Switzerland, finally to Paris.

How, when he found her standing in Notre-Dame Cathedral, streams of light fanning over her, he wondered if she'd been divinely sent. And how it scared him that God might be reaching again into his life, this time without rancor. Maybe even with forgiveness. The thought tasted too raw, the hope pricking his eyes.

He'd debated, then, telling her about himself—about his past, his future. So much of their friendship was spent in the present. But it was that—just a friendship. Until New Year's Eve and the kiss.

The kiss. Quick, but awakening something inside him that told him the truth. Enough to reach out to Cicely to ask her permission.

Which, of course, turned out badly for everyone.

"Have you ever met someone who so completely made you feel like yourself?" The words snuck out to betray him, and yet hearing them gave him resolve. He looked up at Jensen, then beyond him, to the Christiansen lodge. "As if that person awakened inside you the person you've always wanted to be—and should have been all along? And the more you're with her, the more honest and right it feels? Such a person makes you want to lean into everything you could have, reluctant to let it go. You can't envision a life without her because such a life wouldn't be worth living."

He saw Jensen's hand creep across the table to take Claire's. "Yes," he said quietly.

Perhaps Jensen was more an ally than he'd suspected. Indeed, his luck was turning.

Roark put down his spoon. Met Claire's eyes. "Claire Atwood, I know you don't know me. I have blown in off the eastern wind and taken up residence in your town, and I am an interloper. But I am not the scoundrel you suppose me to be, and I am here with honorable intent. I have committed no crimes except for unbearably poor timing and abysmal communication skills. I desperately long to set things right with Amelia, to reveal to her the truth behind our regrettable row. I hurt her, and it deeply pains me."

He swallowed, took a drink of his root beer. Met her gaze again. "However, I promise you this. If Amelia, bearing all the facts of my case, still chooses to reject me, I will walk away and be content to leave her in peace, despite my broken heart."

Something flickered in Claire's eye. A flare of trust?

"I humbly ask if you will give me a chance to prove myself, to do as Jensen suggests and earn the respect of the Christiansen family and win back Amelia's trust. I promise I will not let you down. Nor Amelia."

Claire stared at him. Jensen didn't move.

He felt it then, the weight of what he'd come to do. To prove not only to Amelia, not only to her family, but apparently to the entire town that he could win the heart of the damsel of Deep Haven—and deserved to do so.

Finally, from Claire: "Okay, then. Jens, please pass Roark some more bread."

National Geographic wouldn't come in search of Amelia or laud her photographic achievements after today's not-so-epic shots of Troop 168 and their buckets of sudsy water, but it might be enough to land her the freelance job at the *Deep Haven Herald.*

"Lindy! Alice! Marissa! Show me some smiles and hold up your sponges!" Amelia positioned herself on top of the fire truck, capturing the gap-toothed joy of the soggy Girl Scouts as they scrubbed Edith Draper's Ford Escape. Water sprayed into the cool air, caught by the breeze and turning to kaleidoscope bubbles against the blue sky and laughter of the fifteen-plus girls working the crowd in the Deep Haven EMS parking lot. A small line of locals, pledging their support of the troop's fund-raiser for a playground addition, stood around slurping coffee, holding tenspots, and waiting their turn to get their vehicle sudsed up and sprayed down.

And Amelia caught it all—or most of it—for posterity.

She supposed it could be worse—her tryout for the editor might have been during a council meeting or the annual garden club show. Although extreme close-ups of prizewinning roses did pose a unique challenge. Too bad journalistic photos and macro photography didn't exactly overlap.

Amelia climbed down from the truck and scanned through her pictures. A few of the girls spraying water on each other, a few more with them crowded together, sponges raised. Football coach Caleb Knight and his wife, Issy, eating donuts with the pastor's wife, Ellie—her daughter was one of the older scouts. A couple bubbles drifting into the sky, the sheen of the sun glinting off the surface; she probably wouldn't show those to Lou at the *Herald*.

But nothing epic. Breathtaking. Magazine worthy.

"Amelia, look out!"

She looked up, searching for the voice just as water showered her, cold, sharp, dousing her T-shirt, her jeans. "Hey!" She tucked her camera away, turning fast.

"Sorry!"

This from one of the girls, her blonde hair plastered to her head from the hose war she'd just waged with her cohort.

Amelia forced a smile instead of stringing the girl up by her multi-badged sash. "That's okay."

"Babe, you look good soggy," Seth called from where he was selling raffle tickets for the fire department in the open bay area. Wearing his turnout pants, red suspenders dangling, and a tight white T-shirt, his blond hair tucked under a patriotic bandanna, he probably sold double the usual raffle take. Especially when he grinned, his teeth white against his tanned face.

He should be on a poster somewhere, for pete's sake.

51

Now he sauntered over, picking up a dry towel on his way. Her rescuer.

One of the girls giggled and pointed as Seth wiped her drenched arm.

"They got my camera wet," Amelia said and took the towel, wiping it down.

"Calm down, Red. It's just a little water." He stepped between her and the giggling girls. Lowered his voice. "Hey, I get off shift at six— maybe I can scoot up to the lodge. We'll take a canoe out. Or take a drive. Or something."

She knew exactly what his *or something* meant. And for a moment, the idea of curling up in his embrace in the back of a canoe, staring at the stars . . . it didn't lack in appeal.

But . . . "I told Lou I'd get some pictures to him. Maybe, if I'm lucky, he'll give me another assignment."

Seth's smile dimmed. "Okay. I get it. You want this photo gig. But it's not like anything earth-shattering happens here on a Saturday night. There might be a speeder through town. Or a runaway moose." He leaned against the fire truck, one leg on the running board, reaching out to pull her close. His lips touched her ear. "I miss you. I haven't seen you all week."

That's because she'd spent the week changing sheets, cleaning toilets, and painting flower boxes in anticipation of the resort's Mother's Day kickoff to the summer season. If she never saw

52

another paintbrush again, it would be too soon. She couldn't spend her summer doing laundry and checking in guests.

She untangled herself. "Seth, I'm here to work. I need this job. Please."

"Mmm-hmm." His chocolaty eyes trailed down her, back up. He made a face, glanced away.

She frowned. "What's wrong?"

He cleared his throat. Had the manners to look sheepish. "Your shirt's . . . um, white."

The meaning dawned on her slowly. She looked down, and sure enough, her *Evergreen Resort Welcomes You* T-shirt might be a tad too welcoming.

"Great."

"I got an extra shirt in my locker. C'mon." He wrapped his arm around her shoulders and eased her away from the crowd. Next to him, Amelia felt even smaller, but he tucked her close, then took her hand as he led her into the building, back to the locker room.

A few of the other volunteer firefighters lifted their hands in welcome, and she held her camera to her chest for protection.

Especially when Dan Matthews came out of the kitchen, carrying a plate of cookies. "Hello, Amelia."

"Pastor."

She heard Seth chuckle and swatted him. "Not funny."

53

"Nope. Not at all." But she heard the smile in his voice.

She followed him into the locker room and gladly accepted his navy-blue Huskies football shirt, ducking into the bathroom to change. It smelled like him—wood chips, the faintest scent of pine, and his musky cologne. Familiar and sweet. She sank, just for a moment, into the memory of donning his football jersey.

Maybe it wouldn't hurt to paddle the trail of moonlight with him later tonight.

He seemed to read her mind as he sat down on the bench, pulled her onto his lap. She hooked an arm around his broad shoulders.

"Listen, Red, I know I sort of jumped in fast when you got home. It's just that I've figured out that I don't want to leave here. I like Deep Haven. I like the mill, and my dad's going to sell me half of his stake in it. Someday I'll own the entire thing. I want to build a life here—and I want to do it with you."

Oh. She swallowed.

"I know that you're probably not ready, and that's okay. I'll wait. But I need to know that you'll give us a chance."

When he looked at her with so much emotion in his eyes, what could she say? Besides, what if she wanted this too? What if she'd left Prague because she didn't want the fear, the danger, the bigness of life outside Deep Haven?

Seth certainly had the power to make her forget, help her heal.

She pressed her hand against his cheek. He hadn't shaved today, and his whiskers grew out deliciously red and gold. "Okay."

He rested his hand over hers. "Okay? Yeah?"

"For now—"

But he'd caught her mouth in a kiss, his hand behind her neck. And he tasted . . . like Seth. Diet Coke and the sweetness of a glazed donut and the sureness of knowing who he was and what he wanted.

Familiar. Safe. Amelia let herself relish it, needing him, perhaps.

The alarm broke her free. It blared through the building, followed by the 911 operator. A drowning out on Cutaway Creek.

Seth was up and steadying her even as he pulled his suspenders over his shoulders. She preceded him out the door.

"Where are you going?" he said as he grabbed his jacket, his helmet.

Amelia turned. "Are you kidding me?" She jogged away from him, out to her Kia. Forget the Girl Scouts.

She pulled out as the scouts hurried to clear the lot, catching a glimpse of Seth's frustration as he kicked buckets out of the way.

On the southwest edge of town, just above the bridge, a waterfall dumped spring runoff into a cascading, frothy river that ran through a gorge right into the mouth of Lake Superior, twisting the current into tiny cauldrons. Boulders the size of Smart cars jutted out into the water, tempting tourists to play Frogger, skipping from one bank to the other.

This time of year, with the spring thaw, the creek-turned-river was hungry.

Worse, higher up, where the hiking trail followed the river, pools of cool water tempted hikers to wade in, unaware of the snaking currents.

And when one person went in, rescuers soon followed—too many to their deaths.

Amelia shot up a prayer for the victims as she took the back streets, dodged traffic, and came out southwest of town, with a straight shot to the river. She had outrun the fire trucks, no whine of a siren in her wake.

She'd get there and catch the entire event for the *Herald*. Lou would have no choice but to be impressed.

Good-bye, housekeeping.

She picked up her cell phone just before she hit the highway and left a message on the *Herald* answering machine. No need to send reinforcements—she had this.

A committee of cars jammed the Cutaway Creek lot, tourists now caught in the tragedy. She parked on the side of the highway, scooped up her camera, and ran to the north side of the creek, where onlookers stood back from the rocky edge. She snapped a quick shot of a mother, dressed in khakis and hiking boots, her grade school–age children pressed against her, sobbing. Another of an elderly couple watching from the bridge, hands gripped white on the rails. A third of a young woman, vise-gripping the hand of her husband to keep him from going beyond knee-deep in the water.

On the other side, at least two men were in the water, surfacing, fighting the current to grab at something wedged in the rocks below the surface.

Now, behind Amelia, the sirens wailed.

Her viewfinder scanned the onlookers, took in another family standing on the shore, a woman and her dog, pulling at the leash, and not far upriver, where the rocks jutted out farthest, a little girl standing just outside the spray of water from the nearby falls.

She wore a pink dress—that seemed the oddest—and her fawn-brown hair was in long braids with big red bows at the ends. Rail-thin, she appeared no older than six.

As Amelia watched, the girl crouched on the rock, balancing on her feet, pulling her dress over her knees as if cold. Her expression seemed almost calm, as if she was oblivious to the chaos around her.

Amelia glanced at the mother in khakis, but she

hadn't moved, her gaze on the river. Maybe . . .

She walked over to the woman. "Is that your daughter?"

The woman glanced at the girl. Frowned. "No."

Right. Amelia swung the camera over her shoulder, then headed to the river's edge. "Little girl?"

The girl didn't move, just stared out at the chaos, the men still fighting the current, yelling. The scream of the sirens undulated louder.

Amelia edged toward her, aware of the current eddying up onto the rock, turning it slick.

Maybe whoever was with the little girl had slipped and fallen. Amelia cast a look at the water and saw one of the men surface, this time with a body.

A woman.

Oh no. She glanced at the girl, who watched without a flicker of emotion as the rescuers pulled the woman from the creek.

Amelia crouched next to her. "Honey, where's your mommy?"

The child had blue eyes, which suddenly shook free from her trance and focused on Amelia. But when she spoke, the words were foreign and soft, a lilt to her voice that suggested a question.

Except something made sense—a niggle of familiarity, buried under layers of memory.

Prague. One of her flatmates spoke Russian. Or Ukrainian. Or maybe Polish—she couldn't remember, but it seemed that the words might be of the same Slavic origin.

Of which she'd learned three phrases.

I'm hungry.

I need the bathroom.

And conveniently, *Are you okay?*

The smallest redemption for her broken heart. She tried it out on the little girl, probably mangling the words.

A flicker of understanding. Or maybe just the recognition of an attempt, but it ignited a barrage of words. Unintelligible, but the little girl stood. Pointed at the group of rescuers.

Maybe her father was among them. Amelia shielded her eyes as she scanned the group. She could get their attention, if one of them looked—

The woman lay prone, two Good Samaritans giving her CPR—one administering compressions, the other breaths.

The man at the head—she recognized him as one who'd pulled the woman out of the current—offered a breath, then leaned back while the other pressed her chest.

Now she saw his face.

Oh. No. It couldn't be.

She hadn't a hope of forgetting those high cheekbones. That curly black hair, wet and falling over his blue eyes—so blue they could lift her out of herself, make her believe—

No.

Even the outline of his sopping wet shirt betrayed the truth. *Chiseled,* Ree had said. Yes, Roark had the frame of a man who could dive into a raging river and rescue a lost soul. Delicious biceps, wide shoulders, lean hips, and he leaned down to breathe life into the dying.

Except it was Amelia who needed resuscitating. Hadn't he left? Freed her from the grip of his memory on her heart?

A cold hand touched her cheek and jolted her out of herself.

"*Mamichka*?"

Even Amelia could translate that. "No, honey. I'm not your—"

And then she got it.

Roark St. John was trying—vainly, it seemed—to revive the little girl's mother.

Regardless of what he might be doing back in Deep Haven . . . regardless of the lies and the way he'd humiliated her . . . in that moment, yes, she could forgive him.

She might even love him. Just for right now.

She pulled the little girl close and held her, running a hand over her back. "Shh," she said. "It's going to be okay."

Her hands trembled. Roark couldn't be here. She held the little girl, but her brain tracked to the last time she'd seen him. Leaving the resort, with Darek, Casper, Jace, and Max watching from the driveway.

60

It's going to be okay.

Behind her, the fire trucks arrived, and she turned to watch as the EMTs climbed out—as Seth climbed out—donning life jackets and heading to the river.

Seth hadn't actually met Roark, just heard the story. Over and over.

Oh no. Amelia turned back, but a crowd had gathered around the woman, obscuring the men who'd been working on her. She'd lost sight of the rescuer who might be Roark.

"Amelia? Are you okay?"

She spotted her sister Grace, in a white sundress, her blonde hair loose, running across the rocky shoreline.

"Max and I were coming home to surprise everyone, and I saw your car. What are you doing here?"

"There's a drowning. And I found this little girl. I think . . ." She looked again at the river, where a firefighter had gone in, roped to the shore, and was dragging out another body, male, older. "I think her mother is one of the victims."

As if to confirm, the girl lifted her head. Watched, bearing that same strange, enigmatic expression. *"Papichka."*

Amelia picked up the girl, turned her away, scanned the shore. The rescuers had fanned out as the firefighters and EMTs took over. She saw

Seth attach a safety rope to his harness, wade into the water.

Her throat tightened as the current took him, pulling on his rope. *Please don't die.*

But even as he swam down into one of the deadly pools, her gaze went back to the shore.

She studied each of the soggy civilians who had risked their lives. A burly blond college student. A man—dark hair, stocky, probably belonging to the woman in khakis. The young husband who'd finally wrestled out of his wife's grip.

But no Roark.

She searched the embankment, spied the elderly couple, the young family, others from town she recognized. Pastor Dan, the fire chief, and Joe Michaels, hauling the woman onto a stretcher. Mayor Seb Brewster and another volunteer fire-fighter at the water's edge, belaying Seth, and Deputy Kyle Hueston, taking statements.

But no Roark.

"Let's get off this rock, see if we can track down some relatives," Grace said. She grabbed Amelia's elbow to steady her as they trekked back to safety.

Amelia searched for Roark one final time as she made her way up to the fire trucks. But he seemed to have vanished.

Or maybe he was never there at all. Maybe her stupid, belligerent heart simply refused to surrender him to the past.

• • •

Life, on this blue-skied spring day, had never seemed quite so fragile.

The birds chirruped, calling from the trees over the rush of water cascading in a raucous froth down to the great lake. Mist hung in the air, and just an hour ago, Roark had watched a teenager—no more than fourteen—jump from boulder to boulder across the foamy river.

He could be that boy, had played that game in rivers tucked away in far east Russia. Could nearly taste the carefree danger pooling in the back of his throat.

The parents stood closer to shore, yet still at the edge of a boulder, the father holding the hand of a little girl in braids, her red bows twisting in the wind.

Roark had leaned against the rail of the bridge, working up a strategy—or perhaps just the courage—to talk to Amelia. His conversation with Claire had caused him to rise early, to take a run up the highway until he had to double over and haul in deep, cleansing breaths.

If Amelia, bearing all the facts of my case, still chooses to reject me, I will walk away and be content to leave her in peace, despite my broken heart.

He hated his words then, the very real prophecy in them.

So he'd walked back to his meager flat,

showered, tracked down a pastry at the local donut shop, then made his way to Jensen's suggestion—Cutaway Creek.

He parked with the other vehicles, hiked up to the high falls, then back, sorting through ways to find Amelia alone, to plead his case. At the bridge, he sat on a bench and watched families hike the shoreline. Parents holding the hands of their children, couples taking selfies. The joy of family hung in the air like the cool mist off the river.

"Isn't it breathtaking?" He heard the words from an elderly woman standing nearby, and right then, he was back on the Charles Bridge, admiring the artwork of a local who'd set up an easel, drawing a fresh view of the Judith Tower on the far end of the bridge.

The sun hung low, lighting the red-tiled roofs and turning black the haunting gothic spires of the castle on the hill. The Vltava River was a rich mulberry, the bright lights of riverboats pinpricks against the deepening shadows.

Roark had framed it in his viewfinder, waiting.

And into this magnificent skyline walked Amelia. She wore high boots, jeans, and a black trench coat, an emerald-green scarf twined around her neck, her auburn hair long.

When she pulled a camera from her rucksack, something latent and sweet stirred inside him. Like he'd seen her before, perhaps, and tucked the memory deep inside only to be stirred like a remembered song.

It pulled him to her side of the bridge as she took a few shots, adjusted her aperture exposure. And still he watched.

Until her gaze turned to him, and he'd blurted out the crazy line about wishes and hopes and . . . felt like a fool.

But she smiled and healed the urge to run. He gathered his wits, and his next words came out saner. "Did you know that after the sunset, in about twenty minutes, the sky will light up again? It's even more brilliant the second time around."

She had green eyes. Eyes that could stop his heart, hold it, make him see himself and cringe.

"Really?"

"Indeed. Turn off your auto white balance and switch it to shade. You'll draw all the gold tones into the picture."

He didn't know when he'd become a professor of photography—his own Nikon barely had a scuff on it. But that seemed to impress her, and she tried it.

He wanted to train his camera on her, capture that smile.

"I'll bite—who are you? The local photography bum?"

He liked that. Because yes, it fit. Still, it came with too many explanations, so . . . "I just like the view. You?"

"I'm enrolled in a photography program at Charles University. We're also touring through Germany, Austria, and then over to Switzerland. I think we're even spending the New Year in Paris."

She turned around, framed the setting sun, the trail of gold along the river southwest of the bridge.

His brain, meanwhile, did the math. "Do you mean the course taught by Claude Dupré?"

She lowered her camera. Nodded. "Do you know him?"

Roark was sleeping on his sofa. Which meant, yes, he could probably talk his former schoolmate into letting him tag along.

"Indeed. It seems we are taking the same class."

The first of too many white lies, the trailhead of secrets.

The scream had shaken him out of his memory as he stood on the bridge above Cutaway Creek. He'd watched as the teenager grasped at rocks, tumbling into the current. Then, in horror, as his mother reached out to grab him and fell in too.

Roark wanted to shout, already on his way down the embankment as the father released the hand of his daughter and headed into the froth.

Roark reacted more out of instinct than training, but he had learned to swim in the choppy waters of the Sea of Japan and rowed for two years at Eton.

Point of fact, he didn't exactly remember hitting the water, just that he'd shucked off his jumper, down to his vest, torn off his trainers, and waded in, his eyes on the teenager, now frantic in the water.

"Lie on your back! Put your legs out in front of you!" he yelled. "Ride the current until you can find a rock and brace yourself!" But the river gobbled his words. The icy water stole his breath as he worked his way to the teenager, grabbing at him, missing.

The swell took the boy under the bridge. Roark did get a hand on the mother, however, his grip on a boulder scraping at his other hand.

As his legs went numb in the frigid water, the woman clawed at him, fighting him. "My son!"

Her husband half paddled, half twisted in the rapids, also disappearing under the bridge. Tempests of water would suck them under, relentless in their hunger.

"Ma'am!"

But she shook free of Roark's grasp, kicking him in the gut as she fought. His breath heaved out.

Before he could lunge again, she went under.

The current took her body, sucked her down. Roark clung to the rock, waiting for her to surface.

Waiting.

He finally saw a hand—just a glimmer—peek

from the surface in the middle of a cauldron on the far side of the river.

Another man, older, had plunged into the water beside him.

"She's over there!" Roark pointed to the hole, then launched himself through the rapids toward her.

His feet barely found purchase, pushing at rocks for leverage as he floundered against the current, swimming hard above her.

He landed just below the hole, grabbed the edge of a boulder, and pulled himself to the churning pool.

She had to be down there. Caught. He gripped the rock, tried to reach for her.

A hand closed around his wrist. A younger man perched on the rock. "I got you," he said and lay prone, another buddy holding his legs.

In the distance, sirens whined.

Roark ventured farther, one-handed, letting his rescuer belay him, and ducked under the water. Felt something—a hand, perhaps. Grabbed for it and missed.

He surfaced, pulling against the grip, and sucked in a breath. "She's down there."

He'd stopped shivering long ago, his body heavy in the water. Gulping another breath, he went back in.

He didn't know how many tries it took to finally grab her arm, but he clutched it and pulled her up. Gray and limp, she hung from his grip. He pushed her toward the crowd of men now attending the rescue and let someone pull him from the water.

The group dragged the woman onshore. Stood over her as Roark crawled forward. Someone turned her onto her back and landed a fist on her chest as if shocking her heart.

Didn't any of these blokes know CPR?

Roark crawled to her, turned her on her side, and swept her mouth. He moved to her chest for compressions, but a soggy compatriot knelt beside him and began to pump. When he'd finished, Roark tilted back the woman's head and breathed for her. Water sputtered out of her, and her body shook.

Leaning over her, Roark waited, and the two men fell into a rhythm of breaths and compressions as the circle closed around them.

Time fell away as he begged God—oddly, because he thought he'd run out of chances with God—to deliver her.

Despite the woman's improving color, the EMTs arrived without the woman having gasped a breath on her own. Roark tried not to blame himself as they added oxygen. He scrambled back, climbed to his feet, shivering as water ran off his trousers, his stocking feet dirty, his muscles cramping.

And it was then, breathing hard, feeling life in

its fragile shreds, that he looked up and saw her.

Just like before, standing on a bridge, her hair flame red in the sun, her camera strung over her shoulder.

Amelia.

His heart stuttered.

She held a little girl in her arms and was talking to a local bobby.

The moment crystallized. If pulling a drowned woman out of the unforgiving waters of the north woods could teach him anything, it was not to waste time.

Every breath was sacred, and he knew he'd done exactly the right thing in moving to Deep Haven to repair the hurts he'd caused.

And despite the chaos, the tragedy hanging in the air, the brutal reality of two—possibly three—victims to the torrent of Cutaway Creek, he planned on grabbing ahold of life before it slipped out of his grip.

So he didn't care that he reeked of river water, his body now racked with tremors, his mouth bruised from the resuscitations. He edged away from the trauma, keeping his eye on Amelia as she held the little girl, her head resting on Amelia's shoulder, arms encircling her neck.

Amelia wore an oversize blue T-shirt, dragging low over her jeans, her auburn hair lifted by the breeze. It looked like one of her sisters stood beside her.

Which meant that one of the hockey brutes might not be far behind.

They'd all closed ranks—the brutes, along with Amelia's brothers Darek and Casper—to not-so-politely ask Roark to leave. However, despite Claire and Jensen's warnings, and the brutish circle the clan had drawn around Amelia, Roark didn't much care what they did to him.

Roark's teeth had started to chatter, his vest soaked through, his trousers chafing, his feet cramping against the rocks as he worked his way to the bridge.

"Hey! You need a blanket!" This from a member of the fire brigade, who jogged to the open ambulance bay and retrieved a blanket. He shook it out and returned as Roark glanced again toward Amelia.

She was still talking with the officer, her hand running in circles against the little girl's back.

The fireman settled the blanket over Roark, and recognition dawned. A tall man, black hair, big shoulders. "Seb Brewster, medium white chocolate mocha."

Seb frowned. "You're that Brit who's working at the Cup. You were one of the rescuers? I saw you doing CPR."

"Trying," Roark said. "Not that it did much good." He glanced at the woman, now on oxygen, her chest rising and falling. The EMTs loaded her onto a flat board for transport.

Onshore, another group worked on the man they'd pulled out of the water.

A crowd had formed around them—onlookers, an elderly couple, a family. Roark glanced toward Amelia, walking toward the parking lot, her sister beside her.

"You're a hero," Seb said. "But you look a little shaky. Maybe you should sit down—"

"Seb! We need a hand!"

Roark glanced at the man behind the voice, down on the river's edge. Tall, brawny, blond—a lumberjack, no doubt. As Seb left to help, Roark made his escape, weaving through the crowd.

"Roark, what are you doing here?"

At the sound of his name, he stopped and found Jensen on his tail, wearing a pair of EMT blues.

Jensen grabbed him by the arm. "You're wet and freezing. You could get hypothermia." He dragged Roark toward the second waiting ambulance. Forced him to sit on the end of the bay.

"I'm fine—"

"You're not fine. Your lips are purple; your skin is clammy." Jensen reached for his pulse. "Are you dizzy? Or numb?"

"I'm all right."

"Yeah, well, your pulse is thready. Listen, I have to get back—they've just found the third body."

Oh no. The kid. Roark clenched his jaw against a rush of cold, blunt emotion.

"I'm going to crack a heat pack. I want you to put it next to your skin."

Jensen climbed into the bay and returned with a pack, which he ripped open and cracked. "This will start to warm your core." He lifted Roark's shirt and pressed it to his skin. "Keep it on your chest."

The heat burned against him, a pocket of resolve.

"Don't go to sleep," Jensen said. "I'll be right back." He pulled out a backboard and returned to the trauma site.

Roark found Amelia in the parking lot, talking to her sister and . . . yes, Max, one of the hockey players. So the sister must be Grace.

Amelia set the little girl down, crouched before her. Grace, too, hunkered down. Max shoved his hands into his pockets, wearing a grim look.

Maybe this wasn't the time . . . but when, exactly, did he plan on executing his brilliant plan to win her back?

Apparently his cowardice had followed him across the pond. And glued him to the pavement as the reality of his actions sank in.

He'd really done it. Ignored her father, her brothers—and frankly, even Amelia herself—because . . . because why?

Suddenly his actions seemed belligerent. Bullying. Even . . . selfish.

His words to Claire rang in his head. He did have honorable intent. He did want to make amends. But what if his appearance in town added to Amelia's wounds?

He watched as she drew the little girl into her arms. The gesture reached deep, thickening his throat.

If he truly cared for her, perhaps he'd leave before she caught wind of his reappearance in her life.

He heard voices and looked up to see the lumberjack fireman and the bobby headed toward the fire engine nearby.

The firefighter pulled off his wet shirt and reached for his jacket hanging on the end of the engine. "What's with Amelia and the kid?"

The officer shook his head. Dishwater blond, lean, no-nonsense, this one. "I think she found their kid, although the girl doesn't speak any English. I called Diane Wolfe with social services. She's in Duluth for the night, so Ivy Christiansen is handling a temporary placement. I told Amelia she could take her to the lodge if Ivy approved it—the benefit of having a county attorney in the family."

"Shoot. There goes our plans for tonight."

Roark's head popped up, his eyes on the lumberjack.

"You two are back together?" This from the officer.

"Absolutely. And this time it's for good. No more traipsing off overseas. She'll have a rock on her finger by the end of the summer."

The officer laughed. "Seth, no one would accuse you of pansying around."

"She's my girl. Always has been, always will be." He winked. "I guess I'll have to figure out another time to remind her of that."

Roark wanted to shuck off the blanket, level himself at the bloke, but not only was the man as big as a tree, Roark might have been more affected by the frigid water than he'd supposed. The sky had started to turn fuzzy.

Still, he watched as Seth moseyed over to Amelia, slung an arm around her. Saw his expression as she shook her head. Roark didn't like the way the look settled in his gut, low and tight.

The lumberjack moved away just as Jensen returned, this time helping to carry a body draped in a blanket.

Roark got up and made room for the solemn crew as they loaded the victim into the ambulance. He stood there, stared at the body. Shivered. Listened to the argument in his head.

Yes, he'd hurt her. But what if he went all in, right now, and told her everything? Told her the real reason why she'd found him at the bridge with Cicely and why he'd had to leave Prague so quickly afterward. That would mean, of course, scrolling back further, through the last two years, the fire, and even before that, to Spain. And Russia.

But maybe he could put it all on the table, every last quid, and then let her decide?

Because life was fragile.

Roark threw off the blanket. Fresh air rushed in around the heat pack, raised gooseflesh on his arms. He headed toward Amelia.

He heard the yip of a siren, saw an ambulance inching forward down the highway, and heard someone call, "Make a hole!" He scampered to the side of the road, the sky taking a sudden dip to the right.

And then he was down. A full-on collapse, his hand reaching for the guardrail as his knees buckled.

"Just how long were you in that water?" Jensen came from behind him, caught him under the armpits.

"Twenty minutes?" He blinked back shadows, his eyes on Amelia, but she had loaded the little girl into her orange Kia. "I have to talk to Amelia."

"Not today. Not right now, buddy." Jensen hauled him up, flinging Roark's arm over his shoulder.

"But I have to tell her something."

Except he felt pretty sure his words slurred.

"Declare your undying love later, when you know you'll live."

"No—I mean, yes . . . but . . ." The words seemed to fray around the edges. What was it? "I shouldn't have lied."

"We know that—"

"No, see, I'm not just a bum who broke her heart. I'm . . . the heir to the Constantine fortune . . ."

Suddenly it seemed so ridiculous, the declaration more like babbling than a revelation.

Jensen seemed not to hear him. Until, that is, he got to the ambulance. "Climb in and lie down. There's room for two in here, and I can't let Your Majesty perish on my watch."

Oh, his eyes wanted to close, his body sinking into the gurney. He could feel Jensen covering him up.

"Not . . . royal. I'm rich. Very, very . . . very . . ."

Then the darkness won.

Chapter 3

"I KNOW YOU'RE IN THERE. Wake up already and tell me. Are you rich or not?"

The voice slithered into the darkness, parting it and tugging at Roark. Everything hurt as he shuffled through the cottony shadows toward consciousness. Toward—

Where was he? He'd woken in the cabins of sailboats in the Caribbean, in European hotels, in Russian train compartments and tents perched on the northeast face of Kilimanjaro. On at least two occasions he'd found himself in a local detention center and, once, in a rank French prison. And yes, he'd experienced the surreal moments of waking in a Scottish hospital ward, his head having taken a good knocking on the rugby field.

He blinked, found himself in a cubicle of a room, the window small, framed by pink curtains, a midafternoon sun casting shadows. A cotton blanket was pulled to his chest, an IV pinching his arm, and in the chair beside him . . . Oh, he knew this woman. "Claire?"

"I know you were probably hoping for Amelia, but sorry, bub; you've got me."

"How long have I been out?"

"Five years."

His eyes widened. "Uh—"

"Gotcha." She winked. "A couple hours. Your body temp was dangerously low. But they fixed you up, and you're cooking right along. Out of the woods. Just in time, because I think Amelia's about ready to leave."

He blinked again at her words, trying to push himself off the pillow. "She's here?"

"Oh no, you don't." Claire caught his shoulders. "There you go, Mr. Freeze. Back in the bed until you get the all clear from the doc."

He winced. "You didn't say anything to Amelia about—"

"Your being . . . How did Jensen put it? Rich? Very, very . . . I think there were three *very*s." She shook her head, smiled. "Nope. In fact, let your broken heart rest at ease; she doesn't even know you're here. I saw her come in with the little girl she found at the falls. She and Grace are having her checked out."

He let out a sigh.

"I can run and get her for—"

"No."

That came out sharper than he'd intended. "I think I'd prefer to be standing when we talk." So she could, what? Have less guilt when she walloped him? Because that's suddenly how their conversation ended in his now-aching head. The warmth probably rushing back to fuel his brain with common sense.

He'd come to Deep Haven to win her back. Which meant, sadly, keeping secrets.

And Claire only confirmed it when she folded her arms and nodded. "Probably wise, given the weighty news of your impending inheritance. Because I'm guessing you didn't mean very, very, very rich in *friends,* right?"

He let out a pitiful chuckle. "No."

"So then . . . You said *heir,* which conjures up thrones and kingdoms. Should I address you as Your Highness?"

"Please, no. I'm not royal. I'm just the heir to the throne of the Constantine group of hotels. My grandfather named me as his successor when he passed."

"Successor. Sounds royal. And hotels are sort of like palaces. Which leads me to ask . . . why didn't you mention this when you came to dinner? Rich guy who lives in an efficiency flat over the coffee shop—what's up with that?"

There it was. The very conversation he'd have with Amelia. Inevitably leading to . . .

"My grandfather's money has only caused me heartache, so I like to keep it out of the introductions."

"One of those I-don't-need-or-want-my-money guys. Spoken only by people who *have* money."

"Stop being so rough on him, Claire." Jensen came in, holding two cups of steaming coffee. "Your new boss, Kathy, sent these up. Apparently you're a bit of a legend now."

Jensen handed Roark a coffee. Leaned against the wall. "Okay. I'm ready."

Ready? Oh, right. "It's not that I don't like money—of course I like money. It's just the way people look at you when they *know* you have money." He glanced at Claire.

She frowned. "Touché."

He took a sip of the coffee and felt the heat travel to his belly, fortify him. "And the last woman I loved died because of . . . well, because of me, but also the fact that I have money."

Jensen set his coffee cup down and crossed his arms.

Roark couldn't escape it now. He sighed. "I was an assistant manager at one of our branches in Paris—a five-star, with a view of the Eiffel Tower. On the night before I turned twenty-three, I had a party. Invited all of Paris and more—hosted it in the ballroom. Took the cap off the budget." He blinked hard, looked away. "The place was jammed with guests—most of whom I didn't know. I'd purchased my own fame and drank it in."

He still hadn't pinpointed why he'd needed the adoration of thousands. When he closed his eyes, regret could yank him back to the moment when the screaming began, right after Francesca's toast. "We're not sure how, but a fire started on one end of the ballroom. In the chaos of the fire alarm, I got separated from Francesca, my fiancée."

Claire glanced at Jensen at the word *fiancée*. Roark took another sip of coffee. "We found her after the fire. She'd been trampled."

"Oh, Roark." Claire rested her hand on his arm. "It wasn't your fault."

He met her eyes. "It was my party."

He couldn't bear to confess the rest—how he'd made a few choices that had landed him on the side of God's wrath, and the hotel fire only confirmed it. "So I quit. Left the hotel industry, the infamy of my mistakes, and have been wandering around the world since then, trying to figure out how to live with myself." He set the coffee on his bedside table. "Then I met Amelia. She didn't see me as broken or damaged or even rich. Just as the guy who made her laugh. Who could speak a couple languages, introduced her to Nutella crepes, and helped her see the world through the different f-stop settings on her camera. I wasn't the hotel heir who burned down the Constantine Paris, or the grieving fiancé, but a photography bum on holiday. Who happened to be taking the same course she was."

Jensen raised an eyebrow. "*Happened* to?"

"That might be a stretch, but in my defense, I *was* going to tell her. Just not yet. And not until I'd cleared the way with Cicely, Francesca's sister. The woman Amelia thought I cheated with . . ."

"That's why you didn't tell her who Cicely was," Claire said. "Because then you'd have to tell her the whole story about the fire."

"Ending with the fact that my uncle wants me to report to the board in two months to ease into leadership."

"And you didn't think Amelia would jump at the chance to helm the empire with you?" Claire asked.

"I don't know. I just knew that I'd had enough of women seeing only the euros attached to my name. Amelia didn't . . . and then the omission became gaping, and I didn't know how to bridge it. I'm not sure what to hope now. Especially since she's already dating someone else. A big guy named Seth?"

Claire's mouth formed an O. "Right."

"His family owns Turnquist Lumber, and he's the heir to his own throne," Jensen said. "A sort of Deep Haven royalty, as it were."

Roark winced.

"So when are you going to tell her?" Claire said.

"Tell her?"

"That you're rich to the third power. You know, 'very, very, very'? How rich is that, anyway?"

He sighed. "Add a comma for every *very*."

The room went quiet as Claire—and probably Jensen too—did the math. Their expressions confirmed the resolve inside Roark. In fact, he doubted that they would hear anything else he said. That was why . . . "I can't tell her. Not yet."

"But—"

"No, he's right, honey." This from Jensen. "If he tells her, he'll never know if Amelia loves him for his money or for himself. He has to win her back without the money."

Thank you, Jensen.

"But with Seth in the way, it does get tricky,"

Jensen added. "He has hometown advantage."

"But Roark has you and me." Claire got up and patted Roark's shoulder. "The first thing we're going to do is get you out of this bed, get you back to our place, and fill you with warm stew, Your Highness."

"Claire—"

"I'm just kidding. I'm going to call you Caesar instead."

A guy who just tied the knot with the woman he loved shouldn't feel like he was choking.

Maxwell Sharpe should definitely not feel as if something dark and lethal had climbed inside his chest, waiting, stalking, ready to devour him.

To gnaw away at his joy.

The feeling had started on their wedding night, at a resort on Isla Mujeres, the Caribbean breeze warm through the window, the waves a melody against the shore, singing into their cottage. In the cool, sweet night air, Grace Christiansen—now Sharpe—slid into his arms and became his wife.

Afterward, as he'd stared at the ceiling, her hand on his chest, her blonde hair splayed out on the pillow, her breathing full and deep, Max wanted to weep with regret.

Thankfully, the feeling had died in the sunlight of the day, in the glorious abandon of their honeymoon, and he'd thought himself free of it. They'd flown back to Minneapolis, and he'd agreed to the impromptu trip north to Evergreen Resort to tell Grace's family the good news. Or at least he hoped it would come as good news.

They'd eloped. The word sounded like a gong, a thunderclap of doom resounding louder with each mile northward.

But Grace didn't seem flummoxed by the fact that they'd denied the family a trip down the aisle, a chance to dress up and stand in honor beside them as the couple made their vows. In fact, she thought it might be a relief after the drama of Casper and Raina's recent news and with Owen still on the run.

Maybe he knew her family better than she did.

Because even though the Casper-Raina-Owen triangle seemed soap opera worthy, it all paled when set against the brutal reality of Max's terminal future.

A future that played cruel games, because while right now he proved to be the poster boy for health and vitality, playing forward for the St. Paul Blue Ox, one day his body would ambush him, his latent Huntington's gene striking like a sniper to his future. And sadly, he wouldn't go quickly and easily either, but mercilessly, one languishing day at a time, while Grace cared for him, watching him suffer.

Yeah, Max had no trouble at all picturing her father's reaction to the bombshell of their elopement.

Because he could hardly stomach the shame of succumbing to his own desperate heart, falling in love, breaking his own rules, and marrying a woman who would sacrifice her best years watching him die.

His troubles seemed to vanish, however, when they pulled up to the accidental drowning of practically an entire family. Two members had died on-site, and the mother later, at the hospital—leaving behind a little girl who, providentially, landed in Amelia's care. And was apparently now in the care of Grace Christiansen. Er . . . Sharpe.

"She should be more traumatized than she is, so we're going to watch out for shock," said the doctor on call in the ER, where Amelia and Grace had taken the girl on the advice of Kyle Hueston, deputy sheriff.

The girl sat on an examination table in her pretty pink dress, those red ribbons in her braids loose, kicking her skinny legs against the metal and playing a game on Amelia's iPhone. She hadn't responded to their questions, although Amelia claimed she'd spoken Russian or something like it at the river. She'd finally found a name for her—written on the inside of her jacket. Yulia.

Amelia sat behind the girl, reaching around her now and again to help with the game. Grace talked on her own phone to Ivy, working out the child's sleeping arrangements.

It helped that Grace already had Ivy on her speed dial, as her sister-in-law.

"Weren't Mom and Dad cleared as foster placements last year when they took in my cousin? Don't you think—? Oh, okay. But temporarily?"

Pause, then, "Yeah, me too. Okay, do your best."

She hung up. "Ivy talked with Kyle. They found next of kin, a sister in college in Minneapolis. Apparently her parents recently adopted Yulia from Ukraine. The sister is in no shape to take her, so Ivy's contacting the adoption coordinator, trying to see if we can take her temporarily."

Max glanced at her from where he leaned against the wall, hands in his pockets. He needed air. "Anyone want water? Or coffee? Chocolate?"

Amelia shook her head, frowned.

He escaped anyway, stalking all the way out into the foyer, then beyond, to the cool, pine-scented night, the stars watching as he pressed his hands to his face.

"Honey? Are you okay?"

See, he couldn't hide anything from his wife—not his stress and certainly not his regret.

Imagine her hurt when she discovered her groom regretted marrying her. The thought landed like a knife in his chest, and he bit back a cry of pain. He wanted to keep running out into the night but couldn't when he felt her hand slide into his.

"What's going on?"

Oh, she was beautiful—looking at him with those blue eyes in the way that could infuse a sort of light into his spirit. He reached out and twined his fingers into her silky hair, aware of how rough and big his hands were. "I'm just wondering how we're going to tell your family—your overly protective, in-your-face family—that we eloped."

It had been an impulse, really—birthed after Max's hockey team lost their play-off round. Grace had met him in the tunnel after the game, wrapped her arms around his neck, and whispered, "Cancún. Let's do it."

And with her sweet smell, her soft body against his, her voice like a song in his ear, Max couldn't deny that he longed, with every bone in his body, to be married to her. To take her in his arms, lose himself in her embrace.

He should have pushed her away, let common sense grab hold. Maybe right now, she saw that in his eyes.

"You have regrets," she said, taking his hand from her hair, holding it. "But you shouldn't. You've been putting me off for almost a year, and frankly, I would have married you last fall in front of a justice of the peace with a hobo for a witness, so the fact that you made me wait until after the season ended is pure cruelty, mister."

She lifted her arms around his neck, pulled his

head down. "I don't think I could have waited much longer."

Then she kissed him, and he was a weak man because he wrapped his arms around her, sank into her kiss. She tasted of the lemonade and salty fries from their stop at McDonald's, smelled of the lilacs she'd picked in Minneapolis before their trek north. Her body fit perfectly against his, as if she'd been made for him, or him for her, and when he held her, the world dropped away.

Her touch could heal him. Convince him that yes, marrying her had been a gift to him from God to help him endure, the one thing on earth that could make his life worth living.

She leaned back and said, "I need to get inside and see if Ivy's made any headway with her emergency placement with my parents."

Her eyes glowed with an unfamiliar shine. Max frowned as he followed her inside.

"I think we're done here," the doctor said. "It seems as though your sister-in-law pulled a few strings. The adoption coordinator called and said they would release her into your custody, so she's free to go with you. Just keep an eye on her, maybe check on her in the night."

Yulia ducked her head again, her lower lip caught in her teeth as she played with the phone.

"She seems to be coping," Max said.

Grace crouched before the girl and used a voice Max recognized from when he sank into a surly, defeated postgame mood. "Would you like some ice cream?"

The girl looked at her, wearing a blank expression. Undaunted, Grace straightened and held out her hand.

Yulia hesitated for a moment but then, one hand holding the phone, took Grace's in the other and let Grace help her off the table.

Grace led her toward the parking lot. "Max, can you follow us? I'm going to ride with Amelia."

He nodded, watching his wife climb into the backseat with Yulia and put her arm around the child.

A shadow brushed his heart at the sight.

And settled there as he drove north to Evergreen Resort.

He'd always loved the Christiansen homestead: the two-story lodge with the attic bedrooms, the expansive open family room/kitchen with a stone fireplace. The place overlooked Evergreen Lake, with a deck that could host the entire Blue Ox team, and a fishing dock jutting out from shore.

His wife had grown up here, surrounded by a family that had only seemed to grow stronger with the challenges of the past few years. The wildland fire that destroyed the rental cabins. The accident that left Owen—Max's former teammate—unable to play, and the blowup of his injuries and mistakes that eventually led to the birth of his daughter with a woman now pledged to marry Casper, his older brother. And now, well, Max hoped very much that John and Ingrid would weather the news of their daughter's elopement.

He pulled into the lot behind Amelia and got out, seeing how Grace clutched Yulia's hand as they walked to the lodge.

"Tomorrow, I'll bet Nana Christiansen will make you cookies."

Nana Christiansen?

Grace opened the door, ushered the troupe inside. Max retrieved their suitcases and followed her.

Ingrid Christiansen, her short blonde hair tucked behind her ears, already had Grace in an embrace, the smell of baking—something sweet and chocolaty—filling the air. Max set the suitcases down.

"And Max too!" Ingrid stepped past Grace and threw her arms around his waist.

"Hey . . ." Not *Mom*. "Mrs. Christiansen."

"Call me Ingrid, Max. We've been through this." She caught his face in her hands and gave him a quick kiss on the cheek.

Yeah, he liked Grace's family. Hopefully, after tonight, they'd still like him.

Ingrid crouched before the little girl. "Are you hungry, sweetie?"

"I don't think she speaks English, Mom,"

Amelia said. "We tried—but she seems to under-stand Russian."

"Well, I'll bet she understands the language of macaroni and cheese and chocolate cake."

Max had to love Ingrid for her shower-them-with-food philosophy. Yulia followed her into the kitchen and climbed up on one of the counter stools. A plate of macaroni waited.

Ingrid dug around for a fork, found one. "Your father is out at the accident site—they found the family's car and are towing it to the police station. Darek went home for the night, but I'm sure he'll bring the kiddos up tomorrow."

"I can't wait to see Joy. And little Layla. How are Raina and Casper?" Grace said.

"Good. Raina is still house-sitting for her aunt, so she'll stay there for a while. Casper usually drops by after work—but I think he's itching to go search for Owen."

Max didn't look at Ingrid, the memory of his part in the fight that caused the wounds of his angry, prodigal brother-in-law still raking up too much grief.

"I don't know why Casper's still working at the Wild Harbor," Grace said. "After all, with the reward he netted after his last find, he has enough money to spend his time hunting for more treasure."

"I think he's just trying to help Ned. You know how he is—always coming to someone's rescue,"

Ingrid said. "Besides, I think he has plans for the money. Something that includes building a home as soon as he can marry Raina."

Max glanced at Grace, an eyebrow up. *Now. Tell them now, honey.* But Grace was watching Yulia.

"Poor thing," Ingrid finally said, pouring the little girl a glass of milk.

"I don't know, Mom," Amelia said. "Maybe it's shock, but she didn't seem to care who held on to her, just followed the first person who took her hand."

Ingrid frowned. "She's probably scared."

"It could be an attachment disorder," Grace said. "I've read about that—happens with orphans. They have trouble fixing themselves to one person, feeling that bond."

"Even at the accident site, when they pulled out her parents, she named them but sounded so detached." Amelia scooted a stool next to Yulia, setting her camera case on the counter. "Can I talk you into some macaroni and cheese for the local photojournalist?"

"Oh, Amelia, did you get the job? That's wonderful news!" Ingrid went to the stove and returned to the counter with a plateful.

"I don't know yet, but I got shots not only of the oh-so-exciting Girl Scout Troop 168 car wash, but also the events at the river."

"The whole thing is so sad," Ingrid said.

"Tourists just don't realize how dangerous it is to wade in the rivers and creeks. Life turns ugly so fast. Makes a person want to hold tighter to the happy moments. The joy."

A beat of silence passed.

Then Ingrid said, her tone brightening, "Max and Grace—to what do we owe this surprise visit?"

He glanced at Grace for cues, ready to announce the big news. But she wore a strange expression. "Uh, we thought, since Max's season was over, we'd help with your Mother's Day breakfast-in-bed event. Darek told me how you're making cinnamon rolls for the guests, and . . . we thought we'd help. Right, Max?"

She gave him a smile and for a second, the way the lie slid like honey off her lips made him doubt everything she'd ever told him.

"Uh, yeah."

"Oh, that's wonderful!" Ingrid said. "I'd love some help in the kitchen. In fact, I'll even move aside and let you two Iron Chefs take over."

"You don't have to—" Max started.

"Grace, help yourself to the fridge, and if you don't want mac and cheese, then whip up something for you and Max to eat. I'll make up Eden's bed for Yulia with you and Amelia in the attic. Max, you have your choice—the den or the boys' room."

He glanced at Grace, who suddenly seemed to

forget that, yes, they were married, because she said . . . nothing?

He might regret marrying her, but hello, he had no intention of spending even one night away from his new bride.

Except she met his eyes, a stream of panic in hers.

Shoot. "The den sounds great, Ingrid. Let me help." He thought it came out in a growl, but Ingrid seemed not to notice.

"I'll get the sheets," Grace said. She wrinkled her nose in an I'm-sorry expression.

But maybe she, like him, needed time to get her footing. Figure out how to tell her parents that yes, they'd finally jumped in, both feet, regardless of the sentence looming in front of them.

And while John and Ingrid—the entire family, probably—knew about his diagnosis, he expected a hard conversation with John about how Max intended to provide for Grace when his body no longer could.

Yeah, that conversation, in light of today's tragedy, could possibly wait until tomorrow.

But it didn't mean he wouldn't try to talk Grace into sneaking down to the den in the wee hours. For a moment, that very thought slid a smile up his face.

Grace caught it as she returned with a stack of sheets. He retrieved them, their hands brushing.

Then he winked, and deliciously, she blushed. As if she might be thinking the same thing.

Oh, how he loved her.

She turned, laughing at something Amelia was saying as she jogged up the stairs.

"How about a slice of that chocolate cake," Grace said to Max. Then she patted Yulia on the back, looked down at her, such tenderness in her expression it could stop time.

And in that second, darkness rushed back with a force that felt like a check into the boards as Max figured it out. He didn't fear the news of the elopement or even the future looming before him.

Because he could give his wife everything—his heart, his money, his strength, his faith. But he could never give her what she truly wanted.

A family like the one she'd grown up in.

As usual, her family had swooped in and taken over. Amelia tried not to let the way Grace tucked Yulia into bed, reading her a story as if she'd been the one to find her on the shore, niggle at her.

After all, the little girl needed as much love as she could get. And Amelia didn't really resent her sister's—or her mother's—ministrations. Just that, without a word, they'd assumed she didn't quite have it in her to mother this grieving child.

Yeah, well, she knew exactly how it felt to be in a foreign country alone. Still, she shook away the voices and listened instead to the night sky whispering to her, pulling her away from the speculation about Yulia and out onto the deck, her feet bare against the cool wood. The wind rushed through the trees across the lake, and the lights at Jensen's family's stately lake home peered out like eyes into the night.

She slid onto the picnic table, unzipped her camera from its case, and scrolled through the day's pictures. She couldn't wait to show Lou her shots on Monday morning. The Girl Scouts laughing in the glorious spray of the car wash. It all felt decades away, but there, too, was Seth, strong, tanned, grinning at Amelia, one thumb caught in his waistband.

She heard his voice, his words at the accident site when she'd canceled their date tonight. *C'mon, Amelia, don't let me down.*

Lately that was all she seemed to be doing.

She kept scrolling to the shots of the accident, found the ones she'd taken of the spectators—the elderly couple, the woman in khakis with her children, little Yulia.

And then . . . what? Oh no. The last picture on her memory card was Yulia, silhouetted by a rainbow spray of golden light from the falls.

Nothing of the accident, of the fire engines, of Seth and the others recovering the bodies.

Nothing, even, of Roark. Hours later, she'd decided that whoever she'd seen looking water-logged and exhausted, it couldn't have been him.

How crazy would that be? Roark St. John, European playboy, pulling bodies out of a frigid river in northern Minnesota? Right.

She stared at the screen and wanted to throw the camera—and herself—into the lake. How could she not have snapped at least one shot?

"Honey, are you okay?"

Her mother's voice tiptoed out into the night, the sliding door clicking shut behind her. Ingrid climbed onto the table next to Amelia. The cicadas sang over the rim of the still water, frogs joining the chorus. A loon moaned, low and long.

Amelia set the camera on the table and hung her face in her hands. "I didn't take any shots of the accident today. Nothing. No fire trucks, no rescue. Lou is going to kill me."

Her mother's hand pressed her shoulder. "There was a lot going on. You rescued Yulia. That seems more important than taking shots of the tragedy."

"I don't think Lou is going to see it that way." She could imagine his reaction—especially after her rousing, confident call to him on her way to the river. "I think I'm going to lose this job before I even land it."

"There are other jobs out there. The lodge could always—"

"No, Mom." Her voice emerged more strident than she meant, so she softened it. "I mean, yes, of course, I'll always help out at the lodge, but . . . I wanted something . . ."

"Epic."

She glanced at her mother, saw the softness of her smile.

"Honey, no one blames you for wanting to see the world. I was just like you at your age—wanting to do something more with my life. You know that I went to Ecuador to serve in the Peace Corps for a year after high school, right?"

"I know, but then you came back to Deep Haven. And stayed."

Oh. She winced, hearing how the words laid out. Feeling the heaviness of her mother's silence.

Then, "You clearly see that as a failure."

"Not for you, Mom. But . . ."

"But you hadn't exactly planned on returning."

Amelia tucked her hands between her knees, a breeze rustling through Seth's shirt. She'd forgotten she was wearing it, and now it felt like a sort of betrayal.

Especially since she couldn't seem to scrape the memory of Roark—or the image of Roark—from her brain.

"I just thought I was on my way to something amazing. Maybe it was all those stories I read as a kid, the ones about missionaries smuggling Bibles and chopping their way through the rain forest to find lost civilizations, but I saw myself changing the world. I felt like I was answering this strange voice, deep inside me, the one telling me that there is more out there and I'm supposed to go do it."

"You can still do it, honey. You're just regrouping."

She said nothing for a moment. Then, "I thought I saw him today."

Her mother waited.

"Roark."

"I know who you're talking about." Her mother's hand rested lightly on her arm. "Where did you see him?"

"At the accident. Retrieving the body of one of the victims. I thought I saw him giving her CPR." She swatted a mosquito that landed on her leg. "I know it wasn't him. But you know, sometimes I expect him to show up. To appear at—I don't know, the coffee shop or the donut place. Or maybe in our parking lot. What if he did come back to town?"

"What if?"

"No, it's crazy thinking. There's no way he'd come back here again. Not after the way we treated him."

"We were a little rough on him."

She slanted a glance at her mother. "Really? I thought you didn't like him."

"I don't know him enough to make a judgment. But I saw the way you wanted to defend him when he showed up here. How you nearly leaped into his arms—would have, maybe, if your brothers hadn't stepped between you."

"He came all the way over here and got run off with the metaphorical pitchfork."

"They love you, and he hurt you."

She let that pass. "I regret not talking to him." There, she said it.

In fact, most nights she dreamed about the conversation she longed to have with him, over and over. A conversation that started with her apology for putting them in this mess. For believing they were more than friends and getting confused, jealous, angry, even childish.

She should have realized she thought more of their relationship than he had. She'd simply been a game, a fling.

Except when a guy flew over the ocean and arrived with flowers . . . what did that say? That baffled her most of all.

"What would you say to him?"

That was the problem, wasn't it? "I don't know. It probably wouldn't have worked out between us anyway."

"Why not?"

"I did mention he was twenty-five, right?"

"Your father is older than me."

"Not five years older. And he's British."

"Oh, really?"

"Funny, Mom. But more than that, he's . . . I don't know. Smart. Polished. He spoke French and, I think, German. But I'm not sure I really knew him all that well. I was wooed by the luster of a European man with a sexy accent. I feel foolish for giving my heart away so fast to a man I hardly knew. Maybe it wasn't even love— maybe it was all just an illusion of love. Maybe I wanted love more than felt it."

"That's the biggest part of this. You feel foolish."

"And like a coward for running back to Deep Haven." She leaned back on her hands, stared at the sprinkle of stars against the vast velvet night. "I thought I was brave. I thought I was smart." Her eyes burned and she blinked, feeling moisture on her cheeks. "I thought I was invincible."

"Honey."

Amelia swallowed, the mortality of her dreams pressing a hand against her chest. "I failed myself. How can I ever really trust myself, or my heart, again?"

"Maybe it's not about trusting yourself, but trusting God. He knows your heart better than you do."

"I know. I do. But . . . I guess the big question is, do I know His heart? Maybe if I knew the bigger picture, all of this would make sense. But I feel small, sitting here looking up at the sky. I always wanted to be someone God could use. But I'm wondering if I thought too much of myself. Maybe I'm not who I hoped to be. Now everything is blurry—my future, my feelings for Seth. Even . . . I don't know. Apparently I'm going crazy and imagining Roark too."

"Do you love Jesus, Amelia?"

She drew in the question with a breath. "I do, Mom."

"Then start there. Always start there. Once you have centered your heart on that, everything else comes into focus."

Amelia closed her eyes. Listened to the wind in the trees, the lap of the lake against the canoe onshore. "I do know that I want a man who loves God. A man after God's heart."

"That's a good place to start."

"I can't shake the sense that we were . . . supposed to be together. I know he was a stranger, but it felt right. Have you ever had that?"

Her mother smiled, nodded. "I believed in your father and me long before he did. I knew we were supposed to be together." She put her arm around Amelia. "There is more out there for you. Give it time. God will bring everything into focus."

Amelia leaned her head on her mother's shoulder. "I know what I'd say to him." She lifted her head. "Roark."

"I know."

"I'd tell him we would have to start over. From the beginning. That I wanted honesty every step of the way, no games. And if he lied to me, even once, we'd be over." She rested her head again on her mother's shoulder. "That's what I'd say if he showed up here."

"Which he won't."

"Unless he steps out of my imagination and back into Deep Haven."

Chapter 4

THE SKY COULD HAVE the decency to rain. But no, it arched high and blue without blemish, the gulls crying out, the air redolent with the scents of greening poplars and mountain ash buds.

It all mocked Amelia as she stepped out of the *Deep Haven Herald* office. Fired before she even landed the job. How fair was that?

Apparently, very fair, because yes, Lou had received her message, and no, he hadn't sent out reinforcements to the accident, which meant he had no photos for the upcoming weekly issue of the paper.

Except, of course, front page–worthy pictures of Troop 168 spraying down Edith Draper's Ford Escape. And of Seth.

She should call him back after the five messages he'd left on her phone. Yes, definitely, she'd call him back, let him cajole her out of her surly mood.

Truth was, in Lou's shoes, she probably would have fired herself. But she would have done it nicely. With words like *I know you have talent, and by the way, how's that little girl you helped?* Not, *What am I supposed to do with this? What kind of airhead goes to the catastrophe of the summer and gets pictures of two old people holding hands?*

She hung her backpack over her shoulder and headed toward her car, parked near the harbor lot. Her mother had a slew of preparations this week for the upcoming Mother's Day event at the resort, their kickoff for the summer, with a full house reserved. Amelia had glimpsed the list this morning—plant flower boxes; change sheets, towels, and kitchenware; dust. And that was just her mother's list. Darek would probably stick Amelia at the front desk to take calls. Not that she didn't like talking to prospective guests, but her world seemed to be shrinking in on itself.

Seth. The lodge. The sum total of her shiny future.

Oh, she wasn't being fair to either of them. But . . .

Her phone buzzed in her pocket just as she reached her Kia. She pulled it out, found a text from Ree. **Meet me at the Java Cup!**

Amelia stood a moment, considering her mood—and the hope of commiseration with Ree, who understood better than anyone the fate of being trapped in Deep Haven.

If Ree didn't escape soon, she probably never would.

So, yeah, Amelia texted Ree back and headed to the Java Cup, the smells of the nearby donut/cupcake shop reaching out to entice her. Thankfully, she'd already eaten. At least with Grace home, she got a decent breakfast—her sister had whipped up Belgian waffles and cracked open a jar of their mother's homemade raspberry jam this morning.

Mostly for Yulia, a sort of last breakfast before the adoption coordinator arrived to take her away.

She'd uttered not even a whimper the last two nights, although Amelia slept fitfully, tossing the nights away. Grace seemed restless too and woke her once, shuffling through the room—probably on her way to the bathroom.

In her dreams, Amelia kept seeing Roark, trying to save the life of a stranger. Was he the kind of person to dive into the icy waters of the river, search for bodies? Clearly she didn't know him as well as she should have because she couldn't answer that question.

Except her thumping heart said yes.

The busy coffee shop drew her in like an embrace as she opened the door, the bell jangling overhead. The Java Cup overlooked the lake, with a deck hosting Adirondack chairs perfect for soaking in the view while enjoying a moment of quiet with a mocha and a friend. Inside, announcements of local events fluttered on a bulletin board near the door, and conversation groups anchored by leather chairs and tables made from local birch and pine logs added to the north shore aura. The spill of beans, the churn of a grinder, and a line at the counter evidenced the busy morning.

Amelia studied the specials listed in pink-and-green chalk on the board behind the counter. Today the Becky was featured—a vanilla and caramel mocha named after a town regular.

"Amelia! Over here!"

The voice emerged from the anteroom that jutted off the main area and faced the town's library and yoga studio. She spotted Vivie, today wearing a short tie-dyed dress, brown leggings, and low boots, a scarf at her neck, her hair tied up in a messy, high knot. Vivie slid off a stool pushed up to one of the high-top tables and scampered over. "Just the person we hoped to see!"

"Who is *we?*" Amelia asked, returning her hug.

"The Sawdust Sweeties." Vivie grabbed her hand even as Amelia cast a look around the room for Ree.

She didn't spot her before Vivie pulled her to a table of familiar faces—former classmates, the cute ones who knew how to smile and giggle and probably never failed at love.

Then it clicked. The Sawdust Sweeties. Right.

Deep Haven's annual beauty pageant, held during the upcoming Flapjack Festival honoring the lumberjacks in the area. She'd always tried to erase from her brain the spectacle of local girls in Daisy Dukes, posing with chain saws and axes. But the winner went on to bigger and better competitions, ending at the Miss Minnesota Butter Girl competition and a $50,000 scholarship.

"You did such a great job on my senior photos, I told Vivie you could probably take our Sweetie shots," Colleen Decker said. She'd graduated with Amelia and immediately headed off to play volleyball for the University of Minnesota, Duluth.

"Hey, Colleen," Amelia said. "When did you get back?"

"This is the last week of classes. But Vivie said the deadline for applications is in a week, and we all need pictures, so . . ."

"Please, Ames? No one takes pictures like you," Vivien said.

Oh, well—

"And everyone else costs so much. We're poor college students," Colleen added.

Ah. A *free* gig. She sighed. "Sure. I guess. When do you need them by?"

"We can set up the sittings as soon as possible. Thanks, Ames; you're a doll." Vivie leaned over and gave her an air kiss.

"There you are." Ree's voice came from behind

her, and Amelia turned, accepting the cup of coffee she held out. "I picked you up a Becky."

"Thanks, Ree."

"I got us a seat near the window. Hey, Viv," Ree said as she hooked Amelia's arm. She led her to a table near the picture window with a view of the lake. Amelia sat down, turning her armchair to face the lake and the too-cheerful blue sky.

"So," Ree said, sitting opposite. "Guess what?"

"Chris Hemsworth checked into your motel."

"Sadly, no. We did get a Mr. Melvin Applewood, traveling from Thief River Falls, here for a weekend of bird-watching." She gave a nod of mock approval.

"Okay, fine. I'll bite. What?"

Ree wrinkled her nose, leaned close. "I got a job. A real, full-time job at a newspaper!" She held up her cup. "Congratulate me. I'm moving out of this backwoods joint and off to the big world of journalism."

"Ree, that's fantastic," Amelia said. And she meant it, really. Despite the hitch in her throat. "Where?"

"A town about two hours north of the Cities. It's a resort town like Deep Haven, but bigger. They have a daily. A *daily!* They need a features reporter."

Amelia kept her smile, but, "When are you leaving?"

"A couple weeks—probably after the Memorial

Day rush. My parents need me until then. Unless . . ." She caught Amelia's eyes. "Unless I can find a replacement at the front desk right away."

Amelia stared back until—"Oh! You mean me."

"Well, you do know the resort industry. And you want to get away from Evergreen."

"Not to another resort—Ree, seriously?"

Ree sat back. "It was worth a try. I mean, I just thought with the fiasco at the paper . . ."

"You heard about that? Already?" She took a sip of her coffee. Sweet and bracing. "Sometimes I hate this town."

"Rhonda texted me. Actually, during your very conversation. Apparently Lou was loud."

Amelia watched a couple tourists amble down the street with paper bags of purchases from the local Ben Franklin. "Yeah, well, I probably deserved it. I didn't get any shots of the accident. But that was the weirdest day. When I got there, I thought I saw—"

"Hot guy alert at the counter." Vivie broke into their conversation by sticking her head down, crouching next to their chairs. Amelia started to turn but Vivie grabbed her arm. "Don't look!"

"But you just said—"

"Don't be obvious."

"Oh, my," Ree said softly. With enough weight to her tone that Amelia couldn't help but turn, despite Vivie's warning.

Oh. What—? But . . .

"See. Hot, right?" Vivien said, pulling up a chair beside Ree.

"You're not wrong," Ree said.

No. Not in the least. Because standing behind the counter—wearing a crisp white Java Cup T-shirt under a gray-striped apron, his hair shorter than she remembered but still curly, the dusting of a dark early morning beard on his face, along with the smile she couldn't ever quite pry from her mind—stood a man who appeared to be the spitting image of European heartbreaker Roark St. John, serving a tall latte to Colleen Decker.

Who giggled.

Amelia turned back. Stared hard at Ree. "It can't be him. It just can't be."

"Can't be who?" Vivie said.

"It's 007," Ree said. "The Brit. Mr. James Bond in the flesh, back from over the pond."

Vivie's mouth opened, her eyes big. "The playboy." She gave Amelia a look of delight.

"It's not him. How could it be him? Roark isn't going to get a job at my local coffee shop and learn to pull an espresso shot just so he can, what? Make me a double-shot latte?"

"What about win your heart back?" Ree said. "He was pretty determined."

"And my brothers ran him out of town. No." She shook her head. "It can't be him."

"Go order something. See for sure," Vivie said.

"What? No. Ree, you were at the counter—didn't you see him?"

"Maybe he just got on shift."

"He sort of looks like he's in training," Vivie said, peering past Amelia. "Kathy's showing him how to press the espresso shot."

Amelia hazarded another glance. It certainly looked like him—his arms filling out his shirt-sleeves, the apron outlining his lean torso, the way he listened to his boss, then worked the machine, capable, serious. She traced his high cheekbones, the curl of his hair against his collar. Without a doubt, he wore that musky cherrywood cologne that stirred up memories of a walk along the Vltava among falling stars and the heady hope of tomorrow.

Then he smiled, and her world stopped.

It had always stopped, then tilted just a little, right on that smile.

"Amelia? Is it him?"

She turned back, breathing hard. "I . . . I think so."

"There's only one way to find out."

"No. Ree, no."

Ree leaned back. Lifted her shoulder. "Someone has to go talk to him."

"Me. I'll do it." Vivien was up before Amelia could stop her.

"Viv—!"

But she'd already angled toward the counter

and the dwindling line. Amelia faced Ree. "I can't watch."

Ree grinned. "Fine. She's approaching the counter. Flipping her hair, laughing. Oh, look, he's smiling back. She's ordering, pointing to the menu. He's laughing now. She's touching his arm—"

"She's touching his arm?"

"Nah. Just testing."

"Ha."

"Here she comes."

Vivien sat down, her expression alight. She grinned.

"So?" Amelia said.

"Anyone want a spot of tea?" she said with a wretched accent.

"No," Amelia said. "Seriously?"

"I'd say, old chap, your man has blown back into town."

Ree's hazel eyes widened. "Go talk to him."

"No. I mean, uh . . ." Amelia turned back around, watched him again. He didn't spare even a glance her direction. "What if he doesn't know I'm here?"

"Really, Amelia? We're sitting over here giggling like we're in fourth grade. I promise you, he knows we're here," Ree said. "At least say hi. It might be your only chance before your brothers erect a force field around you."

Hmm.

"I think he could use a friend," Vivien said. "He looks lonely. Oh, wait, here comes Colleen . . ."

"Fine!" Amelia got up and headed to the counter, bypassing the line and stepping right up to the espresso makers, where he frothed a latte.

Up close he still had the power to tangle her brain, reduce her words to babbling. Especially when he looked at her with those amazing blue eyes that could turn at once dark and smoky or twinkle, like they did now.

Then he smiled. Like he expected her. "Amelia," he said with that accent that rippled clear through her. No one quite said her name like Roark.

"Are you out of your mind?" Okay, not exactly the hello she'd rehearsed in her dreams but—

"Probably."

She blinked at him, stymied. "What are you doing here?"

"Making coffee."

"Oh, you're a smart one. Seriously. What are you doing?"

"I believe it is a tall Moose Special, blended," he said smartly.

"Roark!"

"Go out for dinner with me tonight."

She blinked again, but he didn't look at her, just began to blend the mixture. She waited until he finished to keep from shouting.

"What—?"

"I just want to talk." He poured the drink into a cup, added the lid. "Emma?"

Emma Hueston looked up from where she was texting near the door and retrieved her coffee. "Amelia. Hey."

"Hey," Amelia said, glancing at Roark, then at Ree and Vivie, whose expressions made the entire thing feel like an episode of *Big Brother*.

Emma walked away and Amelia pitched her voice low. "No, I won't have dinner with you." Although why those words issued from her, she couldn't say. Didn't she long for this, a chance to talk to him, forgive him?

But what if her brothers—or Seth—found out? She'd call the feeling panic. "No."

To her shock, he lifted a shoulder. "Okay."

"Okay?"

He shrugged again. "I'll wait. I have coffee to make."

"You really moved here to get me to go out with you? Isn't that sort of . . . extreme?"

He looked at her then, his eyes so full of emotion that it swiped away the present, flung her back to that moment only four months ago, New Year's Eve, when he'd leaned her direction, one hand braced against the wall over her shoulder, gaze in hers, searching.

When she could taste her heart in her throat.

"Amelia," he said quietly, so softly she felt it

more than heard it. *"Extreme* doesn't begin to describe what I'd do to win you back."

His words pulled her back to the present: the sounds of the beans spilling, the frothing machine, Kathy barking orders at the counter.

Ree and Vivie laughing from across the room.

He gave her a sad smile, and it settled deep inside her.

Oh, Roark.

She managed a quick, sharp shake of her head and fled to the safety of her friends.

"What do you mean you said no?" Ree said after Amelia ran down their short, brutal conversation. "What more does the man have to do?"

Maybe not so safe after all. Amelia sat there gripping her coffee, the sense of him still like heat inside her.

Roark had returned. For her. *Because* of her.

And Saturday, that *had* been him pulling Yulia's mother from the river, trying to revive her.

"You know, he probably needs a tour guide, being new in town," Vivie said. "I think I'll go offer my services."

"Vivie!" Ree said, but Vivien was already on her feet.

This time, Amelia caught her arm. "If anyone is showing him around town, Viv, it's me." She got up and walked back to the counter.

"Still making coffee," Roark said, not looking at her. "Not going away."

116

"I'll have dinner with you."

He smiled. "I'll come around about seven."

Oh, well—"Meet me at the Harbor Grill."

"Fair enough." He capped another drink. "Chai latte for Vivien?"

"I got that," Amelia said.

"Attagirl," Vivien said as she delivered it. "Now, let's angle our chairs and watch Mr. Bond save the world with coffee."

Apparently Claire Atwood had become his dating therapist.

"So how much do I tell her?" Roark said. He looked into the dusty medicine cabinet mirror, one hand running the shaver, the other holding his mobile. He could hardly believe his fortune— not only seeing Amelia, but getting her to agree to a date on his first day of work.

And Ethan had doubted him. He'd texted the guy, just to set him straight.

"Well, don't mention the *R* word. We already know that. But you have to tell her enough so that she'll give you another chance."

"Right."

"I think the fire story might be too much. You haven't told her that, have you?"

"I omitted that." In fact, he'd omitted nearly everything the first time around—depended on charm and his vast knowledge of the trivial to make her laugh. "I did teach her about wine. And how to crack an oyster."

"What every girl longs to know."

He finished the shave, tucked the razor back into his kit. "I mostly let her talk. She told me about her life—and I listened. I've heard girls like it when you listen."

"You're not wrong," Claire said.

Through the line, he heard Jensen say, "Tell him to take her out to the lighthouse. That's a great place to—"

"Jens! It's a first date!"

Not quite, but it felt that way, the way Roark's stomach had roiled with nerves all day. He'd managed to keep his mind on working his way through the different specialty drinks, pulling the perfect shot of espresso and frothing the latte milk to the exact temperature.

It didn't help that Amelia and her henchmen sat like critics for the better part of the morning. Or that she'd left with nary another word to him. But he held fast to her promise to meet him.

"Reiterate that Cicely was a friend. That she needed someone to talk to, and yes, that you had a history. It's all true."

"I said all that before. It didn't seem to matter. And then I left—how do I explain that?"

"Your uncle had a heart attack—which is true too."

"So play the sympathy card?"

"Have you never faked an injury to get a girl? Jens, this boy of yours could use some pointers!"

"I'm not going to lie to her."

Silence.

"Much."

"Just take her out, remind her of the guy she knew in Prague, and see what happens."

But he didn't want to be the guy he'd been in Prague. He wanted to be better.

"And call me tomorrow with an update. I'm eight months pregnant and you're my only social life." Claire rang off, and Roark laughed as he tossed the mobile onto the bed.

He stared in the mirror, listening to Amelia's words today. *Are you out of your mind?*

Probably, he'd said, but he wasn't. He'd never been surer about anything than when Amelia had walked into the Java Cup wearing jeans and a trench coat, her auburn hair flowing out from under a green beret, and taking his breath away.

Again.

Not unlike their meeting in Old Town Square, two days after he'd first seen her on the Charles Bridge.

He walked out into the main room, trying to choose a shirt, the memory of their first date sweet as it surfaced inside him.

"You again?" he'd said, although he knew perfectly well she'd be there, had asked Claude for the itinerary and details of the class.

He arrived with his satchel over his shoulder, camera around his neck, ready to take notes. To learn. To discover if Amelia had given any further thought to their meeting on the bridge.

"Hi," she said, wearing the same trench coat and boots as the first time they'd met, her hair caught in a cap, her smile lighting up the square. "Isn't it magnificent?"

Of course, she was probably referring to Týn Church, the famous gothic church located just off the square.

He nodded, paying it no mind.

Claude arrived without showing a hint of recognition—good man—and lectured for an hour in the grassy area in front of the fountain on f-stops and apertures. The entire class began to blur as Roark watched Amelia sit in the grass and take notes, twirling one long hair around her finger. They photographed the church then with different settings, and afterward, he invited her back to Charles Bridge because he knew of a café in the shadows. They walked through the cobbled streets, around gardens and monasteries, and he pointed out statues and ancient landmarks.

"You seem to know this city well," she said later, spinning a glass of cabernet. The evening sun setting on the river turned her hair dark, the color of autumn leaves.

"Not well enough," he said. "I went to school in Scotland, so only when I came on holiday." True enough. He and Francesca had traveled here at least twice to visit her family—once for a concert, another time when he accompanied her on a photo shoot.

"By the time I leave, I plan to know all the best hole-in-the-wall cafés in the city," she said.

He made that promise to himself too.

"Where's home?" he'd asked, and she'd leaned in, told him about a hamlet in the north woods of Minnesota—a home pitched at the edge of a lake, three brothers, two sisters, and a life that reached out and entwined him with its charm.

A life that seemed reminiscent of one tucked deep in his memory.

By the time their pork knuckles arrived with creamy garlic potatoes and crusty bread, he'd plunked himself into her life, seeing a future with her.

He'd walked her home, longing to hold her hand, deciding that no, he should probably wait. Hope.

And show up for the next class.

Now Roark chose a blue shirt, pressed it on the bed, then threw on his leather jacket. He forwent the hat, the scarf, and set out for the half-block walk down the street early so he could pick their table. Perhaps order an appetizer.

He found the restaurant—the one located next to the fish shop—nearly vacant. Not odd for a Monday night, and it meant he had his pick of tables; he chose one overlooking the harbor. A schooner, its sails still lashed to the masts, rolled with the waves, and on the dock, gulls wandered, waiting for scraps.

He asked for a lit candle. Perused the wine list, then realized that in this country, Amelia couldn't drink anything alcoholic.

Instead he ordered lemonade and bruschetta.

And at 7 p.m. precisely, his heart stopped in his chest when Amelia walked through the door.

She wore a blue dress, those tall brown boots, a leather jacket, and a teal-and-blue scarf he remembered buying for her in Paris. Her beautiful auburn hair was pulled into a long, sweeping tail.

He stood as she approached. "You came." Oh, he didn't mean for it to emerge quite so desperate, but there it was, his heart beating and raw right outside his chest. He tried to reel it back with "You look so lovely."

She caught her lip in her teeth. "Thank you."

He pulled out her chair. She sat, sighing, her eyes following him into the seat. "You know this isn't necessary, right? I have already forgiven you."

"I wanted to explain."

"I know you didn't mean to hurt me." She clutched her bag in her lap. "Frankly I feel silly for making such a fuss about it."

He sat back, flummoxed.

She didn't look at him as she spoke, not

slowing. "But don't you think this is quite a bit of work for a fling? I mean yes, we had fun but—"

"A fling?" He schooled his voice just in time. The waiter approached with the lemonade, but Roark gestured him away. "Amelia, I do not consider what we had a fling."

She lifted a shoulder, looked out the window, and he saw her swallow.

Steady, boy. This was not the conversation he'd planned. "Darling. Never once did I believe that you were a dalliance. Every moment we spent together was . . . breathtaking. I never meant for you to think otherwise."

She sighed again, and he took the moment to dive in. "That woman you saw me with—her name is Cicely. She is just a friend—"

"It doesn't matter, Roark. I don't care how many female friends you have. I was childish and stupid to be angry over something that is so easily explained."

Oh. But her mouth tightened into a smile that seemed forced at best. "You did me a favor. Did us a favor. See, we never would have worked, not really."

He sat back, stunned. Took a breath. "I don't—"

"You and I are vastly different people."

They were? He wanted to argue then, a match lighting inside. Never had he felt so in tune, so right.

"Listen, I went to Prague to find adventure. And

I found it." She smiled, something genuine this time, her eyes softening. "You gave it to me."

He did?

"We had a grand time, didn't we?"

He didn't quite know—"We did. I *thought* we did."

She gave a small laugh. "You remember when we went on that hunt for apple strudel?"

"You saw it on a television show here in the States and demanded we find it."

"We took three trains, a bus, and walked a mile through a park."

"And when we got there, the store was closed." His sudden hope felt too feeble to smile.

"You bought me a Nutella waffle that night from a street vendor," she said. "We ate them at the park right by the Church of Virgin Mary of the Snows."

"The Franciscan Garden."

"You told me about this place in Paris where you could get crepes the size of American pizzas."

"You remember?"

"Because you took me there when we went to Paris." Her eyes were shining now, free of the shadows that had hovered when she arrived.

He wanted to signal for the waiter, but he feared losing the moment.

"You kept me safe. Showed me Europe. And for that, I'll forever be grateful."

That's when her voice changed. He felt the words coming and couldn't stop himself from reaching out for her. But she kept her hands in her lap.

"But that was a different world, Roark. Your world. This one is mine. And . . . I think we need to recognize what we had for what it was."

He couldn't utter the word.

"A fling."

His jaw tightened, his chest webbing. "It wasn't—"

"Let's be honest. Yes, we kissed, but it was New Year's Eve. Who doesn't kiss on New Year's Eve?"

"I meant that kiss," he said.

"Me too."

He frowned.

"Then. But now . . . I'm looking for something else."

He didn't expect that, and the swiftness of the pain rose up to choke him. "Someone else," he said quietly.

She looked away. Shrugged. The simple action could drive a knife through his heart.

He suddenly wanted to throw down his trump card, see if—

No. Because he couldn't be that desperate guy who used his wealth to lure the girl he longed for.

Mostly because he had a terrible feeling that it

wouldn't matter. He *hoped* it wouldn't matter. But in the end, he couldn't take that chance.

"I can't believe you're working at the Java Cup," she said.

"A guy has to make a living," he said and wished he could give her a better, more truthful answer. "At least I get free coffee."

"You don't even like coffee," she said, shaking her head.

"I do now."

Silence; then she stood. "I don't think dinner is a good idea. I'm so sorry you came all this way . . ." She looked away, wiped her cheek. And poor sap that he was, he hung on to that, because this moment was *not* supposed to end this way.

Movement out the window caught his eye. An animal frolicking on the dock. Amelia saw it too and stilled.

A beat passed.

Then she asked, "Was that an otter?"

"I don't know. Maybe."

She glanced at him. "I want a picture. You don't have to wait for me."

"I'll wait."

Of course he'd wait.

She headed out the door, unwinding her bag from her shoulder. Of course she carried her camera with her. And of course Roark followed and held her bag for her, just like he had across Europe. One last time.

She snapped a succession of fast shots, then changed to a golden light setting and caught the twilight.

And as the sun set, it took with it his heart. Oh, he needed words—any words—to stop the terrible, unexpected rush to the end.

She finally finished. "Thank you," she said. They stood on the dock, the sun low, the sky bleeding out, the shadows long, the breeze playing with her hair. How he wanted to pull her into his arms the way he'd been dreaming of for months.

He'd made a promise to Claire, but—"Amelia, is there anything I can do to prove that we had something more?" He stepped closer and couldn't help himself when he took her hand.

She let him, holding on, and it might have even been cruel, offering more hope than he had a right to.

"It's not you, Roark. I know we had our fight, but I blame myself. I was a silly schoolgirl who found a dashing European and fell too hard for him. I've come to my senses. I know what I want."

"Amelia, it wasn't like that. I fell just as hard—"

"Ames—what are you doing?" The voice, low and dark, came trundling across the deck toward them, accompanied by feet, and then the way-too-large form of Seth Turnquist. He wore a baseball cap backward, a flannel shirt with the sleeves rolled up over his beefy forearms, and a pair of work boots, looking fresh in from the hunt as if he'd just killed a moose.

Not now, mate.

"Seth!"

Amelia dropped her hand from Roark's. With everything inside him, he stopped himself from grabbing it back.

"What's going on here?" Seth stopped in front of them—her—his eyes dark. "I call you constantly since Saturday night and you ignore me and go out with—who are you?"

"Roark—"

"You've got to be kidding me." Seth stared at him. "007. I thought you were asked to leave."

"Seth, we're just having dinner."

"Dinner. As in the dinner we were supposed to have?"

"I don't remember you asking me out for dinner. A drive, yes. Probably a make-out session in the back of your truck, but dinner? Nope. Not a hint of that."

Roark didn't need to hear that. He took a breath, despite his desire to take Seth apart, even with his large-and-I-think-I'm-in-charge size. "I'm going to have to ask you to excuse us—"

But Amelia wasn't finished. "Real men take women out on dates. They wine and dine them. They treat them to music and picnics and art and history. Real men don't consider, 'Hey, babe, let's hook up' a proposal for marriage. And real men certainly don't barge in and start yelling at someone they supposedly care about in public!"

"So, what? You're *dating* this joker?"

Everything Roark ever wanted hung on her next words.

"I might be."

She *might* be? The sky broke open with sunshine and hallelujahs.

"You've got to be kidding me. 007 here couldn't last one week in this town, let alone be man enough for you."

"Really? Well, *007* has climbed Mt. Kilimanjaro. And sailed the English Channel. And run with the bulls."

Well, no, he hadn't done that, but far be it for him to contradict her. So he nodded.

And saw a hint of spark in her eye. "Trust me, he's *man enough* for me."

Booyah, as his American mates would say. And then some. But his ego refused to let him smile at her words.

"He doesn't belong here," Seth growled.

"No, *you* don't belong here, Seth. Not in the middle of my date." She pushed past Seth. "Roark, are you coming?"

Um. "Yes. Sweetie."

Amelia didn't even raise an eyebrow, but Seth narrowed his eyes.

Roark followed her back into the restaurant,

where she sat down at their table. Picked up a menu.

He slid into the seat opposite her, his heart racing in his chest. "Uh, I ordered bruschetta."

"Delicious." She buried her face in the menu.

He stared at the otters. Then at Seth, who stood confounded on the deck. Roark might end up fighting him yet.

"I think I'll have the walleye." She closed the menu. "And could I recommend it for you? It's a local specialty."

He hazarded a smile. "By all means. I love the local specialties."

She leaned back, folded her arms.

"Too much with the 'sweetie'?"

She considered him, and he felt a little like he had at the coffee shop, a specimen still under consideration. He glanced at Seth, who thundered away.

Finally Amelia said, "Okay, here's the deal. We start over. From the beginning. I want honesty every step of the way, no games. If you lie to me, even once, we're over. Can you live with that?"

Even once. Well, a lie by omission wasn't truly a lie, correct?

I've come to my senses now. I know what I want.

He intended to make that answer *him*. "I can live with those terms."

She gestured to the waiter, who brought their drinks.

Roark raised his glass.

"Welcome to Deep Haven," Amelia said.

Every nook and cranny of the lodge smelled deliciously like cinnamon and butter, baked together in the perfection of caramelized rolls.

Max had spent the weekend pulling out all the stops, rolling up his sleeves and diving into the project of producing a gourmet treat for the weekend lodgers of Evergreen Resort. He tested out three different recipes, finally tweaking one—with Grace's help—to create a signature recipe. Then he'd created the rolls and let them freeze in dough form; he'd bake them on Saturday morning.

Tomorrow he'd move on to the breakfast muffins Ingrid planned on offering for sale.

Right now, tonight, he wanted a little appreciation, a little attention for his efforts. From his wife.

Which, still, no one knew. Especially since he and Grace hadn't yet found the opportunity to purchase their rings, with the whirlwind elopement. He'd wanted rings from the island, but she wanted something more profound, wanted to design them. Something theirs alone.

That was his Grace—raising the significant, the beautiful, out of the ordinary.

He'd disappeared into the bathroom—the only part of the house that gave anyone any privacy—and now he texted her. I need help. In the bathroom upstairs.

He smiled as he dropped the cell phone back into his pocket. If anything would bring Grace running, it was a cry for—

"Max?"

See?

"That was quick." He opened the door and found her standing there, wearing an apron and rubber gloves, dripping onto the wood floor.

"What? Are you okay?"

He hooked her around the waist and pulled her into the bathroom. Shut the door with his foot. "No."

"What is it? Are you dizzy? Do you feel sluggish?"

His keen idea died at the panic in her eyes. He should have guessed that she'd go there. To his illness. Maybe he didn't realize how much she lived with its shadow lingering in her mind.

"No. I'm fine," he said, leaning back against the door to the tiny room and drawing her against him. "Sorry. I just missed you."

She lifted her sopping gloves up to keep from dripping on him. "Max! I was doing dishes."

"Dishes can wait." He lowered his lips to her neck, wrapping his arms around her. "Oh, you taste good."

"Max!" She put her hands on his shoulders, leaving damp handprints on his dark shirt. "Really?"

"I miss you, babe." He found her eyes, offered a smile, let her see something of the passion he'd been trying to hide all day.

She blushed and smiled back. "Oh, for pete's sake. You can hardly miss me—you've been baking with me all day."

"That's not what I mean, and you know it." He wound his hand behind her head and drew her lips to his. Sweetly exploring, nudging. She must have missed him too, even a little, because her arms went around his neck and she pressed herself into his embrace, willing for him to deepen the kiss. The exploring turned to desire, something that would quickly lead to more, and the fire inside that he'd banked all day began to flame.

Grace looked up then, aware of him as she was, and shook her head. "I'm not having a tryst in the bathroom, Max." She untangled herself, and he slumped against the door. "It's bad enough that I snuck downstairs the last two nights. I felt positively naughty. Right here in my own house."

"You're my wife!" Max said, catching her gloved hand. "Please, please can't we tell them? What are you waiting for?"

Downstairs he could hear voices—probably

Casper, back from work, possibly with his fiancée, Raina. Or maybe the social worker, finally arriving to remove Yulia into state custody.

"I just . . . With all the commotion the last couple of days, I wanted to wait for a calm moment. Poor Yulia. The whole thing is so sad. The adoption coordinator, Martha, just called and said that the college-age daughter doesn't want custody, and since Yulia is freshly adopted from Ukraine, they might have to send her back."

Max took a strand of her beautiful blonde hair, looped it behind her ear. "I'm sorry for her."

"She needs a family. And for right now, we're it, I guess. Martha asked us to keep her until they sort it out."

"That's tough. Good thing your parents are okay with that."

"Listen." She let him draw her close again. "I'm so overjoyed to be married to you. But it's been crazy here. I know this wasn't the plan. It's just that my mother loves weddings, and I know she'll be hurt."

"Then why did you suggest—?"

She kissed him. And there was something glorious and freeing and whole about having his wife dive into his embrace, Max scrambling to follow. She clenched his shirt in her rubbery hands, pressed him against the door. He finally took her by the shoulders and leaned her back, his breath unsteady, his heart in his throat. "If you really don't want to change your memories of this bathroom forever . . ."

Grace winked at him. "Just letting you know that I'm all in. Even if the thought of telling my parents has me momentarily stymied. We'll tell them."

"When?"

"Uh . . . tonight. Right now."

"Really?"

"C'mon, number 62, let's pop the news." She kissed him again quickly and moved away before he could spark another flame. When she opened the bathroom door, he made to follow, but she put a hand on his chest. "Wait three minutes. Just because, well, I don't want anyone to . . ."

"Think we were rearranging furniture?"

She frowned, then laughed. "Seriously?"

"It's what my uncle calls it."

Grace shook her head, and Max let her go, closing the bathroom door, leaning against it, catching his breath.

They'd break the news, and then would come the sit-down with John. The eyeball-to-eyeball words about making sure Grace was taken care of. And questions about long-term care. And life insurance. And . . . things a groom shouldn't have to worry about, but that he'd already figured out long ago.

Yes, this would be okay. Grace knew what

she was doing, and despite the dark thread still twining through him, Grace was light and hope and he'd be everything he could to her, all the way to the end.

Max took a long breath, then opened the door. Walked down the hallway to the stairs. Spotted Casper sitting at one of the high-top stools, rocking the baby. Not his baby, although he planned on marrying Raina, her mother. Which indeed made the child his, at least in love if not biologically.

Raina stood at the microwave, heating a bottle, her dark hair braided down her back. Grace had snapped off her gloves, was now drying the stack of pots she'd used.

John and Darek were probably outside, working on the last touches to the playground Darek was creating for guests. As for Ingrid and Yulia, he guessed it might be bedtime.

He jogged down the stairs.

"Hey, Max," Casper said. He still wore his work clothes—khakis, a dress shirt imprinted with the Wild Harbor Trading Post logo on the pocket. Out of all the Christiansen brothers, Max liked Casper the best. Owen . . . Well, yeah, he'd played hockey with him, but bad blood might always linger between them because of the accident. And Darek, the big brother of the clan, had a way of intimidating everyone else with a look. Not that he meant it; just the way he carried the legacy of the family resort on his shoulders put everyone off a little.

But his seven-year-old son, Tiger, could cajole a smile out of a curmudgeon, and now the kid ran up to Max. "Uncle Max! Where were you?"

Max scooped him up and threw him over his shoulder, fireman style. "I was just about to take the trash out. Anyone know where I can put this trash?"

Tiger kicked, laughing, beating on his back until he put him down.

Casper chuckled. "You're going to make a fun dad someday, Max."

The words had the power to bodycheck him, right into the boards, leaving him cold and stunned.

Because really, how could Casper know that although Max had made sure he'd never have biological children—and inadvertently pass along the gene—he'd also settled on a truth?

No kids. Ever. They'd had that conversation while lying in bed, the breeze blowing through the window of their suite in Mexico. He'd told her quietly, *I know I said we could adopt, but I just can't bear it, Grace.*

She'd taken his hand, tracing it with hers before she pulled it to her chest. Said nothing as she rolled into his arms, but he could feel tiny pieces of his wife's heart breaking.

Now he watched Tiger run away, then glanced

at Grace. She wasn't looking at him, just quietly wiping the pan. The microwave dinged and Raina pulled out the bottle, began to shake it.

"Yeah," he said quickly. Then he walked around the island, picked up a towel, and grabbed a pot.

Grace glanced at him. "That goes in the pantry, third shelf down."

Now, Grace. Let's tell them now. He put the pot away, then turned to her, that message in his eyes.

She nodded. Put the cloth down. Took a deep breath. Reached for his hand.

The door slammed in the entryway, and everyone looked up to see Amelia enter and pull off her boots. It was the way she sighed, mumbling to herself, that stalled their announcement. Then Grace's question: "Amelia, are you okay?"

She came into the kitchen, dropping her messenger bag on the counter. Then she slid onto a stool and buried her face in her hands.

Grace let go of Max's hand. "Honey . . . ?"

"I'm such an idiot. I just don't learn. The guy has some kind of weird power over me." She lifted her head, looked at Grace. "I was there, had it all figured out, even said the words. But then . . . I don't know—suddenly I thought, what if we're supposed to be together? It was a feeling, really, more than a thought. And then . . . I was just angry."

"What are you talking about?" Raina said. "Did you and Seth have a fight?"

Amelia sighed. "Yes."

"Oh, honey, did you break up?"

"No. I mean, maybe, but probably not. I don't know. It's all so complicated. He's so angry—and I don't blame him, but he's already got us down the aisle and married, and maybe I don't want that. Yet." She pressed her hands to her face again. "Or ever. And he did come all the way here, just to see me."

"Seth?"

She looked up again, her eyes a little red. "No." She glanced at Casper, made a face. "Roark. He's here. We just had dinner."

A beat of silence passed, the kind in which everyone, including Max, traveled back to that moment, almost a month ago, when Roark St. John appeared on the Evergreen Resort doorstep, bearing flowers and jewelry and asking, in his highbrow British accent, for Amelia to forgive him.

Max didn't know why Casper had nearly taken off his head. Something about him stepping out on Amelia, abandoning her, leaving her in Prague with a broken heart. It had been enough for Max to join forces with the brothers and Jace to step between Amelia and the foreign invasion.

"He's back?" Casper said finally, his tone dark even as he took the bottle from Raina. Maybe someone else should take the baby. But Casper rocked Layla gently, humming softly as she ate.

"He moved here. Has a job at the Java Cup."

"He *moved* here?" Max said. "Why?"

"Because he wants me to give us another chance. Because he loves me. Is that so hard to believe?"

He held up a hand. "Whoa. Down, girl. No, and yes. Of course he's crazy about you. Who wouldn't be?" He saw her hackles lower. "But moving here?"

"I know. But he seems . . . honest. And . . ." She caught her lip in her teeth. Glanced again at Casper, who wore a grim look. "I think I still love him."

Casper nodded, looked back at the baby. "I understand having a hard time getting someone you love off your mind."

"Well, it gets worse because . . . it looks like I'm dating two guys." Amelia dropped her head into her arms on the counter.

Grace went over to Amelia, put her arm around her sister. "It's okay, Amelia. We'll figure it out." Then she lifted her gaze to Max, something of apology in it.

And there it was. The look that told him he would be sleeping in the den again tonight.

Alone.

Chapter 5

THE QUIET TICKING of her bedside clock and the gleam of the moon spearing into the cool darkness of her bedroom dissected Amelia's thoughts, laying bare one clean, clear realization.

Roark St. John just might make a fool out of her again.

She rolled over, hit her pillow, then gave up and sat up, pulling her laptop to her legs from where it rested next to her on the floor. Across the room, Grace's bed was empty. In the opposite alcove, little Yulia lay huddled under Eden's pink-and-red patchwork quilt, a bundle of mystery and sorrow. Tonight Amelia had caught Grace singing to the little girl as she put her to bed. She could have used Grace's singing when she sat in her Prague apartment, alone and brokenhearted.

Yes, foolish. She should have listened to her brain, clung to her resolve to dispatch Roark back to England. Send him trotting over the pond once more.

Except for the way his blue eyes latched on to hers, a genuine apology in them. And the fact that he looked so good in that wide-shouldered jacket, his lips tweaked in the slightest of hopeful smiles.

Still, the shards of her broken heart managed to keep her focused, the sharp pain of memory enough to urge the words from her mouth. *I think we need to recognize what we had for what it was. . . . A fling.* The words could make her cringe, and she wanted to wipe from her memory the hurt that flashed in his eyes.

It was a word she'd latched on to the past few months to soothe the ragged wounds of seeing him with someone else. Clearly, however, he meant his soft-spoken yet deadly serious words: *Amelia, I do not consider what we had a fling.*

Oh, Roark. Why couldn't he just leave her to mop up the mess she'd made of her life, her pride, and start over again?

I'm looking for something else. She didn't know exactly where the words emerged from, didn't even know if they were true or just convenient, but she held on to them, a ledge rock on which to perch her Dear John speech.

Because even at the moment, she could feel the something breaking through, pulsing like a heartbeat. The wounded, naive, adventurous side of herself bursting to life inside.

Wait.

Like a breath, the word had gathered inside her, filled her pores until she escaped to take the shot of the otter, just long enough to let it dissipate.

To let her common sense helm her resolve once again.

If not for Seth, she might have walked away, sent Roark out of her life.

She didn't know whether to thank him or hurl her maybe-boyfriend from the dock. Even now, she wanted to knock him upside the head for his Neanderthal behavior.

So, what? You're dating this joker?

Seth always had the ability to ignite in her a sort of fiery rebellion. Like the time he told her she wasn't athletic enough to join the powder-puff football team during homecoming. She joined, played center, and took out the quarterback on a blitz or whatever it was called. So she sprained her ankle—Seth certainly hadn't minded carrying her around school for a week while it mended.

Jerk.

Maybe she shouldn't be so hard on Seth. After all, she had agreed to date him. He just needed to get his inner Neanderthal in check. Needed a little training. European manners.

And just like that, Roark returned to her thoughts—the smell of his cologne, the touch of his hand on her elbow as he opened the door of the restaurant for her.

Sweetie.

Oh, what was she *doing?* She opened her computer, the light cascading onto her lap. She'd emptied the SD card from her camera onto the laptop and now scanned through the pictures in the file—the Girl Scouts, shots of the river tragedy, and more. Leftover shots from Prague in winter. Icing folding over the gothic spires and

Narnia lampposts, the river metallic, the air crisp as it turned words to crystal.

She clicked on a folder marked *Christmas Market* to see a festive gallery of thumbnails depicting the glorious celebration on Wenceslas Square—the soaring evergreen cut from the Krkonoše mountains, bedazzled with lights, and the live Nativity, replete with goats and sheep, a donkey, and actors portraying Mary, Joseph, and the baby Jesus. She could easily close her eyes and stroll through the market, picking out embroidered lace, scented candles, knit mittens, marionette dolls. Smell the hams roasting on spits.

Hear Roark's voice as he tempted her with a fresh buttered *trdelník*.

Roark. From the first day in Prague, he seemed to be always there, embedding her explorations, sharing the beauty. Helping her discover the magic of her great adventure.

Perhaps the magic only happened in Prague. And maybe it should stay there.

She closed the folder and clicked on the remainder of her Prague photos, uploading them to her album on Facebook.

A tapping at her window made her jump. She moved the laptop onto the bed and got up, peering down.

Seth?

He stood, hands in his pockets, peering up into

the darkness, wearing a jean jacket and jeans, his long blond hair like a halo of gold. Then he reached down, grabbed another pebble from their gravel drive.

Oh no.

Amelia grabbed her sweatshirt and tugged it over her head just as the pebble flew to the sash, plinked against it, and trickled down the roof.

She took the stairs two at a time, landing on the slick wood floor, then scrambling toward the door.

She switched on the outside light and pulled the door open as Seth crouched for more ammunition. "What are you doing?" she hissed. "You're going to break a window!"

He dropped the rock. "You didn't mind so much in high school."

Amelia flicked off the light, then closed the door behind her, having slipped on Casper's hiking boots. She tromped over to Seth, the wind whipping through her pajama pants. "We're not in high school anymore. And you can't just come over here in the middle of the—"

He wound his hand around her waist, pulled her to himself. "I'm sorry, babe." Then he ducked his head and kissed her.

She could so easily fall into his embrace. Familiar, his tree-trunk arms curling around her, molding her to the solid planes of his body. He wore the beginnings of a beard, scant copper highlights scruffy against her chin, and when he kissed her, she tasted an urgency, a passion he usually kept banked.

It felt so easy, so terribly like home that she couldn't help but surrender, the moon casting a downy glow upon the night, the cicadas serenading from the shores of Evergreen Lake.

He pulled her closer, deepening his kiss, and the turmoil rose inside her. How could she kiss Seth when Roark too easily filled her mind? She leaned away from him, her hands palming his chest. "Seth, wait—we have to talk about today."

He ignored her words, his eyes finding hers, his hands cupping her face. "I don't want to wait."

"Seth—"

"No, Amelia. Please, listen to me." His voice held a tremor, and the emotion in his eyes cut off her words. "I'm tired of waiting." He let go of her face, clasped her hands in his. "I love you. I've always loved you, and yeah, I know we broke up when you took off for Europe, but—" He swallowed, and her heart could weep for the longing, the sadness in his expression. "But I didn't want that, not really. And now you're back. It's time to . . ." He sighed. "It's time we stopped kidding ourselves. You belong here with me. Seth and Amelia."

"Seth, please." She made to pull away, but he gripped her hands.

"No! Don't you get it? I don't want anyone else. I'll *never* want anyone else. You're my girl."

She caught her lip with her teeth, her eyes burning. "Please don't say that. I'm not . . . I'm not ready. . . . I don't know what I want."

Her words looped out into the night, the spaces filling with her thundering heartbeat. Then he stepped back, his expression dark. "This is about him, isn't it? I thought you might be yankin' my chain tonight—trying to get me to man up and propose by saying you're dating 007. But . . ." He turned away from her, let out a word that made her shrink back.

Then he whirled around to face her. "He's not sticking around, you know. He'll leave once he breaks your heart again, and you'll have no one."

She winced, his words like a slap, and she realized with a jolt how much Seth, too, was embedded in her world.

This world. Deep Haven. Her home.

Seth was the world of evergreen forest, pizza, and football under the stars.

Roark was the glitter of a night market on a cobblestone square, sugary European pastries, and the sky stretching out to forever.

"Seth . . ." She reached for him, her hand on his arm. "I just need time. I don't know why he's here, but . . ."

He hadn't moved under her grip, his chest rising and falling. "Time."

"Maybe I just need to know that—"

"I get it. You want me to be romantic. Buy you dinner? Flowers?"

Well, not exactly, but—

He sighed. "Okay, I'll play your game." He took a strand of her long hair, ran it between two work-worn fingers. "Flowers. Dinner. And you'll see I can be every bit a gentleman. Would you like that?"

"Seth, you don't have to—"

"But then, Ames, you'll have to choose. Me or him. Deep Haven or the world, whatever it is you want out there." He leaned close, his lips against her cheek. "I can be enough for you if you give me a chance."

Amelia closed her eyes as he moved his lips to hers, whisper soft, sweet. She gently pushed him away before he became too ardent.

He gave her a sad smile, then left her alone, shivering as a spring wind dug through her flannel pants, his words swirling through her. *I can be enough for you if you give me a chance.*

Why wasn't he already enough?

She let herself into the house, tiptoeing up the stairs, feeling like a sinner to have gone traipsing out into the night. Especially with Seth's kiss still lingering on her lips.

Until she saw the door to the den open below, light streaming into the dark hallway, followed by Grace, who slunk out of her fiancé's room.

Amelia ducked into her room, scampering under the covers just as Grace crept into the bedroom and slipped into bed.

Quiet as a burglar.

Apparently Amelia wasn't the only one harboring secrets.

The Skype call, ringing through the padding of darkness, jolted Roark out of the quiet place where he relived Amelia smiling at him from across the table.

Welcome to Deep Haven.

Magic, beautiful words—the entire evening had turned out like something he'd only wildly hoped for.

No, she hadn't let him take her hand as he walked her out to her car. Yes, she'd left him standing on the curb instead of responding to his hint that they stroll along the shore. But she hadn't ordered him to leave her town, hadn't continued to taint their past with her use of the word *fling*.

Maybe God had decided to forgive Roark. Or at the very least, leave him alone.

As the ringing continued, Roark reached for his laptop, pulled it onto the bed, and clicked on the icon.

The light could sear his eyes, but through it he saw Ethan sitting in his office, his back to the window overlooking the skyline of Brussels, the sun high, the world of Constantine Worldwide bustling around him. Roark could easily close his eyes and picture his uncle Donovan's penthouse office, see his own expansive office scrubbed and ready for him next door.

Not yet. "Ethan. Do you know it's after midnight here?"

"Sorry, mate. Early morning, and I wanted to let you know that we sold the flat in Paris. I'm dispatching a check to Cicely per your orders." Ethan had cut his hair, wore it short and slicked back, his suit coat draped over a butler's hanger behind him, his shirtsleeves rolled up. As part of the legal team—and Roark's personal barrister— the man probably used the sofa in his office more often than he slept at home.

"Very good."

It was the sigh that stopped him from disconnecting.

"What?"

Ethan made a wry face. "I just wanted to say that I know today's a tough one for you. I'll raise a pint to your family tonight."

Today. Roark stilled, his breath caught behind the place where his heart had stopped, sitting like a boulder cutting off the air to his chest. He didn't have to look at the calendar to know, but the fact that it had so neatly slipped his mind . . . "Quite right. Thank you, mate."

Silence on both sides of the ocean then. "Want

me to reach out to the Spanish police, see if they have any new leads?"

"After twelve years? Probably not." Roark ran his hand behind his neck, massaged a tight muscle. Because really, how could they when their key witness had run from the crime, not looked back?

"It just seems so wrong that they'll never have justice."

Justice. Roark looked out the window to where the night blackened the windows, save for the wan light over the municipal parking lot across the street. "How can there ever be justice for murdering an entire family?"

Well, not an entire family. Roark had lived. Ethan, however, stayed mercifully quiet on that point.

After a brief silence he asked, "Are you ready to come home?"

"No." In fact, at this moment, without much of a shove, he might climb into his rental, push the throttle north.

"Very well. I'll wire your funds to the local bank. Send me the routing number."

"Thank you," Roark said and hung up. He closed his computer and sat back against the cool wood of the headboard, listening to his heart filling his veins, his throat.

He stared out the window into the darkness, watching the waves on the shore. It seemed somehow poetic that the anniversary would arrive just when he might be finding peace. A reminder that he'd never truly escape.

And brutally unfair how easily the memories could pin him to the past, turn him again into a teenager cowering in the shadows, clad in his dripping swim trunks, the slick of the ocean turning to ice upon his skin.

Movement under the lights of the municipal parking lot caught his attention, and he got up.

Was that Casper outside talking with another man? He recognized the frame, the dark hair, and then he turned, and Roark saw his face. Angry. And he had the man in question by the lapels of his trench coat.

Roark was wondering if he should play some sort of ally when, abruptly, Casper let the man go, stalked off to his nearby truck, idling in the lot.

Casper drove away a little too fast, though Roark understood it, his own need to shake free of the conversation with Ethan vibrating through him.

He got up, the floor cool under his feet, went to the kitchen for a glass of water, then returned to the window to sort his thoughts.

He spied more movement in the lot. The same man who'd fought with Casper hung his arm around a woman, walking with her—or was she helping him?—into a truck. She laughed; they kissed.

Roark turned away, climbed back into bed, and stared at the ceiling.

He finally conceded to his insomnia when the dawn began to pale the darkness, and headed for his closet, pulling on running clothes and his trainers.

The fragrance of budding lilacs and new daffodils hung in the misty gray morning, the sun barely lipping the horizon as he jogged downstairs, out into the cool morning air.

He settled into a brisk pace, clearing his head as he ran, reaching for a moment of quiet.

Or possibly just the hope of outrunning his memories.

He passed the fish house, saw early risers heading out of the harbor in their whalers, then continued up the hill, past the senior center and out to the open road that overlooked the silver lake.

It reminded him of the Seine on that crisp New Year's morning, the Eiffel Tower downy with new snow, his heart alight in his chest with the fragile, sweet memory of the kiss he'd shared with Amelia.

Too quick, surprising, but oh, how he'd waited for it. Longed for it.

He ran faster, his feet slapping the pavement.

He hadn't deserved her kiss then. Now he planned on being a man who didn't weave his life from lies.

Somehow.

He stopped, leaning over, breathing hard, sweat tunneling down his back. Closed his eyes.

And he was right there again, hearing his mother's scream as he kicked up sand on his walk in from a clandestine swim.

No. He shook the memory away and settled into a light jog back toward town. The sun now hovered over the horizon, a simmering fire that flooded the sky and turned the clouds a deep rose gold, the boulders along the lakeshore shiny black, some caked with a doily of frost.

I want honesty every step of the way, no games. If you lie to me, even once, we're over.

As he picked up his pace, the smell of freshly fried donuts hit the breeze, luring him along the shoreline all the way to World's Best Donuts. He stopped on the porch of the tiny red building, leaning against a balustrade to stretch.

Inside, he saw movement, then heard, "Hey, aren't you that guy who helped at the river?"

He looked up. Seb Brewster, medium white chocolate mocha. Seb had come outside to flip over the Closed sign.

"Hello, Mr. Mayor."

"Today, I'm the donut man." A smile slid up his face. "I have to appreciate your dedication to early morning donuts."

"A bloke's gotta have his pastries," Roark said as he followed Seb inside, where his petite wife, wearing a red apron, her dark hair under a net, slid a tray of glistening raised glazed donuts onto the display shelf. The smell could leave a man weak.

And he'd left all his money back at the flat.

He must have worn the dilemma on his face because Seb grabbed a donut and handed it to Roark. "On the house. Welcome to God's country." Seb smiled.

Roark matched it, despite the funny churning the words provoked in his chest. "I'll stop by later and pay you."

"Oh yeah. We'll be waiting for that eighty cents. Look out for the knee-breakers." Seb laughed. "I meant it. On the house. *Free.*"

"Right. Thank you." He grabbed a napkin.

"Can I interest you in a cup of hot joe? If you're going to live in America, you have to acquire a taste for coffee." Seb reached for a mug with the World's Best label on it and poured him a cup, black.

"I like coffee. I just prefer it with sugar. And cream. And tasting of tea."

Seb handed him the cup. "You'll find the candy on the tables in the next room." He gestured to the tiny room that served as a gathering place for the locals.

Roark slid onto one of the curved Formica seats.

God's country.

He took a bite of the donut, savoring the sugar that melted, still warm, in his mouth.

He must have emitted a little moan of joy because Seb ducked his head around the corner. "I know, right?"

"This is good," Roark said. "Reminds me of these donuts I'd buy near my uncle's house in Brussels. Like a funnel cake, only with pretzel dough and glaze."

Seb flipped a towel over his shoulder. Slid onto the bench across from Roark without asking. "Brussels, huh?"

"I think they were German, actually." He licked his fingers as he finished it off. Chased it with a sip of black coffee, then made a face and reached for the creamer. "In Russia, we used to add sweetened condensed milk to our coffee. Saves time."

"Russia too? Where haven't you been?"

Roark stirred in the creamer. "Fiji?"

Seb laughed. "Okay, I'll bite. Where *have* you been?"

"Let's see. Born in London, lived in far east Russia until I was twelve, moved to Brussels, schooled in London, did my gap year in Uganda, then attended university in Scotland, worked in Paris, traveled . . . well, all of Europe, over to Australia, with a stopover first in Iceland, swam with the sharks in New Zealand, then a hop to Tanzania to climb a mountain."

"Seriously."

Roark lifted a shoulder, for the first time really seeing it. "I guess I never found a place I wanted to call home."

Seb's wife came over, set a cup in front of her husband, and kissed him on the cheek. "Five minutes and the next batch will be ready to fry."

She left him after glancing at Roark with a smile.

"How long have you been married?"

"Not long enough. We dated—sorta—in high school, and I just knew she was the one. Took me a while to accept it, though. I never really wanted to return to Deep Haven—always thought my best life was over the next horizon. Finally I realized that I hoped it was here. So I came back. It wasn't until then that I saw I was running from the failure of my own expectations."

Roark considered Seb as he took another sip of coffee. "What do you mean?"

Seb lifted a shoulder. "I left here thinking I was going to make a name for myself in football. Blew out my knee, and my career died. I was so angry at God because I thought I'd lost my one chance to make it big, to prove myself to Deep Haven. And to myself. I didn't realize that I could make it big, prove myself every day here, if I had the courage to stop running. I had to figure out that until I forgave myself for letting myself down, I'd never find my way home."

The donut began to sit like glue in Roark's gut. "Some things don't deserve to be forgiven." He wasn't sure he'd said it aloud, but maybe he had because Seb frowned.

Then said, "That's a lie, dude. There's nothing that God won't forgive."

"I'm not talking about God," Roark said quietly. He got up. "Thanks for the coffee."

He turned to go, then stopped and looked at Seb. "And as for God, let's not forget that He's not only love and forgiveness, but also justice and wrath." He tempered his words with a smile but didn't stick around for Seb's retort.

Because although he'd realized that God had definitely found him, for the first time he considered that, if he wasn't careful, someone was really going to get hurt.

The fragrance of pancakes could wake a dead man, lure him to the Christiansen family table, where John, the head of the household and Grace's somewhat-terrifying father, sat reading the morning paper.

Max shot a glance at Grace, who was frying the cakes in a cast-iron pan on the stove, but she offered no encouragement to act on his statement last night, spoken as the moon cascaded into his room, Grace nestled in his arms.

If you aren't going to tell your father that we're married, I will.

He'd said it softly, his lips against her hair, so maybe she hadn't heard him, just on the edge of slumber. But the resolve grew and cemented in his heart when his newlywed bride roused from the sofa bed and crept out to scuttle back to the childhood bedroom she shared with Amelia and Yulia.

Now he tunneled a hand through his shaggy hair—he'd need to shave it soon—and headed over to the counter, sliding onto a stool next to Yulia, who mopped up syrup with a thick blueberry-laden piece of buttermilk pancake. She was still dressed in a nightgown that Ingrid had dug up from her stores of old clothes. Her hair was a nest of tangles around her head, and her bare feet hooked to the sides of the stool. He imagined that, once upon a time, his Grace had been this little girl, snarls and nightgown and pancakes, and it turned his heart soft for the woman he'd married.

Especially since she wouldn't have a little girl of her own. Ever.

"That looks good," he said to Yulia, and she smiled at him, a gap where her front teeth should be. He leaned over and opened his mouth, and to his great surprise, she plunked the dripping bite in.

Max made a roaring sound and gobbled it up, to Yulia's giggles.

"Here you go, honey," Grace said, turning from

the stove with a fresh plate of pancakes. She set the plate in front of him.

If possible, his wife had become more beautiful every morning since the day he'd married her. Today she'd pushed her blonde hair back with a headband, wore a teal thermal shirt and yoga pants. He let his gaze skim over her body, remembering the sweetness of their clandestine union last night. Shoot, but he felt like a teenager, sneaking around like they were misbehaving.

Enough. He grabbed the syrup and doctored his breakfast, then turned to John to suggest a conversation.

But John had already closed the paper and risen, bringing his plate to the sink. "Good morning, Max. Feel like helping me with a project? I need to rebuild the fire pit before this weekend."

John pressed a quick kiss to Grace's forehead before pouring himself another cup of coffee.

"Sure," Max said.

Grace glanced at him, her eyes wide. He shrugged, a covert no-time-like-the-present message.

"I'm headed out to get the backhoe running. Get some work clothes on. Unless—" John glanced at Grace, back at Max—"you want to stay in the kitchen and *cook* something."

"Dad," Grace said, "I promise you'd rather

have Max cooking something and me working in the yard. He can cook circles around me."

John grinned, pulling on a gimme cap. "I doubt that. But yes, I know Max can cook. I just thought he'd like to get outside. It's a glorious day."

"Thanks, John. Yeah, I'll be right out." Max stirred a bite of his pancake into the syrup.

When the door closed behind John, Grace rounded on Max, cutting her voice low. "Max, I know what you're thinking, but . . . I don't know if I'm ready. And—"

The floor creaked upstairs, and she shot a look to the landing. Max followed her gaze, but no one stood there. Just her fears probably.

What was it about telling her parents that had Grace so locked up inside? He cut his own voice low. "Grace, we can't keep sneaking around."

She had turned off the stove, leaving the rest of the batter, and now came around to sit on the opposite side of Yulia. She ran her hands over the little girl's hair. "Should I brush your hair, sweetie?"

Yulia just looked at her, those brown eyes wide.

"I don't think she understands you," Max said, considering adding a bit about how he didn't seem to speak Grace's language either. Instead he voiced a thought that had occurred to him more than once. "Do you regret marrying me?"

The words tumbled out with too much of his heart hanging in them, and he wanted to yank them back.

Or . . . not. Because he understood, and if she said yes, he'd be the first to suggest . . . what? An annulment? That might not be quite possible. But maybe a quick divorce.

The word burned inside him. He should have seen this coming, should have—

"No!"

He raised his gaze, found Grace's urgent and angry.

"Of course not. I'm just savoring the quiet before the storm." Her hand ran down Yulia's hair again, smoothing over the snarls. "She's made quite a mess of her hair. It's going to hurt to brush it out."

Max frowned. "Yeah, I suppose. That's the problem with long hair."

"But it's so beautiful. It's worth the pain. Trust me, I spent years flinching as my mother untangled my hair. I finally convinced her to let me cut it, only to regret it instantly. It took years to grow out, but I didn't complain about the snarls ever again."

She leaned down and caught Yulia's eyes. "*Vakoosna*?"

He recognized the Russian word, something that Vasilley, one of his teammates, said occasionally. It meant delicious or good—although

Vasilley usually said it as a hot rink bunny happened by.

Probably Grace didn't realize that.

Yulia beamed and said, "*Da.*"

Grace glanced at Max. "I downloaded a dictionary of basic Russian off the net, thought I'd learn a few words to make her feel more comfortable." She turned to Yulia. "*Yeshow?*"

More. He got that from the way Yulia nodded, then held out her plate. Grace forked her another pancake and covered it in syrup and powdered sugar. "She's so brave. Hardly makes a peep in her sleep. Smiles like she hasn't just lost everything. I wish we could talk to her."

It wasn't so much her words as her tone that slid between Max's ribs to jab at his heart. And when Grace backed it up by putting her hand on Yulia's shoulder in an affectionate gesture of compassion, he wanted to weep. Because he could have predicted her next soft words, spoken through a tender expression as she slid the pancake plate in front of Yulia again.

"It must be so terrible to be the only one left."

There it was. The awful truth of their marriage.

He'd doomed his wife to a life of grief.

He pushed his plate away. "Grace, maybe . . . maybe we need to think a little harder about all this. Maybe there's a reason you don't want to tell your parents about us."

She frowned, started shaking her head, but he

held up his hand, cutting off her words. "I love you. You know that. But love isn't enough to carry you through our future."

"Yes, it is."

He could see the fire kindling in her eyes, kept his voice low. "No, it's not. You haven't lived through it, seen the damage, the grief. And I should have really thought about that before we said, 'I do' in Cancún. But I'm thinking now maybe it's not too late."

A little of the blood drained from her face. "What are you saying?"

"I'm saying . . . maybe we should get a . . . divorce."

The words seared through him, but he refused to wince. Refused to release the wail building to a crescendo inside him.

Grace exhaled in a shaky stream of pain. "I think you need to go help my father." She flashed a lopsided smile at Yulia when the little girl glanced at her and got up. "I'm going to find a hairbrush and straighten out this mess."

Max slid off the stool, reached for her arm, but she yanked it away, not looking at him. "Leave, Max. Because I'm not sure how to keep from saying what I want to say to you right now, and I don't want my parents to overhear and discover that I've married a man who is so afraid of living, he'd rather destroy the very thing that makes him feel alive."

Chapter 6

A DAY LIKE THIS, with sparrows chirruping from the poplar trees and a fresh, lilac-scented wind over the lake, could clear a girl's thoughts, make her lean into hope.

Cajole her into believing that heartbreak didn't lurk just beyond the horizon.

It helped, too, that the photo shoots of the Sawdust Sweeties had eaten up Amelia's free time over the past three days. Sure, she'd joined in cleaning the Evergreen Resort cabins, airing linens, and planting flower boxes with pansies for the upcoming Mother's Day weekend and fishing opener, but she'd also managed to escape with her camera, taking portrait shots of the pageant girls all over town.

At the harbor dock, with the lake an inviting indigo as a background. On the abandoned railroad tracks west of town. On the hood of a peeling Ford pickup in the woods near Pincushion Trail, and on a stack of hay bales at the Crosbys' farm, just out of town. There, she'd posed one of the girls in a yellow-hubbed tractor wheel, and another with an umbrella in the middle of a field of tall grasses. Then they headed up to the school and took shots in the rickety wooden bleachers on the visitors' side of the football field, and others at the baseball diamond backstop. Finally Amelia took pictures of all six girls eating ice cream cones from Licks and Stuff and gathered around the beautiful street lanterns that bordered Main Street.

She had managed a look inside Java Cup, just to check, and yes, Roark still worked the coffee counter, garbed in an apron, those blue eyes charming the coffee addicts. Or if they weren't addicts yet, they would be, especially when he started taking orders with that too-devastating accent of his.

Even that thought had sent Amelia scuttling back to the resort in a sort of shame.

Two men. A girl who didn't know what she wanted and still nursing failure shouldn't be allowed that much male attention.

Who knew what crazy decisions she might make? Like settle down with Seth? Run away with Roark?

Now Amelia sat on a stool at her parents' kitchen counter, editing the photos, ready to upload them to Facebook. The scent of her mother's chocolate cookies fragranced the house, guaranteed to call Ingrid's children from afar. She had gone out to deliver the first gooey batch to John and Max, their fire pit rebuild turning into an overhaul of the entire beach area.

"Oh, my goodness, look what I found on the front stoop!"

Amelia turned toward her mother's voice, only to find her face obscured by an array of six long-stemmed red roses wrapped in green paper and covered in cellophane. Ingrid set them on the counter. "Who are they from?"

Amelia searched through the bundle, produced a card. "They're from Seth." He'd signed it with just his name, bold, simple, and she found a smile for him.

"Wow, that's sweet." Ingrid retrieved a vase from over the sink, filled it with water, then returned to the counter, scissors in hand.

Amelia unwrapped the flowers and snipped off the ends, adding them one by one to the vase.

She hadn't realized the quiet that settled into the room until she looked up. Her mother was watching her, an eyebrow lifted. "Care to elaborate?"

"He wants us to get back together," Amelia said. "I . . . I don't know."

Her mother let the words sift through the air without comment. Amelia went back to selecting photos to upload, not sure what to think about the flowers.

"Those are nice," her mother said from over her shoulder, referring to the photos. She set a glass of lemonade beside Amelia's laptop, along with two cookies on a napkin. "What are they for?"

"Vivie asked me to take shots of the Sawdust

Sweeties. It sort of got out of hand, but I captured some keepers."

"The Sawdust Sweeties. They've held that competition for nearly thirty years. I remember wanting to enter years ago." Ingrid began scooping cookie dough onto a pan for the next batch.

"Seriously? Mom, it's a beauty pageant."

"With a scholarship as a prize. Some girls pay for college that way."

"I've always thought it was silly. Girls in Daisy Dukes, getting judged on their ability to twirl a baton?"

"Twirling a baton is harder than you'd think." She put the cookies in the oven. Tossed her hot pads on the counter. "Seems like an ingenious way to pursue your dreams."

If she had dreams left to pursue. These days, she seemed fresh out. Amelia checked her notifications and found a number of likes attached to her previous shots of the river. And over a thousand for the photo of Yulia standing on the rock, staring at the waterfall, her ribbons a bright red against the watery backdrop. Someone had left a link with a comment. *Prize-worthy? Check it out.*

She clicked through to the website. "Someone sent me a link for a photography contest called Capture America."

"Really?" Ingrid came over to look, a cookie in her hand. "How does it work?"

"It looks like I submit pictures and the world votes on them. The photographer with the combined highest score after three rounds wins a cash prize. Wow, five thousand dollars."

"Huh."

Amelia returned to her photo, to the comment containing the link. "It was posted by Java Cup."

"Someone at the coffee shop likes your photography apparently."

Her mother's words settled a sweet curl of warmth into Amelia's bones. No . . . it couldn't be, but . . . ?

"Wow, nice flowers." This from Grace, who was coming down the stairs with Yulia, wearing what looked like new jeans and a sweater, her hair braided. "Who are they from?"

"Seth," Ingrid said. "Yulia, would you like a cookie?" She picked one off the plate and handed it to the little girl.

"Trying to keep up with Roark, huh?" Grace said as she swiped one of her own.

Amelia frowned, and it took Grace a second before she followed up with, "Ames, did you not see the flowers in the entryway? They came earlier today. You must've walked right by them."

"Oh, those were for Amelia?" Darek said, walking into their conversation from the resort office. "I thought Mom ordered them for the front entry for Mother's Day." He set his coffee cup in the sink, then went to the entryway.

"Two suitors?" Ingrid said. "My, my."

"Mom, it's not like that."

"I think that's exactly what it's like," Darek said as he brought in the vase of a dozen pink roses. "There's a card here, which I gather Grace already read."

"I was curious."

Amelia retrieved it. *Thinking of you, sweetie. Roark.*

"Sweetie?" Darek said, reading over her shoulder.

She yanked the card away. "Darek!"

"I'm just sayin' . . . 'sweetie'? He sounds like either a Texan or a throwback from the seventies. Who calls their girlfriend 'sweetie'?"

"I'm not his girlfriend."

"Clearly," Grace said, dumping out a puzzle for Yulia on the counter, then turning over the pieces. "Two deliveries of long-stemmed roses in one day? To have your problems."

Darek shook his head. "I feel sorry for Seth."

"What?" Grace said. "Are you kidding me? What about Roark? He came all the way over here to win her back—I think you need to cut him some slack."

"Cut who slack?"

Amelia hadn't heard Casper come in, but he was toeing off his shoes in the entry, dressed in a suit coat, tie, oxford shirt, and dress pants. Raina followed, carrying her daughter, Layla.

Casper took the baby from her and walked into the kitchen. "Anyone want a baby kiss?"

"I'll take that action," Ingrid said and reached for Layla, untying her hat, then kissing her fat cheek.

"I was just defending Roark to Darek, who still, apparently, wants to run him out of Deep Haven."

"I think it's sweet," Raina said, joining Casper in the kitchen. She set the diaper bag on the counter, began to root inside it. "Roark came all the way here, ready to apologize, and you all nearly crucified him."

"He can't be trusted," Casper said in a tone that reminded Amelia that he'd seen exactly how Roark's behavior had ruined her, for a time.

Yes, maybe she should keep that in the forefront of her mind. Still . . . "You guys don't know him like I do. He *can* be trusted." She held up a hand to Casper's protest. "I overreacted in Prague."

"So he didn't step out on you with another woman?"

"We weren't exactly dating—so no . . ."

Darek's mouth tightened.

"And he said she was just a friend."

Even to her, that sounded lame.

"Listen, if it weren't for Roark, I might be human trafficked somewhere. He saved my life."

Okay, she hadn't meant for that information to leak out. But there it was.

Her mother stared at her, wide-eyed. "What are

you talking about?" she said in a whisper that seemed to thunder through the room.

Amelia glanced at Darek, then back to her mother. "If I tell you, promise not to freak out and lock me in a tower?"

Silence.

It appeared that Darek might be contemplating that very action.

"Just for the record, it all ended well."

Casper eased the baby from Ingrid's grip.

"And it wasn't really my fault."

Grace kept turning over puzzle pieces, her expression grim.

"Fine. It was about a week after I arrived in Prague. My roommates heard about an art show across town and asked if I wanted to join them. I thought it sounded fun, and it was a Saturday night, and we didn't have a lot in common, so I decided to go along. Turns out it was more of a graffiti show, with local street artists showcasing their styles in an old, giant warehouse. A band played a mix of funk and fusion—not my kind of music—and the minute I arrived, I knew I wouldn't stay long. My roommates got drinks, started dancing, and well . . . I'm not a great dancer, either."

More silence. Not even a twitter from the audience.

Ho-kay. "So I stayed to watch the drinks. But somehow we ended up scattering, and after about an hour, I decided I wanted to go home. Problem was, I wasn't sure exactly how we got there. So I went out and found a bus—thought it was mine— and ended up in the south end of the city. When it pulled into the terminal, long after midnight, I realized it was the end of the line. I got off thinking I'd find a bus route that led back to Lesser Town, where I lived, and saw that I'd managed to stray into the run-down part of the city. More graffitied cement buildings, feral dogs, trash trickling along the sidewalk in the wind. I walked for about six blocks looking for a different route and . . ."

"You were scared," Ingrid said, her hand now fisted around a cloth on the counter.

"Yeah. And it got worse. A car pulled up, and the driver identified himself as a taxi, asked if I wanted a ride—"

"You didn't—"

"I was desperate. And lost. It looked like a taxi, even had a permit in the window. But when I got in, he didn't start the meter, and I realized . . ."

Ingrid pressed her hand over her mouth.

"I was really scared, and I didn't know what to do, so I got out at the next light and just started running."

If Amelia closed her eyes, the night could crawl over her: the sound of her boots on the sidewalk, the odor of garbage and sewer as she lost herself in alleyways and rutted, dark yards. The taste of fear, metallic and hot in her throat. "I hid behind a Dumpster and tried calling my friends. But no one answered. I'd only met Roark a couple times. On the Charles Bridge, and we had dinner once after class, but he seemed nice. He'd given me his number in case I needed anything, so . . . I called him."

He'd answered on the first ring, with a simple *Amelia*. The way he said it, like he'd been waiting for her to call, was crazy, but she'd heard a calmness, a strength in his tone. It had reached right through her phone and stilled her careening heart.

She could still dredge up the tremor in her voice as she said his name. Still cringe at the way she burst into tears.

Still hear his simple, lifesaving words: *Tell me where you are.*

She didn't know. So she went out into the street and described the landmarks, the stores, the street signs, sounding them out terribly.

He'd kept her on the phone, his voice soothing, as he got into his car and headed south, toward the bus terminal, then worked his way north, following her recollections, all the while telling her about being a new boy at Eton. Just his voice in her ear, soft, with the lilt of a knight, calmed her pulse, and yes, she might have fallen in love with him while huddled in her trench coat behind a Dumpster, avoiding the rats and tomcats.

She definitely gave him too much of her heart when he finally found her, pulling up right alongside her hiding place and venturing into the murky shadows.

"He came out into the night and searched for me," Amelia said to her now-rapt audience. She left off the part where she'd flown into his arms, and the way he pulled her tight, his own breath just a little ragged as if she'd scared him too.

"He drove me home without a word of lecture—"

"Too bad," Casper said.

"And never mentioned it again. Every Saturday night after that, he called to make sure I wasn't sitting at home alone."

Ingrid had folded her arms, leaned back against the counter. "There are some things a mother shouldn't know."

"I know. That's why— "

"But this isn't one of them. You should have told us, Amelia," Ingrid said quietly.

"I didn't want you guys to think I couldn't take care of myself. That I was being reckless."

"Seriously?" Darek turned away, shaking his head.

"Calm down, Dare," Grace said. "She's fine. You can't hover over her, making decisions for her anymore. You have to let her grow up."

He rounded on her. "Stupidity is not a sign of growing up!"

Ouch. Amelia scrambled for a retort—one that didn't sound like she was a three-year-old—as the door closed in the entryway. Amelia saw her father come in, followed by a very grimy Max.

It gave Grace the time to regroup. "What would you prefer, Darek? That we lock her up? Forbid her from leaving the house?"

"What did I miss?" Max said.

John walked over to his wife, put his arm around her. Amelia couldn't fail to notice her mother's white-as-a-sheet expression.

"Oh," Grace answered. "You just missed another infamous Neanderthal moment from the Christiansen boys. Apparently the women in this family aren't allowed to think for themselves, make their own choices about the future."

Max glanced at Darek, Casper. Swallowed.

"I, for one, am glad Roark is back. He's a hero in my book. Dashing and handsome and not afraid to live dangerously, even if it cost him his heart!" Grace returned to fitting together pieces of the puzzle with Yulia, her hand shaking just a little.

Yeah, what she said. Only Amelia had the craziest feeling that perhaps Grace had stopped talking about her.

Clearly, however, Darek didn't catch on. "Roark is just going to break her heart. He doesn't belong here, and he's muddying the waters. Everyone knows that Seth and Amelia belong together. They've been dating for years, and Seth's a great guy."

Darek's words raked up Seth's, still haunting her. *He'll leave once he breaks your heart again, and you'll have no one.*

"There's nothing wrong with wanting to settle down with the woman you love," Casper added. "Especially in Deep Haven."

"But just because she made a mistake doesn't mean she's stupid, Darek," Raina said, handing Casper a toy for Layla. Her gaze darted to Amelia. "I saw 007 down at the coffee shop. He's very handsome."

"So is Seth!" Darek said. "What is it with women and European men? He wouldn't last one day in Deep Haven."

"Seems to me he's been here for a week already." Ivy, Darek's wife, had materialized, probably hearing the conversation all the way in town. She held baby Joy in a carrier against her chest and dropped her satchel on the floor. "And he's something of a hero down at the courthouse. I stopped in today, and Kyle Hueston couldn't stop talking about how Roark refused to come out of the icy water until they recovered the body."

"Oh, for cryin' in the sink," Casper said. "Has everyone forgotten that he broke Amelia's heart? That he's the reason she dropped out of school and came home?"

"He's not the reason I failed, Casper." The

words launched out of her. "I came home because—"

"The cookies!" Ingrid grabbed her hot pads and opened the oven. The acrid smell of burned dough seemed to hit everyone at once as she pulled the ruined, blackened cookies from the oven, slid them onto the stovetop. "Oh no."

John went to open a window.

But Casper hadn't taken his gaze off Amelia. She felt his eyes on her even as she wanted to yank back her words. *He's not the reason I failed.* She didn't exactly know when she'd come to that realization, but the words felt true, albeit raw.

For too long, she'd blamed Roark for cutting her trip short, for sending her home with a broken heart. But if she was honest, the truth could be unearthed from the quiet hour she'd spent in the dank alleyway, waiting for rescue.

She wasn't the heroine of her story. She was exactly what Darek said. Stupid. Or more—foolish. And a coward.

Without Roark, she'd feared stepping outside, feared getting on the bus and ending up lost. She feared making a fool of herself every time she opened her mouth. Feared eating something that might make her sick. Feared, really, everything about Prague.

In every way, Roark had saved her from returning to Deep Haven a week after she'd left.

And in truth, without him, she'd never leave

again. Maybe Darek was right. What was so wrong with settling down with the man you loved in Deep Haven?

Amelia reached for a pink rose, pulled it out, smelled it. Slid off the stool. "I'm going to town. I have something I need to do."

Three days seemed long enough for him to get the message. Worse, Roark had even seen Amelia peering into the Java Cup window yesterday as if looking for him. If not for a line of people at the counter, he might have wadded up his apron and taken off after her, catching up to confirm that she'd agreed to let him back into her life.

Provisionally.

Without the lies.

He set the benching bar on the rack, breathing for a long moment before he got up to add more weights. The weight room at the YMCA reeked of sweaty towels and slick rubber, all mixed with the cloying scent of chlorine drifting from the pool down the hall.

He'd had to admit he didn't mind working at the coffeehouse. Kathy, his boss, let him run the counter, and he'd penciled into his brain the favorites of all the regulars. Jake Goldstein, local floatplane pilot, liked a tall cappuccino. Jorge, who captained the *Fossegrim*, a three-masted schooner for tourists hoping to sail along the rugged shore, preferred a frothy macchiato. And

Roark always had a tray of hot black java ready for the early morning fishermen headed out to haul in the daily catch.

After he'd finished his shift today, he spent some time online, then decided he needed a vigorous sweat to leach the guilt out of his chest. Help him work free of the burgeoning sense that he should jump on the first flight over the pond and resign himself to the fact that he would muck this up.

With the anniversary of his nightmarish past, maybe pitching in the towel made sense. A guy on the wrong side of God's grace had to keep a weather eye over his shoulder, keep one step ahead of catastrophe.

He could admit he'd run on adrenaline and heartbreak since returning to Prague to find Amelia gone, through his relentless search for her and his determination to niche out a place for himself in her town and win back her love.

But was it truly love? What if it *had* only been a fling? Not for him—but for her? He hadn't exactly taken her words apart, examined them from all sides, but . . .

Of course. He was five years older than she was. An eternity, perhaps, to her. At twenty, she hardly wanted to settle down with a man who would be chained to his desk for the next decade. Sure, he'd shown her around Prague, but with the schedule his uncle plotted, he wouldn't come up for air for a good three years. Even then, he might end up in Zimbabwe, manning a hotel under his uncle's "train from the bottom" program.

Roark set the bar on the rack, removed the twenty, and slid a thirty plate next to the forty-five on the bar—not even close to his max. He rounded to the other side and balanced the weight, then settled himself back on the bench and started in on a set of six reps.

He couldn't quite scour from his brain the truth that, for a blinding, triumphant moment, Amelia had used him to dig a knife into her lumberjack boyfriend, Seth. At first, he'd scored it a personal victory.

Now that his brain had stopped the inner cheering, he could see it for what it was. Hurt over Seth's accusation. Which should alert Roark to the fact that she cared, *really cared,* about Seth and their future. High school sweethearts were a far cry from a fling, and a smart man would recognize the writing on the wall.

If Roark hadn't been quite so blind or desperate, he might have seen that, instead of riding in to rescue a damsel who didn't need him. Not anymore.

He removed the thirty and found another forty-five plate, adding it and a ten to the bar, then balanced the weight before signaling to Sammy Johnson, the spotter on duty. A few more bodies grunted—athletes working with dumbbells and at the pull-up bar, another with his back to him, adding plates to the leg press.

Sammy came toward him and Roark lay down, seeing the spotter move into place at the head of the bench as Roark eased the bar off the rack.

He'd maxed out at over three fifty while at the gym in Paris, but two weeks without a nod to the weight room made him feel flabby. Or at least winded.

He pressed through the first rep. Maybe he should just leave. Call the entire thing off, tuck his tail, and scuttle out of town before he made a mess of Amelia's life.

His triceps burned, a band of pain growing around his chest as he grunted through the last rep, spent. He was moving to replace the bar when a hand came out against it.

"Mate!" he said, glancing up. It felt like he took a punch to the chest as he saw Seth the lumberjack standing by Sammy, his blond hair tied back in a black sports band, his oaken arms bare, his T-shirt sleeves ripped off.

"I got this, Sammy," Seth said.

To Roark's dismay, his spotter handed him over to his cohort in crime.

"We need to talk," Seth said, turning his attention to Roark. He didn't remove his hand, and Roark's body quivered, straining against the weight.

"Talk, then," Roark said. Sweat dripped down his face, into his ears, his heartbeat thundering.

Seth smiled, all teeth. "I haven't had the chance to officially welcome you to Deep Haven. You like the sights?"

"Lovely. Especially the local wildlife." His arms trembled, his grip loosening on the bar.

Seth's smile dropped. "Get out of my town."

"Or?"

He lifted a shoulder. "What can I say? You wouldn't be the first to disappear into the woods."

Roark wanted to roll his eyes, but the sweat could blind him. "Righto. Message received." He waited for Seth to move his hand, but he held it in place. Roark's arms began to shake. In a moment, all 245 pounds would crash onto his chest, and the fight between Seth and Roark would come to a swift and bloody end.

"Just so we're clear: I've been in love with Amelia since the seventh grade. I know her and she knows me. We're meant to be together."

"Congratulations," Roark ground out. "I've no doubt who the better man is here."

Seth's eyes narrowed.

From across the room, Roark heard, "Everything okay, Seth?"

"Yep, fine," Seth said, grabbing the bar with one hand and moving it to the rack.

Roark heaved in breaths even as he pushed himself to his feet in front of Seth. He ignored the spinning of the room. "If you want to drop off that welcome basket, I'm living over the Java Cup. Nice little place. I'm going to paint the walls, buy a few plants, set it up. Maybe you can come round for a spot of tea." He clamped Seth on the shoulder. "Nice chat; let's do it again."

He turned, heading for the showers.

Roark stood for a long time under the hot water, bracing himself against the wall, his pulse finally righting into a regular rhythm.

Maybe he wouldn't perish in the men's locker room of the Y. But even as he got out and dressed, he heard Seth's voice. *I know her and she knows me. We're meant to be together.*

Not anymore.

Especially since Amelia hadn't once mentioned a boy back home in the five months they'd spent in Europe. Plus she'd kissed Roark.

And like she said, she'd meant it.

So welcome to Deep Haven indeed, because he did know exactly who the best man was in this threesome. Or at least who the best man could be, if he just figured out how to tell her the truth about himself.

Roark threw his duffel over his shoulder, wrapped a towel around his neck, and headed out into the cool evening. The sun hung low in the west, flames of orange and red bleeding out over the horizon.

Hiking up the rear stairs to his apartment, he

184

didn't look in front of him and almost walked right over her.

Amelia. Sitting on his stoop. Holding one of the long-stemmed pink roses he'd sent her.

"Hi." She could knock him over with a smile, which she delivered slowly.

"Hi," he said, dropping his duffel and settling down beside her. "I . . . It's good to see you."

She twirled his flower between her fingers. Sighed.

"What is it?"

She looked at him, and she was so beautiful, with the sunset lighting her hair, her eyes, that he nearly put his arm around her, nearly folded her to himself to finish the kiss they'd started in Paris.

"I never really told you how grateful I was that you came out that night to find me in Prague."

That night. Oh . . . sometimes the memory of her voice at the other end of the line, tiny and shaking, jolted him awake, slid a cold finger down his spine. She didn't need to know, probably, the danger she'd flirted with that night. Or the panic he'd hidden while searching for her, dreading the worst.

Now he just smiled. "I'm glad I was there."

"That's the thing. You were always there. You never let me feel afraid or alone."

"Of course—"

"But see, that's why I left Prague. It wasn't

185

because you broke my heart, but because, without you, I was stuck in my apartment. I was afraid to leave, to go to school on the bus or even take pictures for my assignments. Without you, Prague turned into a dark, terrifying place, and . . ." She wiped a tear from her cheek. "And that's why I left."

"Because I wasn't there."

"Because I was a coward."

"Oh, Amelia." He reached up to touch her cheek, but she caught his hand.

"Roark, I'm telling you this so you don't have to feel guilty. I will probably never leave Deep Haven again. And you don't belong here; I know this. You're a world traveler, a guy who lives to explore, and I can't give you that. I just . . . I'm not that brave."

She let go of his hand. Looked away. "You should find someone who isn't pretending."

So she could, what? Stay here and marry Seth?

The thought roared up inside him, and he might have even spoken it aloud because she turned to him, eyes wide. "What?"

Oh. "You're not a coward. The first day I saw you, you were hiking through Prague alone, taking pictures. You had a light about you, as if when you saw the world, it took on new shades, new depth. Seeing Prague through your eyes made it come alive, reborn. You dared to live beyond your expectations—"

"Then I failed myself, Roark. And I don't know how to get back to where I was."

He saw her then, not through the lens of Prague or the memories of her laughter as they shivered at the top of the Eiffel Tower, or even hiking along the river Seine, but huddled now in a sweatshirt and jeans, her hands tucked into her sleeves, her hair long and free, the red caught by the sun.

A hot cord of realization ran through him. This was the woman he'd crossed the ocean to find. Not the girl whose heart he'd charmed and broken, the girl who'd kissed a near stranger on New Year's Eve, the girl who made him believe that he could be a hero, but the woman who might understand what it felt like to carry failure, cowardice, in your heart and not know how to forgive yourself.

The one person who might not despise him for his mistakes.

He reached out his hand, holding it open. Amelia considered him a long moment before she took it, weaving her fingers through his.

He stood, pulling her up with him. "Let's take a walk. I have to tell you something."

"I never told you that I really grew up in Russia."

Amelia nodded, waiting for him to go on. Roark walked beside her, spilling out stones with his footsteps, pressing indentations into the beach.

Seagulls rode the waves that lapped the shore, and a chill hung in the air as the sun bundled up for the night, leaving only a tufted gathering of brilliant clouds, like the jet stream blaze of a rocket.

"I thought you lived in Brussels."

"I did, but only after we came home from Russia. See, my parents were missionaries."

He smelled sweet, fresh, as if he'd just stepped out of the shower, and she could admit that his still-wet hair made her want to ring one of the curls at the nape of his neck around her finger. He wore thick stubble—very rugged European—a pair of track pants, and a hoodie that clung to the frame of his body. He looked impossibly young and as he kicked stones out in front of him, if she didn't know better, a little afraid.

Most of all, he held her hand like he couldn't bear to let it go.

"We moved to Brussels when I was twelve so my dad could work for my grandfather. But all my childhood memories up to that point were of Russia—far east Russia. We lived in a tiny village, in a tiny three-room house, with a water pump out in the yard, gas lighting, a coal furnace, and an old four-door Lada my father had to hand crank. My brother and I ran the dirt streets with the other kids, attended a *detski-sod*, then a grammar school, and spent the summers helping our parents run children's camps."

She could see him even as he talked, young, wiry, and strong, his dark hair short for summer, running barefoot, causing mischief and wearing a smile that could charm all the girls in the village.

"My father was a church planter and later on helped raise money for orphanages in the region. I loved helping him visit the orphanages. We'd show up with a shipment of medicines or clothing, and for that day, that moment, we were heroes. My brother and I would go out to the yard with a football—a real football, not the eggball you play here. We'd teach them how to play, or if they had a basketball court, we might shoot some hoops. Everyone loved my father. He played the guitar, and sometimes when he'd sit at the edge of our yard playing, people would wander down the road just to hear him. He spoke Russian so well, one of the town officials asked him how he'd managed to snag a British wife. I thought for a long time that I was actually Russian and that the family we had back in London might be distant relatives."

He stopped at a boulder, settled on it. She slid up beside him.

"I was so angry when we left the field. They sent me to boarding school, where I managed to fight my way into the headmaster's office more than once. Thankfully they'd outlawed caning before I arrived, but my father gave me a decent birching when he came to visit. Not a happy memory for me. Especially since he seemed deeply shaken afterward, even though I'd deserved it."

"I'm sorry."

"I sorted it after that, managed A's, and that summer, begged my parents to take us back to Russia. They took us to Spain instead, a vacation by the sea. My brother, who'd attended a different school, seemed changed. He hadn't loved Russia or the mission field like I did, and suddenly I realized that I was the only one who missed it. Back in Brussels, Mum had fixed up our new flat, and they were laying plans for me to change schools, maybe get a fresh start. The family seemed to be embracing our new life, while I mourned the one we'd abandoned. We were staying at a cabana on the beach, and I snuck out for a swim, furious that they could so easily turn away from our life. Our good, happy life."

He closed his eyes, his breath tremoring out. Amelia gave in to the urge to take his hand in both of hers, not sure why.

"I heard Mum's scream as I was walking back to the cabana. It was late, stars were out, and at first I thought it might be someone having fun on the beach. But when I came up to the house, I heard fighting, whimpering, and then another scream."

His face glistened now, but he didn't wipe it.

"I . . . saw my father wrestling with someone.

190

He was big and wore a ski mask. My only coherent thought was of the kitchen knives. So I ran around the side of the cabana and went in through the kitchen."

He swallowed. "I found my brother in a pool of blood on the floor. It slowed me down long enough to see my father fall in the next room, to see the intruder climb on top of him, a knife in his hand."

She sat perfectly still, her breath cold inside her. No—

"I was terrified. And I did nothing. Just . . . *nothing*. Just stood there and watched as he stabbed Dad a couple times. Or more; I don't want to remember. But he finished and got up, and I knew . . . My father had stopped moving. And Mum had stopped whimpering. I . . . I knew I was next. But still, I couldn't move."

She held her breath.

"Then he looked up and saw me."

Oh—

"I fled. Just lost my mind and ran out into the night, crying, as far down the beach as I could until I threw myself into the woods. Then I curled into a ball, choking back my sobs, praying he wouldn't find me. But by this time, others had heard the noises and the police were arriving."

She couldn't speak. Just held his hand, letting his fingers tighten around hers as he released a long breath.

Finally, softly, she scraped up words, shaky, broken. "I'm so sorry, Roark. Did they ever find the man?"

"No."

Tears brimmed her eyes. Then she got up, stepped in front of him, and pulled him into her embrace.

He closed his eyes, leaned against her, wrapped his arms around her waist, his shoulders rising and falling.

After a moment, he looked up, and the pain in his gaze could steal her breath. "So you see, Amelia, I understand what it means to fail yourself. To loathe your own cowardice."

Oh, Roark. He'd always been the Eiffel Tower at night, glittery and mysterious, captivating and exotic, but in his story he'd become real. Vulnerable.

A man who needed her as much as she needed him.

"You weren't a coward."

She didn't understand the face he made. Half confusion, half disagreement. "Yeah, I was. I never told the police what I saw. I was . . . I was too afraid he'd find me."

"You were a kid."

"I was the only witness. And I ran—frankly, I kept running. I went to live with my uncle and escaped into a new life, not looking back."

He took her face in his hands. "But it wasn't

192

until I met you that I stood still and felt it all drop away—the failure, the haunting regret. You made me feel like I wasn't a coward. With you, I could be . . . your hero. Brave. The person who doesn't hide in the woods."

She pressed her hands to his. "You were my hero, Roark. Every day."

His thumbs caressed her face. "And you were mine."

Words were written in his eyes, a question that formed in his tender expression, and it brought her back to that moment in Paris on New Year's Eve, when he'd caught her eyes with his, the fireworks popping behind them from the balcony like a hallelujah to the moment when he saw her as more than a student.

With everyone cheering, celebrating around them, the night had dropped away, and he'd moved toward her, where she stood against the wall, each step stirring through her an electricity she'd tempered since meeting him on the bridge.

He'd braced his hand over her shoulder, touched her forehead with his. "Happy New Year," he whispered.

"Happy New Year," she mouthed back.

When his gaze dropped to her lips, her heart jumped in her chest. "Kiss me," she said before her courage failed her.

He met her eyes one last moment before he

obeyed. Leaned in and pressed his lips to hers, achingly tender, nudging them to respond.

She dug her hands into his lapels and brought him closer as his kiss deepened, becoming urgent with a fire that suggested he'd wanted to do that for weeks.

Even now, seeing his hungry expression, with the waves cheering behind him, Amelia could taste the memory, the added passion as he'd wound his arms around her, pulled her against himself. Could hear the little noise in the back of his throat, something that sounded like an ache set free.

He might have seen the memory play in her eyes because he swallowed. Released a shaky breath. "Wow, I want to kiss you right now." He dropped his hands from her face. "But I'm afraid you'll only think it's a fling. So I'm willing to wait until you *know* I mean it."

Until this moment, she hadn't realized how her accusation—and her leaving—had wounded him.

She reached out and wiped his cheeks. Smiled. "How would you like another shot at meeting my family? We have a campfire tomorrow night, and I'd love for you to join us."

"Will I need armor?"

"You'll have me."

His smile was eclipsed by a piercing light cascading over them and out into the dark, inky lake.

Amelia held up her hand to block the light, squinting as she heard a car door slam, then, "I can't believe this!"

The voice yanked her out of Roark's hold, made her scramble up the rocky shore. "Seth! What are you doing here?"

That didn't sound guilty. She felt Roark sidle up behind her as Seth charged down the beach.

"I'm driving home, and what do I see but you two cozying up like long-lost lovers. Nice, real nice, Amelia."

He stood in the stream of his car's headlights, like a grizzly in a black sweatshirt, more hurt than angry, judging from his eyes. "I thought . . . I mean, I sent you flowers and told you I love you and . . . I don't get it. What's going on?" He stared at Roark, so much venom in his gaze that Amelia went to intercept, standing between them.

"Nothing, Seth. Nothing's going on." Except the words tasted like poison. Ten more seconds and yes, she would have responded to the question in Roark's eyes. *Kiss me.*

But—really? She'd come to town to tell Roark to go home, that she'd made her decision. That she knew he didn't belong here—and that she wasn't leaving. It only made sense.

Until it didn't. Until he let her into his life, finally unlocked the door to the secrets that she'd known lurked right below the surface.

For the first time the pieces fit. Every second Roark spent with her silenced his demons, and something about the way she depended on him—in what she thought was weakness—only made him stronger.

Only made *her* stronger.

But what would happen when he left? Because Seth was right—Roark didn't belong here.

And now she'd managed to put a knife into Seth's chest.

"I don't know what to do, Ames. You prefer this guy? He's just playing you." His jaw tightened, and he took a step toward Roark. "You're a real piece of work."

Out of the corner of her eye, Roark seemed to encourage Seth's rage, the way he stood there, too casual, hands in his pockets, as if Seth were an annoying child.

She turned back to Seth, touched his arm, where his corded muscle tensed, and kept her voice low. "We were just talking."

Seth's expression was incredulous. "You were holding his hand! He looked like he wanted to kiss you." He glanced again at Roark, a muscle pulling in his cheek. "I warned you, *mate,* and now I'm going to have to take you apart."

She waited for something from Roark to match Seth's bravado, like *I'd love to see you try* or *You want a piece of me?* But Roark just lifted a shoulder, uncaring.

It was the dark confidence, the lurking calm in Roark's expression that made her pause.

This side of Roark she didn't know, and it clung to her, reviving the memory of his mystery in Prague.

She stepped closer to Seth, pressed a hand to his chest. "Listen, Roark and I had something. You know that. But . . . it's over now." More poison. Because in her heart, maybe it would never be over. Just impossible.

She heard Roark's quick intake of breath as the wind caught her words, speared them back to him. Clearly she had more power to wound him than Seth's fury.

But even with his admission, she couldn't escape the truth. So she summoned the right words. "We were saying good-bye."

"We were?" This, softly, from Roark.

Oh no.

She turned.

Roark now bore the same hurt expression. "That's not—"

"Think about it, Roark!" She didn't care that her voice suggested she might be unraveling. "What do you think is going to happen? You make me fall in love with you again—what then? We sail away and see the world? Live on love? What do you want out of life? You have to be more than a professional student someday."

He flinched, and she hated herself for her words,

but in the back of her mind, the question lingered—beyond his classes at Charles University, beyond his vast knowledge of wine, art, geography, and culture, the man seemed aimless . . . a fact that hadn't unsettled her until right now.

She lowered her voice, just in case the entire town didn't want to be privy to their argument. "Seth is right—I have a life here, one that he and I can build together, and I told you, I'm not sure I want to leave Deep Haven."

She felt Seth's hand slide onto her shoulder and shrugged it away, rounding on him. "And you—I need time. Yeah, of course I love you—I have since high school—but I'm not ready to marry you, Seth."

His lips pursed with her words.

"I might be. Someday. But I need time to figure it out, and it doesn't help to have you two fighting like a couple of apes, beating your chests and hoping to scare each other off. I can think for myself, and right now I choose . . . no one!"

The words landed like a slap on Seth, and he recoiled. She glanced at Roark, who stared at the ground.

Nice, Amelia. Way to go from two suitors to none in one day. She blew out a breath. "Listen. I will date both of you—"

Roark looked up, his mouth opening, and she held up her hand. "Amend that. I will go out on dates with both of you. But you have to act like

198

gentlemen. No more ultimatums." She looked at Seth, raised an eyebrow. Then she turned to Roark. "And we start over. Completely. Even playing field. I loved you both . . . once."

Roark winced.

"But there are no guarantees about the future. You're going to have to trust me to figure this out and, in the meantime, behave yourselves. If those terms don't work for you, step out of the ring now."

To her shock, it worked. Neither man moved.

"Super. Awesome. *Smashing*." She backed away from them. "I'm going home now, and if I see either of you sporting a shiner or any other signs of altercation, you're disqualified. Are we clear?"

Seth narrowed his eyes, added a shrug.

Roark stared at her without a smile, resolute. He offered a slow nod.

"Very good. Tallyho, gentlemen."

Chapter 7

WITHOUT A DOUBT, Max knew he deserved to sleep alone. After all, what kind of husband suggested divorce after two weeks of marriage?

A lout.

He hated every syllable of his conversation with Grace and had replayed it long into the brutal, lonely hours of the past three nights, wishing he could simply run upstairs, burst into her room, and declare to the entire family that yes, Grace Christiansen had said, "I do" and changed his world.

Filled it with her hope, her light, her belief that they would live happily ever after, even with the dark hours ahead.

Except he couldn't get past the place, deep inside, that declared he was right.

Annulment. Divorce. Whatever it took to spare Grace from the grief he knew would destroy her.

If only he had the courage to actually go through with it. But indecision—or maybe his own pathetic need—caught him in a no-man's-land between doubt and hope.

Please forgive me, Grace. He glanced at her now, those words in his head, his eyes, as he watched her carry a tray of hot dogs down to the freshly built picnic table just beyond the also-new fire ring he'd crafted with her father.

He'd thought he might be replacing a few rocks. But when John and Darek suggested rebuilding something, they meant from the ground up. Tear out the old stones, sort and clean them, dig a wider footprint, lay a new grate, pour a new foundation, and rebuild the circular stones, adding more until they fit perfectly into each other's embrace.

Then they'd tackled the decade-old benches,

digging them free of the ground and hewing the new logs, ordered from Turnquist Lumber, in half. They'd sanded them and covered them in polyurethane, built new supports, and replaced them around the ring.

The picnic table overhaul emerged as a wild afterthought, but even Max agreed that it fit. Freshly sanded and painted red, it added a festive north shore feel to the campfire pit.

Tonight the Christiansens celebrated the onset of the summer season, a rebirth of the lodge they'd worked so hard to rebuild. A spring chill gathered over the rippling lake, the sun edging below the trees to the west. Max wore a sweatshirt, jeans, but Grace had donned a stocking cap and found another for Yulia, her long brown braids trailing out and making her look like a Russian princess.

Grace bent over beside her, helping her attach a hot dog to her roasting stick, neatly ignoring Max. Ingrid came down the path carrying a bowl of potato salad and set it next to the buns that Amelia began to open. Ivy sat on one of the benches, baby Joy on her lap, bundled to the gills in a pink snowsuit.

Beyond the campfire pit, he spied Casper and Raina, holding hands, Layla in Casper's arms. It lodged a bullet in Max's throat, and he turned away just in time to see John tromping down the trail, driving a wheelbarrow with a fresh supply of chopped wood. Max had spent two hours this afternoon splitting a cord the old-fashioned way—ax and sweat. He got up and helped John unload the delivery into a neat stack nearby. He tossed one of the pine logs onto the fire, the sparks spitting into the night.

Yulia's eyes widened, a smile inching up her face.

"*Otlichno*," Max said, dredging up a word that Vasilley used when he netted a shot.

She nodded, giggling.

Grace looked at them, a tender sadness in her expression.

Well, that was headway at least. She'd barely looked at him since that day in the kitchen when he'd uttered the *D* word.

He went over to Yulia. "*Moshna ya pomoch*?" Probably he was massacring the language, but he thought he'd asked to help.

She grinned and he took that as a yes, leading her to the fire pit. Then, sitting on the bench, he reached around her and guided her hot dog into the flame, finding the coals. She leaned back against him, letting him help her.

Grace rested her hand on his shoulder. He didn't move, fearing she might take it away.

"Hey, Uncle Max! I want a hot dog!" Tiger, Darek's son, came bounding down the path.

"I'll fix you up," Ingrid said as Tiger climbed onto the seat of the picnic table. Max rotated

Yulia's hot dog, the skin prickling, sizzling, the aroma nourishing the clear-skied night.

Tiger came over and stood next to Max, wielding a hot dog on a stick.

"Okay, pal, aim for those red coals along the edge. If you stick it right into the flame, it's going to turn black but still be cold on the inside."

Tiger sat on the bench next to him, worked his hot dog into the space under a leaning log. The fire flickered, sparking as Darek sat opposite him, roasting his own dog. "Let a pro show you how it's done," he said, winking.

Max rolled his eyes.

Grace left, to his great disappointment, but Casper sat down in the ring, two hot dogs on his roasting prongs. "Actually, the mark of a real chef is two dogs at once." He grinned, glancing at Raina, who gave him a thumbs-up.

"Seriously. Does everything have to be a competition in this family?" Ivy said.

Amelia, unusually quiet, sat down with a plate of potato salad.

"I guess now is as good a time as any." Casper stared at the fire. Sighed. "I'm leaving on Monday to find Owen."

Max glanced at Grace to gauge her response. She stood at the picnic table, slowly setting down her plate.

"It's time. The Wild Harbor is ready for summer, and Ned has hired staff to replace me. I figure

I'll head out to Montana, look for Darek's old hotshot outfit, see if Owen has hooked up with them again."

"And if he's not there?" This from John.

"Then I'll keep looking. I'm a pretty good sleuth," Casper said, pulling his hot dogs out, blowing on them to cool them. He put the stick back into the fire. Said to no one, or all of them, "I'll find him. I promise."

He looked again at Raina, a smile of reassurance on his face. And in that moment, Max hated him. Hated that Casper had a life to look forward to, a family waiting for him, with the promise of the happy ending he deserved.

He gritted his teeth, trying to shake away the burn inside. "I think it's ready," he said to Yulia, pulling the hot dog from the fire. She startled but looked at him, and he offered the best smile he could. *"Gatov,"* he said, repeating more of his sloppy Russian.

As he got up to doctor her hot dog, the conversation continued around him with suggestions of where Casper could look—favorite places Owen would visit or things he once mentioned wanting to accomplish. But there was no knowing where anger might take a man when his life was ripped out from beneath him. No accounting for the words he might say or the desperate acts he might find himself doing.

Max blinked, hating the crazy, blinding rush of

heat building in his throat. Clearly marriage made him weak. Emotional.

He hadn't seen that coming.

"I hope you find him soon," Ingrid said. "Layla is growing so fast, I hate for you to miss any of it." Behind her words lingered the suggestion that Owen, Layla's biological father, might be missing it too.

"I don't know what I'm going to do without him," Raina said, sitting down beside Casper and settling Layla, dressed in a sweater and boots, a bunny hat, on her lap. "He's so good with her. She'll be crying and angry, but I give her to Casper and suddenly she's giggling. Betrayed by my own daughter."

Amid the laughter, Yulia came over and sat next to Max at the picnic table, nibbling on her hot dog.

"Looks like Casper's not the only one good with kids. I think she likes you, Max," Ivy said.

"You're going to make a great dad," Raina said.

Max tried for a smile—being the newest in the family, clearly Raina didn't know that . . .

"We're not having kids," Grace said quietly. "Max doesn't want them."

So that's what it felt like to be thrown under a bus. Probably he deserved that.

But not the way Raina or Ivy stared at him as if he might have experienced a psychotic break. Their expressions only ignited the darkness inside, and he didn't mean for the words to tumble out, but he couldn't quite stop them. "No, I don't. Not that it's any of your business, but I can't have kids. And . . . I shouldn't either. Because that's exactly what I *don't* want—a family to mourn me the way I mourned my dad. So no, I'm not having kids. But Grace—she can have kids. She just can't have them with me."

As Ivy's eyes widened, as Raina looked away, as Casper's jaw tightened, and as Darek looked like he might take him apart with a glare, Max got up, brushed past Grace, and headed back to the house.

He might, in fact, just keep going.

He'd made it as far as the end of the path, out of the glow of the fire, when Grace caught his arm.

He spun, expecting anger, maybe even a slap for what he'd said.

Instead, he found her arms wrapped around his neck, her lips against his skin. "Oh, Max, I'm so sorry. I'm sorry."

Uh . . . but he wasn't going to argue with his beautiful wife, not when her full-on embrace knocked him off his feet a little. He stumbled back, landing softly against a tree. "Babe, it's okay—"

She lifted her eyes, tears cutting down her cheeks. "No, it's not. I shouldn't have been so angry."

She caught his face in her hands and kissed him, her lips salty with her tears. She reminded him of exactly what he'd missed these past three days, pouring into him her love, that hope and sunshine that came with Grace Christiansen. He moaned a little, settled back, and pulled her closer, wrapping his arms around her, deepening his kiss.

So familiar, so *his*. His *wife*.

He couldn't take another second of the world not knowing.

She twirled the hair at the nape of his neck, a habit when she relaxed in his arms. Maybe no one would miss them if they—

Grace leaned back, smiled.

Yeah, maybe everything would be okay.

"Max, of course you're scared. I get that. I should have been more patient. Given you time."

He frowned, a sliver driving itself between them. "Time for—"

"Well, to realize that it doesn't have to end the way you see it." She stepped away, just a little.

But he grabbed her hand. "Don't leave."

"I'm not going anywhere. That's the point. We're in this together. And just because you can't father children doesn't mean you can't be a father. Take a look at Yulia. The adoption coordinator called today and said that her adoptive sister is releasing her back into the system. Back to Ukraine. To an orphanage. What about us, Max? We could be her family."

"Grace—"

"Just listen to me. I know that you're going to make a fantastic dad someday."

"And then I'm going to die a terrible death in front of my children. Just like my dad did. You'll be left alone."

"Not alone." She grabbed his face. "Don't you get that? Not alone. I'll have the kids, like your mom did. She survived because of you and your brother."

"She's dying inside every day watching my brother deteriorate."

"Yeah, well, you fixed that—we don't have to pass on the gene. But we can be parents. Okay, maybe not to Yulia—although, Max, she needs a family. But to some other needy child."

He pressed the meat of his hands into his eyes. Shook his head. "Oh, Grace, that's not what I wanted for you." He didn't care that his voice broke. "I wanted you to have a child with your beautiful blonde hair, your blue eyes. A child you could carry inside your body. I stole that from you." Shoot, and now he was crying. He looked away, furious as he wiped his cheek.

She caught his hand. "I knew what I gave up when I agreed to marry you. Don't act like I'm stupid or didn't understand that."

Her tone jolted him. He breathed out, met her eyes.

"I love you. And in the end, if you don't want to have children, I'll figure out a way to keep loving you. But I'm not giving you a divorce, Max. Never. I'm a Christiansen as well as a Sharpe, so you can bet I mean what I say."

She kissed him again, hard, something meant to seal her words. Then she turned and walked out of his embrace.

"Grace—" He pushed off the tree.

To his surprise, she whirled around. "And by the way, I'm tired of sleeping in the attic. It's time to tell my family that we're sleeping together."

He wouldn't have phrased it quite that way. His shock must have shown on his face because she smiled. Held out her hand. "Just checking to see if I can wake up my Max."

"Oh, I'm awake, honey." He took her hand, relief hot inside him. He felt like he'd endured eight overtimes in a play-off game, sweaty, heart thundering, ready for it to end.

They walked down the path toward the fire pit, his mind forming words of defense, apology.

And then he saw, on the edge of the campfire's glow, Roark St. John, bearing a bottle of wine and looking like he had happened upon a band of rogues.

Just when Max thought he was the family villain.

If he ended up at the bottom of Evergreen Lake tonight, Roark would blame it on Jensen and Claire Atwood.

I see the Christiansens are starting their weekly campfire tradition.

Jensen's words, spoken as they sat on his deck, finishing off burgers, the sun going down behind the house. Claire, growing more uncomfortable every day, sat on the wicker sofa, her legs stretched out, a hand on her belly, mulling over Roark's recap of the most recent events.

Seth's weight room ultimatum.

His walk with Amelia along the beach.

The near kiss, the one he could almost taste.

Seth, again, and the way Roark wanted to have a go at the beach, just to work off some frustration.

And most of all, Amelia's words. *What do you think is going to happen? . . . We sail away and see the world? Live on love? What do you want out of life?*

"You can't really blame her for thinking you're a pauper," Claire said finally. "Or like she said, a professional student."

Roark pushed his plate away; his appetite had died halfway through the burger. "It was right there, on my lips. I wanted to stop her, tell her that we could go anywhere she wanted—eventually. Live on love and about nine zeros more. But of course, that means I also take over the business, which means moving her to Brussels. And I'm not sure she wants that. Me working twelve-hour days, her finding her way in a foreign city alone. She was pretty shaken up in Prague and has no desire to repeat that."

He peeled the label off his lemonade bottle. "But when I told her about my parents, something changed between us."

"She saw you," Claire said. "We all need that—someone to truly see us and not flinch."

"If Seth hadn't come along, I might have kissed her, despite my promise not to. I'm simply undone around her."

And this time he would have made it last, lingering, showing her exactly how much he loved her.

"So what are you going to do with the fact that she doesn't want to leave Deep Haven?" Jensen said, wiping his french fries through his ketchup.

Maybe I'll stay. He didn't voice it, but the thought had rooted around his head all day as he worked the counter at the Cup, greeting the regulars with their orders. Seb Brewster came in and invited him to church on Sunday, and he had even considered going.

With good Internet and occasional trips to Brussels, maybe . . .

He winced. "I don't know. I just can't scrape away the feeling that I shouldn't give up. It's like she's got a hold on me, a little more every day."

Jensen glanced at his wife, smiled. Nodded.

"Then what are you doing sitting here?" Claire ran her hand over her belly. "Amelia invited you to the campfire."

"Yeah, well, that was before Seth arrived."

"So. She didn't revoke her invitation, did she?"

Huh. He hadn't remembered that part. "Right. Perhaps I'll pop by—"

"There's a bottle of Yellow Tail in the fridge. We'll donate it to the cause."

Which was how he found himself ten minutes later standing at the edge of the firelight, holding a cold bottle of red wine, facing Amelia's brute squad.

Her brother Casper got to his feet. The older one, Darek, put down his plate. Roark glanced at her father, who just frowned at him.

Retreat!

"Roark!" Amelia hopped up. "You're here. I didn't think you'd remember." She came over to greet him, catching his hand—nice touch—and pulling him into the circle of light. "You all remember Roark, right?"

For a long moment, their previous altercation played on everyone's faces. How he'd shown up over a month ago, flowers and gift in hand. How, for a moment, they'd let him in like they'd been expecting him, seeding way too much hope in a weary, desperate man. How Amelia had stopped at the top of the stairs, even more beautiful than he remembered, her green eyes wide with shock. How he'd bumbled the entire thing by asking her to forgive him. To take him back.

He remembered Casper telling him to leave. Then Darek coming alongside as if he needed an assist. Remembered how their father had remained polite, asking Roark to step outside.

And Amelia, confused, crying, following them out to the parking lot, where the shouting really began.

You have a lot of nerve, pal. He could hear the words, see the fury on Casper's face even now. *Amelia is over you.*

Yeah, well, if he'd felt that was true, he wouldn't have stuck around town, shown up again, faced down Darek, who refused to let him even knock on the door.

He'd heard sirens in the back of his head, stopping him from pushing his way past big brother and his gang of thugs—the in-law brothers—knowing that some things, to Amelia, might be unforgivable.

The sirens roared to life again now. He glanced at Darek, seeing the way the man regarded him with a cool look.

Roark felt a little like Cornwallis at Yorktown.

"Nice to see you again, Roark." Amelia's mother came over, holding out her hand. Ah, the family diplomat.

"This is Casper's fiancée, Raina," Amelia said.

She gestured to a woman with dark hair, holding a baby. Roark nodded.

"And, uh, Grace and Max." She motioned and he turned, finding the couple standing in the path. The ambush from behind.

He offered a smile.

"Okay, everyone, just breathe. Roark isn't here to entice me to elope."

On the contrary, the thought didn't sound so terrible at the moment.

"I invited him so we could start over. All of us. So be nice, and I promise you'll like him."

He smiled at Amelia, and she met his gaze, smiled back. *"Thank you,"* he mouthed.

"I brought wine," he said, looking at Ingrid. "It's not a 1961 Château Palmer Margaux, but it's an okay pairing with a burger and chips."

He expected a burst of laughter at the ludicrous thought of pairing a burger with a Bordeaux instead of a frothy pint, but no one seemed to get it.

"Oh. Uh, why, thank you." Ingrid set the wine on the table. "I will put it away for . . . a special occasion."

"Would you like a hot dog?" Amelia asked.

"I ate at . . . I ate already." He didn't know why, but he thought exposing Jensen might come back to haunt him. "Thank you."

John handed him a can of Coke. "Amelia says you're working at the Java Cup?"

He opened the can. "I've never been a barista

before, but I'm enjoying it. I took the flat above the shop and it looks out over the bay. The most glorious sunrises. Reminds me of the sunrises over Pilot Bay in New Zealand."

Crickets.

Why did he say that? Nerves. He mustered up a smile. "I'm also acquiring a taste for World's Best Donuts."

John nodded. "They're addictive. Have you traveled a lot?"

He longed to hold Amelia's hand, but she'd taken a seat, now finishing her potato salad.

"Yes. Some. I . . ." He glanced at Amelia, and she gave him a smile, a nudge. "I grew up as a missionary kid in Russia. But I went to secondary school in Great Britain. I worked for a bit in the hotel industry before traveling."

"You lived in Russia?" Grace seemed to come alive as she sat down next to a little girl who looked somewhat familiar. "Could you . . . ? Do you speak Ukrainian?"

"It's different from Russian, but some is the same. Why?"

Grace tucked her arm around the girl. "This is Yulia and she doesn't speak much English."

The girl smiled at him, and for a moment, his youth caught up to him, the memory of the children in the orphanage. She had the big, wide eyes, the wary smile. Hope. He knew exactly how she felt, and knelt in front of her.

"*Zdrastvootya*," he said. "*Menya zavoot* Roark."

There was the smile. "Yulia" came a tiny voice in return, and in that moment, he felt the postures around the fire ease.

Never would he dream that his past might actually come in handy.

"Can you tell her that she's safe here and that we'll take good care of her?" Grace said.

He translated and got a small, hesitant reply in return. "She says her other mama died? I don't know what she's referring to."

"You pulled her mother from the river," Amelia said softly and knelt beside him.

He felt a little sick, thinking of it now. "The woman. Did she lose her entire family?"

Amelia nodded, and strangely, his chest filled with the oddest urge to pull the child into his arms.

Amelia's touch on his arm brought him back. She caught his gaze in hers. "But she's not alone."

Maybe someday that truth would finally sink in. "I'll be glad to translate if you need me to," he said as he got up.

Grace mouthed a thank-you.

"You really worked in a hotel?" This from Darek.

"Yeah. I was the . . ." Well, why not? "Assistant manager."

"Wow," Casper said. "So why the urge to travel?"

This was harder than he thought. "I found the

industry to be more challenging than I expected and was given the opportunity to spread my wings a bit, so I launched out on an extended holiday. It's lasted a bit longer than I supposed, but I have discovered a few beautiful surprises along the way." His gaze again fell on Amelia, who gave him such a sweet smile, it made the interrogation worth it.

"And now? What's next for you?" John asked. "Pulling espresso shots in Deep Haven?"

He didn't hear indictment but still nearly rose with a retort, defensive words ready on his tongue. He dismissed them fast with a sliver of shame. So his family's company owned hotels from one end of the planet to the next. It didn't mean that they were any more successful than the Christiansens.

In fact, maybe the Christiansens simply defined success differently. Better, perhaps.

"Hey, I'd trade a day of managing rates and keeping guests happy for pulling shots any day," Darek said, oddly coming to his rescue. Roark didn't exactly net a smile, but the man seemed less likely to wrap his hands around his throat. Darek even added, "If I'd known what I was getting into . . ."

"You grew up in the hotel industry, Darek. The hard work can hardly be a surprise," Amelia said. Dressed in a sweatshirt, baseball hat, and jeans, she seemed so . . . American. Friendly. Willing to laugh and sink into the camaraderie of her family.

For a second, the easy humor, the acceptance—though maybe not of him—and the community they shared touched a familiar, long-buried memory. And a dream he longed for but couldn't put his fingers around.

"Yeah, well, maybe I'm just not quite as good as Mom and Dad yet," Darek said.

"You will be, Son." John winked, and the pride in the gesture hit Roark full on the chest. He drew in a breath.

Amelia's hand was on his arm. "You okay?" she said quietly as Darek listed off the projects they still had to complete.

He nodded but pressed his hand against hers on his arm.

"The biggest issue is we're triple booked for day trips next weekend. I thought Casper would be around, but with him leaving to find Owen, we're a man short. I'd ask Grace, but she was never one for canoe trips."

"I can carry a canoe with the best of them," Grace said, and for some reason this elicited laughter.

Darek glanced at Max. "I don't suppose you're sticking around?"

"Not yet. I have a final meeting with the team next week; then I'm free for the summer. Grace will be here, but . . ."

"Which gives us Dad to guide one fishing trip,

and me on the other, but leaves the group of Boy Scouts who want to go canoeing without a guide."

"I could take them," Roark said. Oh, blast. He glanced at Amelia. "Sorry."

"Why? That's a good idea."

Apparently not a soul agreed with her. More silence.

Then Darek offered, "Thanks, Roark, but—"

"He climbed Mount Kilimanjaro, for pete's sakc. He is capable of taking a few boys paddling for an afternoon," Amelia said.

"Seriously? You climbed a mountain?" Casper said.

"Took the Lemosho routc, from the west. Eight days to the summit."

Casper made noises of approval.

"Spectacular views. I'm also a first responder and am accreditcd with the ISAF."

The fire spit into the sky, a log falling.

No one? "The International Sailing Federation."

"That's not a canoe," Darek said.

"I rowed for two seasons at Eton. Perhaps that will do." There it was again, the defense. He blew out a breath, hating himself a little for trying so hard.

Amelia's hand tightened, and he glanced at her. She was grinning.

"Listen, I know you don't know me and probably think I'm off my rocker, but if you need help, I'd like to give it a go. Amelia could come along, take photos for that contest she should enter."

When he felt her go still beside him, he asked, "You saw the link I posted, right?"

She bit her lip. Nodded. "I wasn't sure it was you."

"Of course it was me. Your photos are brilliant. You could win, Amelia." He caught both her hands, the rest of the crowd dropping away. "You're such a gifted photographer. Remember that shot you got of the Eiffel Tower?"

He turned to the group. "She set up her camera at the Trocadéro just before sunset with her f-stop on the lowest setting for the widest aperture. Then she adjusted the bulb function for the longest shutter speed and set the camera on a tripod and timer for the steadiest shot. The tower at night displays a glorious spectacle of light, and after a few tries, she caught the most incredible shot of the lights blurring against the velvet background of the sky. Ingenious."

He hadn't meant to wax on, but the memory seemed to snapshot in his mind. Now he faced her. "Please say you'll enter the contest."

She swallowed, glanced past him, and he hadn't realized how he'd put her on the spot. He looked at her mother, searching for reinforcement.

Ingrid wore a soft, enigmatic smile as she met his gaze.

"Yes, she'll enter," Grace said from her perch on the picnic table. "I agree, Roark. She's a rare talent. And who knows but she might win."

Amelia made a face. "I don't know."

"It's five thousand dollars toward your dream. You don't have to spend it today, but give yourself the opportunity to choose," her mother said. "I agree with Grace. Enter. And I cast my vote for letting Roark and Amelia take the Boy Scouts into the wild. It's only a day trip—what could go wrong? Amelia's paddled that lake with her brothers dozens of times. Besides, they'll have their leader with them."

Her smile was warm as it fell on Roark. He wasn't sure what he'd done to merit the sudden favor of Ingrid Christiansen, but he returned it.

"It's usually the den leaders who are the most trouble," Darek said. "But, okay. Please promise you'll bring everyone back in one piece."

"Scout's honor," Roark said.

"Very good," Ingrid said. "Now, Roark, have you ever, in all your travels, eaten a s'more?"

Chapter 8

A GIRL SURROUNDED by her family, spilling over into a second church pew, the sun gleaming through the sanctuary windows as if in divine approval as the praise band rousted any sleepers with the Celtic version of "Be Thou My Vision," shouldn't have this much turmoil in her heart.

Especially after the way her family seemed to relax their guard around Roark the moment he spoke to Yulia. She couldn't believe Darek would really let him—them—take out a group of tourists.

She had to admire the sheer courage it had taken for him to show up at Friday night's campfire. She should have put up a bigger fight for him at the beginning.

It brought back the words he'd spoken at the coffee shop that first day. Extreme *doesn't begin to describe what I'd do to win you back.*

And when he'd told the story of that night under the Eiffel Tower—how they'd *together* captured the perfect shot—he had no idea that she would have never been in that place, never had the courage to venture out, if he hadn't pushed her.

Apparently, however, he was also serious about not kissing her until she knew he meant it because when she walked him out to his car, he hadn't leaned in, hadn't pulled her to himself. He'd pressed a gentlemanly kiss to her hand that left her heating from the inside and wanting him to stay. To watch the stars together, wrapped in an embrace at the end of the dock.

But right then she vowed not to kiss either of them—Seth or Roark—until she knew in her heart what she wanted.

" 'Be Thou my Vision, O Lord of my heart; naught be all else to me, save that Thou art.' "

Next to Amelia, Max raised his voice with the rest of her family—Casper down the row and Darek in front of her with his growing tribe, Tiger standing next to him, singing his seven-year-old lungs out. Her father stood next to them, his arm casually around her mother, and the sound of their tenors raised together stirred a longing in her she couldn't name.

Or maybe she could. . . . *I do know that I want a man who loves God.* Her words to her mother, on the deck, rose inside her. Somehow the cry of her heart had faded in the heady mix of attention from Roark and Seth.

But if she stayed quiet, she could still hear it, a whisper inside. She did want a man who wanted to love God, serve God. Be His man.

" 'Be Thou my Wisdom, and Thou my true Word; I ever with Thee and Thou with me, Lord.' "

She felt a hand on her arm and looked over to see Vivie, in a pretty yellow sundress, her lips painted red, looking like a throwback from the sixties. "Scoot in," she said.

Amelia bumped Max, who moved into the row, leaving a space for at least half of Vivie.

"Can't you ever be on time?" Amelia said.

"This is on time, darling," she said before raising her voice into the song.

" 'Thou in me dwelling, and I with Thee one.' "

"How's it going with Roark?" Vivie said under the start of the next verse. "I saw him yesterday in the coffee shop. He had a lineup of admirers."

"Thanks for that. And fine. He came to our campfire on Friday night."

Vivie's eyes widened.

Max nudged Amelia with his elbow and she wanted to nudge him back, something sharp right in his gut. Because yes, she'd seen Grace sneak out of their room again last night. It felt a little hypocritical for him to be singing about "Thou and Thou only, first in my heart," when he and Grace had so much compromise going on.

" 'High King of heaven, my treasure Thou art,' " Amelia sang and glanced at him.

He frowned at her.

But movement on the far side of the sanctuary snagged her attention. Seth and his parents, sneaking into the only available room on the far end of the front row. He'd cleaned up for worship, wearing a pair of dark jeans, a white oxford with sleeves rolled to the elbows, his glorious blond hair held back with a rubber band. He towered over his mother but put his arm around her as he began to sing.

Oh, that's right. Mother's Day. With the resort full, Max and Grace had baked cinnamon rolls for each guest, filling the house with the redolence of Christmas. Amelia didn't look forward to the days ahead of turning over the cabins for the coming week's fishing groups, but seeing her parents—and especially Darek—overjoyed with the turnout tempered the drudgery to come.

And then she had Saturday's outing with Roark waiting for her like a reward.

" 'Heart of my own heart, whatever befall, still be my Vision, O Ruler of all.' "

The song ended and Pastor Dan offered greetings before they took their seats, Vivie scooting tight next to her. She breathed into Amelia's ear, "I see Seth."

Amelia put a finger over her lips.

Vivie rolled her eyes.

Pastor Dan continued with announcements as Amelia's eyes drifted to Seth again—old habits, hard to break. She'd probably loved him even before he started flirting with her in seventh grade, before he began to taunt her on the playground in fourth grade, all the way back to when they fought over the rocking horse in the nursery. She didn't know a life without Seth teasing her, then later, turning his hundred-watt attention on her.

Of course they belonged together. Everyone knew it, and he seemed to sense her eyes on him because he looked over his mother's shoulder and met her gaze. A slight smile pulled at his lips.

She couldn't help but return it.

"Today we have special guests. Barb and David

Gunderson, our missionaries to Uganda, are visiting us, bearing a report from their work at Hope Children's Village."

Amelia checked her program, found pictures of the missionaries dressed in traditional African garb. Onstage, they looked all-American, David with dusty-gray hair, about the age of her father, Barb with short black hair, wearing a jean skirt and T-shirt. As a slide show played pictures of whitewashed buildings and adorable, dark-skinned children in pretty pink-and-yellow dresses or oversize Chicago Bulls T-shirts, her mind began to wander.

What if she married Seth? She might one day have her own row—or two—of children, carrying on the legacy of two families whose ancestors built Deep Haven. And Seth—yes, he could be rough-hewn, but he had a tenderness that had made her crazy about him in high school. So when did that change?

Maybe it hadn't. Maybe she'd simply been sidetracked by the exotic allure of Roark, the sense of adventure. But a girl couldn't build a life on adventure, right?

What if Roark stayed in Deep Haven? The thought churned through her brain, trying to fit him into her world. What exactly would that life look like?

The slide show ended, and David gave a recap of the year's activities.

Seth's words began to burrow inside Amelia. *He'll leave once he breaks your heart again.*

But what if she went with him?

David introduced his wife, and Barb took the mic. Amelia shifted in her seat. Checked her watch.

" 'Be Thou my Vision, O Lord of my heart.' We sing it, but do we want it? Do we believe it?" Barb stepped out from behind the pulpit. "I used to sing it loud and proud, but I didn't really want it. Sometimes I still don't want it. God's vision sounds terrifying. What if He sends us somewhere we don't want to go?"

Amelia glanced again at Seth.

"We're satisfied to get a glimpse of His vision, and then we seek out the places where we can accomplish it on our own. And frankly, that's why we live empty, frustrated lives. Pursuing God's vision requires faith in *God* to work it out. It means turning our hearts to Him fully, undivided, focused on loving Jesus with every part of ourselves. I can't do that on my own. Truth is, I don't even want to. Loving God like that takes courage and the surety that He won't fail us."

She looked at the audience, the first pew. "Sometimes it feels like God fails us. Many of you prayed for us when we lost our middle son. A freak moment we couldn't have stopped—he stepped on a black mamba and died in my arms, sixteen years old, his entire life ahead of him. In that moment, I believed God failed.

"But did He? God didn't promise safety for me or my children. He didn't promise me riches or a home. He promised me Himself. He promised me eternity. He promised me hope. That is the vision. It's only when I lose that vision that I begin to call God a failure. I've lost my focus.

"I don't know what call God has put on your life, but if you have tried to answer it on your own, you will find yourself wandering. Lost. Overwhelmed. Afraid."

She stepped back, reached for her husband's hand. " 'Heart of my own heart, whatever befall, still be my Vision, O Ruler of all.' The answer is in the song."

Next to Amelia, Max shifted, sighed, and on the other side, Vivie tapped her phone against her lap.

The congregation stood for another hymn, then the offering, and Pastor Dan dug into a sermon on the book of Mark.

I don't know what call God has put on your life, but if you have tried to answer it on your own, you will find yourself wandering. Lost. Overwhelmed. Afraid.

The service ended with a hymn about trusting Jesus; then Amelia found herself being towed by Vivie out to the lobby and into the bathroom.

"Okay, dish. Are you back together with

Roark?" Vivie planted a hip against the sink, folded her arms.

"I don't know. Not really. Roark and Seth had a fight, and I told them I would date them both."

Vivie's reaction, eyes wide, mouth open, betrayed a little of how Amelia felt, overwhelmed and foolish.

"But maybe I shouldn't date either of them?"

"Now that's stupid. Two swoon-worthy men vying for your heart? I wish I had that kind of attention."

Someone pushed into the bathroom, and Vivie turned to the sink, fixing her lipstick.

"Hello, Mrs. Draper," Amelia said and headed back to the lobby.

God's vision sounds terrifying. What if He sends us somewhere we don't want to go?

She spied the missionary couple surrounded by a small welcome committee in the vestibule and went to join them. Their oldest daughter looked about her age, and she stood holding hands with a young man who sported a fresh haircut. Amelia introduced herself.

"Esther," the young woman said in return. "This is my fiancé, Mark. We're meeting with your pastor after the service to talk about marrying us in a couple weeks."

"Are you heading back to Uganda with your parents?"

Esther shook her head. "God called them to

overseas missions. He has different plans for us. Mark just got a job as a history teacher in Blue Earth."

"I have a buddy I met at Vermillion from Blue Earth." Seth's voice cascaded over Amelia's shoulder. He reached past her, hooked Mark's hand. "Played football for the Buccaneers."

Mark said something about the Blue Earth team, but Amelia missed it, caught by the way Seth seemed almost jovial. And when he turned to her, he wore the smile that could always leave her a little weak.

He drew her away from the group, pocketed her in an alcove, one hand braced on the wall. "You look pretty today."

She did? An unexpected blush rose in her cheeks. "You look nice too." She straightened his tie, smoothed it against his chest.

"How about later I come around and take you out for a picnic? You know, a real date."

He smiled again, a hint of tease in his eyes, but they landed on her with such affection that he seemed a different man from the one she'd seen Thursday night on the beach.

"Yeah, okay."

"Perfect. I'll be there around five." He winked and walked away.

Amelia looked around for her parents. Instead her gaze landed on Seb Brewster and the man he was introducing to Pastor Dan.

What was Roark doing in church? Yes, they'd visited Notre-Dame and a number of cathedrals around Europe, and he'd professed a belief in God, but other than the time she'd found him sitting alone in the middle of a monastery garden in Prague, lost in thought—or maybe prayer—she hadn't seen him attend church.

He had grown up as a missionary, however.

She headed toward him, her heart thumping.

Tiger ran up to her, holding a treat in a napkin. "Want a cookie, Aunt Amelia?"

"Thanks, Tiger." She took the cookie and looked back toward Roark, but he had just stepped outside, moving toward his car.

Pursuing God's vision requires faith in God *to work it out.*

What if she left it up to God to decide? Because the harder she looked, the more her vision seemed to cloud over.

"I'll take you to Europe if you want, Ames. I mean, I like castles and history. I'd go for seeing Normandy beach." Seth sat up on the picnic blanket and threw a rock into the lake. It startled the loon feeding just offshore, and the bird disappeared under the water.

"Seth!" Amelia lowered her camera, searching the dappled lake for the loon's black head.

"Sorry," he said. "You can take a picture of me." He grinned as she turned the camera on him, the

231

sun catching his golden locks, his warm brown eyes. He wore a black T-shirt that outlined his powerful torso, those burly shoulders, thick biceps. Her lumberjack. And he did photograph well.

True to his invitation, he'd arrived at 5 p.m. to pick her up, heading north, toward a picnic clearing on Poplar Lake, a blue lake rich in walleye that she'd fished a couple times with her father. Seth had unloaded from his pickup truck a blanket and a basket full of sandwiches, fruit, and bottled lemonade—a feast that she knew had taken some preparation.

The gesture had touched her, as did the egg salad sandwich he'd handed her. "You remembered."

"Hello, you drove me crazy our senior year—the Thursday special at the deli."

She'd grinned. "We did have fun trying to make our Thursday deli runs in time to get back to school."

"To this day, I avoid the strip of road in front of the school—I just know Kyle is waiting for me to gun it so he can slap me with another $200 ticket." He'd dug into his Italian roast beef.

"Yeah, well, you would have gotten more of them if it weren't for me. His kid brother had a crush on me."

Seth rolled his eyes. "Who didn't have a crush on you, Red?"

Now, their dinner eaten, the sun falling lazily

into the horizon, Amelia lay back to trace the clouds and finally responded to his offer. "I'd love to go to Europe with you."

"I'm just saying, you don't need James Bond to see the world. I can take you." He rolled onto his side, propped himself up. "It's not like I didn't expect you to want to travel."

She glanced at him.

"Sheesh, don't you think I noticed you buried in the church library on Sunday mornings, reading those missionary books? I'd go in, pretend to check out a Left Behind book, and you wouldn't even look up."

"They were about Bible smugglers. I used to dream I'd be a spy for God, hiding Bibles in the back of my tricked-out motorcycle."

Seth laughed. He picked a long piece of grass and tickled her neck with it.

She swatted at him. "Beyond playing lineman for the Minnesota Vikings, didn't you ever have any dreams? And driving NASCAR doesn't count either."

His smile fell, and he nodded, suddenly serious.

She waited, but he flopped onto his back, staring at the sky.

"What?"

"I don't want to tell you."

"Seth."

"It's silly."

"It's me. I'm not going to laugh at you."

233

He turned to her, his eyes suddenly rich with unshed emotions. "I used to dream that I'd build us a house out here. On Poplar Lake. I even drew it, had plans made."

She sat up. "You wanted to build us a house? Here?"

"*Want* to, and brace yourself because I already own this patch we're sitting on."

"Seth!" She stood and turned to survey the sloping hill down to the lake, covered by towering birch, white pine, and poplar.

He stood next to her, settled a hand on her shoulder. Pointed. "I'm going to put the house there, with a deck that overlooks the lake. The house is open and big, so we can fit your entire family and more, and it has two stories, lots of bedrooms for our kids. It'll be easy for me to get the logs—I thought I'd skin them and build it myself. It might take a couple years, but we can live in town until then, right?"

Amelia swallowed, the vision too vivid—the sound of kids jumping into the lake, the smell of campfire. The life she'd grown up with, for the next generation. She looked at him, and her eyes blurred.

He thumbed the corner of her eye. "What is it? Did I say something wrong?"

"No. It's so . . . right. It's perfect."

A muscle pulled in his jaw. "Except I have a feeling that's not a good thing."

"It's a great thing!" She looked away. "It's just—"

"You don't want it. At least with me."

She closed her eyes. "I *do* want it with you."

"Then what's the problem?" He turned her. "Help me understand what you want!"

She couldn't put it into words, this simmer inside, a sort of ethereal sense of something bigger. "I want Jesus. I want that passion, that vision Barb Gunderson talked about today. I want to know what 'Thou in me dwelling, and I with Thee one' feels like."

She'd rendered him silent.

She bit her bottom lip, shook her head. "I know I don't make sense, but I think that girl who longed to be a Bible smuggler is still inside me. Maybe that's why I went to Prague."

"Okay, fine. I get that. I know you wanted to leave Deep Haven, have some kind of grand adventure. But, Amelia—you had it! And came home, remember? Isn't that enough? What more do you want?"

"I want all of it. All that God has for me. All the vision, in faith. I—"

"And that doesn't mean me." He was trembling, and she hated herself for destroying this perfect evening.

"It might. I just don't know yet."

He raked his hand through his hair. "Silly me for thinking you could have Jesus and me."

"Seth—"

"Fine. When will you know? A week? Two weeks? A month? A year? You have to make a decision, Ames. You can't just wait around for your life to happen. You have to *make* it happen." He reached out and took her hands. "I'm trying to be patient—"

"I know you are."

"But you're killing me here." He put his forehead to hers. "For the record, I want what God wants too. I just happen to think it's you."

He started to kiss her, a whisper against her lips, and for a long second—too long—she ached to simply lose herself again in Seth's embrace. To lounge on the blanket with him under the twilight and accept his words as her answer. *I want what God wants.* Wasn't that a man after God's heart?

Maybe—but her hand came up anyway against his chest.

"Ames!" He tore away from her, his eyes reddening. "What?"

"I can't kiss you. I mean, of course I want to, but I can't kiss anyone until I know. It's not fair."

"You mean it's not fair to Roark!"

"No! It's not fair to me! It just confuses me. I love kissing you, Seth. Too much. So . . ." She shook her head, started to pick up the picnic supplies. "I think I need to go home."

"Ames, c'mon . . ." His voice held too much pleading, but she steeled herself against it.

"I'm tired of wandering, Seth. I came home from Prague because I lost my vision of why I was there. And now I don't have one. But I'm going to figure it out. I promise."

She heard his intake of breath, then his quiet movements as he packed up their picnic. He wrapped it all in the blanket and carried it to the truck, dumping it in without ceremony.

Then he climbed into the cab, both hands on the wheel, driving her home in stony silence.

When they reached the resort, she got out but paused at the open window. "Seth—"

"Call me when you figure it out," he said sharply and drove away.

Amelia stood there in the dust a long moment before she went inside. Her mother sat on the deck, reading, most of the weekend guests departed. She guessed that Darek had gone home for the night, and through the window she spied Grace and Max teaching Yulia to fish off the end of the dock.

She headed upstairs, sat on the bed, pulling her computer to her lap and inserting the SD card from her camera. Then she uploaded the pictures from the picnic—the loon, Seth, the sun ablaze across the lake. Editing a couple of her favorites, she uploaded them to Facebook, tagging them to Evergreen Resort. Darek would be thrilled.

She couldn't help but notice the contest link, still on her home page.

Give yourself the opportunity to choose.

She closed the computer before she did something foolish.

Roark didn't know what had possessed him to go to church with Seb, but the effect of it lingered all week. Everything from the hymns to the fact that Darek had come up and shaken his hand.

The crazy sense of acceptance by the Christiansen family had clung to him, fueled his week. By the time Saturday rolled around, he'd purchased a pair of hiking boots, a rain jacket, Gore-Tex pants, and a compass for his trek into the woods with the Boy Scouts.

It helped that Amelia stopped in twice for her Becky—a medium caramel-vanilla mocha.

He arrived at the lodge just as the sun edged above the horizon, the day crisp, the faintest hint of breath gathering in the air, lacy dew in the ferns growing in the garden along the stoop. He passed John and his crew of fishermen, on their way to some remote northern lake for the season's fishing opener.

Darek came out of the garage carrying poles, life jackets, and tackle boxes. He loaded them into the resort pickup, then came over to Roark. "The forecast calls for rain, so we provided ponchos along with your gear." He pointed to a collection of lumpy oversize backpacks.

"What are those?" Roark asked.

"Duluth Packs—especially made for canoeing. The scouts packed them yesterday as part of their merit badges. You should have everything you need for lunch. We added some gorp—a kid favorite—and some of Mom's hardtack with peanut butter, but there's a hot lunch. You just have to build a fire, heat up water, and add it to the individual packs. I think Amelia packed ravioli."

"It's not beans and toast, but it'll do."

Darek raised an eyebrow, not getting his humor. "Okay. So Amelia has the map—you'll take them up to Hungry Jack and Bearskin, onto Rose Lake, let them explore the waterfall, then back. It's a nice trip and they'll be worn out by the time they get back. Their leader is named Mike—nice guy. He's an Army veteran, but I'm not sure he'll be a lot of help. Amelia knows what she's doing; just get everyone back safely." He held out his hand, and Roark shook it. "Thanks, Roark. We appreciate your help today."

Darek's clients arrived, and he pulled away. Amelia came bounding outside, dressed in cargo pants and a fleece, her hair covered with an orange bandanna. "When did you get here?"

She looked so cute, it stole his breath for a moment.

She didn't seem to notice as she walked to the Duluth Packs, picked one up, and hauled it to a trailer stacked with canoes. She threw it in.

Roark grabbed the second one. "I didn't realize you were such an Amazon woman."

She offered a muscle and a smile. "Amelia Christiansen in her natural habitat."

He laughed, but he hadn't quite thought about that. As she loaded in paddles and counted life jackets, he realized that she carried herself with a confidence he hadn't sensed in Prague.

He picked up another stack of paddles, loaded them into the truck. "I'm starting to feel like maybe your brothers were humoring me when they agreed to let me tag along."

"Oh, you're going to earn your keep, Mr. St. John, when we start to portage."

When they did *what?*

She tossed him a green T-shirt, and he held it up, read the Evergreen Resort logo on the front. "Really?"

"Time to earn your Evergreen merit badge." She winked just as a crowd of boys dressed in brown shirts, jeans, and jackets arrived, their leader in tow. An older man, carrying extra girth and sporting a white goatee, he reminded Roark of his uncle Donovan, if only for the way he trundled along the path, fearful of breaking a sweat.

He introduced himself to Roark as Mike McGuire. "Ah, a Brit. Served with a crew from England in the Gulf War," Mike said. "Very good, then," he said, affecting a dreadful British accent.

Roark forced a smile.

Mike opened the van door for the boys to climb in.

"Mike's been bringing up Troop 126 for the last fifteen years," Amelia said as she got into the driver's seat.

Indeed. Mike regaled the eight boys with stories of previous trips, then started a round of "Ain't No Bugs on Me," followed by a thousand choruses of "Be Kind to Your Web-Footed Friends." By the time they reached Hungry Jack Lake, Roark quietly hoped that Mike and his memories would end up in a different canoe.

However, Amelia sang along, seeming joyous. "'Be kind to your fur-bearing friends. For a skunk may be somebody's brother . . .'"

Roark offered a grim smile that only made her sing louder.

"C'mon, Roark—'be kind to your friends wearing stripes . . .'"

When they arrived at Hungry Jack, he launched himself from the van, unloading the paddles, the life jackets.

"Let the boys take the canoes—it's part of their merit badge requirements," Mike said as he untied one of the canoes and helped two twelve-year-olds lift it from the rack. Roark cringed as they nearly dropped it, the aluminum hull scraping against the rock with a squeal as they slid it into the lake.

While he tried to untangle life jackets, Amelia handed out paddles and gave the boys a lesson. Then she dispatched them to their canoes, girded up in their flotation devices, and pushed the first two boats out onto the glorious indigo lake.

Mike, thankfully, climbed into the stern of one of the remaining canoes.

For a wonderful moment, Roark thought he might get to share a canoe with Amelia, but she took the stern of a fourth, leaving him with a skinny boy who looked like he spent most of his time playing video games in the basement, his face pasty white, eyes round with fear as he climbed into the boat. He leaned too far over the edge, and Roark had to grab it before the canoe tipped.

"Ahoy, matey, let's not go in the drink!"

The kid looked back at him as if he might be a pirate.

"It's okay. Just take a seat." Roark pushed off from shore and got in, taking his paddle. Amelia and Mike had already paddled toward the middle of the lake, catching up with the other two canoes.

He dug in, paddling hard, but quickly found that he'd angled away, moving toward the western shore.

"Hey there, Your Highness, how about heading this direction?" Mike's voice carried across the lake, along with the sound of his laughter.

Roark blew out a breath as the kid at the bow turned to look at him. "Switch sides," he said quietly.

Right. He knew that. But he put the paddle in on the other side and steered the canoe toward Amelia, correcting as he went.

He finally pulled up alongside her. "Getting my sea legs," he said.

"No problem." She bore nothing of criticism in her expression. He didn't look at Mike.

Amelia pulled out a map. "This is where we're going." She indicated their destination on the map and then pointed out the indentation in the shoreline. "Thankfully, this side of the BWCA wasn't affected by the fires. It's a pretty paddle; then we'll portage into Bearskin and finally head into Rose for lunch."

"Off you go," he said, his mood lightening.

She led them out, and the crew began to paddle to the portage across the lake. The quiet nudge of the canoe through the water, the bump of the paddle against the frame of the canoe, the call of loons in the still morning—he could find a sort of peace here.

From across the lake, probably from Amelia's canoe, he picked up a song, this one familiar.

" 'Riches I heed not, nor man's empty praise, Thou mine inheritance, now and always . . .' "

The hymn from Sunday's service. It had found purchase in his heart, dredging up an old memory from his camp days in Russia. If he listened hard, he could still hear his father's voice as he worked out the chords on his guitar. *"Thou and Thou only, first in my heart, High King of heaven, my treasure Thou art."*

Except God hadn't been first in his father's heart—not really. If He had, he never would have sold out his calling to grab a job co-running Grandfather's vast business.

But like father, like son, because Roark had his chance to serve God, to follow the High King of heaven, and had turned away at a full-out sprint.

He noticed Amelia had reached the portage, followed closely by Mike, then the two other canoes. He tried not to let his dismal skills horrify him as he pulled up last. Mike and Amelia had already hauled their canoes from the water, loading one onto two of the scouts and sending them on their way up the trail.

Mike propped the next canoe on two more scouts and took the third himself.

Which left a Duluth Pack and two canoes to divide between Amelia, Roark, and Skinny.

Roark's eyes widened as Amelia positioned herself at the middle of the canoe, dragged it up her legs, then, with a hitch of her hips, hoisted it onto her shoulders. She balanced it with one hand, turning. "You okay here?"

He stared at her. "Seriously? You're going to carry that?"

"Try to keep up." She took off up the path.

Skinny grabbed the pack and followed her, which left Roark with the canoe. He shoved the paddles against the gunwales, then reached over and, mimicking Amelia's movements, hauled it onto his shoulders.

He hadn't expected the weight. Or the unwieldy balance. He turned the canoe to follow her and crashed the bow into a skinny birch. The sound bellowed across the lake and shivered into his bones. He straightened the canoe out, hoping no one heard, and headed up the path.

The portage trail wound through the woods, and he nearly tripped on a slew of roots, bare and winding like snakes across the path.

By the time he reached the output, sweat dripped down his back, his shoulders screaming. But he swung the canoe down and set it gently in the water.

Skinny sat on the Duluth Pack, arms folded. Amelia and the rest of the crew floated offshore, waiting.

"Sorry."

"My mother can portage faster, dude."

Roark refrained, barely, from pitching Skinny in as the lad took his position in the bow. Roark pushed them off, and Amelia and the gang started for the next portage while he managed to zigzag his way across the lake. By the time he arrived, only Amelia remained, waiting for him.

"You okay, Roark?" She sat in the sun, her fleece tied around her waist, the sleeves of her Evergreen staff shirt rolled up to her shoulders.

"Right as rain," he said darkly.

She raised an eyebrow but stood and did her canoe-carrying ballet move. He wanted to load the canoe on Skinny, but the coward grabbed the Duluth Pack and took off at a run.

Nice.

The portage climbed a thousand steps up the side of a mountain—or seemed that way as sweat saturated his shirt, ran in rivulets down his face. But the view from the top could heal him, the lake stretching out before him, flanked by high cliffs. He heard laughter and the sound of rushing water and worked his way down the portage to find the scouts wading in the pool below a waterfall.

The canoes rested against a tree nearby. Amelia sat on a rock, capturing the scouts' activities with her camera. Rainbows of sunlight arched in the spray of the waterfall.

Roark set his canoe down, crawled onto the rock next to her. "I am woefully out of my element here, love. I'm about as useful as a sieve in a rainstorm."

She lowered her camera and laughed. "You're doing fine. We'll cross the lake, make lunch, and the boys will work on their knots. You can teach them a stevedore knot."

He glanced at her. "That's a sailing knot."

"Or a knot we use for our tarps." She caught him in her viewfinder. "Smile."

He tried for something that didn't look like a grimace.

"Oh, Roark, you look like you're in pain," she said, reviewing the shot, her hand over the screen to shade it.

"I'm in agony over my wretched paddling skills."

She laughed and rounded up the Boy Scouts. "C'mon, guys. Let's get going."

They set up camp for lunch an hour later, at a clearing across Rose Lake. Roark managed to stay ahead of his own chagrin by building a fire, then boiling water for lunch.

After a less-than-gourmet meal of freeze-dried ravioli, during which Mike led the boys in a chorus of "On Top of Old Smokey," Roark and Amelia taught the scouts the figure eight, carrick bend, bowline, bowline on a bight, and stevedore.

He was helping one of the scouts with a running bowline when Skinny came running over. "Something's wrong with Big Mike!"

Amelia got to him first, Roark close behind. Mike sat with his hands over his chest. His breath came in hitches, his face contorted.

"Big Mike, you okay?" Amelia said.

He shook his head, leaning back. "My chest hurts."

Roark crouched beside him. "Where does it hurt? Your arm, your neck?"

"Yeah." His breathing became shallow. "I think I'm going to faint."

Roark looked at Skinny. "Open the Duluth Pack and get out a couple ponchos." He took the man's pulse as Amelia helped retrieve the ponchos.

"Lay one out on the ground; cover him with the other."

She spread out the first poncho, eased him back. "Is that better?"

Mike shook his head.

"Mike, have you had a history of heart trouble?" Roark asked. He pulled off his fleece jacket and draped it over the man, covering him with the second poncho. Then he gestured to another scout for the Duluth Pack and used it to prop up the man's legs.

"No. Nothing. I mean, sure, I get a little indigestion every once in a while but . . ."

"Okay." Roark patted his chest, then turned to Amelia, walking her a short distance away. "The fact that his pain hasn't gone away has me worried. I'm not ready to say he's having a heart attack—"

"Oh no! I was thinking that as you were talking to him. What are we going to do?"

He took her by the shoulders, feeling useful for the first time today. "We should get him some help. And as we both know, you're the better paddler."

"I can get cell reception at the top of the portage between Rose and Bearskin. I'll call the Deep Haven EMS."

"Good." He wrapped an arm around her neck, pulled her to himself in a fast hug, pressed a kiss to her head. Then he let her go. "Hurry."

He didn't watch her paddle away, just mobilized the boys. "Let's pack up camp and load the canoes."

"Don't let me die," Mike said, his voice a whisper.

"Are you kidding me? Who's going to teach me the next wretched verse of 'On Top of Old Smokey'?" *Please, God, did You hear him?*

Only then did Roark glance up and spot Amelia halfway across the lake, on her knees in the middle of her canoe, paddling like she'd been born in the wild.

He checked Mike's pulse again. Skinny came over, crying, clearly afraid.

Roark put his arm around him, directed him back to the campfire, where the other scouts sat, shaken.

"Hey, how about a song? Who knows 'Do Your Ears Hang Low?'"

The next time he looked up, Amelia had reached shore, was scrambling out of her canoe and running up the trail to the top of the portage.

And right then Big Mike gasped, cried out, and fainted.

Chapter 9

THE SKIES PARTED and unleashed a rumble of doom as Amelia ran up the trail to the apex of the portage, the highest point between Bearskin and Rose Lakes. She already had her cell phone out, watching the bars. *Please.*

Lightning, then droplets of rain dribbled down from the sky. She slipped on a root, landed hard on her hands and knees, splitting her lightweight pants. Pain speared through her wrist, but she shook it off as she scrambled to her feet and pushed harder up the portage steps.

Please, God, let Mike live. She'd known the leader—a fixture at Evergreen every summer, leading a fresh group of recruits out for a taste of wilderness—for most of her life. He couldn't die on her watch.

On Roark's watch.

Breathing hard, she reached the top of the portage. The drizzle from the steely-gray clouds grew steady, heavier, becoming drops that slid down her hair, her back. She should have grabbed a poncho.

No, she should have paddled faster. She lifted her phone and found a bar. If she stood right here . . .

"Deep Haven Emergency Services."

Seth. She took a breath, pushed every thought but Mike from her mind. "Seth, help. We have an emergency."

"Amelia?"

"I'm on Rose Lake with the Boy Scouts and their leader might be having a heart attack. I need a medevac from the campsite across the lake from the falls."

"Okay. Breathe. Is he still experiencing chest pains? What's his pulse rate?"

"I don't know. I had to paddle to the portage to get a signal." She stepped out of the pocket, heard his voice cut off, and for a second she thought she'd lost him. "Seth!"

"Amelia, listen. The chopper is out. There was a drowning on Gunflint Lake, and they flew the victim to Duluth. You'll have to bring him in."

"I . . . I have a bunch of sixth graders. I can't—"

"You left them alone?"

"No! Roark is with them." She heard the quick intake of breath, but she couldn't help it. "We need help. We can't carry him out on our own."

"Okay, Ames, breathe. I'm on my way. Sit tight. I'll bring a team as fast as I can. But with the storm and the road conditions, it might be two hours."

"Please hurry, Seth." She hung up, the rain lashing over her now, soaking her to the bone. *Please give Mike two hours, Lord.*

She scrambled down the portage, nearly running, praying she didn't slip as she jumped from root to root. A low-hanging branch slapped her face and she tasted blood on her lip. She fell again, sliding in the mud, but scrambled back up, ignoring the pain in her wrist.

She reached the canoe and pushed it onto the water, too aware of the lightning crackling in the sky as rain pelleted the surface of the lake. An aluminum canoe made for a terrific lightning rod on open water.

She ducked her head and dug in, pushing through the burn between her shoulder blades and in her upper arms and knees, grinding against the bottom of the canoe. *Two hours, Lord. Two hours.*

Or more, really, if she were honest, for the EMTs to get over two lakes, two portages, and paddle to their campsite. They should move Mike to the base of the portage between Rose and Bearskin, but she couldn't jeopardize the lives of the kids in the thunderstorm.

She could see them now, huddled in their ponchos onshore, under a makeshift shelter made from the emergency tarp Darek had added to the pack. A puny fire crackled under the shelter, smoke peeling out from under the tarp, a marker for her to follow.

And singing. Was that—? Yes, she made out the tune: "The Battle Hymn of the Republic." But the words were new. " 'He jumped out without a parachute from twenty thousand feet . . .' "

She heard a voice shouting as she came closer, and one of the scouts came down to help catch the canoe, pull it onshore. The scout held it steady as she climbed out, soaked to the bone, shivering.

"He died, Ms. Christiansen," the kid said.

Her heart stopped. No—

"And then Roark brought him back to life!" The kid was scrambling up behind her, leaning on the paddles.

Brought him back to life?

Mike lay on his back, still wrapped in Roark's coat and the poncho, his legs elevated, his eyes closed. Roark knelt beside him, holding his wrist, checking his pulse against his watch.

He looked up, and she read the stress on his face. But he turned to the group. "C'mon, guys, where's the chorus?"

They mustered up words to their battle hymn tune.

" 'Glory, glory, what a heck of a way to die, suspended by your braces when you don't know how to fly. Glory, glory, what a heck of a way to die. And he ain't gonna jump no more.' "

Given the circumstances, Amelia wasn't going to judge Roark for his song choice. She dropped to her knees beside him, cut her voice low. "How is he?"

"Barely with us," he said, equally low. "His heart stopped, so I had to administer CPR. But I got him breathing again."

"Oh, my—you really did bring him back to life."

"For now. Please tell me you got ahold of EMS."

"Yeah, but the medevac is already taking a drowning victim to Duluth. We have to get him out on our own. Seth is bringing in a crew, but it could be hours."

"He doesn't have hours!" He glanced at the crew of wide-eyed scouts. "C'mon, boys, don't let my fire die."

She couldn't help but be impressed with the way Roark had mustered the boys, having them pack their gear, bring the canoes onto shore, overturn them so they wouldn't fill with water. Keeping them calm.

A couple boys added wood to the fire, stirred the coals.

"I don't know what else to do. We could try to bring him out, but with the storm, it's not safe to be on the water."

"Do you know CPR?"

"Yes, of course."

He checked Mike's breathing once more. "Good. I'm going for help." He stood. "I'll be back as fast as I can."

"But—what? Are you hiking out?"

"No. I'm going to get us a medevac."

"How—?" She got up, chasing him half down the shore, her voice shaking. "Don't leave me!"

He rounded and caught her shoulders. Found her eyes. "Amelia. You are more than capable of handling yourself. Do what you know to do."

Rain pelleted his black thermal shirt, pasting it to his body. She probably appeared just as waterlogged. He must have noticed her shiver because he rubbed her arms. "You're hurt." He touched her lip with his thumb, then pushed her hair behind her ear. "You were very brave."

She licked the blood from her lip, reached up to wipe her cheeks. "I don't feel brave."

"It's not about how you feel. It's about what you do." He pulled her against himself, pressing his lips to her forehead. "I'll be back with help; I promise."

Then he let her go and headed down to the canoe. As he grabbed a paddle and pushed her canoe into the lake, he seemed a different man from the one she'd seen this morning, trying too hard to impress her. He sat in the middle, crouching on his knees, just like she had, and his long, powerful strokes carried him out into the lake, over the cresting waves. Lightning still zagged in the sky, followed by the roar of thunder.

Please, God, keep Roark safe.

Amelia crouched beside Mike, the fire flickering under the misty air, and laid a hand on his chest, felt it rise and fall. *And don't let Mike die.*

Then she turned to the boys, sitting around the fire, their faces drawn. "What's the next song?"

She kept her eyes on Roark as he shrank to a speck across the lake, crossing it in half the time she had. He might have never canoed before, but he'd become a pro by the time he landed it, disappeared up the trail.

They'd sung through "Boom Chicka Boom," "Greasy Grimy Gopher Guts," and the entire length of "I Met a Bear" by the time he reappeared.

He set out across the lake again, the wind bringing him toward her. She could make out his tall outline, like a voyageur bent against the wind and rain as he fought the waves. His black hair streamed back from his resolute face.

Mike began to moan, reviving.

"Shh." Amelia caught his wrist, found his pulse weak. "Hang in there, Mike. Help is coming." *Please.*

" 'The prettiest girl . . .' " Mike's voice emerged in a whisper.

She leaned down near his mouth. "What?"

" 'The prettiest girl . . . I ever saw . . . was sippin' cider . . .' "

Oh, another song. One of the scouts picked it up. " 'Through a straw.' "

Mike smiled.

Roark came ashore, hopping out of the canoe and dragging it with one hand. He jogged to the site, crouched beside Amelia. Exertion flushed his face, his body shivering even as the thermal shirt outlined the corded muscles on his arms, his stomach. He pushed his hair back as water ran in rivulets down his face. "Help's on its way."

"Did the flight come in?"

He shook his head. "I found another plane."

"What—?"

He stood. "Boys, we're going to need to get your scout leader ready to transport. That means we need a makeshift gurney. Colin, Darrin, I want you to get me all the paddles. We're going to lash them together."

Two of the scouts scampered to the overturned canoes.

"Mark, you and Evan start unloading the Duluth Packs."

"What are you doing?"

"We'll use them to create the body of the stretcher."

"I can walk," Mike said.

"Shut it," Roark said to Mike but added a smile. "We have it sorted."

The boys brought over the paddles. "Shoelaces," Roark said. "I need as many as you have."

The boys began to untie their shoes.

"We could probably carry him," Amelia said quietly.

"And steal from these boys a great story of how they saved their scout leader with their shoelaces?" He winked at her.

Oh. But she had to admit the mood changed suddenly from doom to anticipation as they worked together to lash the paddles, then cut holes in the Duluth Packs—she'd have to sew on patches later—and wove the wooden paddles through the packs to create stretcher poles.

"Lay the stretcher down next to him."

In the distance, a low drone hummed above the roar of rain. It seemed, too, the rain had started to die, the thunder now an irritated growl.

"We're going to roll him onto the stretcher. Boys, I want two of you at his head, two more at his feet, and I'll pick up his body."

"I can move."

"Sit tight, Mike." Roark directed the boys into position, then on three, rolled Mike to his side. "Colin, you and Evan push the stretcher under him."

They obeyed, and Roark rolled Mike onto the makeshift stretcher, made with three Duluth Packs and six paddles.

Amelia covered him again just as she heard a floatplane drop from the clouds and skim across the lake, bouncing against the waves.

It motored to shore, dropped anchor ten feet away. The door opened and the pilot poked his head out, waved.

"You called Jake Goldstein?" Amelia said.

"Yes." Roark got up and headed toward the water. "Jake!"

Jake waved. "I brought an EMT like you asked."

The passenger door opened, and Seb Brewster

jumped out from the backseat, wearing his orange rescue jacket.

Amelia didn't have time to sort through the questions. Or even argue as Seb waded to shore and, with Roark, lifted Mike and hauled him across the cold water to the plane. Jake met them, and they managed to load him in before Jake climbed back into the cockpit. Roark ran ashore, sopping wet. "Amelia! You have to go with him." He grabbed her day pack, her camera, and shoved them into her arms. Then, before she could protest, he scooped her up. Strong arms pressed her against the planes of his chest.

"What are you doing?"

"You're freezing, and you could get hypothermia. And from the way you're favoring that wrist, you need it looked at."

She clutched her pack to herself, throwing an arm around his neck as he waded out again into the lake. "I can walk!"

"I don't want you to get wet."

"I'm already wet." But it did no good to argue as he marched her to the plane. "What about Seth? He's on his way."

"He can help me bring out the scouts." Roark reached the door, set her inside. "He can learn a couple songs."

She didn't want to imagine how much Seth might love that.

"Seb, take a look at her arm, will you?" Roark

said as he buckled her in. He called up to Jake, "Thanks again."

"No problem," Jake said as Roark jumped off the float into the water.

See you at home—the words nearly emerged from her mouth, but how silly did that sound? Almost as silly as *Be careful.*

"I'll get them home safely!" Roark shouted before she could figure out a decent response. He closed her door.

She pressed her hand on the window. Watched as he waded to shore. Jake pushed the throttle forward, and the plane skidded across the water.

As they lifted off, she saw Roark standing onshore, a dark, wet, heroic outline.

And as they arched over the lake and flew south, she made out Seth's crew, just topping the ridge over Rose Lake.

By the time she dug out her phone, the rescuers had descended out of service.

Of the handful of people Roark would not want to see paddling through the low-hanging mist as an early twilight cast shadows over the lake, top of the list would be Seth Turnquist, local hero, rescuer extraordinaire.

Roark stood onshore, pausing from rallying the scouts, who, behind him, took down the tarp, doused the fire, and packed up the supplies in the remaining ponchos, turning them into plastic, lumpy knapsacks. The chill of the day had begun to find his bones right about the time Amelia vanished into the clouds with Jake Goldstein and a good chunk of Roark's monthly allowance. But he hadn't quite known how to persuade Jake to jump into his plane in a lightning storm except through a generous financial motivator.

No one had to know, either, because Roark paid for that too—Jake's silence.

But someone would find out, judging by the darkening look on Seth's face as he drew closer and spied Roark standing in the drizzle. Roark lifted a hand to the four men, in two canoes with EMT supplies piled in the middles.

Seth wore a sensible bright-orange rain poncho and paddled a fiberglass canoe with wooden paddles—safe passage in a lightning storm.

Roark caught Seth's canoe as it came to shore, softening the bump against the rocks, then holding it while Seth and his partner climbed out. Seth reached for the medical kit.

"No need. They flew out of here over a half hour ago."

Seth's mouth tightened. "The floatplane."

Roark nodded.

"She should have mentioned that when she called me."

She called him. Not EMS, but *Seth*. He tried not to let that rattle him. "She didn't know."

Seth frowned at that as the other canoe bumped

up. Roark guided it to shore, held it as the crew climbed out. He recognized a couple men from the Cutaway Creek rescue—a guy named Joe and the pastor, Dan.

Dan pulled his slicker on over his head. "What happened?"

"The scout leader had what seems to be an AMI. His heart stopped, I revived him, but he was in serious condition when he left."

"You called in Jake, then?" Dan said.

"And Seb Brewster came along."

Dan nodded. "Let's get these boys home so they can check on their leader."

Seth stood considering Roark, who had started to shiver. Then he reached into his pack and pulled out a thermal shirt, contained in a plastic bag. "I brought an extra." He tossed it to Roark, then marched past him, heading up to help the Boy Scouts.

The sky stopped weeping as they loaded the youngsters and crossed the lake, Roark managing to at least stay caught up to the scouts and the second EMT canoe. Seth's canoe had streamed out ahead, maybe moving under its own fury.

Twilight fell around them like a sheet as they cut across Bearskin, then portaged through the murky forest into Hungry Jack. By the time Roark loaded up the canoes and followed Seth's EMT truck from the forest, his jeans had dried, his legs chafing, his body sore.

Seth continued south into Deep Haven, while Roark turned onto the resort driveway. Behind him, the Boy Scouts had fallen quiet, some of them sleeping.

Darek stood in the lot as Roark pulled up, dirty, tired, and solemn. "Amelia called us from the hospital. Mike's stable, but you probably saved his life. Don't you answer your cell?"

Roark dug it out of his pocket. Dead. "Sorry, mate."

Darek blew out a breath, clamped him on the shoulder.

"You did good, 007." This from Jensen, who came out of the lodge toward them. "You had us all worried. Darek was just gathering the troops to head into the thicket and flush you out."

Darek had begun to unload the supplies, handing the tied ponchos to the Boy Scouts. "Leave them in the outfitter's shed, then go into the lodge. Mrs. Christiansen has supper for you."

A few cries of approval. Skinny—aka Colin—came up to Roark. "Thanks, man," he said. "You're not so bad." He held out his fist, and it took Roark only a second to figure it out. He bumped it.

Colin grinned and went inside.

"I think I'm headed to the hospital," Roark started.

"Not until you have some food," Darek said. He was climbing into the truck. "I'll move the canoes and unhook the trailer. You get inside and change clothes."

Roark hadn't realized that he'd begun to shiver again.

"You're a little taller than Owen, but I think Mrs. C. can dig up some clothes," Jensen said, directing him toward the house.

"Owen. He's the one just older than Amelia, right? The one who is missing?"

"Let's say he's trying to find himself. And don't bring him up in front of the family," Jensen said, opening the lodge door. "I found a castaway!"

Amelia's family greeted him like he might belong, Ingrid coming up to him with a smile and an unexpected hug. Grace turned from where she was dishing up spaghetti to hungry Boy Scouts to say, "Hey there, Bond."

"Bond?"

"I told them about your nickname," Claire said from her perch on the sofa.

"Someone best dash upstairs and find some trousers for this one," Jensen said.

"Please cease with the vile accent. My ears are bleeding," Roark said to Jensen's back.

"Jensen, dig around the boys' room and get him some trousers. And a jumper! He's positively trembling!" Ingrid said with her own shameful accent.

Roark cringed, and Grace laughed as Jensen headed upstairs.

Ivy came down the stairs. "Okay, the baby's asleep," she said. "What did I miss?"

"Roark saved the Boy Scouts," Claire said. "And we're indoctrinating him into the American inability to speak in an accent that sounds remotely like British."

"Speak for yourself, darling," Darek said as he came into the house.

Claire laughed, and Roark managed a smile. He took the plate Grace offered him filled with spaghetti. "How's Mike?"

"They're keeping him overnight, and tomorrow they'll take him to Duluth. They might have to put in a stent, see if they can open the arteries. His family's driving up from the Cities right now."

"And Amelia? How's her arm?"

Silence.

"She did mention that she hurt her arm . . ."

Ingrid put down her plate. Shook her head.

"Oh. Of course not." Roark took a bite of spaghetti, then another, trying to finish it off.

"What do you mean?" Darek said.

"You know. She doesn't like to worry you all. She thinks you hover too much—"

"Hover?"

Uh-oh. "Or perhaps simply—"

"No, they hover," Claire said. "It's like the family motto: Protect Amelia."

"That's not true," Grace said. "We just don't want her to repeat our mistakes."

"I'd definitely call it hovering," said Ivy, who poured a glass of milk and carried it toward the den, calling over her shoulder. "What else would you call the great fort-in-the-wood fiasco?"

"Hey now, that was just—" Darek started.

"Hovering," Ingrid said, raising an eyebrow. She handed Roark a glass of milk. "Amelia was seven. She made a fort in the woods down by the lake—a cute little shelter—and was so proud of it. She hauled her sleeping bag out there and asked her father and me if she could sleep there. We could see the shelter from the house, and John figured at the height of summer, if she had Butter with her—"

"Butter was our dog. She passed away this winter," Grace said.

"Right. We figured Butter would keep her safe. Besides, we honestly thought she wouldn't last much past dark."

"No one asked me, however, what I thought," Darek said. "Amelia is a Christiansen. She's stubborn."

"She gets it from her big brother," Ingrid said.

"Hardly, Mom. I think you and Dad are a lethal combination." Grace pulled a pan of brownies from the oven.

"Exactly," Darek said. "So it's about ten o'clock, and I know she's out there, and it's eating at me. I was sixteen, and I couldn't believe Mom and Dad were letting this happen. So I grabbed my sleeping back and snuck outside, setting up about twenty-five feet away from her."

"Except he made so much racket, Casper woke up and decided he'd tag along. When they got out there, they found Eden wrapped in a blanket on the dock," Ingrid said.

"With me," Grace added. "Eden thought Mom was nuts, so she rousted me out of my warm bed and made us sit on the dock, watching the shelter."

"Owen woke up around midnight, saw that we were gone, and came looking. He saw Casper's sleeping bag in the moonlight, thought he might be missing a party. He came outside and tripped over me," Darek said.

"Which sounded like waking a bear from a sound slumber." Grace began to plate the brownies. "Darek howled, which woke up Eden and me."

"So John and I wake to this terrible howling and then shouting, and we race downstairs thinking something horrible has happened to Amelia."

"They get outside and find Casper, Owen, and Darek all in a wrestling match, not sure who they're really fighting," Jensen said, coming downstairs holding a pair of track pants and a sweatshirt. "The screams are echoing across the lake to our cabin—"

"And my grandparents' cabin," Claire said. "They get up, along with everyone else on the west end of the lake, thinking that someone is dying, and my grandma calls the police."

Roark set his finished plate on the counter, smiling.

"Meanwhile, John pulls the boys apart. Grace and Eden are completely freaked out, and in their panic, Grace falls in the lake," Ingrid said.

"Totally Eden's fault. She was running to Amelia's shelter, didn't see me, and body slammed me out of the way."

"So now we have Grace in the lake, a couple of the boys bleeding, and the police heading up to the resort. Not to mention that we've woken our guests."

"It was chaos," Darek said. "But in all of it, no one had seen Amelia."

Silence fell, and they looked at Roark, Darek grinning, Grace shaking her head, Ingrid chuckling.

All at once, Roark got it. "She was already asleep inside."

Claire nodded. "She'd gone inside to bed, asleep in the den long before Darek stumbled out to save her."

"And that is how the Christiansens *don't* hover," Jensen said. "Leave no man unscathed."

Grace made a face, turned away.

"So we hover a little. Amelia's the youngest," Darek said.

"And extremely capable," Roark said. "You

should have seen her today. She is so at home in the woods—knew exactly what to do."

"But you're the one who got Jake Goldstein to fly in. Slick move," Darek said.

Yeah, well, it didn't take a hero to dole out cash. Roark finished off his milk. "I'm headed to the hospital to check on Amelia."

It was Darek's expression that stopped him. "What?"

"Well, it's just that . . . Amelia called, and Seth's there. He's bringing her home."

Roark opened his mouth in a round, silent O. He sighed, reaching for the sweatshirt Jensen had brought him and pulling it on over his soggy, borrowed thermal shirt. "Maybe I shouldn't be here when they get back."

"Stay," Ingrid said. "I'm sure Amelia would like to see you."

Even so, he probably couldn't bear seeing her hug Seth. Thank Seth. After all, when she needed someone, *really* needed rescue, beyond what bottle of wine to order or what f-stop to use, she'd called her trusty lumberjack, Seth.

What did he expect? Seth had grown up in these woods like Amelia. Had built a lifetime of trust with Amelia, was so embedded in Amelia's life that her instincts simply took over.

And Roark couldn't compete with that, could he?

He sank onto a stool, trying to ignore the stares

269

of the curious Boy Scouts at the kitchen table. What an arrogant, desperate fool he was to think he might compete with Seth, with this world.

He clung to a future that he could never have, one where Amelia left Deep Haven to live in Brussels, maybe even travel the world with him.

Ethan was right. He was completely off his trolley.

"Are you okay? You look a little pale there, 007," Jensen said.

"I think I'm just hearing Amelia for the first time," he said. "She keeps telling me that we're from two different worlds. I'm realizing now that maybe she's right. She belongs here."

And he didn't. He didn't say it, but the reality seemed to march into the room, sit down in front of him.

Claire, his new guidance counselor, seemed undaunted. "So can you. You just have to be willing to . . . well, stay."

He glanced at her, and she raised an eyebrow, completely understanding that *stay* meant a whole new set of rules.

A whole new life.

But maybe that's exactly what he needed. A restart, instead of dragging around his past, dodging divine retribution.

He glanced at Jensen for reinforcement and found him nodding. And then, to his surprise,

Darek added, "No one is kicking you out of Deep Haven."

It struck Roark that for the first time, they'd invited him to . . . stay. The sense of belonging—or wanting to—to this hovering, loyal, brave clan felt . . . like home. Like something he might have been searching for all his life.

It knocked him a little off-kilter.

"You know, if you really want to impress Amelia, to show her you belong, you could enter the annual lumberjack games," Darek said quietly.

"Oh, Darek," Ingrid said. "I don't think—"

"It's perfect, Mom." Grace turned to Roark. "Seth won last year, but Darek won a couple years back and he could teach you all the tricks."

"What is it?"

"It's a competition held during the annual Flapjack Festival about three weeks away. The events are based on lumberjack sports—chainsawing, chopping, team broad sawing, and birling."

"Birling?"

"Logrolling," Darek said. "It's not a full-out competition, just smaller events designed to stir up excitement for those competing in official events around the state. Brings out the locals, maybe a few contenders who want to sharpen their skills. But it's serious enough around here that you need to know what you're doing."

"I haven't a clue."

"Yet," Darek said, a gleam in his eye. "At the very least, you'd show Amelia that you're willing to fit into her world."

He did want to fit into her world. After all, he'd taught her how to belong to his. Maybe it was his turn to join hers.

Who knew? He might even impress himself.

"Okay, you're on," he said to Darek. Then he turned to Grace. "How about another plate of spaghetti?"

The puck pinged off the crossbar, the sound reverberating through the arena. Max chased it, scooped it up, and headed to the other goal, slapping the shot wide.

It slammed into the boards.

Jace Jacobsen, his brother-in-law and line coach, former enforcer of the St. Paul Blue Ox, brought the puck down the ice. A good six inches taller than Max, Jace appeared every inch his reputation as a former bruiser. What most people didn't know was his soft side, the side that despised his reputation and led him to spend hours volunteering in the children's ward at the university hospital.

He circled around Max, who'd stopped, sweating despite the chilly air of the practice dome at Blue Ox HQ. Max propped his hockey stick on his knees, leaning over, breathing hard.

"Something eating you, Max?" Jace said. Of

course, his slap shot landed dead-on in the center of the net.

Max straightened, skated toward Jace. "Grace and I are married."

"Wow. So you *did* elope. I mean, you hinted at it all season."

"Three weeks ago, right after our last game."

"Three *weeks* ago? And my wife doesn't know yet? Oh, Eden's going to be livid."

"Yeah, well, she can get in line. We haven't told anyone. Not Grace's parents, no one."

Jace skated over to the bench. Picked up a towel. "Wait—didn't you spend last week at their house?"

Max skated with the puck around the boards, behind the goal, tucking it in. Finally.

He skated in to the bench and grabbed another towel. "Yeah."

Jace regarded him with a smile. "And you didn't tell anyone? So that means . . ." He dropped into a chuckle. "Fun."

"No doubt. Grace was afraid to tell her family, so she slept upstairs with Amelia all week long. I hung out in the den."

Jace's laughter echoed through the arena. "Dude! What a way to spend your honeymoon."

"Tell me about it. Grace would sneak down at night sometimes, but let's just say that I'm ready for the wrath of John Christiansen if I can spend the entire night with my wife."

"You gotta bite the bullet and confess. John and Ingrid like you—they'll be thrilled." Jace picked up his water bottle.

Max didn't answer.

And right there, hanging in the silence, was the truth.

"I'm not so sure. I mean, yeah, they said they gave us their blessing, but now that it's done . . . After all, I'm dooming their daughter to grief."

"I thought we went through this." Jace grabbed his skate guards, worked them on, then headed off the ice with Max following. "You have to let go of that, let her choose whether to love you or not."

"I know. But . . . it suddenly got real the day we said, 'Till death do us part.' And it's worse now." They entered the locker room, empty of the cacophony of his teammates' voices, a sound Max loved to lose himself inside.

Jace sat on the bench, loosened his skates.

"Grace wants to have kids."

Jace looked up at him. "I thought you . . . uh, took care of that."

"She wants to adopt."

Jace pulled his shirt off. "Makes sense. The second Eden and I got home from the honey-moon, she started talking about kids. Of course Grace wants to be a mom—"

"I don't want to be a dad." There, he said it straight out, even as the words seared through him. Someday, if he said it enough, his heart would accept what his brain knew to be right.

Jace tossed his shirt into the hamper, grabbed his bottle of soap. "Never?"

"I can't bear to leave a family behind, grieving me."

Jace stopped at the door of the showers. "Max. You're going to leave people behind. It's inevitable. And they don't have to be family to grieve you."

"Kids. *My* kids. Leaving them without a father. I've been through that. No thanks." He threw off his own shirt. "I just wish Grace would get that."

"I think she probably does. But the good thing about Grace is that she's not alone. You married into a family with a team of overbearing brothers. Do you think they wouldn't help her?"

Jace had a point. Even now the family's immediate welcome of Yulia into their midst rose up to confirm his words.

"I think you need to consider what you're truly afraid of." Jace stepped into the shower.

"I'm not afraid of anything!" Max said, grabbing his own soap.

Jace said nothing further until after he was dressed and waiting for Max in his office, just off the lobby of the arena.

Max came in, flopped into a chair. "Okay, yes, I can admit not looking forward to getting sick, deteriorating in front of my family. Don't shoot me for wanting to protect Grace from adding more to the stress of taking care of me."

Jace closed his laptop. Since moving to the coaching staff, he seemed older, maybe more responsible, and now he looked at Max like a brother. "Dude. Who are you really trying to protect here?"

Max shook his head.

"You've cemented a reputation of being the guy who doesn't get involved. Doesn't have long-term relationships. Suddenly you find a girl who looks past all your demons and loves you anyway, and you actually let yourself fall in love."

Max wanted to cringe, but Jace's smile eked out his own. "Yeah, okay. I got lucky."

"You scored big. But now you've got a chance to love beyond yourself by putting it all out there for a family, and that scares the stuffing out of you."

Max started to shake his head again, but Jace cut him off.

"I get it, Max. I used to think that I couldn't let a woman close, because when she got a glimpse of the true me, she'd run. But Eden proved that theory wrong, and she's got me believing that a baby is a good idea. I can't help but think that I've lost my mind, but another part of me can't wait to know that we've created a life together. To hold our child in my arms, to teach him—or her—how to shoot a puck. It's crazy, but I want it, man. And you do too, if you let yourself admit it."

"Grace deserves to have her own child growing inside her. Not be saddled with a guy who's already stolen that from her."

"So what? You leave her? Divorce her?"

"I suggested it."

Jace's expression had him thinking he should flee at full tilt from the building. Max held up a hand in defense. "I know I'm an idiot."

"Thank you."

"But I can't get past the fact that she won't have what she desperately longs for."

"Having a biological child is only one way to be a parent, and if any two people are suited to adopt children and create an amazing family, it's you and Grace."

Max managed a slight smile, followed by the sudden, sweet image of Yulia sitting with Grace as she worked a puzzle, or Grace braiding her hair, or the way Yulia had pocketed herself into his embrace at the campfire.

Maybe.

"Stop trying so hard not to be happy, Max," Jace said, rising. "And start trusting the life God is giving you. It just might knock your socks off."

Chapter 10

SATURDAY'S STORM had littered trees and debris from Hungry Jack Lake all the way down to Deep Haven, overflowing the riverbanks with frothy, murky brown water and stirring the big lake into a turmoil as it threw flotsam upon the shore.

Three days later, the air still hung heavy with mist. Amelia sat in the coffee shop, needing an escape from the lodge. How she hated house-keeping. With a full house booked for Memorial Day weekend, she wanted to summon a cheer, but her summer loomed ahead as an endless cycle of making beds, washing sheets, cleaning bathrooms, and mopping floors. She still nursed her sprained wrist, encased in a brace.

"Where's Roark?" Ree sat opposite her in an overstuffed chair, holding a blended vanilla mocha. "I thought 007 would be here. I was looking forward to the view."

Amelia looked up from the screen, where she had been clicking through her photographs of the Boy Scout trip. The shot of Roark, his hand up, grimacing, made her smile with the memory of his wretched paddling skills. Until, of course, everything faded away and he'd become her hero.

She wouldn't easily forget the image of him

standing onshore, hands on his hips, his shirt wet against his chiseled outline, watching the plane as if she carried his heart with her.

She'd expected him at the hospital, or later, at the resort, but she hadn't seen him since he'd spoken those words into her ear, the ones that stirred the feeling he'd seeded all those months ago while she stood on a bridge in Prague. *You are more than capable of handling yourself. Do what you know to do.*

"He must have gotten off his shift early." She couldn't brush the disappointment from her voice.

Ree must have noticed. "No more sending him packing?"

"Not so much," Amelia said. "He was . . . Well, he probably saved Big Mike's life. I'm not sure how he talked Jake Goldstein into flying him out."

"How are you? The whole thing made the papers—even in Duluth. Said that the EMS crew hiked in." Ree gestured to Amelia's braced arm.

"I'm fine. I fell trying to get help. And yes, Seth and Pastor Dan came in with a crew. Seth wasn't real thrilled that I'd left them behind when he showed up hours later at the hospital."

"The papers said he evacuated a troop of Boy Scouts."

"I think that might trend toward fiction. Roark had it under control. Even had the boys singing camp songs. You should have seen him—he went from being a duck waddling over the lake to . . . I don't know, a rescuer, I guess. Unflappable. I bet that comes from his days as a missionary kid. Which makes him, by the way, probably poor and not remotely a European playboy."

"And mysterious. And exotic. Very James Bond," Ree said.

"Yet, unlike Bond, he probably doesn't have two quid to rub together."

"So you live on love."

Amelia's own words at the beach tumbled back to her. But the thought didn't sound so crazy. Live on love, or maybe run their own resort somewhere around Deep Haven? Didn't he say he had hotel training?

No. He wouldn't consider staying here permanently, would he?

Ree ran her thumb down her cup. "Did you meet the folks from Uganda? They stayed at the Mad Moose while scouting out a place to have their daughter's wedding. By the way, I gave them your name for wedding photos."

"Thanks. Anything to get away from washing sheets."

"I don't think I could ever be brave enough to be a missionary," Ree said.

"Me either," Vivie said, approaching from the counter. "Not to mention, that's what I call over-kill. You can serve God without doing it halfway across the world. I promise there are enough unsaved, lost people in Deep Haven." She sat next to Amelia wearing jeans and a blue blouse tied at her waist, her hair in a high ponytail.

"You're looking very Betty Rizzo," Amelia said.

"Perfect. Sal is coming into town today." Her red lips curled up. "He says he wants his car back, but I think he misses me."

"I have no doubt," Amelia said. "But really? You think it's crazy to be a missionary?"

"I mean, you have to be cut from a special kind of cloth to cross the world to tell people about Jesus." Ree stirred her drink. "And Vivie's right—there are plenty of lost and needy people here."

"But what if you're—I don't know—called to go to Uganda or Rwanda or someplace off the map?"

"I would think that it doesn't matter if you're called or not. You have a choice in the matter, right?" Vivie said. "You can say no."

"Say no to God? Who does that?"

Ree stared at her. "Are you kidding me? We say no to God more often than we say yes. Or at least normal people do. Maybe not Amelia Christiansen." She winked.

But the words stung as they dropped around Amelia.

"I think my answer would be no. Hello—

snakes," Vivie said, making a face. She turned to Amelia. "Do you have those photos?"

"Yes. I edited a few of them." She angled the computer toward her. "Tell me which ones you want and I'll send them to you."

Ree leaned over, examining the screen. "I love the ones on the farm. And of Colleen in the tractor wheel. They're beautiful, Amelia. You're so talented. You should so enter that contest."

"What contest?" Vivie said, scrolling through the pictures.

"The link someone put on the pictures she uploaded last week. It's a viewer contest—you vote for your favorite photographer."

"It was Roark. He posted the link," Amelia said. "The contest is called Capture America. I post ten pictures of my American life, and then people vote on the ones they like. There are three rounds, each one with a smaller group, and the one with the most votes wins $5,000 and an offer to visit their offices in New York."

"New York City?" Ree's voice rose. "Amelia, you have to! Vivie can show you around, right, Viv?"

Vivie wore an odd smile but lifted her shoulder. "Sure."

"I don't know."

"What's not to know? You could go to a photography school with the money—or back to Prague. You could escape Deep Haven."

"I'm not sure I want to leave," Amelia said softly.

A knock on the window made Amelia look up. Seth stood outside, waving, smiling, wearing a red T-shirt with *Turnquist Lumber* stamped on the front. She waved back, wrestling out a smile.

He'd been so attentive, worried. So sweet when he'd practically charged into the hospital, wet, grimy, and every inch her rescuer.

Ree looked at Seth, back to Amelia. "Are you back together?"

"He's been hovering since the accident."

"And Roark?"

"I haven't seen him. He delivered the Boy Scouts to the resort and left." She'd tried not to feel like he'd reverted to the man she'd known in Prague—taking off without explanation.

"Not a word?"

"I keep wondering if he saw the real me and made a break for it."

"Ames—that's not right. He came all the way over here, got a job, is braving your family . . . What was it he said?"

"That *extreme* didn't begin to describe what he'd do to win me back."

"Exactly. That doesn't sound like a man who's going to easily throw in the towel and head for higher ground," Ree said.

"But I'm not the same person he met in Prague. I'm . . . I'm a hometown girl."

"Whatever," Vivie said, adding a roll of her eyes. "You went over to Prague and came back with your tail cut off. So what? The Amelia I grew up with, dreaming of an epic life, is still inside there. It's the same girl who's probably clicked on the Capture America link, won't let it leave her brain."

She *had* clicked on it, looked at the other photographers' work, been debating which pictures she'd enter, and that truth probably showed on her face.

"I knew it," Vivie said. "Just like I know that you are destined for bigger things. Beyond Deep Haven. Maybe Roark is here to save you from a life you would too easily embrace. Seth is a full-blooded alpha male, and I certainly wouldn't run away from him on a dark, starry night, but Seth is safe. And, Ames, I'm sorry, but deep down, you don't want safe. Roark is just exotic enough to bring back the Amelia we knew nine months ago, boarding an airplane."

"You don't understand, Vivie. I thought I wanted that, but once I got there, I was . . . I was a wreck. Terrified. Without Roark, I might have hopped a plane home that first week."

"Maybe," Ree said. "But everybody gets in over their head. Eventually we would have turned you around and shoved you back on the plane until you stayed. Until your outside matched the Amelia we know is inside."

It's not about how you feel. It's about what you do.

Amelia stared at Vivie, who was trying so hard to become the movie star on the outside she believed she could be on the inside. At Ree, launching out to grab ahold of her journalism dreams.

"One failure does not a lifetime make," Ree said. "That's the best Yoda I've got."

Amelia had a crazy urge to hug both of them. She turned the computer. Clicked on the Capture America link.

"The deadline to enter is today," Ree said, reading over her shoulder.

"It's a sign," Vivie said.

"No, it's not," Ree said. "It's Providence. God is in this. Enter, Amelia."

"I won't win."

"You could win." Vivie wiggled her eyebrows. "You could win, and suddenly you get to see the world. You'd have opportunity and choices. A doorway to your future."

Amelia glanced at Ree. At Vivie. They nodded, her own personal cheering squad. Plus, she had more—an entire family of fans. And Roark.

Do what you know to do.

Yes, maybe, for the first time in months, she did know.

Even before Darek's crazy suggestion that Roark become a lumberjack, the idea of staying, of starting over here in Deep Haven, building a life with Amelia, had begun to seem . . . maybe not so crazy.

And the longer he spent with Darek, training for a contest he didn't have a prayer of winning, the more the life of the Christiansens drew him in. Took root, settled deep, became sane. He saw himself belonging, taking kids out on the trail with Amelia, or toasting s'mores by the fire.

He could even help with the lodge, teach them how to manage rates and revenue. Maybe they could expand. Open another resort.

"So you're saying that you used to change the rate every day?" Darek was saying. They stood in the gravel pit a few miles from the Evergreen property where Darek had decided they should train. Just in case Amelia should happen home, unexpected.

Roark tried not to let the word *lying* into his head.

"Yeah, depending on how many rooms we had, the occupancy of local competition, the time of year, the day of the week, and how much we needed for our projected ROI. It's easy once you plug all the values into a formula. Then you change your rates on your reservation software system, and it changes them globally across all your online and off-line platforms."

As Roark talked, Darek affixed a skinned log vertically between two clamps, raising it to knee height. He wore steel-toed boots, had given Roark a pair of Casper's boots, and fitted them both with shin guards.

To think Roark believed yesterday's lesson on hot sawing had been challenging. He could still feel his hands buzzing from the chain saw.

Darek had picked up an ax, now set it down. "We don't have a reservation software system. We issue rate cards at the beginning of the year, then record the reservations in a guest book, designated by nights."

Roark stared at him, trying to imagine a system that required someone to flip pages, to manually record all the information without the convenience of a computer. But lodges like Evergreen Resort had managed exactly that way for centuries. Still . . . "We need to get you an RDP system. It'll change your life."

"And this will change yours. Have you ever chopped down a tree with an ax?"

"I hardly think that learning how to swing an ax—"

"It's called the standing block chop, and it's the first of the four competitions in the lumberjack games," Darek said and handed Roark the ax. "By the way, I know I'm all gung ho, but you should know that you don't have a snowball's chance in Texas of winning the logrolling, although I'll do my best. I think our strategy is to hone the block chop, the hot saw, and the double buck. Let's be thankful that there's no pole climb, because I am not a fan of the ninety-foot height."

Uh . . . "Me either?"

"With the standing block chop, the goal is to cut away the scarf on each side until the block is severed. You're in luck because technique and skill trump brute strength. I won two years ago, was runner-up the year before that. Seth, he's all about the brawn in this event."

He gestured to the ax. "That's called a racing ax. It's lighter than a regular ax and razor sharp. And—" he smiled—"it was my father's."

Nothing like holding the legacy of two generations in his hand. The hickory handle fit into Roark's grip, and Darek showed him how to put both hands together at the end of the handle. Then he demonstrated his stance. "Everyone is different. Some like the wide stance; others like a narrower stance. I like to keep it wide so I can utilize the power in my legs and hips. Keep your knee back a bit so you can use your weight to distribute the power." He took the ax, demonstrated the upswing.

The ax struck deep, smooth as butter into the wood. Darek stepped up, grabbed a marker, and drew four equidistant lines on the log. Then he drew an oval, centered on each side. "This is your scarf, where you'll be chopping. These lines help you set your feet. If you line up exactly the same on both sides, you should have an even chop.

This stance will also protect your leg in case you skid your ax down the stump."

He demonstrated again, standing in position. "Now, the bigger the arc, the harder the hit. You want to reach back as far as you can, keeping your eyes on your target. If you're casting a down hit, you let gravity do the work. Once it hits, pull the ax out, let it fall to the ground, then loop it back up and strike again. Think of a circle motion. When you're striking an up hit, think of the ax like a pendulum. You'll hit, pull it out, let it fall, then bring it back in nearly the same place. You'll repeat this technique for both sides until the block is chopped in half.

"You want to bend your legs into the up hit, stand tall for a down hit, getting above the block and using your shoulders to power into the strike."

He handed the ax to Roark, who positioned his feet, then brought the ax down. It sat in the groove, about half as much as Darek's strike.

"Don't be afraid to really hit it," Darek said. "We're sort of conditioned here in the States, and maybe even Britain, to pull our punches. You don't have to do that when you're power chopping. Give it all you've got. I usually start with about four up hits, then two down hits, and I keep that rhythm as hard as I can, as fast as I can. It's fun."

Fun? Maybe it was as Roark threw his

shoulders into the next hit. Chips flew as he sank the ax deep, then yanked it out. The rush of adrenaline burned through muscles he'd forgotten existed. "This could get tiring."

"Good thing you have almost three weeks." Darek stepped up to the wood again and explained the art of cutting scarfs, the way the underhand cuts should carve out trapezoid chips. "But the most important thing is to nail the technique before you work on speed."

Roark tried the underhand cut. Realized that it took a bit more finesse to aim the ax in the right slice. "You can feel the weight of the ax head engage about halfway through the swing," he said, giving it another go.

"That's a good sign. Means you're doing it right. Now, when you feel that weight, add a little whip action with your wrists and it'll sink even deeper."

He tried it, the ax sinking to the head. Darek made a noise of approval. "By george, I think he's got it. Give it a few more goes; then I'll teach you about covering your corners."

The wood came off in twenty-four blows, the top skidding into the gravel. Roark set the ax down, breathing hard.

"Not bad," Darek said, reaching for another block. "If you can get it off in twelve, you'll have a contending time."

He helped Roark mark the wood, then sat on

the bed of his pickup and directed, corrected, and encouraged as Roark attacked the block. "Nineteen. Better."

The chops echoed through the pine trees into the sweet summer air. Roark's hands burned, his shoulders cramping with the upper hits. He set the ax down again and took a breath.

Darek dug a cold can of Coke out of the cooler in the truck. He tossed the can to Roark, who opened it and drank deeply as Darek lifted another block.

"Not a lot of chopping at that prep school you attended?" Darek said, affixing the block. He marked it, then grabbed the ax.

"Eton. And no. We did some outdoor survival, but no lumberjack games. Cricket. Polo. Yachting."

Darek attacked the block and had chipped out half of it in six blows. "So where'd you learn first aid?"

"My gap year." He watched as Darek attacked the other side. He had the block apart in five more blows. "I went to Uganda to work in a refugee camp. They needed so much help, I got a hands-on course in basic triage. And I did a lot of nursing."

"Where did sailing and Kilimanjaro fit in?"

Darek set up another block, this time handing the ax to Roark.

He stood, sized up the log, considering how to answer Darek's question. He'd sealed the past inside so long; maybe he'd let a little of it leak out. He drew in a breath and landed the upper hits perfectly. "I needed some space after an accident in my hotel. People died, and it was my fault."

He arched the down hit, and it slid into the wood with a satisfying thump over Darek's silence behind him.

He glanced over his shoulder. Darek seemed to be considering his Coke can. He looked up, met Roark's gaze. "Keep chopping."

Oh. He threw himself into another chop. "I just . . . I needed to get away, so I started traveling." He cut out the corners with the next upper hits, and a nice wedge of wood fell out.

"New Zealand is pretty far from Paris," Darek said.

Roark didn't add that his uncle had a hotel in Wellington. Instead he threw down another blow and sliced out a hefty wedge of wood, feeling strong. "It wasn't far enough." He moved to the opposite side. "I could still hear the screaming, smell the smoke." Could still taste what his arrogance had wrought. Feel the futility of trying to outrun God's wrath.

"I'm sorry. I know a little about trying to run away from mistakes," Darek said quietly. "Although if it was truly your fault, you'd be in jail, right?"

He hadn't thought about it that way. "Right. I suppose that's a bit overstated."

For some reason, the quiet exchange loosed

something inside. He placed the next two cuts fast and hard, then added two down hits. "I eventually headed to Africa. Decided I'd climb a mountain." He surveyed the wood, then swung down with everything inside him. The top spiraled off. He looked at Darek. "That didn't quite work either. I came back to Europe and ended up in Prague."

"Where you met Amelia."

"Yes. And for the first time, it felt as though I could finally start over. Stop running."

Darek crumpled his can. "Evergreen Resort is a good place to stop running." He took the ax from Roark. "I should know."

It was the second time he'd dropped a bread crumb Roark desperately wanted to follow. Instead he said, "Why are you helping me, Darek? It wasn't too long ago you might have taken that ax to me."

One side of Darek's mouth curled. He looked at the ax as if he might still be considering it. "You're right about the hovering. We spend a lot of time in this family meddling in each other's lives."

"Some would call that caring."

"We do too, but the fact is, we know each other so well, it's easy to be cemented in by the expectations of the family. Seth is that expecta-tion. He's been in Amelia's life so long it seems only logical that she would settle down with him. But you . . . you're unexpected. You . . . see her.

Not the Amelia we expect her to be, but maybe the Amelia who has been trying to break free. My mother always says that my sister is trying to escape our shadow. I think, in Prague, she finally did. And you were part of that."

He walked over to the stump. "Besides, seeing your devotion to Amelia has made me realize something. Seth is smitten with the idea of him and Amelia together." He looked up and met Roark's eyes. "You're smitten with Amelia."

Indeed.

"Wait until she finds out you're taking on Seth." Darek wore a strange grin. "I can't wait to see her face."

"We don't have to tell her . . . yet." Even as Roark said it, warning flares lit in the back of his head. Still, set against his other secrets . . .

"Oh, I love it. We'll get you into shape, then surprise her."

Roark wanted to rewind, recast his words. "Maybe—"

"Listen, I think we're done here. Why don't you come back to the office and show me what you mean by reservation software. You can stick around for dinner."

"Uh, I've been invited for dinner to Jensen and Claire's."

Darek considered him, wearing an enigmatic expression.

"What?"

"I just put it together. Jensen's your inside man. The one who convinced you to return, got you a job, fixed you up at the Java Cup. I was trying to figure out how you two met."

"I got my own job, thank you. But yeah, Jensen suggested that maybe your bark was worse than your bite."

Darek shook his head, chuckling. "He was always for the underdog."

"I'm not the . . ." Okay. "Maybe I am." The thought stirred him. He'd never, ever, been the underdog.

It felt . . . empowering.

"But not for long."

"No doubt." Darek was standing there, not moving, staring at the wood.

"What?"

"By the way, I did the count." He turned to Roark. "Eleven hits. Lucky, maybe, but with a little practice, you might just win this thing."

Then he clamped Roark on the shoulder. "Maybe we'll even let you stick around."

"Yeah, well, I might even be willing to stay."

Jace's words bugged Max more than he wanted to admit.

Stop trying so hard not to be happy.

Fact was, he'd spent so many years angry, so many more trying to pretend he didn't care about happiness, that when he finally found it . . . he simply didn't know what to do with it. It felt unwieldy. And he couldn't trust it.

Not with so much stacked against him.

Max touched his brakes as traffic slowed along the Superior lakeshore, just north of Duluth. Two hours out of Deep Haven, and the Memorial Day weekend traffic had jammed the highways, probably doubling a five-hour trip. Now, with the sun tucked in for the night, the moon rose to watch him over the inky waves of the lake.

Who would have thought that a guy with his quirks, emotional barricades, and dismal future would find a woman like Grace to marry him? To love him, until death—his death—would part them?

Yeah, if he stripped away the guilt, the fear, even the anger, he could find happiness. Joy.

It simply didn't look like the version so many people dreamed of. A family, grandchildren, a fiftieth anniversary, fading into the sunset.

But hadn't he learned that a happy ending didn't have to contain the same ingredients as others had?

Traffic finally lurched to a stop. Ahead, he made out a construction traffic light, burning red as the road narrowed to one lane.

Start trusting the life God is giving you.

Grace. And, yes, her sweet, nurturing heart that wanted to love a child.

What if he gave that to her? She knew the

consequences. If she wanted to adopt a child, perhaps that was a gift he could give her.

The line of oncoming traffic passed him, and the light changed. He followed the traffic in front of him, inching along as they crossed through the construction zone.

That gift started with telling her parents they were married. Tonight. He wasn't going to wait a second longer to declare to the world exactly how blessed he knew he was.

Just for fun, he turned to the Elvis station. Sang along. " 'When no one else can understand me . . .' "

He didn't hear the text come in, only found it a half hour later as he stopped to refuel. Grace, asking when he might arrive.

He texted his dismal ETA and ran into the convenience store, grabbed some chips and a soda, then hit the road again.

To more construction zones, spent with the entirety of Minnesota, who'd decided to head north for the weekend. He finally hit the hill above Deep Haven close to midnight.

He stopped again before continuing north to Evergreen, before he lost cell service. On my way. See you in ten.

When Grace didn't text him back, he feared that maybe she'd gone to bed.

He pulled up to the quiet lodge, the parking lot jammed with SUVs, glad to see that finally, the resort had hit its stride with twelve cabins occupied. He found a spot in the grass, climbed out, stretched.

The moon hung full in the sky, the stars so brilliant he could pluck them from the heavens. The scent of pine hung in the air, reaped from the shoreline on the opposite side of the lake, and the finest hint of campfire smoke evidenced a recent Christiansen family s'more fest.

After a winter of traveling, fans, interviews, and pressure, yeah, he could easily dive into spending the summer helping around the resort, cooking with Grace, and learning to live happily ever after.

From behind him, hands went over his eyes. "You're late."

He caught her hands and turned. Grace smiled at him, arching her arms around his neck. "Welcome to Evergreen Resort."

Then she kissed him, her lips soft, molding herself to his body, warm and intimate. He wrapped his arms around her, not realizing he'd been this hungry until he had her close. How could it be that he'd forgotten how amazing she smelled, how she tasted, and how, in her arms, the world stopped, folded in around the edges, and pocketed him in that quiet place of joy?

Yeah, he'd definitely stop trying so hard not to be happy.

She leaned back, grinned at him, stroked his cheek.

"Please tell me this isn't the greeting you give all your guests."

She lifted a shoulder. "Only the especially handsome ones."

"Nice, Mrs. Sharpe."

"I like how you say that." She kissed him again, then ran her hand over his freshly shorn hair. "The summer cut, I see."

"Reboot. It'll be long enough by camp." He set her away from him so he could pop the trunk and pull out his duffel. "And speaking of a reboot . . ." He closed the trunk and caught her hand, meeting her beautiful blue eyes. "How about we revisit that conversation about adopting. Just give me some time, babe. I think it's totally on the table. I just need to get used to, well, us. And before we do anything, please, we tell your parents."

She folded her fingers into his, walking with him toward the house. "Absolutely. First thing in the morning."

"Aw, Grace. Seriously?" He stopped, pulled her close again, pressed his lips against her hair, then leaned down and whisper-kissed her neck, his voice turning husky. "I've missed you so much this week."

She curled her hands into his shirt, trembling a little. "They're already asleep, so no one will notice if I sneak into your room. But you have to promise not to let me fall asleep. I can see it now—me coming out of the den, dressed in your hockey sweater, to my family eating pancakes."

"Oh, I'd like to see that." He grinned.

She gave him a swat on the shoulder. "Max! I can promise you, you wouldn't."

He caught her around the waist and kissed her again, right there in the moonlight. "You make me so happy, I could cry," he said, real moisture crazily in his eyes.

"Oh, Max," she said softly, her hands cradling his face.

"Listen." He touched his forehead to hers. "I promise you we will live happily ever after. Regardless of what it looks like to everyone else."

She gave him a slow, glorious nod before she leaned in and kissed him.

As it turned out, he hadn't packed his hockey sweater. Grace had her own clothes anyway, her yoga pants and T-shirt. But as the sun cascaded in through the den window, as the sounds of the family breakfasting in the next room nudged him awake, he kissed his beautiful wife with frowsy bed head and took a tight hold on her words.

"Babe," he said as she shot up, fully awake, her eyes wide. "Stay calm. I've got this."

Chapter 11

HER LOVE LIFE had gone from feast to famine in a week's time.

Amelia sat at the breakfast table Saturday morning with her laptop open, choosing the ten allowed photos for the first round of the Capture America contest, having been accepted into the running with her application photo.

She was painfully aware that her Friday night had consisted of writing an e-mail to the Gundersons about their daughter's upcoming wedding/photo shoot in Deep Haven, watching Grace teach Sorry! to Yulia while checking her phone for texts from Max, coloring Ninja Turtles with Tiger as he waited for his father to finish checking in the guests arriving at the resort for the weekend, and occasionally checking her own cell phone. Just in case someone—namely a tall, dark, and charming Englishman—might call.

Nothing. Nada. It was as if, after picking her up, carrying her to Jake's plane in those strong arms, leaving behind a trail of desire that only deepened with each memory, he'd vanished.

Not a call. Not a single flower. Not even a glimpse of him at the Java Cup in nearly a week.

"You haven't seen Roark lately, have you?" She addressed it to her family—her father, mother, and Darek, who hung out at the counter, diving into a pan of sour cream coffee cake her mother had baked this morning. She'd made twelve smaller batches, one for each cabin, and the smell could probably revive the dead with the belief all would be well in the world.

And with the sky arching a pale, cloudless blue overhead, the sun bright, the buds on the lilacs open and fragrancing the warming early summer air, one might be justified in believing that.

At Amelia's question, Ingrid shook her head, but John shot a look at Darek, then took his coffee and walked to the sofa, where he set the cup on a side table and picked up the paper.

Huh.

"Darek?"

"I . . . He came up yesterday, but you were in town."

"And you didn't tell me? You didn't ask him to stick around, say, for dinner?"

Darek took a sip of coffee. "Don't get your knickers in a knot there, Sis. Yeah, I did, but he had plans."

A beat. "Plans?"

"Dinner with Jensen and Claire."

"Now he's making friends? In Deep Haven?"

"Did you expect to be his entire world, Amelia? He's trying to belong here—and that means getting to know people," Ingrid said. "I think his efforts are admirable. He's even—"

"Mom." Darek cut his mother off.

Amelia looked at him, frowned. "What aren't you telling me?"

Darek sipped his coffee. Glanced at their mother.

"Oh, great. More secrets. I warned him—even one secret and it was . . ."

But her words died as the door to the den opened. The room went silent, deadly silent, as Max emerged, holding Grace's hand.

They looked freshly woken, Grace's hair mussed, Max's shorn short, signaling the end of hockey season. He wore a T-shirt, one that accentuated all his hockey training, and a pair of sweatpants. Grace wore the same clothes she'd been in last night.

Oh, my. She'd noticed Grace's bed was empty when she rose but thought her sister had taken an early run into town for supplies.

Amelia watched as her father slowly put down his paper. A muscle tensed in his jaw.

Grace gave a feeble smile, first to her father, then to her mother. She glanced at Amelia, who shook her head.

Busted.

Sure, they were engaged, but Grace, along with every other member of the family, had pledged to wait until she was actually married before staying overnight together. More than a Christiansen family rule, it was a promise based in their faith.

Not that others hadn't broken it—namely Darek and Owen. But Grace had always been the holy one, the one most likely to hear and obey God.

Yet Grace had shattered her promise, right there, in front of everyone. No wonder she looked a little white.

And Max—yeah, by the look on Darek's face, he'd better head at a full sprint out the door. Not put his arm around Grace, pull her close.

"I know this looks bad," Max started, and that's when John got to his feet. "But we can explain."

"Really? Please don't tell me you were watching a *Doctor Who* marathon. Or honing your Dutch Blitz skills," John said in a quiet, lethal tone. "It's fairly clear what's going on here."

"Dad," Grace started.

"I got this, honey," Max said.

Darek put down his coffee as if to free up his hands.

And while Amelia had suspected . . . well, exactly this . . . to have her sister and Max so brutally outed in front of the entire family gave her the strangest urge to get up, maybe stand beside Grace, who at the moment looked like she might cry.

This could get ugly, fast.

"We haven't . . ." Max glanced at Grace with such a tender expression, it only added to the confusion in the room. "We haven't done anything you wouldn't approve of."

John cocked his head to one side. Darek's eyes narrowed.

"Because . . ." Max drew in a breath. "We're already married."

Silence. Amelia's heart hiccuped a beat in her chest.

"What?" Ingrid said, and suddenly Amelia feared her mother unraveling more than her father. "What did you say?"

Grace's arms went around Max's waist. "We eloped. About a month ago."

"A *month* ago?" This from Darek, but it could have been voiced by any of them, including Amelia. "You got married a month ago, and you didn't tell anyone?"

Max nodded. "We kept trying to, but . . . there was the accident at the river, and then Yulia came to stay, and then Roark showed up, and there was never a good time—"

"What? Were you going to wait until Christmas?" John looked undone. "Max, you stayed under my roof for over a week . . ."

"Grace snuck down to his room."

It just came out of Amelia, an almost-involuntary spurt, driven by the anger, the betrayal forming in her chest. "Every night, she'd sneak downstairs, then back up again before morning—"

"Amelia!" Grace glared at her, a layer of fury forming in her eyes that Amelia hadn't seen since their growing-up years.

"It's true—"

"Should I mention again that we are *married?*" Max gave Amelia a look he probably reserved for a game. "We were waiting for the right time—and no, it wouldn't have been Christmas. In fact, we were going to tell you all today. Just not . . . right . . . now."

Ingrid let out a ragged breath. "Where . . . ?"

"We flew down to Cancún right after Max's last game." Grace unlatched herself from Max, went over to Ingrid. "It was just getting so complicated. Max wanted something small, but I wasn't sure how to cut our guest list down, and with the resort opening and everyone so busy, we couldn't find a date. And . . . yes, we were a little selfish. We wanted to be married as soon as we could. . . . Please understand, Mom."

Ingrid still wore a wide-eyed, pale expression. Her eyes glistened. "But now your father doesn't get to give you away. . . . I don't get to see you walk down the aisle."

Amelia's stomach tightened at her mother's disappointment. Yeah, she got it—with the threat of Max's disease, every moment was precious. And maybe she shouldn't have told on Grace like that, but the fact was, she'd stolen that moment from the family, a moment that could never be repeated. Not unforgivable, but selfish.

"You lied to us," Amelia said as Grace let go of her mother. "You snuck around and lied to us."

306

Grace frowned. "I . . . I'm sorry, Amelia. I didn't mean to hurt anyone—"

"You couldn't have told me? I share a room with you. I thought—" She glanced at Max, then back to Grace. "I'm not a child, Grace. I kept Casper and Raina's secret about the baby until she and Casper told the family. He trusted me— why couldn't you?"

"What? I was going to tell you before I told Mom and Dad?" Grace said. "Sorry, Ames, I didn't mean to hurt you, but I guess telling you wasn't my first priority."

Her words ignited something deeper in Amelia, something she couldn't name, that came out in a strange, ugly diatribe. "Of course it wasn't, because no one tells me anything! Roark comes to visit me and Darek refuses to mention it, and now Roark and Darek are keeping some kind of secret from me. Mom's in on it—probably Dad too. Apparently my entire family thinks I'm still a child who can't handle the truth!"

She was on her feet now, shaking, her words reverberating through the room.

She had the vague sense of wishing them back.

Especially when her father turned to her. "No one is treating you like a child except you right now," John said quietly. "Your sister has a right to keep her secrets—although, yes, Grace, Max, you should have told us earlier instead of sneaking around. And as for Roark—well, that business is between you and him. If you want to know what he's up to, I suggest you ask him."

"Maybe I will. If he hasn't already left town, that is. Please tell me the big secret isn't that you scared him off—"

"Take a breath, Ames," Darek said. "We like Roark. A lot. Especially after he helped us out last weekend. So if he leaves, it won't be because of us."

He left the rest silent. Like it might be because of her actions—or inaction, perhaps.

Suddenly it occurred to her that maybe she'd been the one to drive Roark away in Prague. After all, he'd shown up at her door, begging to explain, and she'd slammed it in his face, embracing betrayal instead of explanation. Fleeing instead of forgiving.

She closed her eyes and took that breath Darek had suggested. Turned toward the window. She was so concerned with making another mistake, being foolish in front of her family, that maybe she was driving away the one man who didn't see her as young and naive. Even when she acted like it.

"I'm sorry," she said quietly.

She felt Grace's hand on her shoulder. "What's the real problem here?"

Moisture wicked her eyes. "I don't know. It's just, he came all the way over here for me. He believes in me—more than I believe in myself. He's lived this big life. He's not going to want to live a small one, here. What if I'm not enough for him?"

She pressed a hand to her mouth, horrified that she'd let those words sneak out, especially in front of her family.

Grace wrapped her arms around Amelia's shoulders. "Trust me. You're enough."

Amelia said nothing, sifting Grace's words through her brain.

"Do you still love him?"

Amelia sighed. "Not like I did in Prague. There, I was all big cycs and wow and dependent on him. Here . . . I don't know if he fits into my life. But when I was with him on the canoe trip, I remembered the way he made me feel in Prague. Confident. Like together we could tackle any-thing. When I am with him, it seems like I'm a better version of myself. I want him to fit into my life . . . I think."

"Give him a chance," Darek said. "You might be surprised."

Amelia looked at him, a frown on her face. "Since when did you become a fan?"

"I think we're all becoming fans."

Grace let Amelia go, walked over to Max. He kissed her forehead, and the action reminded Amelia of Roark's confession about his parents, the night he seemed human and real. *I want to kiss you right now. . . . But I'm afraid you'll only think it's a fling. So I'm willing to wait until you know I mean it.*

She wanted a man like Max, who wasn't afraid to stand up for her to her parents, her brothers. To declare his love.

Yeah, she'd gotten that in Roark. And frankly, in Seth too.

"You know why he hasn't called, don't you, Darek?"

Darek sighed. "Go talk to him."

Amelia nodded. "No more secrets."

"I think this has gone far enough, Roark." Ethan, in one square of the Skype screen, shook his head, a glass of something amber in his hand, the view of some clubhouse behind him—a sprawling lawn, the occasional laughter of the highbrow set relaxing after a round of golf. "You're properly out of your mind."

In the other square, Uncle Donovan sat in a leather chair at his office, the view behind the window one of gray skies and penthouses. "I concur. We've put this off long enough, Roark. It's time to settle this business and come home. I understand you have feelings for this girl, but staying there is quite out of the question. Enough foolishness. Sort it out and get on a plane."

"Uncle, I promise you, I'm not being foolish. I think this is something I've been considering a

310

long time. Probably since Paris, but maybe even before—"

"You're not going to bring up that nonsense about Uganda, are you? Son—"

Roark tried not to cringe, but somehow, when Uncle Donovan called him *son,* it only raked open the old wounds.

Uncle Donovan continued without noticing. "I know you've had a rough go of it, but two years is long enough to nurse your wounds. You've blown through your monthly allowances like water—"

"He gave most of it away, Donovan." This from Ethan, always his protector. "Early on to Francesca's family and the victims in the fire. Then, pretty much wherever he went, he seemed to find something worthy of a fortune—"

"It wasn't that much," Roark argued. "Not after Eton and university and the flat in Paris . . ."

"And the Ferrari. Let's not forget about that," Ethan said.

Maybe not so much of a protector as Roark thought.

"Exactly why you need to pack up and head home, my boy," Uncle Donovan said again. "I've already told the board you'll be there for the quarterly meeting. Don't make me break my word—again."

Roark sat at the table in his flat, overlooking the view of the lake, the fishing boats just returning to the harbor, seagulls circling in anticipation. Soon the fish house would fire up and fragrance the entire harbor with the scent of hickory wood and smoked lake trout, herring, and cisco.

"I'm afraid you'll have to, Uncle. But this time it's for good. I . . . I've found what I'm looking for. Something more valuable than money or a position at the Constantine Worldwide helm."

Uncle Donovan rolled his eyes. "You sound just like your father."

What—?

"Right after university, he came home and told your grandfather he didn't want to join the company. Made us all feel like guttersnipes for our club memberships."

He had? "It's not like that. I promise."

"You have a responsibility, Roark. To your father and your grandfather."

Roark glanced at Ethan, who had fired up a cigar. He raised an eyebrow, like *Don't look at me.*

"I think if you take a good look at this, Uncle, you'd agree that maybe you don't want me anywhere near the family business. If you haven't noticed, I'm cursed. The farther away I stay from Constantine Worldwide, the better."

"One accident—"

"An accident that cost a dozen people their lives and burned down an entire city block. Don't be trite, Uncle."

Uncle Donovan's eyes narrowed. "Fine. Then how about this. Have you lost your mind? There is nothing left of your inheritance, and if you walk away from your grandfather's place at the table, you'll have nothing. That's millions of euros in stocks and bonds."

No. He'd have peace. A home—one he'd longed for since his family died. If, that was, Amelia decided that yes, he could stay as a permanent part of her life.

The word *if* suddenly took up all the oxygen in the room. Gave him pause. Made him slow his headlong rush into financial martyrdom. "Okay, I'll think about it. In the meantime, you draw up a list of replacements. But I'm not going to make the mistakes of my father and surrender to the call of money."

"You might not be so self-righteous if you knew your father came home because your mother had cancer. He couldn't afford the medical costs. So he asked me to create a position for him in the family business. He couldn't afford to live on a dream, and neither can you, Roark."

His uncle's words put a fist into his sternum, stole his breath. His mother'd had cancer?

He didn't know where to file that information. Instead, he answered, "I have a job."

"You live over a coffee shop."

Ethan nodded, the traitor.

"Roark, you need to think about this. You've

had everything you needed—and wanted—since you were twelve. Cars, vacations—and these past two years, you've squandered everything with the hope that you might escape your mistakes and, apparently, find absolution. Or even peace. But there is no peace in this world, not without security. And you can't have that without money."

"There's more to life than money."

"Says a rich boy who can't remember living without it." Uncle Donovan shook his head. "Don't get preachy on me. But think about this: when you need it, you've always had the money to obtain it, whatever *it* is. You walk away, and that's gone. *You're* gone. Position, power, and wealth *make* you someone. Give you influence. You *can* help people and change the world with money. That's what your father finally figured out."

Donovan's quiet, precise words pricked the back of Roark's throat. "I know you mean well but—"

"I do mean well. I always have. End this business and come home." Uncle Donovan disconnected before Roark could argue further.

But Ethan stayed on the line, his face filling the screen. "Your uncle is right, mate. You can't walk away from your entire life because of one girl."

"Amelia doesn't want to leave Deep Haven. Her life is here."

"So she says. But this is not hard, Roark. You tell her you're wealthy. She asks, 'How wealthy?' You answer, 'Very, very wealthy,' and she says, 'When do we leave?' This is not hard!"

"You're forgetting that moment when she says, 'You lied to me.' "

"She'll get over it when she sees the view from your flat in Brussels."

Roark shook his head. "Not Amelia. She's . . . I'm not sure it would matter to her. And if I tell her now, I'll never really know, will I?"

"But you'll have the girl, Roark. It doesn't matter *how*. Just do it. It's like a Band-Aid—you have to rip it off."

A knock at the screen door behind him. Roark turned.

Amelia stood on the other side of the screen. "Sorry to interrupt."

Blimey, he should have closed the door after his run this morning. But with the cool breezes off the lake, the aroma of fresh-brewed coffee floating up the stairs . . . "Be right there," he said, trying to keep his voice tight, not let fear trickle out.

How much had she heard?

"Gotta run, Ethan." He closed the cover on his laptop without a proper good-bye, but probably Ethan had seen everything.

And knew how close Roark's life was to truly falling apart.

He stood, his entire body still aching from his run, and managed a smile as he hobbled to the door. "Amelia!"

She stood, hands on her hips, wearing leggings, her running shoes, and an oversize sweatshirt, her hair in a messy bun, looking so impossibly young, it struck him again that she was just turning twenty-one.

He heard that *if* in his mind again. *If.*

"I was going to—"

"Roark, tell me the truth. Are you leaving town?"

He frowned, shook his head. "No. I, uh—"

"Because Darek seems to know something about you that I don't."

She cocked her head, and his smile fell. "Ames—"

She froze, her eyes wide. "You've never called me Ames. I was always Amelia to you. Until right now."

"Amelia. Sorry—"

"Oh, I can't believe I didn't see this." She sank down on the stairs. "I'm such a fool."

He stood there, stymied. "See what?"

She looked up at him, defeated. "You don't look at me the way you did in Prague."

"Of course I don't!"

"I used to be Amelia the traveler, Amelia the brave. Now I'm Ames, the kid sister of Darek and Grace. In need of protecting." She got up, but he grabbed her arm.

"What are you talking about?" He had raised his voice; now he cut it low. "I don't see you as a child—I never did. And of course you're not the same person you were in Prague. There—yeah, I thought you were brave and beautiful, and I loved every minute we spent together. But there I was the protector. Here . . . here *I need you,* Amelia. I need the woman who stands up for me and believes I can live in her world. I need the woman who makes me think I'm no longer cursed!"

She blinked at him. "Cursed? Roark, what are you talking about?"

There he went, blurting out the truth, letting it hang there, raw and brutal and horrid. He hadn't quite meant for it to come to this. "God has cursed me."

Her voice softened. "Why would you say that?"

"Maybe *cursed* is the wrong word, but He certainly doesn't like me, and for good reason."

She just frowned.

"You don't get it, Amelia. You . . . you see God through eyes of hope and expectation. But I'm on the other side. He's . . . Well, you know my parents' story. They turned away from His calling, and for it . . . they were murdered."

Her eyes glistened. "God didn't punish your parents."

But he barely heard it, his throat thickening as he looked away, sat on the stairs. "And I only made it worse."

"What are you talking about?"

He sighed. "Do you ever wish that you could go back, change one decision, and then your life might fall into place?"

She swallowed. "Yes."

Wait. What if it was—?

"I should have never run away from you in Prague. I should have let you in, forgiven you." She sat next to him. "I acted like a child, and I regret that."

Oh, Amelia. "I think we were both to blame in Prague. I wasn't . . . Well, I wasn't completely honest with you. I was afraid that if you knew the truth, you'd run."

"Why would I run?"

He closed his eyes. "Because I'm not a brave man. Because, at my core, I am a coward."

"Roark—"

"I've been running from God since that day on the beach, when I let my parents' killer go free. God gave me plenty of opportunities—even called me into missions in Uganda, but . . . I said no. Only a coward says no to God."

Her mouth opened. Closed. "That's not true."

He didn't want to argue with her.

"Tell me what happened. How did you say no to God?"

He couldn't look at her, the memory so ugly, it might show in his eyes. "I told you about the refugee camp I worked at in my gap year. What I

318

didn't mention was that I loved it. I felt, for the first time since my family died, that I might have recaptured what we'd had in Russia. I knew I was supposed to do something, that God was calling me to something bigger. So I went home and told my uncle that I wanted to join a seminary. He went off his trolley. He had different plans for me and intended that I follow them."

"What kind of plans?"

This is not hard, Roark.

Except it was. "He wants me to take over the family business." He gave a rueful smile. "Hotels."

She gave him a curious look. "Your family has a hotel?"

"More than one. Brussels, Paris." And about ten other countries.

"What happened when you told your uncle you wanted to be a missionary?"

"I behaved rather beastly and told my uncle to snuff it. Then I took off for Italy."

"Why Italy?"

"I'd met a girl in camp during my gap year, and I thought she shared my call. Turns out, she didn't care for the poor-missionary version of me."

Her voice turned tender. "Then she was a fool."

Maybe he could believe that with Amelia's beautiful eyes in his.

He looked away. "I ended up broke, sitting at a

train station, calling my uncle to wire me money. I went home and enrolled in university and ended up in Paris."

A beat passed as he blew out a long breath.

"I have a feeling that's not the end of the story, is it?" She tilted her head. "What happened in Paris, Roark?"

So maybe he would just yank off the Band-Aid, as Ethan had suggested. "You're right; I can't be a professional student forever. In fact, I never was."

She went very still.

"I never told you why I left Paris. Why I spent the past two years traveling. Or who you saw me talking to in Prague."

"Hugging."

"Quite right. Hugging. She was the sister of my fiancée. I wanted her permission to fall in love with you."

She blinked at him. "I don't . . . I don't understand. You're . . . Please don't tell me I'm that stupid."

"No—I'm sorry; that came out wrong. Francesca is dead. She died in a fire—a hotel fire."

"Oh . . ." And then she got it. "Oh! Roark, how awful."

She made to reach for his hand, but he pulled away. "You might not like this part. It was my fault. It happened on the eve of my twenty-third birthday. I had a party—a big party. There was a fire, and people got trampled trying to escape. Francesca was one of those people."

"Roark, you can't believe that Francesca's death was somehow your fault."

"It was completely my fault. Because my family is cursed. My father turned away from God's call, and so did I."

"Do you think that your parents' deaths, and the fire, were God's punishment?"

His jaw tightened.

She pressed her hand to his arm. "That's a bit extreme, don't you think?"

"Tell that to Jonah."

"Jonah—and the whale? God wasn't punishing Jonah—"

"What would you call three days in a fish's belly?"

"Getting his attention?"

He gave a laugh, nothing of humor in it. "Well, he certainly got mine. Reminded me that I had failed Him. I left Paris and didn't look back. I've done everything I can think of to forget, outrun the grief, the curse."

"Are you still running? Is that what Darek knows? Are you . . . ?" She swallowed, looking impossibly vulnerable. "Leaving?"

"No." He drew in a breath. "What he knows is that I want your life, Amelia. I want the world you live in. You have riches here you have no idea of. I think perhaps, finally, God has given me another chance, because why else would He put you in my life, send me to this backwoods hamlet, but to tell me I can start over?"

Her eyes widened.

"I know that the man you met in Prague isn't the one you see before you today. But hopefully you know enough of me to believe me when I say I am not going anywhere. Not without you. You stay; I stay." He took her face in his hands. "You are not a fling, Amelia. For me, you are the reason to stop running."

She gave him a look, the same one she'd given him almost five months ago, across a crowded room in Paris. New Year's Eve, a night of new beginnings, and he saw it again now, on her face, an answer, perhaps . . . Yes.

"Oh, Amelia." He had no choice but to kiss her. He tried to hold back, to keep his touch light, soft, but she wasn't having it that way. She made a little noise of surprise, then something more, deeper, and ran her arms around his neck, curling herself against him.

That's all it took for Roark to dive in, kissing her like he'd imagined for five months—maybe longer. Really kissing her, with his hands in her hair, his heart so full in his chest it might explode. *Amelia.*

This was the only fortune he needed. This woman who made him feel rich, who didn't see his mistakes.

He loved her. The entirety of his feelings rushed over him.

He'd loved her in Prague for the possibility of who she might be in his life. Today he loved her for herself—the brave, forgiving person who could set him free.

He leaned back, his breath shuddering out, his thumb caressing her cheek. "I've been wanting to do that for a while."

"I told Seth I wouldn't kiss either of you until I knew . . ." She swallowed and looked away, but he caught her chin.

"Does this mean—?"

She suddenly frowned, pulled his hand away. Took the other and held them open. "Roark, your hands. What does Kathy have you doing?"

She ran her fingers along the row of broken, rough blisters, some turned to calluses.

He didn't want to lie to her—not anymore. But everything in this moment had sorted out so perfectly . . . Maybe she never needed to know about the inheritance, the life he wanted to cast aside for her. "You have to promise not to be angry."

"Seriously?"

"Fine, okay. It's from chopping wood."

"Chopping . . . wood? What—?"

"I've been working with Darek—"

"He's got a lot of nerve, roping you into free labor."

"—in the afternoons. At the gravel pit."

She frowned again.

"I'm in training for the lumberjack games."

Her eyes widened, so he kept talking. "I know it sounds crazy, but I guess there's a part of me that wants to fit in here and . . ."

"This is all about Seth!" She hit her feet. "What is wrong with you two?"

"I know—I *know*." He stood too. "It's just that—"

She held up her hand. "Fine. I get it. I have brothers. I should have guessed. Who put you up to this? Please don't say you had another run-in with Seth."

"Darek."

"What? I thought he liked Seth."

"I think he doesn't like how Seth believes you belong to him."

That must not've been the right thing to say because she cocked her head, raised an eyebrow. "Trust me. I can handle Seth."

"Quite right, sorry."

She considered him. "So. Are you any good?"

"Darek seems to think I have a chance. At least for the hot saw and the standing chop. He's going to be my partner for the double buck, so if I can keep up with him . . . But it's the logrolling that's got me in a knot. I'll likely go into the drink first round out but—"

"Now I'm really mad."

Oh.

"Darek should have told me. Because while he holds the local title for the hot saw and can probably teach you how to throw an ax, you're looking at the Deep Haven two-time junior birling champion." She grinned. "Suit up, 007. You're officially in training."

Chapter 12

THE COUPLE MARRIED on the beach, just the families witnessing the ceremony as the sun crested over the bay, and Amelia caught the glorious sunrise, the rose gold lighting the sky behind them.

Such a simple, beautiful wedding, sacred vows before the heavens. It caught Amelia up in the mystery even as she stood back and snapped the moments with her camera.

"Okay, I need Esther standing on the steps, and Mark, you stand just below her, holding her hand." *Thank you, Ree, for the referral.* And good thing they'd chosen a Saturday morning for their pictures because she planned on spending the afternoon at Evergreen Lake. Teaching Roark how to logroll.

It had taken a week to find space in the training schedule Darek had Roark on—apparently her brother expected him to simply forfeit the birling.

Not on her watch. She'd talked Darek into hauling out her old training log, dug out Casper's wet suit from the basement, and found an old pair of shoes for Roark to wear.

She felt a little deceitful, siding with Roark, but the truth was, she loved an underdog.

Loved . . .

Did she love him? Maybe it hadn't been a fling, but what they had in Prague didn't compare to the well of feelings he stirred in her with his story of his own failures.

He could break her heart with his belief that he was cursed, with the brutality of his past. Put against hers, she'd lived such a sheltered, perfect life.

No wonder she'd stumbled in Prague. Thankfully, right into Roark's arms.

For me, you are the reason to stop running.

With those words, something had unlatched inside her. That dark band of fear, maybe, that she would choose poorly.

Seth had waited for her. Roark had chased her here, needing her in his life.

The reason to stop running.

Oh, she just needed a clear answer. She'd take anything—writing on a wall, a talking donkey, angels from heaven, even the voice of God in the middle of the night—just to give her some direction as to which of the two amazing men God wanted for her.

She owed Seth an apology, maybe, for the way she'd nearly leaped into Roark's arms, kissing him with too much of herself.

And Roark, with his *You stay; I stay* declaration, had made the decision that much muddier.

The fact was, she could see herself building a life with either man. Seth, with his beautiful home on the lake. Roark, running a hotel, treading the path of her parents.

Living happily ever after. With *one* of them.

She snapped a picture as Esther posed on the steps up from the beach to the roadway, holding out her hand to her groom. She wore a simple, ankle-length white gown, Mark in a gray vest, dark trousers. The families stood behind them, watching as Amelia asked Esther to bend down and kiss her groom.

Amelia framed another shot, snapped it, and then the couple laughed, and she caught that too.

"Are we done?" Esther said again, her eyes shining as she glanced at her groom.

"We just need the family shots." Amelia scrolled through the photos of the day as Mark helped Esther down the steps.

Barb, her mother, wearing a bright-blue dress and sandals, trekked over to Amelia. "Thank you so much for helping us at such short notice. They wanted to get married before we left for the field again, and only got engaged a month ago."

"It turned out beautifully," Amelia said. "I've

never seen a dawn wedding, but look at the pictures." She held up her camera to Barbara.

The first shot silhouetted the couple against a backdrop of brilliant orange, the sun's rays a halo of golden light.

The next number caught the ceremony, the simplicity of the bride walking down the beach to her groom, holding a bouquet of daffodils wrapped in twine, her hair loose, no makeup.

A lone guitarist sang a version of the song Amelia couldn't seem to escape these days.

"You are my vision, O King of my heart. Nothing else satisfies, only You, Lord."

"You are a very talented photographer," Barb said as she finished scrolling to the last, the pictures on the stairs.

"Oh, I had nothing to do with these epic shots. I simply showed up. God did the rest."

"That's the way it is when we step back and let God put the picture together." Barb cast a glance at Esther and Mark, sharing a private moment on the beach, away from the family. "I never thought I'd survive losing Caleb. The loss felt overwhelming. It paralyzed me. I thought I could never go back to Uganda. Then I realized that I didn't have to be brave. I simply had to look to Jesus."

A seagull landed nearby as more soared overhead. The wind drew the waves onshore, the smell of summer in the fresh-cut grass of the nearby park. Esther was walking along the beach, holding hands with her groom.

"It wasn't until I said yes, not knowing how I might find the strength, that I recognized Jesus holding me in the middle of the storm." Barb sighed, smiled. "And days like today, He's still holding me."

"I'm so sorry about the loss of your son."

"Thank you. But he's not lost. He's just watching from a different place." She winked at Amelia. "But we did bring a picture to add to our family photos."

Amelia gestured the family over, and they assembled with their backs to the harbor. The sun had crested the horizon, the sky edged in gold and lavender. She took shots of each family, then both together.

Then, finally, Esther and Mark, wrapped in a spontaneous intimate moment.

"Perfect," Amelia said, almost under her breath. She walked back up the beach, following the families, Barb and her husband holding hands, their youngest son throwing rocks in the lake, his dress pants wet to the ankles.

She took shots of the family, silhouetted by the horizon, as she pondered Barb's words. Jesus holding her in the midst of the storm.

How long had it been really since Amelia had felt that kind of peace? Before Prague, maybe. Or maybe that day she and Roark strolled through

Paris, took shots of Notre-Dame. When they'd ventured inside to the ethereal hush of the cathedral. For a moment, she'd stared at the icons of Christ, and something moved inside her. A longing. A restlessness.

"You're my soul's shelter and You're my high tower. Come raise me heavenward, O power of my power."

She sat on a boulder and drew in a breath, watched the rising sun caress the waves. *Oh, God, I want You to be my vision. My shelter. Heart of my own heart, whatever befall.*

The thought wove through her like the song, nurturing.

Footsteps spilled on the beach behind her. She turned and smiled as Barb approached, holding something in a napkin. "I brought you a piece of wedding coffee cake."

Amelia took it, suddenly ravenous. "Thank you."

Barb leaned on the rock next to her. Drew in a breath. "It smells fresh here. Rich."

Amelia nodded.

"Uganda smells of grasses and wide-open sky. . . . I'm not sure why, but I feel I'm supposed to tell you that if you ever want to come to Africa, we'd love to have you. Even for a visit or a short-term trip." She got up. "Bring the camera. You never know what epic shots are waiting."

Amelia watched her trek up the shore to where the families waited in their cars to depart to the brunch reception at nearby Naniboujou Lodge. Barb caught her daughter around her waist, gave her a hug. Kissed her son-in-law.

Amelia lifted her camera and snapped a picture.

Four hours later, Amelia wished she still had the camera around her neck as she watched Roark wriggle into Casper's old wet suit, pulling it over his wide chest. "Are you sure I need this?" he said, his face in a knot as he tugged the skintight neoprene over his body.

She tried not to look at his sculpted shoulders, the ridges on his stomach. Whereas she'd grown up seeing Seth shirtless after a workout or swimming, this might be the first time she'd truly seen Roark's chiseled form.

Yeah, okay, she didn't look away. And didn't mind how the suit outlined his body, a glove over his thin hips, strong back, biceps.

"The water's about sixty degrees at best," she said. "So yes."

The benefits of living on a lake: they could do their training off the dock at the resort. The sun had burned off the clouds, offering a glorious, seventy-degree day, the lake so ridiculously blue that it seemed impossible not to dive in, despite the early summer chill.

The wet suits muted the cold, and she wore her old rolling shoes as she pulled the log to the dock, tied it up.

Roark finally secured the wet suit and sat beside her to put on his dock shoes—or rather, Casper's. The wind caught his dark hair, held back from his face with a red bandanna.

"Okay, some basic instruction first." She stood and put her hands on his shoulders. Then she pushed.

"What—?"

"You stepped back with your right leg. That's your dominant leg."

"You're tricky," he said.

"Just getting started. Now let's imagine one of these slats is the log. You're going to want to stand with your dominant leg to the outside."

He lined up, his right leg back.

"Good. When we get on the log and start rolling, you have one rule."

"Don't fall in?"

"You wish. No. Don't look at your feet."

"How will I stay on the log?"

"By instinct. You need to concentrate on the other end, where your opponent is standing. If you look down, your center of balance will be thrown off. It's also instinctual to look down, so you'll have to fight it. But you'll get used to it. Focusing on your opponent helps you anticipate his strategy because you can watch his feet. And you'll be able to see the log and his body movements in your peripheral vision."

"I think the only thing I'm going to see is water in my eyes as I go under."

"Not after I get done with you."

"I'm depending on you, coach."

His eyes, so impossibly warm, stole the words from her. Far from the man who'd been her lifeline in Prague . . . yes, this man needed her. Imagine.

Heat rushed through her at the thought of his kiss, only a week ago—the kind of kiss that kept her awake and deepened her guilt.

She should feel guilty for the way, suddenly, she wanted Roark to win this competition.

"The most important thing in logrolling is to keep your feet moving—fast. If you don't, you're doomed. Moving your feet, lightly, in small steps, helps you keep your balance. You want to bend your knees—yeah, like that—and hold your outside arm slightly forward in front of your body. Your inside arm should be back. The arms are important, but more important is your core."

He affected the stance, and oh, she wanted a picture.

"Your main job today is to keep your body centered and stay on top, using small, fast steps. Micro steps, either forward or backward. Once you learn how to stay on the log—"

"Sometime next year."

"Today. Then I'll teach you the three main

skills of birling—the front and back steps and the transition."

He sighed, put his arms down. "I don't know about this. I'm just going to be a fool out there."

She went to him, took his hands. "A heroic fool. I love that you are doing this. I'm not sure why, but the fact that you're willing to go so far out of your depth makes me believe you—that yes, we weren't a fling. That . . . that—"

"That I just might be the best thing that ever happened to you and you must marry me immediately?"

She grinned. And with a push, sent him off the end of the dock into the water.

Roark sputtered to the surface, pulling the soaked bandanna off his head and shaking out his hair.

She shrieked at the spray of water, laughed. Then leaned over. "Maybe."

He grinned and, before she could react, reached up and yanked her into the lake.

The water sucked her under, a blanket of bracing chill. But she felt Roark's hand on her arm, lifting her.

She burst to the surface. Wiped the water from her eyes.

Roark floated beside her, looking so sweetly mischievous she couldn't help but splash him. Then she took off, and he came after her, swimming hard.

He grabbed her foot and dragged her close. She splashed him again, laughing. "Roark, this is no way to treat your coach!"

Snaking an arm around her waist, he drew her against himself, his eyes suddenly serious, desire pooling in them.

"Quite right. Perhaps this is better." He kissed her, diving in without the tentative exploration of his previous kiss, his touch resolute, filled with longing.

Everything dropped away. The turmoil of choosing between Seth and Roark, the guilt of loving two men, the ragged indecision that tied her in knots. Just Roark and the sunshine and the water in an embrace around them as her arms encircled his shoulders and she let him deepen their kiss.

It brought her back to Prague, and walking hand in hand in Paris, but so much more—his heroism with the Boy Scouts and his broken heart, and the fact that while he'd been a mystery in Europe, she knew *this* man. Knew his fears, his heart.

In fact, she loved this man, who would be a fool for her in front of her entire town to prove he could stop running, would make his life fit hers.

He tasted of freedom and their tomorrows and the kind of person she'd longed to be when she'd flung herself into her Prague adventure.

Brave. Strong.

Loved.

She leaned back, captured his wet face in her hands. Droplets had gathered on his long eye-lashes, and the sun twinkled in his eyes. "I love you, Roark."

His breath caught, and he swallowed, his expression becoming impossibly tender. "That's the first time you've said that."

She touched her forehead to his, then kissed him again. He softened his ardor this time, capturing her head in his hands, his touch gentle, lingering. Igniting a sweet swirl of desire through her.

He leaned back, breathing a little hard. "Maybe we should commence with the lesson."

"Quite right," she said, quoting him. "What lesson?"

He laughed and let her go, leaving her just a little shaky in the water.

His long, fluid strokes brought him to the log, tethered three feet from the dock, in thigh-deep water. He climbed over one end, straddled it, then levered himself to a standing position like he might on a surfboard.

"Move your feet, tiny steps," she said, swimming over. She stood in the water, holding the log steady, her heart still afire in her chest. The answer seemed so utterly clear to her.

Roark could be the one. She could almost see herself staying here, running their own resort, finding herself every morning waking up to this amazing man.

Almost.

Something, however, still seemed out of focus.

"Let go of the log. I think I can keep it stable."

Amelia let go, and he began to move it, first forward, then slowing and moving it backward.

"Roark, you're a natural."

"YouTube," he said, looking down at her, winking.

And that's when he lost it, falling off the log backward, splashing into the water.

"You have to keep your peripheral vision on the log, like I said. Don't lose focus."

He got up, held out his hand to her as she steadied the log. "I can do this. But this might be a great shot for your photo contest. Life in the north shore."

"Really? You don't mind?"

"Not in the least."

"Good, because I made the top 100 list—and I'm in the second round!"

She'd tried not to obsess about the stats since uploading her photos Saturday morning, but, well . . . "I need five more pictures by Friday."

He straddled the log. "I think an Englishman making a fool out of himself as he goes into the drink just might be a keeper."

A swell of tenderness filled her throat. "I'll be right back."

She climbed out of the water, grabbed her towel, and ran up the path to the lodge. Standing in the entrance, she slipped off her soggy shoes, then, still wet and ensconced in the towel, headed upstairs for her camera.

She was standing in the alcove beside her bed, making room for more shots on her memory card, when she heard a vehicle pull into the gravel drive. She glanced out the window, expecting a guest.

Instead, she recognized the Turnquist Lumber logo printed on the car's door.

She froze as she watched Seth park, then get out of the car. He walked up to the house, the bell dinging.

Amelia couldn't move as she heard her mother answer the door.

"Hello, Mrs. C. Is Amelia here? I need to talk to her."

And of course, since her mother hadn't seen Amelia dash inside, she sent the lumberjack right on down to the dock.

Amelia loved him.

Her words settled deep inside Roark, nourished him, and the moment she said them, her arms locked around his neck, her perfect body molded against him, her beautiful eyes in his, something unlocked inside him.

As if he'd gulped sweet, fresh air after holding his breath for years.

She loved him. Just him. Roark St. John,

failure, coward, broken and desperate, yet she looked into his life and saw something worth loving.

Without his wealth. His legacy—good and bad.

Yeah, he could take a deep, full breath, and his lies no longer made him ache. Because he didn't need them anymore. Whether rich or poor . . . Amelia loved him.

Which meant the great *if* had vanished.

He pushed up on the log, balancing with tiny steps as it rolled. Amelia had affixed some kind of training device in the middle, a sort of paddle wheel that slowed the turn of the log. Remembering her techniques, he managed to steady himself. He moved the log forward, faster, then slowed it and moved it the opposite direction.

He tightened his core, keenly aware that, thanks to his recent hours with the ax, he'd strained every muscle in his body.

He didn't have a prayer of winning the competition; he knew that. And right now, he didn't even care about entering, except for . . . *I love that you are doing this.*

Probably he could also be called a fool for suggesting Amelia take his picture, but she had no idea how talented she was, how she could pan a scene and capture the magic in a perfect shot.

So yeah, he'd enter. And try not to embarrass her and the entire Christiansen clan.

He was just climbing back onto the log after falling off again when he heard footsteps on the path. Shaking the water from his eyes, he glanced up, expecting Amelia to snap his picture.

Not Amelia.

"Hey, Seth," he said, pushing his hair out of his face.

Seth stood on the dock, dressed in cargo shorts, a green T-shirt, and aviators that reflected a rather warped picture of Roark.

"What are you doing here?"

Roark jumped into the water and pulled himself onto the dock to get even footing. "Sunbathing."

Seth refused to be affected.

"Clearly I'm learning to logroll," Roark finally said. "Just for sport."

A slow smile slid up Seth's face. "Nice. Oh, this is *fan*-tastic." He glanced at the log, then at Roark, and chuckled. "Now we're going to have some real fun."

"Seth!"

Roark glanced over Seth's shoulder at the sound of Amelia's voice, but Seth kept looking at him, wearing that grin. "I think this calls for a wager. If you win, I back off. You can stick around Deep Haven, and I won't tear you limb from limb."

"Jolly good. And if you win?"

"Easy. You leave. I get Amelia."

Roark let out a laugh bearing nothing of humor. "You must think I'm daft. And from some pre-historic, hair-dragging tribe to think I'd wager the heart of the woman I love over a contest I know I'm doomed to fail. I'm sorry, Seth. I respect and care for Amelia too much to win her in battle."

"Then how about this? Walk away. Today. Or it's going to get ugly."

"Hardly. I believe you're the only one making it ugly. You can trot back to your den now."

Seth didn't move. "Last chance before I destroy you."

Every nerve in Roark's body tensed. "Please," he said quietly. "Let's have a go. Finally."

Seth's mouth tightened to a dark, lethal line. "You know, I'm not an idiot. I know you might think so because I drive a big truck and occasionally chew with my mouth open, and no, I don't talk with a fancy British accent. But after you hired Goldstein to fly in for you, I got to thinking. Jake isn't going to hop in his floatplane and fly to an inner lake during a storm just because you asked. Or offered him a free cup at the Java. So yes, I used my rather small brain to figure it out. Jake dished on you, said you'd dropped a cool 10K on that fly in. So I fired up my computer and used both my thumbs and did some checking. Surprise! Even the redneck from the woods knows how to google."

Seth took a step closer, his voice cool. "I found you, pal. I found you and your group of rich-boy friends and the fact that you're a billionaire hotel heir."

Roark's voice pitched low. "That's none of your business."

"It is my business if the woman I love is being lied to. Don't you think she should know that you're not remotely some European bum, but a guy worth . . . What did the Internet say? Nine billion?"

Over Seth's shoulder, Roark could see Amelia now, emerging from the trail.

A fist closed around his chest, squeezing. But he kept his voice cool. "I hardly think my financial status will dissuade her."

"Really. So you're saying she won't care that you lied to her?"

Roark drew in a breath.

"That's what I thought. Last chance for a wager."

"Tempting, but I guess I'll treat Amelia like an adult and win her heart the old-fashioned way."

"Oh," Seth said, taking off his glasses so Roark could see the venom in his eyes. "Like with the truth?" He smiled again, slow, dark. "Have at it, dude."

A breeze found Roark, chilled the wet suit, raised the skin on his neck.

Amelia caught up to them. "Seth! Uh . . . hi. I can explain."

If she wanted to wound Roark, punching him in the stomach would have done less damage. Because she looked genuinely worried that she might have hurt Seth.

Nice.

Seth grinned at her. "I came by to see if you wanted to grab a pizza tonight. Maybe eat it at the point?" He winked and made sure Roark saw it.

"Oh . . . uh . . ."

"But I think you and Roark have things to discuss."

She looked at Roark, then back to Seth. "We do?"

"Yeah. Tell him to buy dinner. He can afford it." Seth leaned down and kissed Amelia on the cheek. "I'm just a phone call away." He walked up the path, hands in his pockets.

Amelia turned. "Roark? What's he talking about?"

She had such pretty eyes. Trusting. Honest. Ethan's words pinged in the back of his head. *This is not hard.*

Yeah, she'd told him she loved him, but the words were so fresh and young and . . . he'd only just become her hero again.

Seth! . . . I can explain.

Maybe the *if* hadn't quite vanished.

"He's jealous because . . ." He scrambled, came

up with an errant conversation, something he'd fully intended to do. So not quite a lie. "Because I booked the *Fossegrim* for a twilight sail next week. I thought you needed a proper date."

She smiled. "Are you sure? Seth's right—that's expensive. Probably a month's pay at the Cup."

"You're worth it." True, but his lie burned inside him.

She gestured to the water. "I can't believe he wasn't angry about you entering the lumberjack games."

Roark let out a laugh, something sharp. "I think he knows that I don't have a hope of defeating him."

"Ha. Maybe it's not about who wins, but how much courage it takes to lose."

He gave her a look.

"No? Okay, let's put it a different way. Are you man enough to show up and stay in the fight, even if you could lose?"

He stared at her, wishing too hard he could turn time back, tell her at the get-go, *Listen, I'm wealthy.*

"Let's get you back in training."

How wealthy?

"You really think I can learn this in two weeks' time?"

Very, very wealthy.

"Enough to impress the crowd. And me." She

344

winked at him as she lifted her camera, took a shot of the coward at the end of the dock.

And she says, "When do we leave?" This is not hard!

Oh, blimey.

Chapter 13

WITH THE SOFT PATTER of rain dripping from the roof, the distant roll of thunder, the cool breeze lifting the curtains of the den . . . how Max longed to stay nestled in the pullout, his wife cradled in his arms.

Grace nudged him again. "You promised you'd take Yulia fishing. Roark even explained it to her. Her hopes are up."

He rolled away from her onto his back, forcing his eyes open to stare at the ceiling and the gray skies outside the window. "But it's gloomy out." He kissed her shoulder. "Wouldn't you rather I stay here?"

His lips touched her arm next, eliciting something inside him that, in a moment, might be challenging for him to say no to.

Grace knew him too because she turned, pushed on his shoulder. "Max . . . she's probably out there waiting for you."

"She doesn't even understand us, Grace." He rolled her over, kissed the soft place behind her ear. "We've been speaking to her for nearly a month now, and she hasn't said a word in English. If it wasn't for Roark, we wouldn't know anything about her—or her, us."

She caught his chin, forcing him to meet her eyes. "She's just scared. She'll speak when she's ready. But she can still communicate. I can read her, Max. I know when she's happy or sad." She ran a finger down his cheek, touched his lips. "And I know she likes you."

He hoisted himself up on one arm. "What's not to like?" He winked and she laughed, leaning in to give him a quick kiss.

He chased her for more, but she held him back and climbed out of bed. "I have breakfast to make. And twelve German coffee cakes on my list of to-dos." She dressed in her yoga pants, a T-shirt, and tied her hair into a ponytail.

Then she leaned over the bed and touched her forehead to his. "The walleye bite best on cloudy, dark days. Go fishing—I promise it'll be worth it. Just for an hour. When you come back, I'll make you waffles."

"Sure you will. You'll make Yulia waffles. I'll get the leftovers," Max said but let her go. He could admit to more than a little worry about the bond Grace and Yulia had formed. The girl followed Grace around the house, helped her cook, and Grace indulged her with too many puzzles, games, and read-alouds.

After a month, the agency still hadn't found an American placement for the girl. Apparently with Yulia's so-called attachment disorder, no one wanted to risk the energy of loving a child who couldn't love them back.

No one except Grace, of course, who excelled in loving people who couldn't—or shouldn't—love her back.

With no news about Yulia's future placement in over a week, the Christiansens seemed to be operating on a no-news-is-good-news policy. He didn't blame them—Max excelled in denial as a form of coping.

He rolled out of bed and stretched. His body ached, the crossbar of the pullout leaving a permanent crease on his spine. That, or carrying Sheetrock into Darek's house yesterday. With Grace helping her mother put away frozen baked goods for the summer season, he'd volunteered to help Darek and John finish the interior of Darek's new place.

He could admit that he'd started to miss the apartment in Minneapolis. He couldn't wait to lie in bed an entire Saturday, eating pizza, watching BBC America reruns, and relishing this pocket of nothing before training camp started.

A year ago, he'd been in Hawaii, trying to figure out how to walk away from Grace and all the complications of falling in love. Today he couldn't imagine living without her. She added

347

the smile to his day, gave him a reason to want to wake up, want to have faith. To believe in hope.

Yes, someday he might be ready to adopt a child, for Grace's sake. But not yet. Call him selfish, but he didn't want to share her.

He pulled on a T-shirt, jeans, and grabbed his socks, then padded out into the family room. The rain cast a pallor of gray over the room, the lamplight puddling over John as he sat on the sofa, reading the paper. His father-in-law looked up, nodded at him, his face solemn.

It brought to mind the moment, nearly two weeks ago, when Max had shuffled out with Grace and announced their news. John and Max had yet to hash out the conversation Max dreaded, the one about the future and just how he'd prepared to take care of Grace. In the meantime, Grace had consented to a reception at the lodge over Christmas, a family get-together that they all quietly hoped might include Owen and Casper.

Grace and Ingrid worked in the kitchen, brewing coffee that added a morning aroma. Grace looked over her shoulder at him, then inclined her head toward the far end of the room.

He followed her gaze and found Yulia standing at the sliding-glass door to the deck. She faced away from him, staring out at the lake, the rain, the dismal skies. Hope of hopes, maybe she didn't want to go fishing either.

He walked over to her, crouched beside her. "Hey there, Yulia. It's yucky out, isn't it?"

When she turned to him, his heart gave an extra tharrumph, then became stone in his chest. Tears trailed down the little girl's cheeks, pooling at her jaw, dripping onto an oversize sweatshirt Grace had dug out of the hand-me-downs. The sleeves were rolled up, but only her fingers stuck out. Her hair lay in a tangled mess, escaping from her long braids, and if Max read his women right, her tiny heart was shattered.

He rested his hand on her shoulder, small, breakable. "What's the matter, honey?"

She just stared at him, blinking, her bottom lip caught in her teeth.

"Do you want to go fishing?"

She turned back to the window, her finger tracing raindrops on the glass.

"Did you think, because it was raining, that we wouldn't go?" And oh, he felt like a jerk for even thinking it. She trembled, swallowed, her tears still leaking out.

"Didn't you know the walleye love rain?" He stood, held out his hand.

She looked up at him, her eyes wide, so much hope in her cherub face that it could knock him over. Then she drew her arm across her face, wiping it. With a hiccup, she pressed her hand into his.

An unfamiliar feeling lit inside him, cascading through his heart into his chest.

He couldn't breathe, not with her looking at him with those immense, impossibly trusting brown eyes.

They were going to catch a fish if he had to dive in and bring one up with his teeth. "C'mon," he said, turning her away from the window.

Grace's eyes were on him, along with Ingrid's, wearing matching expressions of tenderness.

"Have fun, you two," Grace said, winking at Yulia, then smiling at Max.

So maybe the sun would come out after all.

He found Yulia a rain slicker in the closet, and Ingrid dug up a pair of boots. She patted Max on the cheek, her eyes warm, forgiveness part of her smile. "Thank you. Don't forget life jackets."

Of course.

Yulia headed outside just as the phone rang. Grace picked it up as Max walked out the door.

An hour later, he'd netted two small walleyes and shrieks of joy from Yulia, who seemed not at all disgusted by the slimy fish writhing on the floor of the boat. And as they walked back to the house, carrying the stringer of fish, she slipped her small hand in his again.

Once more, that unfamiliar curl of tenderness wrapped around him.

They entered the house, and Yulia kicked off her boots and ran into the kitchen, holding the fish.

"Oh, look at you!" he heard Ingrid exclaim.

Max followed her in. "She caught them both."

In an eerie déjà vu moment, he saw Grace standing by the sliding-glass door, like Yulia had been earlier.

"Honey?" He walked over to her, listening to Ingrid slide out a stool, fix Yulia breakfast.

Grace dashed her hand across her cheek. He touched her shoulder, turned her. She hazarded a broken smile.

"What's wrong?"

"Martha called as you were leaving. We were right. They can't find a placement for Yulia." She glanced at Yulia, then back to Max. "Next week sometime, she's going back to Ukraine."

"I can't believe that Seth actually threatened to tell Amelia your secret." Claire sat on the bed with the glow of a new mother about her.

Not a hint on her face of last night's labor and delivery, the 2 a.m. birth of her and Jensen's daughter, Ruby: six pounds, eight ounces of perfection. Roark stood at the end of her bed, having brought flowers for Claire and a Subway sandwich for Jensen, who sat in the rocking chair, smiling at the swaddled little girl.

Now he looked up. "I'm more hung up on the fact that Roark is logrolling. Really, dude?" He made a face that betrayed the craziness of Roark's entering the competition. "Good thing you didn't take that bet."

"It's not hard to figure out how Seth put it together," Claire said. She reached for a cup of water. "Smooth move, hiring Goldstein. He's like a thirteen-year-old girl—if you wanted to keep it secret, you'd have more success telling Edith Draper."

"Who?"

"Never mind," Jensen said. "Can you win this thing? Are you any good at all?"

"I can stay on the log. And yes, I'm getting better. Much better. Amelia and I practice every day after work. Between that and Darek's lessons on the bucksaw and the chopping, I might not make a ninny out of myself."

"But are you going to tell her?" Claire said, clearly not caring about the competition. "Seth knows, and you can bet he's not going to let it drop."

"With Darek on the bucksaw, you might stand a chance. And the hot saw is all about concentration and technique."

"You know, she might not be as angry as you think. It *is* billions."

"The entire competition is scored by points, so even if you end up second or third in one category, you could win the overall if you do well in another. Or if he bombs the logroll."

"I mean, what's going to happen next, Roark? You're not actually thinking of sticking around, right? At some point, you have to tell her—"

"Seth's always been one of the first out in the logroll. I think Claire could beat him and she's never even stepped foot on a log."

"Hey!" Claire said. "I could totally hand it to him."

"Maybe you should have taken him up on his wager," Jensen said, laughing.

Roark stared at the pair. "Clearly you two need less caffeine."

They frowned at him.

"Okay, Jensen. I respect Amelia and care too much about her to leave it up to a contest I'm doomed to lose. And yet, Claire, I fear that I'm doomed to lose her anyway if she finds out I've been lying to her. All the same, I'm disgusted with the thought of keeping this secret from her one more minute."

"Then it's time," Claire said.

Roark walked over to Jensen, studied their daughter. "She has your eyes, Claire."

"She has baby eyes. But Jensen's nose, bless her heart."

Roark ran a finger over her cheek.

"Want to hold her?" Jensen asked and handed her into Roark's arms. She snuggled in close, making baby sounds that could wreck him.

He sank into a chair. Held out his finger, and she wrapped her tiny hand around it.

"I daresay, Jensen, that he likes her," Claire said softly.

"She's . . . brilliant."

Silence, and when he looked up, Jensen and Claire wore soft, patronizing expressions.

"What?"

"You need to tell her," Jensen said. "Because I've never seen a guy so ready to have his own kids."

Roark shook his head. "No. That's not—"

"You totally are, Roark. I can't believe I didn't see it until right now. I should have, for the way you've been fighting to be a part of Deep Haven and the Christiansens. No wonder Amelia came home crazy about you," Claire said.

He liked how their words landed on him, watering the hope, the belief, that Amelia had seeded all week. The moments in the lake when she splashed him, when he caught her in a kiss, when she sat with him on the dock and stared at the stars, holding his hand.

She hadn't said it again—*I love you, Roark*—but he felt it.

As for himself, he couldn't put a finger on the shift inside him, the way that when she looked at him, he ached all the way to his bones.

He wanted so much for her. And for the first time he feared, properly feared, that he couldn't give it to her.

If he turned his back on his family, he would have nothing.

No way to provide.

The thought swept through him. No wonder his father had given up faith for finances. But maybe his uncle was right. Money gave him the ability to help people, save the world.

Except not from Deep Haven.

"By the way, we voted. Loved the picture of you falling off the log into the water," Jensen said. "I see she landed in the semifinals."

"I loved the silhouette of the bride and groom on the shore," Claire added. "Perfectly captured a north shore sunrise."

"She's so brilliant. For all my struggle to stay here, I can't help but think she should leave. She's so brave, and she doesn't see it. And I don't know how to show her." He sighed. "My uncle has found a successor for his position should I decide to resign."

He had to admit, he hadn't quite seen it coming—Ethan's name at the top of the list. But perhaps it made sense. Ethan's father had been in the company, on the board until his recent death. Ethan was practically family.

"Roark, no, are you serious?" This from Jensen.

"I want a life with Amelia. And it seems she wants to stay in Deep Haven. My dad did it—left home and lived without the family wealth. I want what we had, a family. A better life." He stared down at Ruby, watching her eyes try to focus. "The problem is, I don't want her to know what I gave up for her."

"Roark!"

He looked up at Claire's outburst. "I don't want to be the guy who used his money to buy friends. Even Francesca, I believe, never truly loved me. We had a terrific row the night of the fire. I thought she might be seeing another bloke. It's a terrible thing not to really know if you're loved for yourself or your net worth. Or worse, to use it to win women and friends. It took my uncle Donovan three tries before he found a woman who loves him. I can't be that guy."

"You won't be because you never were." Jensen got up as a nurse came into the room, strapped a blood pressure cuff on Claire. "Think about it— you miss your family. You wanted that sense of belonging. Of course you used what you had to try to get it. But that doesn't mean the roots are bad. Who you are isn't about your money or power but how you use what you're given. And it shows by your fruit. You're a guy who cares about people, about family, and your *very*s don't change that."

Roark glanced at the nurse, but she appeared not to be listening.

"I just don't want to guilt her into . . ." Oh, he'd already said too much.

"Guilt her into loving you?" Claire finished for him as the nurse unstrapped the Velcro. The noise startled the baby and her eyes widened.

"Uh, I think we're headed for trouble here,"

Roark said as Ruby squirmed, her face knotting. "Jensen—"

Jensen came over to retrieve the bundle. "No worries, Roark, I got your back."

Amazing how the baby calmed almost immediately in her father's arms.

"You're taking her out tonight, right?"

"I rented the *Fossegrim* for the evening cruise."

"Fancy."

"Yes, well, she thinks it's costing me a month's pay."

"You walk away from your inheritance, and it will," Jensen said, his hand patting the baby's bottom. He glanced out the window. "The storm seems to have cleared up the sky. It's going to be a glorious night."

It could be.

"Roark, you listen to me." Claire reached now for her baby. Jensen settled the infant into her arms. "You told me I could trust you—"

He made a sound and she quickly said, "Ah, ah—I do trust you. But you also said that Amelia was the one. That you can't envision a life without her. Do you really want to walk into your future hiding your past? You do that, and you'll never really stop running."

The baby in her arms began to squirm, let out a cry.

"Want my advice?" Jensen said. "As Darek would say, it's time to go big or go home. Put it all out there. Show her exactly what those dollars—or pounds—can do. My guess is, she'll forgive you."

"But . . . I'm not that guy."

"I beg to differ," Claire said. "You're 007, man of mystery. Lumberjack *and* European playboy. But at the heart, you're Roark St. John. Show her that you can be lavish and still be the same guy, and I'll bet you end the night with a woman who loves you."

She nodded to the door. "Now you need to skedaddle while I feed my daughter."

Jensen followed Roark into the hall. Stood for a moment, considering him. "You're a good man, Roark. Everybody can see that but you." He clamped him on the shoulder. "I have experience in this department. You gotta trust the girl." He gestured with his head toward the room. "Mine— and yours."

Oh, how he wanted to lean into Jensen's words.

But yes, if he wanted to win the girl, she had to see all of him.

Amelia *knew,* and the feeling of it, the immense peace of deciding, settled into her bones, could make her strong.

Brave.

Even brave enough to break Seth's heart.

It had never been her intention to hurt him, to destroy the life he'd planned for her. She simply couldn't have predicted falling in love with Roark not once, but twice. The European Roark, Mr. 007, the spy who decided to also be a lumberjack.

She'd made Seth no real promises, although their three years of dating in high school could be a sort of pledge.

But not all the way into the future.

This, tonight, was the future. She stood in front of the mirror, wearing a long-sleeved teal dress that turned her auburn hair nearly copper. She'd tried it up, then down, and decided to pull it into a loose ponytail. Added flats for sailing and a white sweater, and she recognized the girl who roamed the streets of Prague in search of the perfect shot.

She grabbed her camera case, stuck it in her backpack, and headed downstairs.

Roark was in the kitchen, listening to her father, something serious by their solemn expressions. He looked up when she appeared at the top of the stairs.

And his smile could stop the world on its axis, scatter a girl's thoughts.

"You clean up well," she said. "No longer the lumberjack." He wore a pair of dark trousers, a blue sweater over a white oxford. His dark hair curled behind his ears, and he was tan from a week of working in the late-afternoon sun.

More, the hours practicing his hot saw, his

chopping techniques, and the two-man bucksaw had added bulk to his shoulders, carving out the muscles in his biceps, his torso.

Yeah, he cleaned up well.

"Right here—" he pointed to his heart—"deep inside, I'm still a grizzly bear."

"Sure you are," she said.

John held out his hand, and Roark shook it. Amelia frowned at the exchange. But then Roark crooked his arm toward her and winked. "Your yacht awaits."

"Really? I think it's more of a fishing schooner," she said as he led her out to his car. The question of how a man who drove a used and rather unimpressive Ford Focus could afford a three-hour twilight cruise on the harbor had her wishing he'd just ordered her pizza.

She wasn't a fancy girl, didn't need a fuss.

Although, as he drove them to the harbor, helped her out of the car and across the dock, she could admit she appreciated the effort.

It confirmed everything she'd finally let herself believe. Not a fling. And the way he'd let her inside over the past month, really let her take a good look, only made her realize that no, she hadn't been foolish to fall for him.

Just to run away.

The three-masted schooner, painted a rich green with crimson sails, listed against the dock.

"Your carriage."

She laughed but took his hand as he helped her aboard and settled her on a bench in the back. Two crewmen welcomed her, then untied the *Fossegrim* from the dock.

The sun hung low, just over the horizon, rays reaching out into the mottled lavender clouds like the arms of heaven, the brilliant orb cutting a swath of fire over the lake, spreading out molten lava across the placid surface, spent after the storm. A balmy, sweet wind ruffled the sails.

Amelia lifted her camera.

"Not much wind tonight. We'll have to motor out of the harbor," the skipper said.

Amelia settled back into the cushions and held on to the rail as the skipper cast them off. Roark sat beside her, his hand next to hers on the rail. Otters trailed them out, past the boulders protecting the inlet and the lighthouse jutting from shore.

Then the *Fossegrim* hit the big lake. A wind picked up out here, but not enough to do more than jostle the boat. The captain cut the motor and hoisted the sails, tying them off.

Roark produced a basket and reached inside, pulling out a bottle. "In honor of this night, I wanted to track down a bottle of Château Mukhrani. However, since you're still underage in this country—as much as it pains me to admit that—I found a beautiful gewürztraminer juice. It'll pair nicely with tonight's hors d'oeuvres."

"What is gewürztraminer juice? I can't even say it." Amelia laughed.

He took a corkscrew and began to open the bottle. "Grape juice. Not as good as the Saperavi cabernet I wanted to get you from Georgia, but we'll have it next year."

"I didn't know they had wineries in the south. I thought they were only in California."

He grinned. "No, darling. Georgia, as in the country. South of Russia. The vintage I had in mind was served to the US president during a state dinner at one of the Constantine hotels. We'll simply have to use our robust imaginations."

He finished uncorking the bottle of grape juice as the name hit a memory.

"Is that one of your family's hotels? You said you had a couple, right?"

He made a sound of assent and reached for a cabernet glass. He poured a portion for her, then a second glass for himself, and held it up. "*Na zdorovie!*" He leaned in, met her eyes. "To your health."

"And yours." She clinked his glass and allowed herself another small sip.

The schooner had turned north, sailing along the shoreline of Deep Haven. She waved to a couple standing on Artist's Point, a peninsula that jutted out from the rocks surrounding the bay. The lake washed up on the rocky island shoreline, pockets of water captured like fire in the wells of the ledge rock.

Roark unwrapped a tray of cheese from his magic picnic box. "Asiago, some Huntsman, Le Gruyère, fontina. I know these are dessert cheeses, but we'll have dinner later. For now, let's enjoy the sunset."

She took a slice of the Huntsman. It looked like a piece of layered cake: white filling, yellow encasement. "What is this?"

"It's a combination of two different English cheeses, Double Gloucester and Stilton. Eat the layers together. You'll find they're pungent and creamy in one bite."

She took a taste, let it mix together in her mouth, chased it with the juice. "Delicious. Where did you find this?"

He lifted his glass. "The important part is that you like it."

They'd rounded the point now, were heading along the shoreline, where the resort homes of families who lived in Minneapolis or Chicago and frequented only on holidays nestled.

"I've always wondered what it might be like to live in one of those grand homes." She pointed to a three-story A-frame timber house with arching windows and an expansive deck that appeared to wind around the entire structure. A boat launch onshore hosted a yacht longer than the schooner.

"A lot of worry," Roark said, and she looked at him, frowned.

"Think of it. Whenever they leave, they have to have a security system, probably a cleaning service."

"You're too practical. Think of the view you'd wake up to every morning." She turned her face to the wind and felt him move behind her, his arm circling her shoulders. She leaned against him, his chest warm.

"Is that what you want, Amelia? A house with a view?"

"I don't know. Someday, maybe." She took another bite of cheese. He always made her feel so . . . cultured. Like she might be royalty.

The sky had darkened as the sun fell away, and now, in the distance, she could just make out the sprinkle of stars. "When I was a little girl, I used to read stories of missionaries and spies. My daydream adventures were always in foreign lands."

"That's why you went to Prague."

"Yeah." She ran her finger around her juice glass. "Sometimes, recently, I've been feeling it again. That stirring for something . . . I don't know, more maybe. Like a voice deep in a place I can't quite hear is calling me."

"Are you saying you want to leave Deep Haven?"

The question lingered in the air. "I don't know."

Really, did it matter? Roark loved to travel, didn't he? He'd be the first to sign up for some adventure overseas.

And with him holding her hand, she might just make it.

The waves, slight as they were, lapped against the boat. Amelia put her feet up on the couch, letting herself lounge against Roark. He smelled of his cologne, and if she closed her eyes, she could be tucked against him as they stood at the Eiffel Tower and gazed at the city. Safe.

"I could get used to this."

He made a noise, something of agreement, perhaps, that rumbled deep inside his chest.

He said nothing more as they sailed along the shore. As his silence drew out, it began to thrum inside her.

She retraced her words and wanted to cringe. Here he'd spent who knew how much to give her a beautiful evening, and her comments felt ungrateful. Like she wanted more. She sat up, turned to him. "Roark, this is perfect. Right here, right now. But I don't need this. I would have been happy with pizza. Or homemade cheese and baloney sandwiches. As long as I was with you."

He blinked, looked away, his Adam's apple bobbing in his throat.

She longed to make it better. "I know that you are probably comparing yourself to Seth, and even my family, but I don't care that you have nothing. We . . ." She swallowed, her words suddenly too naked. "We have each other, right?"

Something enigmatic entered his eyes, and she couldn't bear the sense that she'd hurt him. So she leaned in and kissed him. He seemed surprised but in a second had woven his hand behind her neck, holding her there as he kissed her back, sweetly, the taste of grapes upon his lips.

She moved back and finally got the smile she'd hoped for. He was so handsome when he smiled, the world could stop, sing a song. "Roark . . ." She caught her lip in her teeth. "I need to tell you something."

The time seemed perfect to tell him that she'd made her choice. It had always, probably, been Roark, but seeing him tonight only reminded her of the world he'd shown her in Europe. How he'd been her hero, squiring her from one castle to the next.

And here, taking on her family and Seth, making her believe he needed her just as much as she needed him.

They were a team, she and Roark. Seth needed her to fit into his world. Roark made his world fit around her.

"Darling, I need to tell you something first."

And then it hit her. The moment with her father, the handshake.

The boat, the lavish cheese, the romantic night.

366

Roark was going to propose.

She sat up, her eyes wide, not sure—

"You can have this life," he said quietly.

He took her hand. Drew in a breath, cleared his throat. Yes, she could feel it coming. *Will you marry me?*

"I've kept a secret from you."

Oh. Uh.

"When I said my family owned hotels, I let you believe that we owned a couple."

"Okay, so it's three, right? No problem—"

He had a firm grip on her hand, his face strangely resolute. "The Constantine group owns 4,386 hotels in 91 countries. Last year we had a net revenue of 9.72 billion euros."

Amelia stared at him, the world dropping away around her. "Excuse me?"

He took another long breath, still with that hold on her hand, almost as if he were afraid.

"My uncle, Donovan St. John, is the CEO and principal stockholder, although we're a public company. When he steps down, I was—am—supposed to pick up the reins."

She tried to shake his words around in her head, find the pieces that fit. "Are you saying—?"

"I'll be quite wealthy, should I decide to helm the family business, as my uncle intends."

"Quite wealthy . . . I thought you were poor. I gave you clothes to wear. I thought . . . ." She yanked her hand away.

367

The floating puzzle pieces crashed down, fitting perfectly.

Professional student. Cultured. Paris hotel. His crazy stories about sailing and climbing a mountain and . . . "Oh, my. You *are* a playboy!"

"What?" He recoiled at her words, but she scooted away from him, the cheese and juice pitching together in her stomach, nauseating her.

"You lied to me. You really, really lied to me. This is . . . *epic* lying!"

His mouth tightened into a grim line. "I know. But I had to know if you loved me without the portfolio. And now I know—"

"But you . . . you came here. You got a job. At a coffee shop! What was that? You mocking us?"

"No! I—"

"What was with the lumberjack competition? You must have been laughing at me every moment, trying to help you defeat Seth, making me believe you were the underdog, needing my help—"

"I do need your help!" His voice echoed across the water.

"You can buy a fleet of professional birling coaches, Roark. You hardly need my help for anything."

"But that's just it, Amelia. You don't see me as a man with means—"

"Believe me, yes, I do. I see exactly who you are. And I can't believe I didn't see it sooner."

"Does it mean nothing to you that I came all the way over to America, tried to live your life? I'm the same man with or without my inheritance."

"No, you're not. Because a man without his inheritance would have no reason to lie to me. But apparently you think because you're wealthy, I can't see past that? I'm so shallow that money might speak louder than . . . honesty? Character?"

Based on his expression, that's exactly what he thought.

Perfect.

Her voice fell. "Yes, it does mean something that you came here. It means my stupidity has no borders. I can be a fool on both sides of the ocean." She was standing now, gripping the side of the boat, looking for the captain. He turned from where he stood at the helm. "Take me back to shore."

"But your cruise isn't over."

"It is over." She stared at Roark, her stomach hollowing, only horror remaining. "It's most definitely over."

Chapter 14

MAX WAS QUIETLY DYING. Not physically—not yet—but as the days had ticked down to Yulia's departure, he wondered what would kill him first: watching his wife suffer with the worst of faux smiles painted on her face, or seeing Yulia's naiveté as she wove her way into their lives, not knowing that in a few hours from now, she would be torn away from them.

"Which one do you want, Tiger?" Darek crouched at the edge of a baby gate separating them from the squirming golden retriever puppies. The litter climbed over one another, eager to reach Tiger's outstretched hand. Tiger giggled when one found his finger and started to gnaw with its sharp puppy teeth.

The tiny yips, however, made Yulia pull back, and for a moment, she turned to where Max knelt behind her and cowered into his shoulder. He put his arm around her, glanced at Darek, who shrugged.

"Shh. It's okay," Max said, drawing her close. "They won't hurt you."

In some ways, she seemed so strong, facing the sudden loss of her family without blinking. Yes, she'd known them only for a week, their trip to the north shore having been a celebration of her arrival stateside. Still, she seemed more bonded with the Christiansens than she had with her former adoptive family.

Probably he could blame Grace's pampering, the endless batches of pancakes, cookies, pies, and cinnamon rolls the little girl helped make. Ingrid had even sewn Yulia her own apron, with pink ruffles and a giant pocket in front. She now pulled up a stool every time Grace entered the kitchen.

Max could also blame himself for Yulia's new culinary skills. After he'd cleaned the walleye, she'd helped him bread it, and they fried it up. Then he'd made homemade steak fries and let her shake the bag of seasoning.

It turned into a sort of dance, thanks to the local radio show, and apparently started a tradition because now whenever the music played, she leaped into his arms and expected him to do a clumsy waltz around the room.

Which he didn't mind.

Especially when Grace looked at him with a shine of approval in her eyes.

He could also blame Ingrid for hauling out all the old picture books that he'd started reading aloud to Yulia. Not that she understood, but she seemed to like the pictures and settled upon *The Story about Ping* and *Go, Dog. Go!* as her favorites. Which he now had memorized. But he wouldn't exactly complain about whiling away his evenings with her on his lap, her head on his shoulder as she dropped off into an exhausted slumber.

She smelled like talcum powder and fresh laundry, and although clearly she had decided not to speak, her giggles sweetened the air and turned the clouds to sun.

Now, as the puppies yipped, she trembled in his

arms. "Yulia. Sweetie. It's okay. They won't hurt you."

Darek scooped one up under its belly and held it out to Tiger, who approached the animal. It licked his face, and he backed away, laughing. "It kissed me!"

Yulia looked up, her brown eyes big.

Max gestured to Darek, who handed him the puppy. About a month old, the animal wriggled its entire body, writhing to get away. Max held it to his chest, cupping his other hand over the body to soothe the pup. He got the puppy to settle down, then told Yulia, "You can pet him." He kept his voice soft, his body still.

She reached out her hand, two fingers touching the puppy's back. The animal curled its head, trying to lick her.

She yanked her hand away.

"He won't hurt you. He's just a baby." How much she understood, he couldn't know, but maybe his tone bore enough calm for her to reach out again. This time she touched the pup's nose, giggled when he licked her fingertips. She glanced at Max, her eyes brightening, and he nodded.

She touched the puppy again, running her hand down its head, then moved closer to Max, still giggling.

"I don't know, Max. I think you have a new member of your family."

For a second, Darek's words stopped him cold. What? No, he wasn't—

"Grace would love a puppy. She's mentioned it at least twice since I said Tiger was picking from the litter."

Oh. Right. Max manufactured a smile, something easy, as if Darek's words didn't still have a vise grip on his heart.

Because, for a second, a long second, even after Darek clarified, the image of Yulia in their lives lingered. Her laughter, that sweet smile, the way she looked at him with so much . . . trust, maybe. Or adoration?

No. It wouldn't work. Couldn't work. They weren't ready. And despite Grace's tears at the thought of Yulia returning to Ukraine, she hadn't mentioned adopting her, not once. As if she, too, knew it wasn't quite time to add to their family.

Someday. Not now. But soon, before his health started to take up too much room in their lives.

Tiger had already picked out a different pup— bigger, rounder. "This one, Dad. I think his name is Raphael."

"Why not Butch or Duke?"

"Dad. It's after the TMNTs."

When Darek raised an eyebrow, Max shook his head. "Dude. Teenage Mutant Ninja Turtles."

"Right. I feel so old," Darek said. "Okay, pal. We'll put your name on this one. You can pick him up in a couple weeks."

Max stood to put the puppy back in the cage, but Yulia grabbed ahold of his arm, shaking her head. He paused. "What is it, honey?"

She bit her lip, pressed close to the puppy, then put her head down on its back.

Darek waited, frowning. Max's throat turned thick, itchy. "Sweetie, we have to give him back. He doesn't belong to us."

Her bottom lip began to tremble, and he felt it like claws raking over his heart. Because his very words tore through him.

We have to give him back. He doesn't belong to us.

He took a breath as he put the puppy in the pen. Yulia stood silently, fighting her trembling lip. Then she turned away and headed to the door.

"I think she's mad at you," Darek said, pulling out his checkbook for the breeder.

"I'm mad at me," Max said, not sure exactly why.

They got in Darek's truck and headed to the resort, Tiger talking with wild hand gestures, and without pause, to Yulia in the backseat.

"You okay?" Darek said quietly to Max.

"Yeah. Why?"

"I was just thinking that *you* might be thinking about the fact that Yulia is leaving today. And that you happen to be kind of attached to her."

Max looked away. "She's cute. I've done my part in trying to take her off Grace's hands while they were packing her things. It's going to be hard enough on her—seeing them pack up her stuff will only make it worse."

"Mmm-hmm," Darek said.

"What?"

"Nothing. It's just that you, of all people, don't have to live by the rules. You get to bend them. And nothing says that you can't adopt a six-year-old a month after you're married."

Crazily, Max's eyes burned. "Yeah, well, I . . ." Shoot, his voice sounded wrecked. He swallowed. Cleared his throat. "We're not ready. Maybe someday but . . . not now."

"Yeah. Totally get that." Darek drove for a while, then said, "When will you be ready exactly?"

"Shut up."

A soft chuckle on Darek's side of the car died as they pulled up to the lodge. As Max saw Grace in the driveway, talking to a woman with short black hair, in khakis and low heels, holding Yulia's new duffel bag.

Darek put the truck in park, glanced at Max, then at Yulia. She danced one of Tiger's Ninja Turtle action figures up and down her leg.

Mercifully, Darek said nothing. But they'd all known that this day would come and had savored every moment with Yulia.

So why did it feel as if a hand had reached in, grabbed ahold of his lungs? He got out and opened the door for Yulia, who slid out of the cab and almost instinctively took Max's hand.

Heaven help him, he held on.

Grace met his eyes as he walked over. She stood with her arms wrapped around her waist, her eyes hollow and red, but she smiled, even while clearly fighting tears.

The adoption coordinator turned, and in that instant, Yulia froze. Just stopped walking, her breath catching, her hand tightening in Max's.

The woman crouched. "Hey there, Yulia. Remember me? Martha?"

Yulia began to tremble.

It cost Max everything to crouch down beside her. To pull her into his arms. "Shh. It's going to be okay." Except it wasn't, was it? In a few days' time, they'd put her on a plane and ship her back to Ukraine, where she'd wait, hope, probably in futility, for another family to adopt her.

Oh, he couldn't think about that. Or the way she almost mechanically bent into him, stiff, already withdrawing.

See, this was why he just couldn't believe in happiness. Because it always turned on him, betrayed him.

Especially when he wasn't looking.

He had no more words for her. Nothing to soothe her, because inexplicably his own heart seemed to be serrated. Especially when Grace touched his shoulder.

And then Yulia pushed away. She let Grace hug her, almost wooden in her response. Martha took her hand, leading her to the car.

Grace's quick, hiccuping intake of breath nearly did Max in. He straightened and searched her face. "Grace," he said raggedly. "We can't . . . We just got married. We're not ready."

She said nothing, just pressed her hand to her mouth. Nodded.

He had to be right, didn't he? Because two weeks ago the thought of adopting a child, any child, had seemed almost a crime when he stared down the road to his future. But what about right now? The years he had that would be good? Full of joy? Wouldn't they be even better if he had not only Grace but . . . ?

"We can't—"

He was about to say it—*We can't let her go*—when suddenly he heard a cry behind him. High and broken and dissecting the wretched silence of his own fear.

"Papa!" Yulia yanked her hand from the social worker and whirled around. Tears dragged down her cheeks.

"Papa," she said again, a whisper.

Max couldn't stop himself. Didn't even want to. Just crouched and opened his arms, and Yulia launched herself toward him.

She hit him so hard, it nearly knocked him over, but he swept her up, holding her tiny body to himself as she sobbed, *"Nyet. Pshaulshta, nyet."*

He heard it himself. *No. Please, no.*

Martha set the duffel in the car. Gave him a pitying look even as she headed over to him.

He held out his hand. "No . . ."

"Max. Grace. I understand. Of course you've bonded with this child. But you're not even the foster parents here—your parents are. You have no right to Yulia."

"We have every right," Max said, finding his voice again. He set Yulia down, and she ran to Grace, clutched her around the waist. By the look in his wife's eye, Martha didn't have a hope of prying Yulia away.

Max stepped in front of his girls, the eerie sense of protectiveness surging through him. "We love her. And she needs a family. She needs us. We're her family." He steeled himself, just in case the emotions wanted to work their way up his throat. "She doesn't have to go back to Ukraine. We could—we will adopt her."

He felt Grace's hand in his, and he curled his fingers around hers. "Show me what we have to do."

Martha sighed, her lips tight. "It'll take time. And she can't live with you while you apply for adoption. You'll have home studies and you might have to be approved by the Ukrainian governmental agency. I don't know, Max. I do know that Yulia has to come with me today if you have any hope of adopting her in the future."

She could have taken a knife to his chest and it would have hurt less.

Martha extricated a distraught Yulia from Grace's arms. When Yulia fought her, Max had to swoop her up, hold her against himself. Soothe her.

"Shh." He put his forehead to hers. "Yulia, I will find you. You will come back. I won't let you go; I promise."

He didn't know if she understood, but he prayed it, repeated it, and gritted his jaw against the tears that rimmed his eyes as he himself put her in the car.

"*Nyet, Papa. Nyet.*"

He closed the door on her, her eyes so big, so hurt, that he wanted to howl.

Grace took his hand, probably holding him up, as Martha drove away, Yulia's little hand on the window.

But Max heard her words echoing over and over inside, along with his own brutal cries. *Nyet, Papa. Nyet.*

"I clearly need a Mohawk and more flannel. Whose idea was this?" Roark held his free Flapjack Festival T-shirt to his chest, his prize of entry into this blasted event that he should have backed out of a week ago.

Right about the time Amelia had slammed the

379

door in his face, left him standing in the dirt where he'd started two months ago.

"It was my idea, and stop your yappin'. You're going to do just fine." Darek led him away from the sign-in booth. One look at the competition and Roark knew the train had truly left the station. He was in for a right walloping.

"Do you see that man over there? Roughly the size of a barge?" Roark pointed to a man who looked like he might eat a full moose for dinner. He had a handlebar mustache; his red-and-black flannel sleeves were cut off at the shoulders, revealing the kind of muscle a man only got from dragging real logs around in the woods. Not the pitiful weights Roark pumped on a regular basis at the gym. "There are women here whose arms are bigger than my legs."

"Calm down, 007," Jensen said as he approached, holding two fish burgers. He gave one to Roark. "Have a local specialty. You'll feel better."

He made a face. "Please, have mercy."

"I'll take that action," Darek said. "How long before he makes his official appearance?"

"What?" Roark said.

"You'll be introduced on the grandstand with the other competitors," Jensen said. "In about fifteen minutes."

A specimen to be mocked. "No. That's not happening." Roark was already searching for an exit from the crowded park, past the grandstand thick with spectators wearing novelty hats with axes in the top and shirts with Stihl and Husqvarna logos.

Too many appeared as if they could wrestle Sasquatch and win.

Main Street had become a carnival, with cheese curds, Chinese food, gyros, and popcorn stands all muddled together in a collision of smells that could turn his stomach. Face and henna painters decorated the cheeks and arms of youngsters, and a small carnival of kiddie rides played a tinny tune from a nearby parking lot.

Smack in the middle was a tent with endless rounds of flapjacks sizzling on a griddle the size of a pickup. The feast spiced the air with the smell of bacon grease and sweet maple syrup.

For the lumberjack games, organizers had brought in a pool of water for the birling competition, and a stage hosted the giant logs for the hot saw. On another platform, smaller logs waited for the standing chop.

Away from the food vendors, the air smelled of fresh-cut wood. Music from a nearby band, the Millers, a group of Celtic players, drifted on the breeze.

"Whoa there," Jensen said. "Don't disappear on us. I see that look on your face. It's done. And it's already official. It became official the minute you didn't cut and run after Amelia left you on the front porch."

Darek took a bite of the fish sandwich. "You should have seen him, Jens. White as a sheet." He looked at Roark. "When Amelia came in, I have to admit, I've never seen her as truly angry at anyone as she was at you."

Roark glanced at Jensen. "I blame you and Claire," he said. "I do believe this is a grand plot to make me look a fool in front of the entire community, get me right good for—"

"Lying to us? Acting like you're some poor bloke in need of a job and a roof over his head?" Darek took another bite of his fish burger, glanced at Jensen. "Billions?"

"9.72."

"Stop," Roark said.

"I'll bet you have a Porsche, don't you?" Darek said.

"I need something stiff to drink."

"Or an Aston Martin."

"Please." The oily odor of the fish burger had started to make him nauseated. "Take that thing away from me."

"Indeed. Only filet mignon for Your Royal Highness."

Roark shot Darek a look.

"He's a little sensitive about the royal thing, Darek," Jensen said, hiding a smile.

"I'm not royal. And right now, I believe I've flipped my lid to think I could do this." He started toward his flat.

"Hey, Roark," said a girl who passed him. He recognized her as one of the regulars—tall vanilla latte.

"Colleen Decker," she said when he didn't respond. "Are you competing?" She indicated the T-shirt in his hands.

He wanted to rip the blasted thing to shreds.

"I haven't quite decided."

"Oh, you should! It's great fun. And stick around for the Sawdust Sweeties pageant." She winked and headed toward the mini donut stand, giggling when she caught up with girlfriends who gave him a long once-over.

"Roark!"

Roark ignored Darek's voice and kept walking. Jensen caught up. "Dude. Don't chicken out."

That stopped him. "I'm not chickening out—"

Darek came up to him. "Yeah, actually, you are. We train for three weeks, I bust my backside this week teaching you how to logroll, wear myself out in the double buck, trying to get you to keep up, and you're walking?" He blew out a breath. "I admit it, I didn't see that coming. Not after everything you've done to show up—and stay—in Amelia's life."

"She hasn't talked to me for a week. And she's not going to. Apparently I'm right back where I started."

" 'I'm *rich.*' That's not so hard to say." This from Darek.

Roark's mouth tightened.

"But here's what's harder. Sticking around. Because if you really love her, be a fool for her. She wants the guy who took a job pouring coffee just to be in her life. I think she loves that guy; she just has to figure out how to get past the one who keeps getting in the way."

"The rich one, from Europe?"

"The one who thinks he has to lie to get her to like him. I think the real Roark St. John is the guy who helped rescue Boy Scouts and learned how to stay on a log, the guy who isn't afraid to fight for the girl, even if it means he's about to get chippered—if it means helping a girl realize she wasn't a fool to fall in love with him twice."

Amelia's words floated back to Roark, her voice rough-edged, her eyes flush with tears. *It means my stupidity has no borders. I can be a fool on both sides of the ocean.*

He'd wanted to be sick at the thought of how much he'd hurt her.

Darek held out the shirt, and for a second, the gesture brought back John's words the night he'd taken Amelia out on the boat.

I was wrong about you. Thank you for sticking around, for showing us you were worthy of her.

Darek waited. Jensen, who'd finished his fish burger, wadded the wrapper into a ball.

Roark heard the announcer call the contestants onstage.

"You could at least wish me the best of British." He headed toward the stage, his shirt tight in his grip. The other contestants had already pulled theirs on, but he marched onstage, too wound up to comply.

Even when Seb, as mayor, took the stage. He glanced at Roark, smiled. Roark offered him a thin smile in return.

Seb welcomed everyone, gave a rundown of the weekend's events, starting with tonight's street dance, the classic car show, the pageant, tomorrow night's Flapjack Ball, the chainsaw carving contest, and then the lineup of lumberjack sports—the hot saw, the chop, the birling, and the double buck. "Top scorer overall wins the Flapjack Festival title. Let's meet our competitors."

He introduced the women first, six competitors who ranged from women who could bench-press Roark to lean athletes with sinewed arms.

Then the men. Seb started at the top, alphabetically, and the men stepped up, some of them waving to the crowd, pointing at sweethearts as the applause rose and fell with each competitor.

And then Roark spotted Amelia. The fact that she'd come rocked him. He hadn't really contemplated what he might do if Amelia appeared in the audience. Her eyes were hidden behind sunglasses, her hair up in a ponytail and threaded through the hole at the back of her baseball hat.

She wore a black shirt, a pair of ripped jeans, and looked about as American as a girl could get.

He ached, every inch of him, to replay the past month—no, the past nine months. More, at once he didn't care, not really, if she loved him for himself or his money. He just wanted her. Wanted her laughter, her solid belief that he could do anything. Save her from thugs in Prague, teach her wine pairings, and yeah, also win a stupid log-chopping competition.

He wanted her smile. On him. For him. Forever.

"Unbelievably, folks, our next contestant hails from . . . Europe. Where is it, Roark?"

"Brussels," he said quietly to Seb, his eyes on Amelia. Her mouth had tightened almost imperceptibly. But Roark saw it, and his heart sank.

Clearly he'd harbored a sort of crazy hope that she might be impressed. *Are you man enough to show up and stay in the fight, even if you could lose?*

He wanted to be.

He stayed right there, rooted to the stage, as Seb announced his name.

A cheer went up from the audience—probably Darek and Jensen—but to his surprise, it was followed by a rising cascade of applause. He recognized Colleen Decker and her mates, as well as Kathy, his boss from the coffee shop, and Jake, the pilot, plus a few other regulars he'd managed to befriend.

In fact, he'd received just as much applause as any of the locals.

Amelia shifted. Beside her, Vivie stuck two fingers in her mouth and let out a whistle.

Roark lifted a hand, waved, and it elicited a few more cheers.

"I guess we have some BBC fans here," Seb said.

Roark couldn't help but smile.

"And our last contestant, a veteran of the Flapjack winner's circle, a logger by legacy, our own Seth Turnquist!"

Applause, of course, which Roark couldn't help comparing to his own. When Amelia didn't cheer for Seth either, Roark tried not to find satisfaction in that.

Until Seth stepped forward and took the microphone from Seb's hand. "Hey, everyone. I just want to say that this year, my win is for my girl, Amelia Christiansen." He pointed to her, and the crowd erupted.

The earth could have opened up, swallowed Roark in a gulp, when the smallest of smiles went up Amelia's face.

Seth handed Seb back the microphone. Seb closed the announcements. Then the competitors left the stage.

Roark stood watching as groupies surrounded Seth, dearly hoping Amelia wasn't among them.

"Did you hear the crowd? They love you!" This

from Jensen, who came up to him with a closed fist.

Roark ignored the fist bump. "What is he thinking, dedicating the competition to her?"

"I think he's going for the win, dude," Darek said.

That was all it took. Roark marched over to Seth, weaving through the crowd right to where the lumberjack stood, a few feet from Amelia.

"What?" Seth snapped, obviously annoyed at being torn away from his groupies.

"You're on," Roark said.

Seth frowned. "What?"

"The wager. You win, you get her. I win, you walk away."

Seth let out a harsh laugh. "Right. Okay, dude. May the best man win."

Roark walked toward Darek and Jensen, who stood there, nonplussed. He pulled out his wallet. "I think I'll have one of those fish burgers."

He smoothed the fiver between two fingers, then turned to Darek. "By the way, the car you were looking for is a Ferrari 599 GTB Fiorano."

Jensen grinned.

"Oh, he so has this," Roark heard Darek say as he headed to the fish stand.

Yes. Yes, he did.

Chapter 15

"JUST ONE MORE TIME, for me. How rich is he?"

"Oh, Vivie, give it a break." Amelia sat balancing a cup of bracing coffee between her hands as the sun turned the shiny sawdust produced by the chain saws into a rainbow of light. Vivie sat beside her, wearing a pair of overalls, her costume for today's talent show and pageant interview on the main stage.

"I'm just sayin', he's only gotten better-looking since he picked up an ax. If you're still mad at him, I'd start looking at the big picture. Brains, brawn, and bucks. And please, let's not forget the accent. What's the question here?"

"He lied." Amelia took a sip of her coffee as Vivie waved to a couple contestants, gearing up for their turn on the hot saw. And yes, her gaze lingered, just a moment, on Roark.

He wore Casper's steel-toed boots, a pair of faded jeans he probably borrowed from Darek, and the black Flapjack Festival T-shirt that sculpted every inch of his torso, reminding her exactly how it had felt to lean against him in the schooner. A gimme cap sat backward on his head so his curls fed out under the brim, behind his ears.

He probably smelled manly.

Shoot.

But that's just it, Amelia. You don't see me as a man with means—

Funny thing was, right now she could agree. She never saw him as a man of means. Just the guy who showed up in her life to make her believe in herself.

She blew out a breath, looked away. He was a liar. And the fact that he was still mocking her by competing had her wanting to run. But she'd promised Seth she'd stay.

Seth, who'd found her last night and asked her to dance. Who'd wrapped her in his arms and told her that he'd win today for her, and she'd never have to worry about Roark again.

What, because Seth planned on humiliating him?

"Does he own a yacht?"

"Vivie!"

"Or a palace?"

"I don't know, okay? Maybe. I googled him finally—something I probably should have done at the beginning—and Roark St. John is all over the Internet. Pictures of him at Eton and the University of St Andrews—"

"Isn't that where Prince William went to school?"

"It is, and for all I know, he had tea with the queen and bested the future king in polo. And yes, he played rugby and rowed, just like he said.

Then I looked up their company, Constantine Worldwide, and they do have four thousand-some hotels. And are worth something like nine billion euros. But the Roark I know drives a Ford Focus and lives above the coffee shop as a pauper."

"Claws in, sheesh. I was just curious."

"Yeah, well . . . I'm trying not to think about it." Amelia blinked back the sting in her eyes. Because seeing how amazingly rich Roark was only did strange things to her. Like made her want to weep for a guy who felt like he couldn't be loved if she knew he was rich. Or the guy who had lost everything, twice. And the guy who felt as if God had abandoned him—no, *cursed* him, to use his words.

So much for trying to scrape him from her mind.

Please, let this day get over fast.

"Here he comes! Pick up your camera!" Vivie grabbed her arm as Roark took the stage, fitted his ear protection, and grabbed the chain saw, one of Darek's with the engine taken and modified from his old snowmobile. He'd no doubt tuned it to perfect racing condition. Roark and another contestant—thankfully, not Seth— would compete for times, sawing the horizontal log through from the top down, then from the bottom up, keeping the cuts straight, then down a third time, for three "cookies."

She reluctantly centered Roark in the viewfinder, just on the wild chance he didn't make a gigantic fool of himself and she could sell a few shots to the paper.

Roark pulled the string, starting the saw. To her surprise, he handled it like a man who'd spent his life in the woods.

Good job, Darek.

Roark positioned the saw, revved it. Didn't even look her direction.

The gun went off and he dove into the cut, starting over the back, just like Darek taught him, then slowly, steadily pulling the saw through the cut. If he came off max power, even for a second, he'd lose momentum.

He leveled out as he reached the bottom, and the cookie fell off in a solid thump. Without breaking, he started up from the bottom, in closer at the front, evening out on the back side as he came up to the top.

"He's ahead!" Vivie said, grabbing Amelia's arm. She hadn't noticed the cheering increasing as Roark ripped through the top, but when the second cookie fell, the roar began to swell.

Sweat ran down his face, and the sight of him, fighting through the log, his jaw tight, his legs straining at his jeans, sawdust layering the fine hair on his arms . . .

Who was this man?

The final cookie dropped off, and Roark cut the power to his saw, dropped it, breathing hard.

His competitor had just started his third cut.

"He beat Seth."

"What?" Amelia looked at Vivie, who had the score sheet from her program open.

"By 2.3 seconds. He beat him."

"No, he didn't."

But yeah, as Roark jumped off the platform into the high fives and fist bumps of Darek and Jensen, it appeared Roark, the Brit, had bested Seth. Especially when she caught a glimpse of Seth, his eyes dark on Roark, a moment before he turned and stalked away from the audience.

Amelia couldn't help a strange surge of pride. Especially when she scrolled through the series of shots she'd taken.

The man actually looked like a bona fide lumberjack.

"C'mon. Seth is chopping next."

Right. Amelia scrambled off the benches and headed over to the platform for the standing block chop. On the way, she and Vivie picked up a bag of cotton candy, sharing it between them.

"I have to run after this and get ready for my talent," Vivie said.

"Which is?"

"Guess." She sighed big. " 'Do you know what I intend? I intend to be a queen. When I grow up, I'm going to be the biggest queen there ever was, and I'll live in a big palace, and when I go out in my coach, all the people will wave and I will shout at them, and . . . and . . . in the summertime I will go to my summer palace and I'll wear my crown—'"

"*You're a Good Man, Charlie Brown.* Senior year."

Vivie winked.

"You were the perfect Lucy."

"If I had half the talent for acting that you have for photography, I wouldn't have to try out for a silly pageant. I'd be in Hollywood right now, reading scripts with Chris Pine. Please tell me you're going to win."

She'd thrown herself into finding the perfect shots this week for the finale in an effort to keep her mind off Roark and his revelation.

Here she was, trying to win a paltry five thousand dollars. He was probably laughing at her behind her back.

Laughing at all of them, maybe. It made her feel small and simple, her life in Deep Haven, their resort, provincial.

Once again, he'd humiliated her. "I hope so. I made it to the finals, and I have until Monday to submit three final shots. I'm not sure what it is that America loves about my photos—"

"It's your subject matter. And speaking of, the mighty Seth just picked up his ax." She hooked Amelia's arm and pulled her over to the standing chop.

Seth lined up, his stance textbook, something

394

she knew from all those hours watching Darek once upon a time. He competed for time against a burly man who looked like a Wisconsinite.

When the gun sounded, Seth slammed his ax into the wood, two blows to the bottom. Looking like Thor with his golden mane gleaming in the sunlight. Two more blows into the top, and a perfect trapezoid wedge chipped out.

He had the shoulders of a lineman. Sturdy, solid. The kind of man she could depend on. Who would never leave her, never lie to her. Husband material. Father material. A happy life in Deep Haven material.

His fourth and fifth chops took out the rest of the wood on the front, and he stepped around the back, just ahead of his competitor.

He wore jeans, a white shirt, the arms ripped at the shoulders, and red suspenders. And he took the top of the block off in four more blows. It went skittering into the audience, who roared.

Vivie recorded his time. "Twenty-eight seconds. Not a world record but it's good."

"It's fantastic. Darek got a 29.3 once and we had to call him Mighty Dare for a week."

Vivie laughed. "I gotta run and get ready for the show. Here's my gift to you. Words to live by."

"Yeah?"

" 'I forgive you, Roark.' " Vivie squeezed her hand and climbed off the bleachers.

Amelia watched as two more competitors came

up, both of them nearing Seth's time, neither beating it. Then she spied Roark. He stood with Darek and Jensen, head down, getting final words.

Her brother's arms hung on Roark's shoulders as if they were in a pregame huddle or praying, even. She had to admit that her anger cooled enough for her to feel the stirring she'd felt in Roark's arms on the boat. Staring at the stars with a sense of electricity or anticipation, as if all might be awaiting her, just behind a veil.

Waiting for . . . what?

Two more competitors and her breakfast donut had turned into a ball in her stomach.

Especially when, as Roark stepped up to the block, Seth slid onto the bench beside her. "Hey, beautiful."

She looked at him. He hadn't shaved today, the finest layer of reddish-blond whiskers adding to the lumberjack aura.

"You were amazing out there."

"Best time yet."

She nodded, trying not to glance at Roark. But the gun sounded and she couldn't help it.

He lined up with his back to her, corded muscles rippling in his arms as he threw his first blow. It sank deep, but it took him a second to yank it free.

The next, an underhand blow, sank farther, a better hit.

He raised his ax for a down hit, and to her horror, it skimmed down the front of the log, the angle off. The crowd gasped as the blade plunged into the deck, narrowly missing his leg. Thanks to Darek for teaching him the right stance.

But Roark looked shaken.

Darek yelled at him from the side of the stage, and Roark looked over at him, nodded. He picked up the ax, blew out a breath, and brought it down.

A perfect blow, and he yanked it out, down, around, and back into the wood. A beautiful trapezoid chinked out of the wood. He added another up hit, two more down hits, and the wedge came out.

His competitor had moved to the other side, his hits hard, but his V seemed lopsided.

Roark lined up, wood chipped on his shirt, and drove in an up hit, then another.

Then he rose up as tall as he could and brought the ax down, severing the top from the wood.

It skidded off just as his competitor finished his log.

Amelia glanced at Seth, saw his mouth in a tight, dark line. But it vanished as he glanced at her. "Want a fish burger?"

No. What she wanted was a chance to talk to Roark. To find out exactly why he'd decided to stick around and challenge Seth. Did he seriously think that he could ever belong here, in this tiny town?

And what was he doing with her? He'd dated a supermodel. Amelia had seen her photo online—Francesca, a tall, shapely blonde who belonged on magazine covers.

Roark's time came up, and Seth let out a breath. Thirty-six seconds.

"C'mon," he said, taking her hand, and she slid out of the bleachers with him, almost out of habit.

They ate their fish burgers while watching Vivie recite her monologue, then answer her interview questions.

She smiled at her audience, pretty, poised. Quintessential Vivien.

Mona Michaels, owner of the local bookstore, played the role of moderator. "Okay, Vivien. Tell us this. When is the last time you failed? How did you handle it?"

Vivien blinked, and Amelia couldn't tell for sure, but it seemed her smile faded for a moment. Then she sighed. "Actually, it was quite recent. I dropped out of acting school. Something I always longed to do, and I blew it because I was afraid. I . . ." She swallowed. "I actually ran off the stage during an important audition, got into my friend's car, and drove all the way back to Minnesota."

Amelia stared at her, unmoving.

"So I guess the answer is, I came home. But you see, that's the thing about home. It's here. It will always be here. It's not failure to come home and regroup. I've discovered that coming home helps you remember exactly who you are and what you want. Home gives you the courage to leave again. At least, that's my theory because I'm not giving up. Hollywood or bust." She winked, and when she did, it landed on Amelia.

A few cheers went up as Mona moved on to the next contestant. But beside Amelia, Seth asked, "Did you know she dropped out of acting school?"

"No." She closed her eyes. Poor Vivie. But she got it. She'd wanted to hide when she got home too. But coming home had healed her. And was starting to show her that maybe she didn't have to stay.

"I gotta go. Birling next. *Brr.*"

Amelia laughed. "Good luck." She got up, wandered over to where Vivie stood offstage. Wheedling in past a couple organizers, she caught Vivie in a hug. "You should have told me," she said.

"Aw, I . . . was ashamed. Here I was, acting like I was a big shot, and I was really just a failure."

"Neither of us are failures. We're regrouping."

Vivie nodded. She looked over Amelia's shoulder. "Is that Roark up on that log?"

"No, it's Seth—"

But Vivie took her by the shoulders, turned her.

And her heart stopped for a second as she watched Seth climb up opposite Roark.

"Oh no."

"Yeah, this isn't going to be pretty."

Vivie took her hand, and they cut through the crowd as the two balanced, duking it out. Seth had changed, wore a pair of athletic shorts, a T-shirt. Roark wore what looked like biking pants, a sleeveless shirt. And a pair of soccer cleats, which looked new.

Seth had always been clumsy, no finesse when it came to birling. Roark, on the other hand, had grace, and he toyed with Seth, rolling forward, then slowing, jerking the log, and rolling back. Twice he kicked the water, a ploy that worked the second time.

Seth tumbled off hard into the bath.

Roark jumped down, rolled the log over to the edge of the pool.

The officials held the log as the competitors climbed up, using poles to push out from the edge. They let go, balanced, and the gun went off.

Almost instantly, Seth jerked the log hard, and Roark went down with a splash.

"Oh, my," Amelia said. "He looks mad."

"Seth?"

"Roark." Indeed, Roark came up hot, shaking his hair from his face, huffing out a breath.

"Just one more, Roark. You got this." Darek, from the far end of the pool.

Seth looked at him, frowned. "Thanks a lot, Dare."

Amelia stepped a little behind Vivie.

Roark and Seth climbed up. This time, Roark was ready when Seth tried to jerk the log. He stayed on and countered, pressing the log backward fast, running in micro, almost tiptoe steps. Seth clomped on the far end, low in the water. Slowly he took control, decreasing the speed, moving the log the opposite direction. Roark now ran backward, his arms trying not to flail.

Keep low; keep your center. Amelia let out a breath and realized she'd been holding it.

Suddenly Seth slipped. His foot went out, and he kicked the log. It jerked out from under him and he went flying. But the action toppled Roark, who hit the water first.

No.

Roark came up and almost instantly turned to the officials. Amelia wanted to scream at the injustice when they gave the win to Seth.

As Roark climbed out, Jensen met him with a towel. Seth's pal Sammy Johnson stood at his ready.

"Wanna stick around for Seth's next round?"

Amelia sighed. "I should."

But really she wanted to follow Jensen and Darek as they wandered toward the food shacks to grab a bite, rest.

Relaunch for the final event, the double buck.

No, what she *really* wanted was to tell Roark that it didn't matter who won. That he'd shown her exactly the kind of man he was—the kind of man who kept his promises, even in the face of defeat. And apparently he'd been right when he said *extreme* didn't begin to describe what he'd do to win her back.

"I have to go find out who made the finals in the pageant," Vivie said, squeezing her hand.

Amelia climbed onto the bleachers, cheering as Seth fought through the next round but was handily beaten by a wiry man from Duluth.

He'd still earned enough points to rise against Roark, at least on the leaderboard.

Roark couldn't believe he hadn't done something stupid, like chop off his foot or saw off his leg. His name hung on the leaderboard, three notches below Seth's, thanks to his fall in the pool. But he'd seen Amelia watching him. Cheering for him. And angry for him when he went into the drink.

He planned on winning. Because there was no way he was walking away from her. Not when he saw that expression on her face. She still loved him; he just knew it.

Tossing his wet clothes into a rucksack, he climbed onto a picnic bench and cracked open the cold Coke he'd purchased from a vendor.

He drank it half down before Darek stopped him. "You need water, not soda." He grabbed Jensen's bottled water. Handed it to Roark.

"Hey."

"It's for the win. Go get him one of those corn on the cobs." He motioned Jensen toward the stand.

"I'm not your lackey."

"Our boy needs sustenance."

Actually, Roark couldn't eat a thing, but with the double buck still an hour away, maybe he needed somewhere to put all this adrenaline.

"I should have won that."

Darek raised an eyebrow. "Seriously, the fact that you stayed on and won even one round was—"

"No, I can do better. Have done better, against you."

"I let you, dude. Confidence building."

"Hardly. I know cheating when I see it. You were in for the win, and I sent you into the lake."

"Whatever you want to believe." Darek tossed the can into a nearby bin. "But more importantly, we gotta win that double buck. You're on the leaderboard, and whether you win or not, the key here is—"

"I gotta beat Seth."

"I was going to say that you've already earned the respect of Deep Haven. And Amelia. I saw her watching you that last round. You're golden, bro. I think you've already beaten Seth in that department."

Roark shook his head. "If I don't win, it won't matter. Because I'm an idiot."

"Let me count the ways. But seriously, why this time?"

"I wagered Seth . . . uh, well, Amelia."

Darek stared at him a long moment, then let out something that sounded remotely like laughter. "As her brother, I should probably be angry, but the very idea that either of you could think you could wager Amelia—like she isn't the most stubborn person on the planet, the one person in our family who seems to always get her own way—is downright laughable."

"I know. I . . . He just set me off."

"So drive your Ferrari over him. Don't do something like say you'll wager my sister, whatever that means."

"If he wins, I promised to leave town. And he promised to step out of the picture if I won."

"Roark, if you believe for one second that Seth would walk away from Amelia if you won this match, you are more naive than we were to think you weren't serious about Amelia. He's in this, wager or no wager, until she says no. Out loud. Until she stands up and declares you the love of her life."

Roark nodded, trying to get behind Darek's words. He picked at the label on the water bottle.

"Oh no. Don't give me a 'my word is my bond' speech. You Brits, all about honor and country."

Roark sighed.

"Okay, so it's simple. We win. We've been practicing the double buck for a week now, and if you can keep up, we got this."

"I can keep up."

Darek smiled. "When we win, do I get to drive the Ferrari?"

"Oh, for pity's sake—"

"Two corncobs and another bottled water," Jensen said, sitting down. "By the way, I think Vivie made the finals." He nodded at the judges' booth on the platform, and Roark turned to see three contestants, dressed in overalls, waving to the crowd. "I think they have to look pretty for tonight's ball."

"They're not the only ones. We'll win this thing, and then, Roark, we expect you to show up in something . . . Bond, James Bond. It's time for the true Roark St. John to come out of hiding."

If only he knew who that might be. But today, during the hot saw, during the standing chop, and even during the birling, it had all felt so . . . elemental. Good, clean fun, without the posh accoutrements of his upbringing.

Or maybe it *was* his upbringing. Simple village living, chopping coal, pumping water, fixing the car.

"C'mon, let's go check out the chain saw exhibits." Darek hauled him up before he could dwell.

They walked around the festival grounds, watching the children riding ducks on the merry-go-round, the face painters, the few vendors selling chain saw art or watercolors on swaths of birch bark. Seagulls waddled in the street, scavenging for scraps.

Chain saws buzzed in the air, which held the smell of flapjacks against sawdust, the freshness of summer. Roark finished his corn, wandered down to the harbor, watched Jake fly in and out, cutting through the indigo waves.

He wanted to stay. To build a life here. The urge could take him under, drown him with its intensity.

But not without Amelia, and he didn't know how to fix that.

"We're up, dude," Darek said behind him.

Roark tossed his water bottle in the bin as he headed toward the stage.

Working together, he and Darek would use a two-man bucksaw to cut through a twenty-inch-diameter white pine log. Apparently the best times were under ten seconds. He and Darek averaged under twenty, which he'd thought nearly miraculous but, when he watched videos on YouTube, became downright slothful.

With only eight contestants, the judges had lined up four logs across the expansive stage, each team sawing at once, three rounds for the grand finale.

Sunlight cascaded over the logs, stretching their shadows out to eternity as Roark followed Darek onto the platform, picked up his end of the saw. The crosscut saw had mean five-inch teeth, razors that tore through the wood with a violent bite.

Roark flexed his hands inside his work gloves as they settled the saw into the starting cut on the log. Two blocks of wood nailed into the platform gave his feet leverage as he stretched them out, one in front, the other in back, twice as wide as his shoulders, drawing him low to use his core and hips for maximum power.

"Rhythm," Darek said opposite him as he hunkered down. "Remember to keep it level, steady, and . . ." He grinned. "Try to keep up."

Roark heard the crowd's cheers rise around him but dared not look for Amelia.

Seth and his partner, one of the blokes Roark recognized from the gym, manned a bucksaw next to Roark and Darek. Seth faced him, of course, and sent him a grin, all grizzly teeth.

Roark ignored him. Darek pulled the saw out, maximum length toward himself, and Roark bent over, ready to draw it back.

For Amelia.

The gunshot sounded the go, and just like they'd practiced, Roark pulled back, steady, even, as Darek pushed. At the end, he powered into a push, which Darek matched. Their early practice attempts had Darek bowing the saw, pushing into the wood harder than Roark pulled, with Roark pulling up instead of bearing down into the wood, but now Roark matched Darek's speed and power. Not unlike rowing in the rhythm, only faster, brutally faster.

The cookie fell off in what seemed a blink, and he looked at the clock: 12.6 seconds.

Seth's cookie, however, had fallen off at 12.2.

Darek stood, wiped the hint of sweat from his brow. Glanced at the times as the crowd roared. Roark's heart thundered, adrenaline thick as the judges notched the next cutting mark.

Hazarding a look into the crowd, Roark didn't see Amelia.

"Ready?" Darek said, assuming his stance. This time, they started with Roark at the initial push.

He nodded, took a breath. Tensed.

At the gunshot he dove into his push, matching Darek, even perhaps besting him. He dug into Darek's pace, faster than before. Back, forth, his arms burning.

When the cookie fell, he hunched over, breathing hard.

With a time of 10.8 seconds, they'd bested Seth's team by 2 seconds.

Darek grinned, and Roark imagined he heard Amelia's cheer over the crowd noise. Sweat dribbled down his back, his heart still in his lungs.

They notched the log for the final heat.

"Under eight," Darek said, straightening, shaking out his arms. "Right?"

Roark nodded and took his position.

Under eight.

"For the win." Darek hunkered down, pulling the saw out.

The gun went off and they set a perfect rhythm, the saw biting through the log so fast, they were halfway through in seconds.

Then suddenly the saw caught.

It happened so fast, Roark didn't know who to blame. He slammed the saw forward into the push, and it bowed. He nearly went over the log but righted himself, and Darek worked it free.

He settled back into rhythm to finish the cut, but before he could cut through, the cookie broke off. Only a lip remained. One fast cut and it too fell off, but the crowd had hushed.

Clearly they'd finished their cut before the competitors, easily beating Darek's eight-second goal. The board listed their time—7.6.

Except Darek was shaking his head.

"What?"

"We broke the cut."

Roark frowned.

"We're disqualified."

Disqualified. The word landed like a punch to his sternum as Roark glanced at the leaderboard. Sure enough, their time blinked to red, then erased.

Dropping their team to the bottom.

Seth raised his fist in the air at his 8.2-second time.

The crowd roared for the hometown favorite even as Darek came over to Roark, shook his hand. "It happens."

"It was me. I pushed too hard. I bowed the saw."

Darek clamped him on the shoulder, but Roark could see his disappointment. "Next year."

Roark had no words. He stepped back as Seb Brewster mounted the stage, taking the microphone to announce the winner. The totaled points appeared on the scoreboard. With Roark's loss in the double buck and the catastrophe in the birling, he'd dropped to sixth.

Seth's name appeared at the top of the board.

Roark mustered up a smile, harkening back to his schooling, fighting the urge to run from the stage. Or better, to take Seth off with him in a full-out American football–style tackle.

Especially when Seth stepped up to receive his trophy and took the mic. "I told you all that I planned on winning for my girl, Amelia."

Roark rolled his eyes.

"And in case I won, I had a little surprise . . . Amelia, could you come up here?"

Roark's chest began to tighten. He searched for her in the audience, which parted around her. Oh, there she was, hiding. In fact, she wore her sunglasses again.

Amelia's mouth opened and she gave the slightest shake of her head, but hands pushed her forward.

She hesitated before she mounted the stage. Roark wanted to reach out, grab her hand, but she walked right past him without a word, a nod, an acknowledgment that he existed.

And then, if this day could nose-dive further, he watched as Seth got down on one knee.

No. Roark glanced at Darek, who was shaking his head.

"Amelia Christiansen. I've loved you since I was twelve years old."

This could not happen.

"The years we dated in high school and afterward were the happiest of my life. And when you left me for Prague, I was in agony. I've realized I never want to let you go again. So . . ."

He was not sticking around for this. Roark pushed past Darek, headed for the end of the platform.

"Would you do me the honor of becoming my wife?"

Roark didn't turn, didn't wait to see her answer, just hit the ground and pushed through the crowd.

But something died inside when he heard the spectators begin to clap, the applause swelling.

Apparently the best man had won.

Roark cleared the crowd and continued down

411

the street, away from the festivities and the town's delight at their hometown prince getting his girl.

He felt a hand on his arm, grabbing him, and wished it might be Amelia. But no—Jensen, who stopped Roark cold. "That's it? You're done fighting for her?"

"Clearly she's made her choice."

"Roark—"

"Leave it." He shook out of Jensen's grip, kept walking.

"Where are you going?"

The words came out like poison, burning through his chest. "Where I belong. Home."

Chapter 16

"SO ARE YOU ENGAGED OR NOT?" Grace slid a plate of flapjacks in front of Amelia, doctored in syrup and powdered sugar as if that might balm the crash and burn of her love life, not to mention her reputation in the annals of Deep Haven events.

"It depends on who you talk to. The crowd would say maybe. From Vivie, the answer would be a resounding yes. Especially after Roark stormed off the stage—"

"Could you blame him? From what Darek said, you didn't even look at him as you walked by.

After he'd practically taken out his heart and pinned it on his rather muscular chest."

"Whose side are you on?"

"Yours." Grace poured her orange juice. "And Roark's."

"Thanks. Thanks for that."

"I just want you to be happy." She smiled, but Amelia could see the sadness marked by the red cracks in her eyes. Since Yulia left three days ago, it seemed nothing could free Grace—or Max, for that matter—from the shadow of grief. As if they'd truly lost their own daughter.

Max had finally gotten ahold of his lawyer this morning and was pacing his way across the deck, just beyond the sliding-glass door, gesturing his frustration as he talked.

Grace kept glancing his direction, and Amelia's heart went out to her. "You'll get her back," she said, reaching out to touch Grace's hand.

Her sister nodded, nothing of conviction in it, then returned to the stove, flipped the pancakes cooking in the cast-iron pan. Keeping with the theme of the weekend, Grace had stirred up her own tasty version of north shore flapjacks and given the dry ingredients in a bag to each guest cabin. How Amelia had missed this—sampling Grace's experiments.

Her mother came into the kitchen, fresh from delivering breakfast baskets to the cabins. "We're running so late I don't know if we're going to make it to church today. . . . Oh, Amelia, you're up."

"I hardly slept."

Ingrid pressed a kiss to her daughter's forehead. "This too shall pass."

"Mother, I don't think the town will soon forget Seth's proposal. I bet it makes the paper today."

"The local Girl Scout car wash also made the paper. It doesn't mean it will live in infamy. This is not your legacy."

It felt like it. One epic, foolish moment after another.

Her bite of flapjack and homemade syrup melted in her mouth. "For the record, I didn't talk to Roark because I was terrified of what Seth might say. And what was I going to do—throw my arms around Roark right there in front of everyone? Especially since *Seth* invited me onstage." She said this for Grace but also for her mother, who'd probably gotten the entire disastrous rundown from Darek.

"Did you think he was going to propose?" Ingrid asked. She opened the fridge and took out a package of hickory-smoked, thick-cut bacon.

"Of course not! We sat together at the competition, and I cheered him on, but . . ." She stirred a bite around in the syrup. "I just didn't even know what to say."

No. No, Seth. She should have mustered the

courage right there, instead of her stumbling, awkward reply.

"Mom, it was awful. He was on one knee. Had declared his love for me in front of the entire town. He even produced a ring. And the hope in his eyes . . . I just couldn't bear to hurt him in public."

So she'd made it all worse.

She sighed. "I said, as discreetly as I could, 'I can't talk about this now.' Just loud enough for him. He looked at me, really hurt, and said, 'Is that a no?' "

"Oh, Ames," Grace said, plating her current pile of pancakes.

"I know, right? I couldn't embarrass him in front of everyone."

Ingrid pulled out a synthetic cutting board, laid the bacon on it. "Except he'd just done the same to you." She wore her mouth in a tight bud of disapproval. "I find the entire thing manipulative."

Amelia frowned. She hadn't thought about that before.

In fact, if she took a close look, she might say that Seth had tried to manipulate her from the moment she arrived back in Deep Haven. With his ultimatums and the picnic, the vision of the house, and his proposal at the competition.

The thought brushed through her that Roark had done just about anything he could not to manipulate her. He'd lied, or something like it, about his pedigree, yes, but because he didn't want to skew her feelings his direction.

"So why did Seth kiss you?" Grace poured more batter into the pan.

"Because when he asked if my answer was a no, I said . . . no. Right then I didn't know what to say. Or how to say it, and I just wanted to get off the stage. Which he assumed meant my answer would be yes."

"That's a pretty big leap," Ingrid said, cutting the bacon with more oomph than necessary.

"Maybe. I . . ." She frowned.

Good enough for me, he'd said. Then he'd kissed her. Wrapped her in his sweaty arms and kissed her good. While the audience cheered.

"I left as soon as I could. He was being congratulated and I just . . . I left."

"He's called here three times. I suspect he'll be on our doorstep anytime today," Ingrid said. "He's probably at church right now, hoping you'll show up."

"Which is why I'm not going. That's just what I need—for Seth to make an announcement to the congregation."

"Honey, you have to find the courage to tell him no."

"But what if . . . what if I should say yes? What if that is the logical, right thing to do? On paper—"

"No." Ingrid set down the knife. "It's not about

what looks logical. Or even what's in your heart. Amelia—what do you hear God telling you?"

Amelia stared at her cold pancakes. Then back at her mother. "If I tell you something crazy, do you promise not to laugh? Just be my friend and not my mom—or my sister—for a moment?"

Ingrid wiped her hands. Nodded. Amelia waited for an accompanying nod from Grace.

"Okay. I know I've said this before, but ever since Roark and I met, I've had the strangest sense that we belong together. That God wanted us together. And that despite our differences, our destiny was out there—not here in Deep Haven. That sense has only grown since Roark has been here. I was so convinced he was the one a week ago. Until he lied. The problem is, I want a man who loves God, and Roark is . . . well, he's hurting. And Seth . . . he's a good man, a Christian man."

"But something is still tugging you toward Roark," Ingrid said.

"Yeah. Maybe it doesn't matter, though." She tried not to let her words choke her. "Roark's gone. Darek said that he told Jensen he's leaving, and I tried to call him. He didn't answer."

Ingrid leaned over. "Your friend would say, give him time. And your mother would say the same thing."

"So would your sister," Grace said. "Because she remembers you talking about how he came here, ready to rumble, or whatever Brits do—

maybe duel at dawn for your heart. So she would say that he's not a coward. Not a runner."

But that's exactly what Amelia feared. They didn't know Roark like she did. In her heart, she just knew he was halfway to Brussels by now. She didn't respond.

"You need to get out of this house. Clear your head," Ingrid said. "Don't you have photographs to take? Grace tells me you made it into the finals of your competition. The top ten in the nation? What do you get if you win?"

"Five thousand dollars. And a trip to New York City if I want it. But . . . I'm not going to win. There's this guy who lives in Nevada who has the most gorgeous shots of the desert. And a woman from Chicago who can capture the soul of the city. Besides, what would I do with that money?"

"See the world?" Ingrid picked up her knife again. "Follow your dreams?"

"Mom—"

"You need something epic," Grace said. "Did you get any shots of yesterday's competition?"

"My camera's in my bag." She nodded toward her backpack, hanging in the entry.

Grace plated the last of her pancakes, then went to fetch it. She came back with the camera, scrolling through the pictures. "These are great. Roark looks like a superhero. You'd never know the man was worth millions."

"9.72 billion."

"But who's counting," Ingrid said, looking at Amelia. She took the bacon to the stove, switched on the burner, then layered it in.

"Mom, seriously. I was kidding. It doesn't matter to me."

"Really?" Grace was still scrolling through the pictures. "Not a smidgen?"

"I don't like that he lied about it."

"I think it's forgivable," Ingrid said, turning from the stove.

"Because he's rich?"

"Because he loves you. And he wanted you to love him without the money. You know, money is a cruel taskmaster. It doesn't play fair. The lack of it leads a man to foolishness; the abundance, to paranoia. In the end, a man ruled by it is not his own. I think this was Roark's attempt to not let money rule his future."

"Except it did. It destroyed us."

Ingrid returned to the sizzling bacon. "That part's up to you. It seems to me that maybe you're the one letting money make your decisions for you."

"I don't care about being wealthy, Mom. He made a fool out of me. Again. And again."

"I'd say he made an even bigger fool out of himself." Grace showed her a picture, perfectly captured, of Roark flying into the air, on his way to a dunking in the birling pool. Arms up, he looked like a child.

She advanced to the next picture, the one where he came up out of the cool water, sodden, his mouth open, gasping for air.

Amelia allowed herself a smile. Oh, why hadn't she gone after him when he marched off the stage? Told him she'd forgiven him?

Because she realized now that she had. Or wanted to.

But it was too late, wasn't it?

Ingrid came over, carrying two crisp pieces of bacon in tongs. She put them on Amelia's plate, then reached for the camera, looked at the shots. "He is handsome, isn't he?"

"Mom!"

"I have eyes. He's got a little bit of Casper's dark locks, Darek's determination, and maybe even some of Owen's impulsiveness. And your father likes his protectiveness." She handed the camera back to Grace. "Very tall, dark, and dangerous."

"Nice, Mom. You watch too many spy movies."

"I was thinking of your father." She winked and returned to the stove.

Tall, dark, and dangerous.

Yes, he had been. Dangerous to Amelia's heart because he suddenly fit into every picture she had for her future. Here in Deep Haven or taking pictures of an ancient castle or . . .

So much for being meant for each other. She'd slammed the door in his face once again.

"I like this one of Tiger eating a stack of pancakes," Grace said. Amelia remembered it—had picked it for one of her final entries. Her nephew sat at a picnic table with a stack on a paper plate, syrup dripping off his chin. Ivy had stood just a few feet away, rocking baby Joy and watching, the ever-protective mother bear of her adopted son.

Bear . . .

What if she did win the contest? Amelia picked up the bacon. Slid off the stool. Grabbed her camera. "I gotta go. I have one more epic shot to find."

"Attagirl!" Ingrid said. "Don't forget—we're having a family campfire tonight."

"I'll be back, I promise."

The sun had already dipped below the horizon as Roark drove along the shoreline, the wind blowing into his ears through the open window. He'd cracked it just to inhale the last of the north shore's fresh, piney breeze before he entered the city limits of Duluth.

He'd be in Minneapolis in a few hours, back in Brussels by tomorrow evening.

And in his office the next morning, rolling up his sleeves, ready to do . . . well, he wasn't quite sure what after his phone call to his uncle last night.

He'd waited until midnight to place the video

call. Until after all the revelers had dissipated from Main Street, the artists' displays emptied, the sawdust swept, the vendors packed up. Until he'd let the searing pain in his chest dull to an ache, pervasive and clinging to his every breath.

Probably it always would.

What a fool he'd been to think he could outrun God. To believe that finally God had turned his direction with the face of forgiveness or even mercy.

His family legacy decreed the truth. A man didn't walk away from God's call without repercussions.

Roark had known it was early when his uncle Donovan answered while eating his morning grapefruit. Aunt Gisela hummed in the background, joining him when Roark started with "I'm coming home."

She'd always treated him like a son. And she gave him the sympathy a son should have. "She doesn't deserve you, Roark. I've always thought that."

He didn't argue, despite the truth. "I know it's probably too late—"

"The board has preliminarily approved Ethan to take over. But come home and we'll sort it."

"I don't care what I do, Uncle. I'll be a bellboy. I'm just . . . I'm done."

"Jolly good news, Roark, even if it has been painful. It takes a few lemons to find the right one." He kissed Gisela, who smiled. "When will you be back?"

"I have to give Kathy notice, so it might be a couple days or more."

"Smashing. Cheerio."

As it was, Kathy had let him go without a fuss. He'd put in a call to Jensen, gotten his voice mail, debated calling Darek, and decided against it. So he'd booked his flight, packed up, cleaned his flat, given the key to Kathy, and left.

Old habits. He fell into them easily. Leave; don't look back.

Except this time it hurt to breathe.

He slowed as he came down the hill, the aerial bridge in the Duluth harbor shiny in the night. The city served as a sort of corridor to the rest of civilization, the world beyond the enclave of the forests of northern Minnesota.

Next to him on the seat, his phone buzzed. He slowed, then pulled into an overlook and picked it up. "Hello?"

"I dearly hope that Amelia is with you."

Darek? "What are you talking about? No, of course she's not with me."

"She's missing. She left this morning to take some pictures and hasn't returned. We have no idea where she might be."

It took a second for the words to register. "What do you mean, *missing?*"

"She took the Evergreen truck, and we've

423

looked all over town, in all the places she likes to shoot pictures. Even called her friends. She's . . . vanished. We had our family campfire and she never showed. We'd hoped she was with you."

He'd hoped she was with him too. He glanced at the time. After 9 p.m. "I'm in Duluth."

"What?" And then Darek sighed. "Okay. I get it. Really. I had just hoped that . . ."

Roark said nothing, watching the lights of a laker anchored offshore, like eyes in the darkness.

"Listen, I know it looks like she said yes to Seth—"

"Leave it, Darek. It doesn't matter. I'll be there shortly."

"You're two hours—"

But Roark hung up on him. He turned his Focus around.

An hour and a half later, he pulled behind the Java Cup, where Darek told him Seb and the EMS workers had assembled. Cars and trucks, parked at crazy angles, overflowed the lot. As Roark walked into the building, he locked eyes with Pastor Dan, giving a briefing at the front of the packed room.

Darek, John, and Max sat together at a table, dressed for the search with headlamps, rain jackets, backpacks. A water bottle hung from a loop of Darek's pack, connected with a carabiner. A blanket stuck out from the top.

When Darek motioned him over, Roark sidled up behind him, listening to Dan.

"We're not sure where to look. We know she went out to photograph—she took her equipment with her. Grace and Ingrid seem to think she went inland, although it's anyone's guess. Right now, we're looking for the green Evergreen Resort pickup. It's getting late, so our best bet is to drive the back roads, see if we can spot her, hope she's hunkered down someplace for the night. But there's a lot of territory out there, so we'll have to split up."

Dan handed out maps, search grids. "I've separated us into teams. Seth, you and your group head east, on the county roads. Darek, you and your family head up the Gunflint Trail. We have others searching farther west."

Nearby, Seth shook his head, seeming not to care that Roark had walked in. He muttered to his friend, "There are thousands of miles of back roads. We're never going to find her. It would take an army, and we don't have the resources for that."

Roark leaned over to Darek. "What does he mean, we don't have resources?"

"Searches cost money, lots of it, and we're a small town. We can't afford airplanes and SAR dog teams."

"Let's hope we don't need them," John said.

Except what if they did? Because according to Roark's calculations, the night temps dropped to the fifties, even the forties in June in northern Minnesota, and who knew if wolves or bears or . . . ? Well, he didn't exactly want to let his imagination run, but what if Amelia was hurt?

Yeah, they needed armies. Squadrons of airplanes, if the search went into daylight, and all the SAR canines he could find.

"This is not hard," Roark said. He stalked outside, pulling out his cell phone.

Amelia was going to die in the woods, and no one would find her body. Ever.

Unless they decided to go blueberry hunting in the clearing overlooking beautiful Twin Pine Lake, exactly twelve miles northwest of her house, on the back roads where the gravel pit turned in and the caribou hiking trail led to the Twin Pine Point lookout.

Or maybe they could simply look for the carrion, the crows filleting her body.

Nice, Amelia. But she couldn't help the thoughts of doom as she curled up in the darkness, staring at the faint light filtering through the ravine into which she'd fallen. Taken a header, really. The crevasse smelled rank, as if she might not have been the first to fall—and perish—in this gully. She'd landed so hard in the hidden ravine that she blacked out, and when she came to, the pain could double her over. In her ribs, her wrist, her knee.

She managed to push herself upright, the world churning around her, and felt her head, where a bump rose above her hairline. Her fingers came away sticky and wet.

She crumpled back down, trying not to panic. Piecing it all together.

She'd been running for the trailhead. It happened so fast, the entire thing was a blur. She must have set some sort of land speed record as she sailed over the ground, through the brambles of blueberry bushes, away, just *away* from the rearing black bear.

A rearing *mama* bear . . . and her babies. Two cubs chomping down on the blueberry plants in the clearing. Ingrid's favorite blueberry-picking spot and, of course, the best place to capture black bears.

Also known as Amelia's award-winning shot.

She'd found a perch upwind—a novice mistake in the woods, brought about by the fact that she'd been waiting for so long, the wind had shifted. That, and the distraction of a very vivid image of Roark, chasing her down the dock, his words churning in her mind.

I am the man you suppose me to be. But how exactly did you imagine I'd work the truth into the conversation?

Not a good defense, and she'd told him that. Now as she fingered her wrist, deciding it must be broken, she could admit that maybe the fact of his wealth *would* have changed her. She did look at him differently. Which frankly wasn't fair.

It didn't matter anyway because he'd already left Deep Haven.

And she was going to die in this ravine.

Alone. Her stupid self, trying to be amazing.

She'd found her camera in the darkness, not far away, and miraculously, it had survived the crash. Now she aimed it at the heavens, took a shot of the moon and stars, barely denting the blackness of the ravine. Tears wet her cheeks as she reviewed the photo.

She began to click back through all the places she'd captured. Or rather, people. Roark birling and a couple of Seth too, during his hot saw. Darek and Roark working together, a clear sign of her family's acceptance. Tiger and Ivy and the baby. The sailboat and the beautiful sunset, right before everything changed.

In that perfect moment, she'd felt as if she stood on the edge of her still-unseen future, Roark beside her, a hum of expectancy under her skin.

In fact, she knew the feeling: a stirring of something more, a taste of the epic, a glorious anticipation of the view just beyond the horizon. She'd felt it when she'd left for Prague.

Where sadly it had vanished.

Strangely, however, when Roark showed up on her doorstep, it seemed to reignite.

In fact, even now, she could taste it.

Wetness fell into her ears.

She kept scrolling back to shots of the lodge, her mother and Grace in the kitchen, Yulia in her apron, grinning as she licked a cookie beater.

Then the sunrise wedding. The family holding a picture of missing Caleb. Barb's soft voice. *It wasn't until I said yes, not knowing how I might find the strength, that I recognized Jesus holding me in the middle of the storm.*

She flipped to the next picture: Esther and Mark kissing.

She had no doubt that God had sent Roark to Prague to save her. To hold her in the middle of her storm. But what if He'd also sent her to Roark?

What if Roark wasn't the answer but a piece of a bigger picture of what God wanted for her? And likewise, what God wanted for Roark?

I knew I was supposed to do something, that God was calling me to something bigger. Roark's words, but she lingered on them. What if God was still calling him?

I think perhaps, finally, God has given me another chance, because why else would He put you in my life, send me to this backwoods hamlet, but to tell me I can start over?

Amelia bit her lip, found it fat and caked with blood. She trembled, hearing her mother's voice. *It's not about what looks logical. Or even what's in your heart. Amelia—what do you hear God telling you?*

Roark. It had always been Roark, a man who desperately wanted to follow God but feared he'd lost his chance.

Oh, Lord, I'm sorry. I shouldn't have pushed him away. When I asked You to decide, I should have listened not to my heart or my fears, but to You.

He'd asked her to love His Jonah back to his true calling.

Her true calling.

Suddenly it all came into focus.

Amelia hadn't *failed* in Prague. She'd simply smacked face-to-face with the truth. She'd always seen herself as that Bible smuggler, brave and adventurous. And maybe she would be. But she couldn't do it alone. She'd gone to Prague brimming with her own confidence, her own strength, and fallen hard.

So God had sent Roark, His emissary, to show her the truth: she was never alone. Maybe she no longer had Seth. Or Roark. But she didn't need them to be brave.

She simply had to look at Jesus. Who would show up. Who had always shown up.

Who, really, had never been away from her.

Amelia put the camera down and leaned back. The cool air in the ravine seeped over her body, had already started to turn her feet, her knee, mercifully numb.

Don't sleep. The thought ran over her, through her. *Don't sleep.*

She stared at the stars, which seemed to gather above her, winking.

The song arrived without effort, filling her head, as if a divine hand had pressed Play, and the words nourished her as the night deepened.

"Be Thou my Vision, O Lord of my heart; naught be all else to me, save that Thou art— Thou my best thought, by day or by night, waking or sleeping, Thy presence my light."

Chaper 17

AS DAWN CRESTED over Evergreen Lake, the gold rays leaking into the gray swell of darkness, Roark tried not to let his hope fade with the night.

Base camp had been set up at Evergreen Resort, where teams might assemble and fan out, based on Amelia's projected path of travel. Darek and John had just returned, having driven a scenic road that overlooked a nearby waterfall. Meanwhile, others had checked out all the campsites, lakeshore landings, and even a few nearby hiking trails.

However, in the darkness, who knew what they'd missed. Sun would burn off the pervasive chill that embedded the night and give rescuers keener vision.

Roark wore his leather jacket, had changed into jeans and his trainers and donned the cap Darek let him wear, but a shiver still blew through him, finding his bones.

Please, let her have survived the night.

He knew exactly who he wanted to beseech, but as the hours grew long, fury had banked his words.

Why, oh, why, couldn't he learn?

God hadn't sent Roark to Deep Haven to set him free, but to torture him. He'd never escape the belly of the whale.

Not even his vast resources seemed enough to pull him free.

During the night, he'd hired a fleet of private search planes to scan the back roads, the lakeshores. He'd hired search-and-rescue teams, sent them out with their dogs. And he'd taken out a PSA over the radio and local television station, alerting the public to her disappearance and asking for volunteers.

People began to arrive in the wee hours, and now the entire county seemed to have mustered up to find Amelia.

However, he'd started to realize that he could blow through millions at this effort and never find her.

Worse, God knew where she was—but wasn't telling.

"We have five private planes landing at the

Deep Haven airport, and Dan is giving them search grids," Seth said, coming up to Roark in the parking lot of the resort, wearing an orange-and-gray rescue jacket.

Somehow, in the middle of the night, Roark's animosity toward the man had perished. He didn't care who Amelia chose.

As long as she was alive to choose.

"Jake is searching this quadrant here." Seth indicated the northwest lake area.

"What about the volunteers?"

"We've split them up, and they're driving every road in the county."

"And beyond?"

"We'll spread out if we need to, but I can't help feeling that she's nearby. Just . . ." Seth turned away as if hiding a rush of emotions.

"You really love her," Roark said quietly to Seth.

Seth looked at him. Frowned. "Yeah. She's my entire life—has been for years."

Roark nodded. "We'll find her."

Seth drew in a long breath, folded the map. Shoved it into his pocket. "For the record, thank you for this. I know you love her too."

"I do."

Seth held out his hand, and Roark shook it, then let him go as he picked up a radio to check in with the teams.

Roark walked over to Darek, who cupped his

hands around a mug of coffee his mother had brought out to him. "Where to next?"

"I don't know. I've talked to my mom, trying to figure out their last conversation. She said it was mostly about you. Whether Amelia would forgive you."

Roark couldn't hear this. Not now. "It doesn't matter."

"You don't think she went to your apartment or even something silly like drove to Duluth to catch you, do you?"

"Do you really think she'd do that?"

Darek shoved a hand into his pocket. "No. She's . . . she's a Christiansen. Might suffer from a few pride issues."

"Don't we all." Roark glanced away from him toward where Ingrid was wandering down the dock.

Something he couldn't name seemed to nudge him to follow. Maybe it did matter what Amelia had said.

He followed Ingrid to the dock slowly, watching as she sat on the end, a blanket wrapped around her shoulders. The action seemed so private, he nearly stopped. Would have if she hadn't turned suddenly as if he'd made a sound.

"Roark."

"Sorry; I—"

"Come." She patted the space beside her, and he obeyed.

He sat, his feet just above the water, and watched the mist rise off the lake. A water bug dragged a trail along the surface of the water.

Ingrid's hand touched his and squeezed.

A crazy burning filled his eyes. "I just feel so helpless," he said and tried not to hate himself for the way his voice wrecked at the end.

"We're not helpless. We're waiting. She went out to take that last photo, and while we don't know where she is, God does. He sees our girl, and He'll take care of her."

"I wish I could believe that. I *would* believe that if it weren't for the fact that this is my fault."

"Why on earth would you think that?"

"It's because . . . I love her. And whoever I love, God takes away. Wherever I go, He sends a storm, and the only way to escape it is for me to run. Keep running. God is again reminding me I failed Him."

"That is the craziest thing I've ever heard and a lie from the pit of hell."

Huh?

He tried to pull his hand away, but she held on. "Satan wants you to believe God is vindictive and cruel. God is just, yes, but He tempers that with love. The Bible talks over and over about how He stays His hand, how He gives His servants chance after chance. It's our pride that makes us believe God's favor depends on us, on our actions. If that were true, that would make

435

God an equation—we obey; thus, He must love us. Or even that God does 90 percent of the work of salvation and we have to put in our 10 percent to reap the fruit. But God is above the equation of our minds. He loves us simply because He finds joy in loving us. And no amount of our running, our disobedience, our mistakes will keep that love from us. God requires nothing from us but to turn and embrace Him."

She still had ahold of his hand. "I don't know why you believe you are not worthy of God's favor, but I might remind you that God's blessings fall on the wicked and the righteous alike. It's our response—our embrace or our rejection of those blessings—that determines whether they bear fruit in our lives. Yes, you can walk away from God. But He will never walk away from you."

She cupped his hand with her other. "You know what I see, Roark? A good man with a servant's heart. The problem is that you want to serve God without having to interact with Him. I think you are deeply angry at God, and instead of blaming Him, you've blamed yourself. Told yourself that you're not worth God's favor. You want to be a good man, but your wounds keep you from trusting God. From receiving His grace. It's time to turn around, receive the grace God wants to give you."

Ingrid lifted her face to the morning, closed her

eyes. " 'In my distress I called to the Lord, and he answered me. From deep in the realm of the dead I called for help, and you listened to my cry. You hurled me into the depths, into the very heart of the seas, and the currents swirled about me; all your waves and breakers swept over me.' "

Roark recognized the passage, heard his father's voice, picked up the verse from memory. " 'I said, "I have been banished from your sight . . ." ' "

Ingrid gave him a soft smile. " 'But you, Lord my God, brought my life up from the pit. When my life was ebbing away, I remembered you, Lord, and my prayer rose to you, to your holy temple.' "

She let go of his hand and got up. To his surprise, she pressed a kiss to his head, then walked away. However, she stopped at the end of the dock.

"Jonah's prayer, in the belly of the whale. It's never too late to say yes to God."

Roark turned back to the lake, his breath caught in his chest.

Never too late . . .

He'd spent his entire life looking at God through the lens of his parents' deaths, the last few years seeing God as an avenger, thanks to the hotel fire.

But what if God hadn't forsaken him?

God requires nothing from us but to turn and embrace Him.

437

His breath grew ragged, his jaw tight.

Please. He let the word break free inside, tried again. *Please, oh, God, help me not to cling to my pain, but to reach for grace. Save me from myself.*

But even that prayer felt so . . . selfish.

Instead . . . *Please, God, find Amelia. Keep her safe. Bring her back to us. Whatever You require of me, I will do. What I've vowed long ago I will make good. Please, just save her.*

Just save her.

He sat at the end of the dock, watching the fog burn off, and in his memories, his father's voice rose again. Solid, reading the Bible at their kitchen table by the wan glow of the light.

"The engulfing waters threatened me, the deep surrounded me; seaweed was wrapped around my head. To the roots of the mountains I sank down; the earth beneath barred me in forever."

Except no, that memory hadn't been at the table in Russia, but at the beach house in Spain. His father praising God even after he had left his life's calling.

Or had he? Maybe Roark needed a different lens.

"But you, Lord my God, brought my life up from the pit."

"Roark!"

Darek's voice, then footsteps thundering down the path. "Roark, they found the truck!"

Roark scrambled to his feet and sprinted to the

house, where Darek had already climbed into his truck. Roark jumped into the cab. "Where is she?"

Darek rammed the truck into gear, backed it out. Roark saw John and Ingrid getting into their vehicle as they pulled out.

"A local called it in to the police station. Found the truck at a gravel pit about twelve miles from here. It's near Twin Pine Point." He glanced at Roark. "Bear country."

Of course. She'd gone after the final photograph for the contest.

Which she never would have entered had it not been for him.

Please, God. Whatever You want of me—for her.

Darek fishtailed his way to the gravel pit, kicking up a cloud of dust, Roark holding on, trying not to urge him faster. Finally they slid into the drive, where they found a rescue truck, two more vehicles, and a small band of volunteers.

And Amelia's truck.

Roark barreled out of Darek's truck before it stopped. John got out next to him, and Roark asked, "Where does this trail go?"

"There's a small grouping of cabins not far from here, along Twin Pine Lake, and the upper path goes to an overlook."

"She's at the overlook," Ingrid said. "It's my favorite place to hunt for blueberries."

She hadn't finished speaking before Roark took off up the wide, grassy path. About a hundred yards in, it veered to the left, to a cabin set back from the lake. He turned the other way, kept running, Darek on his heels.

The path spilled out into a wide clearing, filled with brambles of blueberry plants, fallen logs, and a clear view of Twin Pine Lake.

No sign of Amelia.

"Amelia!"

His voice dissipated in the air. "Spread out," he said to Darek, and now John, Ingrid, and the other searchers.

They began to walk through the brambles. "Amelia!"

Trees edged the clearing, the perfect hiding place for wolves or bears.

"There's fresh bear scat over here," Darek said, about twenty feet away.

"I found her jacket!" Ingrid stood on a fallen tree. "And the grass is trampled. I'll bet she was here, waiting . . ."

Roark glanced at Darek, then at Ingrid, then at the trail. "If she was sitting there, and a bear came ambling up . . . why didn't she run down the trail?"

"Maybe there was something in her way," Ingrid said. "Like a cub."

"Where would she run?" He looked toward the edge of the field. To the cliff.

No. Please.

Darek seemed to have the same idea. He started off at a run. "Amelia!"

"Darek, stop!" This from John, who stood twenty feet ahead of them. "There's a ravine here. It's hidden in the brambles." He walked along the edge away from them. "It gets wider."

Roark approached the ravine, a narrow slit at the top of the field, growing wider as he ran along it. Thirty feet down maybe, darkness gathered at the bottom, along with boulders and debris. More brambles jutted from the edges. "Amelia!"

He heard Darek calling, all of them peering into the shadowy slit.

"Here! There are broken branches!" John, peering over the edge, got on his knees.

Darek ran up beside him.

"Do you see her?" Roark jogged to the edge. Here, it seemed the bottom might be even farther, forty feet, a desperate distance to fall. *Oh, God, please . . .*

"I'm going down there," he said. "Darek, give me your rescue pack." Blanket, water, flashlight, first aid. Of course, in his haste Roark had left his in the truck.

Darek shrugged it off.

"Are you sure? Maybe we should wait until the rescue squad gets here," John said, but he lacked conviction.

Thank God—really—Roark had learned how to climb.

"Get the rescue squad!" He turned himself inward to the cliff, stepped down.

"Please don't fall," Ingrid said.

Roark wedged his hand into a crevice. "There are plenty of handholds here. I'll be fine."

It was then that a scream lifted from deep inside the ravine. Haunting. Feral.

Hurt.

Ingrid pressed her hand to her mouth.

"Hurry," Darek said.

Amelia had used her last breath on that scream. Hadn't quite realized she had it in her after dropping into exhausted unconsciousness. But something roused her. A nudge inside the darkness, her name in the wind, pulling her to the sunlight.

She'd pried her eyes open with not a little pain, a groan starting at her belly, working through her bones to emerge out of her throat via an involuntary shudder.

She couldn't feel her legs or her arm, but that might be merciful. She heard her name again, wanted to shout, but nothing emerged. *I'm here.*

That's when she tried to move, to sit up or maybe throw something. She turned her head, now throbbing, trying to locate a rock.

It took a second for her eyes to register what she

saw, lying ten or more feet away from her. Pants, dress shoes, a shirt, and inside it all, a mangled body or what was left of it.

Another scream bubbled out, hard and fast, leaving her heart thrumming, fat and hot in her chest.

A body. A decaying dead body, and she'd spent the night with it mere feet away.

She flopped back, breathing hard. Her eyes began to close, pain tunneling up to swallow her whole. Oh . . . "Help me," she said, her voice a whisper.

"Amelia!"

That voice. She knew it. It had found her once before as she huddled, afraid, and it reached out to find her again.

"Amelia!" Closer now.

She wanted to open her eyes, to help him. *Here. I am . . . here . . .*

"Oh, my—I found her!" Footsteps on the rocky, moist ground. Then hands on her, behind her head, checking it for injury.

"Amelia, sweetie. Hang on."

Her mouth moved, but nothing came out.

Water, fresh and cool, touched her lips. She tried to swallow, but it spilled over her chin. Still, it loosed her tongue, soothed her parched lips.

She felt a blanket go over her, pulled up to her chin, but it did nothing to warm her. She blinked, fighting the light that pierced her brain. "Roark—"

"I'm here."

And he was. He leaned over her, such tenderness in his expression that she wanted to weep. "You . . . found me."

He made the funniest noise, a sort of moan. He kissed her forehead softly, then moved back, his eyes glistening. "Oh, God, thank You, thank You."

He turned away from her as if hiding his face, but she saw his palm go into one eye, then the other.

When he turned back, he tried and failed a smile. "Yes," he said, his voice thin. "I'll always find you. I promise."

Then his face wrecked, and he leaned over her again, weaving her fingers into his. He kissed her hand, held it to his cheek. "Please, Amelia. Don't die. Please don't die."

She swallowed. "No . . . worries." It had gotten harder to breathe as the night waned, before she passed out. Now her lungs felt as if they were squeezed in a vise. "We have . . . more . . . to do."

"Yes, darling. So much more. We'll go anywhere. Do anything."

"Coming down!"

She heard something falling, breaking trees, and Roark got up. "I'll be right back."

More shouting, Roark hollering back. Gray filtered into the edges of her vision. "Roark—"

And he was there, close, his hand in hers again.

444

"I'm right here, darling. They're coming. The rescue guys will be here any moment, just hang on."

"I know . . . I know who . . . I'm supposed to be . . . with. . . ."

"I know. And I understand. I just need you to be okay. That's enough for me."

More voices and now footsteps.

"I think she has a collapsed lung. She seems to be having trouble breathing." Roark moved away from her as a face she should recognize came into view.

"Hey, Amelia. Remember me? Joe Michaels? We're going to give you a little oxygen now, make it easier for you to breathe while we figure out how to get you out of here."

He put a mask over her nose, mouth, but she reached up, hiccuping breaths, and pulled it away.

"R-Roark." She'd started to shiver, especially since they slipped off the blanket to check her vitals.

"I'm here. Put the mask back on." He moved in next to Joe. "I'm right here."

"I . . . want . . ." Her breath caught. Joe set the mask over her face, but she fought it. "I want . . . you. You." She breathed out, leaned back.

Closed her eyes.

Roark, I want you.

"We need that backboard now!"

Movement on her arm made her cry out.

"Careful," Roark growled.

"I think her wrist is broken. And there's head trauma."

Hands on her, around her neck, and a brace snapped into place. She groaned again, the gray turning to black.

But . . . wait . . . She opened her eyes, gulping in the fresh, sweet air, longing for it to fill her lungs, fighting the terrible anvil that pressed down, harder, harder.

Roark. She met his eyes, tried for a smile.

Roark's hands cradled her face, his lips on her forehead. He backed up, met her eyes, his own fierce.

"No, Amelia. You will not leave me. I have crossed an ocean for you, and you're right: we do have more to do. Much more. But you have to stay alive. Be brave. Hold on." His face crumpled, his voice ragged. "Please."

But the darkness was creeping in. She blinked, reaching up for the light, but it crept away.

"We're losing her!"

Chapter 18

MAX WALKED DOWN THE HALL, abandoning the family in the waiting room. He'd been checking his text messages all day, waiting for the right news. Now he burst outside into the sunshine. The cloudless day had no right to be so spec-tacular. Or maybe it did. Because maybe they needed it.

He searched the parking lot. A seagull flew overhead, calling as if in anticipation.

Max stuck his hands in his pockets. How he hated hospitals, always had—the smell of them embedding his skin, the sense of despair, the long hours of nothing to do. He'd read every magazine on the tables—everyone had—and paced the halls, unable to look at Ingrid and John one more minute. The hope in their eyes every time the doctor walked in. The grief when he walked away.

It wasn't supposed to be this way. Not for Amelia. Not for any of them. If anyone was supposed to go first, it was him.

He recognized the person walking toward him and raised his hand. "Pastor."

"Max." Dan gave him a smile, something reassuring. Of course, he'd worn the same smile for the last two days. How could he be so hopeful when they knew so little?

Amelia's lung had collapsed down in the ravine, and while Joe had managed to relieve the pressure, to drain her chest, they'd had to reinflate it at the hospital. Then her heart stopped. Twice, as a matter of fact. And there'd been so much internal bleeding from her fall that they'd had to give her a transfusion.

They'd set her wrist, set her ankle, x-rayed her swollen knee to find it only bruised, and given her a CAT scan. Thankfully, the head trauma had proven to be less than they feared. Still, she hadn't woken up. Two days, and she hadn't yet woken up.

"Family's inside," Max said.

Dan nodded and headed in.

She'd had a slew of visitors over the last two days. So many volunteers had offered their time to find her. Roark managed to raise an army. No one mentioned it, but overnight he'd become a Deep Haven legend. Mostly because everyone knew it cost more than the town's entire EMS budget for a year.

Poor Roark was in so much pain Max could hardly bear to be in the same room as him, watching him sit with his face in his hands, despair bowing his shoulders. He got up now and again, walked the length of the corridor, sometimes pressed his forehead to the window glass as if seeing some escape from the nightmare.

And right next to him had been Seth, equally distraught. He'd left a few times to shower but always returned, sitting just two chairs down from Roark.

Allies in pain for the woman they loved.

If Amelia didn't wake up today, the doctors would transport her to Duluth, put her in ICU there, start running more tests.

Something had to happen soon. They needed something—anything—to brighten their spirits, give them hope.

Max saw the car as it appeared over the hill, followed it with his eyes until it turned at the driveway. A smile formed inside his chest, worked its way to his mouth, and by the time the sedan pulled up to the entrance, he wore a full-out grin.

Martha got out of the car. Gave him a nod. And then she opened the door to the backseat.

Yulia flew out, already unbuckled. "Papa!"

She'd said it again. He'd thought he'd dreamed it the first time, but now it fell into place—the word, the name he knew belonged to him.

He dropped to a crouch and opened his arms, and she launched herself into him, clinging to his neck.

He wrapped his arms around her and twirled her. "Yulia," he said. "I promised that you'd come back."

"Papa. Papa."

Gently dropping her to her feet, he took her hand, walked over to Martha. "Thank you for bringing her back. We really needed her."

"I understand the paperwork will take some time, but with your in-laws being foster parents, it should work just fine. I don't know how you managed to smooth out the legal process, but I have to admit, I'm glad we didn't have to put her on a plane."

He was too. "Once I found out that her adoptive sister had been given guardianship, it was simply a matter of transferring the adoption to us instead of Yulia going back into the system. My lawyer says it's called re-homing. Taking a child from one home and adding her to another."

Martha nodded. "It's rare for that to happen, but it can work."

"Well, she's home now, and she's never leaving."

"I'll be in touch." Martha got in the car.

"Thanks a lot." Max looked down at Yulia. "Ready to go see . . . your mama?"

That felt right too.

Yulia nodded, smiled as if she understood.

He led her into the hospital, then paused, bent down. Probably she needed briefing.

"We're at the hospital because Amelia—you remember her, Grace's sister—had an accident. She fell a long way. She's sleeping right now, and we're all very worried about her. But I promise you, everyone will be so glad to see you. And we won't stay long. We'll go home soon."

Yulia stared at him with beautiful brown eyes and gave a small nod.

Max took her little hand. "Okay then." He walked her down the hall, turned the corner to where the family sat. An alcove, really, where they all jammed in among chairs and coats, purses, take-out containers. The lot of them, just sitting, waiting.

Ingrid looked up first.

Max met her eyes.

Her mouth opened. "Oh," she said, her voice shaky.

It elicited a response from John and Ivy, Darek. And then Grace.

His wife gasped, jumped to her feet. "Oh. Oh, my." She advanced, falling to her knees as Yulia unlatched her hand from Max's and ran to her.

Yulia caught Grace around the neck, and Grace fell back onto the floor, laughing. She ran her hand over Yulia's hair. "What are you doing here?"

Max answered, "It was time for Yulia to come home."

Grace sat up, kissed Yulia's cheek, caught her hands. "Yes, you're home. Finally." Then she looked up at Max, her blue eyes changing from amazement to warmth to a deep joy. "Thank you, Max."

He helped her off the floor, keeping hold of her hands. "I realized something when we lost her, then sitting here the last few days. It's time to be happy, to trust in the life God gives me. I'm not afraid to love life anymore. Life isn't worth living if you don't have the people you love with you. Love makes me stronger and better, and I know I will survive longer if I have both you and Yulia—and God—to hold on to."

"Yes, you will," Grace said. "And when you can't hold on, we'll hold on for you."

He touched her forehead to his, and she kissed him, the kind of kiss that held promise and the hope that their tomorrows would be just as rich as today.

I want . . . you.

Amelia's words, softly spoken, had settled inside Roark like a rock, the only thing he had to cling to as the hours slipped into a day, then two.

He should have found her sooner—why hadn't he found her sooner?

Rather, he never should have left her at all. Because he could have been there for her, could have gone with her, protected her. Instead he'd let his own broken heart drive him away from the only woman he'd ever truly, without reservation, loved. Leaving her alone to pursue her dreams.

We have more to do.

Yes, they did. Anything. Everything she wanted.

Roark sat in the tiny hospital chapel, staring up at the cross. He felt prayed out. How many times could he say, *Please save her, Lord*?

If God was listening, He clearly knew what Roark wanted. And Roark prayed He *was* listening. He had to be, right? Because they *had* found Amelia. Miracle of miracles, they had found her. God had given him that much.

He wanted to believe God was so good that He'd give Roark more. Forced himself to believe it because he had nothing else.

He dropped his face into his hands. Breathing, just breathing. Waiting. Listening to his own heartbeat.

He'd called his uncle about two hours after he found Amelia. Told him that no, he couldn't return to Brussels, not now or anytime soon. That he was sorry for again going back on his word. Strangely Uncle Donovan seemed to understand.

"Hang in there, son," he said. "We'll be praying for her." Terminology his uncle didn't normally use.

Roark should probably go back out to the family, sit with them, but they had each other, and for the first time since meeting them—well, since being a part of their campfire and their lives—he didn't quite belong. He sat at the outskirts. They tried—Darek came after him a couple times, and they pulled him into their prayer circles, but Roark stayed away, the intimacy too much for him. Somehow it felt easier to bear it by himself.

That's always how it was, wasn't it? Him bearing his own grief. His own guilt, his own shame. Alone. Staring up at God and shaking his fist.

There would be no shaking his fist today. Just him on his face, praying.

He heard footsteps behind him.

Ivy, the baby on her hip. She looked tired, although she'd gone home a couple times to sleep and to look in on Tiger, who was staying with his other grandparents.

"She's waking up," she said.

Roark leaped to his feet. "Oh, please—"

He didn't wait for Ivy, just sprinted down the hall. A small hospital, so few rooms—he arrived in seconds, pushed into the tiny two-bed ICU, and found Amelia's family gathered around her.

Ingrid held her hand. John stood behind his wife, his hands steady on her shoulders.

Oh, Amelia looked beat-up. Of course, he'd seen her before, numerous times, but now it seemed too brutal. Her beautiful face had turned purple around one eye, where she'd smashed it into the ground. Thankfully, nothing fractured, her wrist taking most of the blow. Her other eye blinked against the light. Her lips, too, had swelled, cracked and purple. An oxygen cannula fed air into her nose, plaster encased her arm, and a cast bound her ankle. Machines beeped around her, indicating life. She'd suffered two broken ribs, one that had nicked her lung, slowly releasing air into her body, crushing her. If Roark hadn't found her when he did, she would have suffocated.

Darek, arms folded, mouth grim, leaned against the wall. Grace stood by Amelia's head. Ivy and baby Joy had stayed in the hall. Even Raina held vigil, texting updates to Casper, who was somewhere in Montana.

Seth was nowhere to be found, probably, unfortunately, on one of his trips home.

"Hey, honey," Grace said. "We're all here." She leaned down and kissed Amelia's forehead.

"You're going to be okay. You're going to be just fine," Ingrid said, her voice strong, clearly hiding the fear that Amelia might, again, drop away from them.

"I . . . ," Amelia began, her voice low, raspy.

"Shh," Ingrid said.

Amelia's eye closed. She swallowed with effort.

Roark longed to get nearer, to talk to her, but he wasn't a part of—

"Roark." His name passed her lips, shuddering through him, catching his breath.

"I'm right here." He moved alongside the bed, next to Grace. Leaning down, he pressed his lips to an unbruised part of her face.

"You found me," she whispered, just an exhale of breath really.

"Of course I found you," he said.

"Hey." Her breath leaked out.

Please, Lord, don't let her die now.

But she caught it back up.

"I love you," she said.

"I love you too." He closed his eyes before his tears could overflow and embarrass him in front of her family. But he felt Grace's hand on his shoulder, tightening.

He looked up, and she met his eyes, tears running down her cheeks.

"Of course she loves you," Grace said.

"We should have seen it all along," Max added. "That you were the one when you came barging back into her life. Refused to leave. When you fought for her and made a fool out of yourself for her. We all should have known."

Roark turned to John. "How could I let her go? I love her."

"Yes," John said. "You said that. We know."

Okay. Okay then.

Amelia's eye opened again. "I saw . . . a bear . . . and . . . cubs."

"Yes, I know. We saw the pictures." Downloading her amazing shots of the bear and her two cubs eating, along with the scenic panorama of Twin Pine Lake, the close-ups of the still-ripening berries on the bushes, and the night sky overhead, had given him something to do to keep the crazy at bay.

He didn't know much about editing—didn't need to because she'd caught it all with such clarity that he'd simply uploaded them to the Capture America site.

And then, because he had to, he'd written something about her accident. About how a person dedicated to the things she loves will go all out, sacrifice herself, her life, for what she believes in. How Amelia was that kind of person and how he admired her.

He asked people to pray for her. It seemed silly, really, to ask strangers to pray for a person they didn't know, but he asked anyway.

Ingrid gave Amelia a drink of water through a straw, and she settled back into the pillow.

"Roark?"

"Yes?"

"God was there, in the ravine."

"Yes, of course He was. He helped me find you."

"He did?"

"Well, yeah. You were lost to us, and . . ." He licked his dry lips, glanced at Ingrid, back down. "We prayed. *I* prayed. And God brought you back to us."

It felt awkward to say those words, but even as he released them, the truth of them settled inside.

God, in His goodness, had given him back Amelia. And Roark would keep his vow. *Anything for You, Lord. Anything.*

"Yeah, but He was with me all night," Amelia said, her gaze almost fierce. "I could hear Him singing to me."

A strange emotion rose through Roark. A tingle. A stirring of anticipation, almost.

"I realized . . . ," she said and lifted her hand. He caught it. "I know what God wants from us. I know why He keeps putting us together."

Roark did too. Because he couldn't imagine a life without her. She made him better and stronger. She made him believe in himself. That he was a good man. That someday he could bear good fruit.

"I think God wants us to be missionaries."

Silence.

Roark swallowed. Not moving.

"See, it came to me that I've been wanting to do this my whole life. I love photography, and maybe I'm supposed to do that too—I don't know. But I grew up on missionary stories and the stir of adventure and the desire to do something epic—it's all part of His calling. When I finally realized that this call was what I've been afraid to say yes to, that all I have to do is point my eyes at Jesus and focus on Him, it all came together. I saw the picture. I think God is calling you too, Roark. And I think you know that."

She seemed stronger now, her grip on his hand unbreakable.

"I think your whole life you've wanted to be a missionary. That's why you were so happy in Uganda. But you're afraid to let God down. And

I think deep down you're afraid to walk away from all you have, only to fail."

No. Oh, Lord, not this. Anything but this.

"But you didn't let God down. You can still say yes to Him."

He closed his mouth, his breath coming out in a wisp. "Right. Of course." His words lacked conviction, so he tried again. "You get better, and we'll . . . we have so much left to do." He used her words because he didn't know what else to say. "Just get better."

"I will, Roark." Her eyes gleamed. "And then we'll go do amazing things. You and me, for God."

He felt as though a hand had closed around his lungs, his heart.

"Yes," he said. "Of course." He kissed her forehead.

Amelia closed her eyes and faded into sleep, her breathing steady. Ingrid wiped a tear off her cheek and looked at Roark.

"Excuse me," he said. He pushed past them out into the hall, his breathing ragged.

Pressing a hand to the wall, he leaned against it, bracing himself. A *missionary*. He closed his eyes, rested his forehead against the cool plaster.

In a way, it made sense. In fact, if he were to step back and take a good look, maybe that's why he'd been so attracted to Amelia. Because she reminded him of his mother or his father or maybe even himself. That desire, that longing, the hunger and thirst for more, to do something significant. And her family brought him back to the days when he'd had a family too.

But why a missionary? Of all things, a *missionary?* Of course, God would require of him the one thing he couldn't give.

Behind him, the door opened and closed. Then he heard a voice. Deep, resounding. John.

"Roark, you all right?"

Roark stepped back from the wall. "I'm more than all right. I feared she wouldn't wake."

John nodded. "Yeah, me too. But there's more, isn't there? Something that she said."

Roark looked at him, considering. "I can't be a missionary, John. I just can't be." He shook his head. "I know what she asked, and I know what I said. I know what I promised God, but I can't believe God would ask that of me. Yes, I'll do anything for Amelia, and for God too, but . . . but not this."

"I don't understand."

"My own father, who loved God, let Him down. Let the worries of the world pull him away from his calling . . ."

"Why is this so hard, Roark?"

Roark closed his eyes, turned away. "Because my uncle is right. I've lived most of my life with wealth and opportunity, with the power to do anything I want. Now God wants me to leave that all behind and trust Him. To go out into the unknown and follow Him. It's a blind sort of faith." He shook his head. "It's one thing to surrender my position at the company and exchange it for what you have here. The richness, the family, the life. But to abandon the world I know for a world that could be disastrous . . . it's too much to ask."

"I see." John went quiet behind him for a moment. "So the problem is, you're willing to trust God if He agrees to your parameters and as long as He obeys the rules. Is that what you're saying?"

His words fell on Roark, stung.

John sighed. "God wants you to obey Him not because of what you get in exchange, but simply because He asked. To give up everything simply for the wonder of knowing Him, experiencing Him, believing in Him. The wonder of chasing after Him and abandoning all for Him."

Roark swallowed because he had nothing.

"When you came after Amelia, you didn't know if she was going to say yes. She could have turned right around and said, 'No, never, get away from me.'"

Roark closed his eyes. "In fact, she did."

"And yet you pressed on. You refused to give up because you believed in Amelia and her love for you. You believed that love was worth pursuing. It was not a fling for you, and it was not a fling for her, as she has told me. Yet you're treating your relationship with God like a fling. As if it means nothing to Him and nothing to you. As if you can walk away from each other. But God doesn't operate that way. When He sent Jesus to pay for your sins, He was all in. And when you turn to Him for salvation from death, He isn't just offering you a onetime moment, but a lifetime of joy. Of peace. Of hope. You don't have to see the future to trust in God's goodness, in His love for you. You simply need to turn around and take a good look at what He's already done. Then you can let the wonder of His love for you draw you to Him."

He wanted to hear John's words, but . . . "I've spent a lot of time running from God."

"In all that running, what have you learned about Him?"

What had he learned? He'd learned that God wouldn't let him go. That whether he was in Australia or Tasmania or on the streets of Prague, God would pursue him all the way, including giving him a woman who saw beyond his hurt— and even his wealth—to his heart.

"I guess, that He doesn't seem willing to give up."

"And why would God not want to pursue you? Why would He not be concerned about a child who so desperately wants to love Him but is afraid?" He walked past Roark to the window, where the sun had risen high into a cloudless sky, then turned back. "You're a part of our family, and you can bet we're not going to let you go either."

"Neither am I."

Roark stilled at the voice behind him, turned. It couldn't be.

There in the hallway stood his uncle Donovan. Tall, balding, a little rounder than he had been two years ago. He wore a simple jacket, a pair of jeans—pressed, of course—and trainers. Dressing down, apparently, for his trip across the ocean.

"What are you doing here?"

As Donovan came up to him, Roark saw warmth in his uncle's eyes that he'd forgotten. "I was worried about you," he said. He put his arms around Roark. "Son."

Roark closed his eyes. Let himself embrace his uncle. *Son.* He'd been Donovan's son longer than he'd been his own father's, and he should probably face that. Donovan had been a good man, a good father for him.

"Thank you for coming," Roark said and backed away. He looked at John. "This is my uncle."

John shook Donovan's hand. "Glad to meet you." He wore a funny smile as he disappeared into Amelia's room.

"You're . . . here," Roark said.

"Of course I'm here."

And it settled upon Roark that yes, Uncle Donovan had always been here. He'd shown up in the hospital after his family died, been there for his rowing events and rugby matches, and had picked him up for every break, attended his graduations. He'd believed in Roark enough to give him a job he didn't deserve and let him roam the planet for two years, wallowing in his grief and anger.

"I'm sorry, Uncle," Roark said suddenly. "I'm so sorry. I should have come home—"

"It's okay, Roark. I understand. You have the same wandering spirit as your father; I know this about you."

"I don't believe I'll be joining the ranks of—"

"Yes, I know you're not coming back. But there's something that you probably need to know also." Donovan took a breath. "I've been holding out on you."

Roark frowned.

"I overheard you talking; you probably don't realize that being a missionary is in your blood, just like your father."

"My father turned away from missions."

"No, he didn't. Not at all. I should have told you about that." Donovan shook his head. "I was greedy, and I wanted you for myself. But when God gave you to me to take care of, I should have realized that He would want you back. Your heart is your father's heart. Your inheritance is your father's inheritance—a love for God. I should have never turned you down when you wanted to stay in Uganda. And for that, I'm sorry."

"I don't understand."

"As much as I've hoped for the day when you would take the helm of Constantine World-wide, it seems that is not your destiny. Instead, perhaps, you should finish what your father started. Yes, your father returned from the mission field because he needed medical assistance for your mother. But he also had his priorities in the right place. He was in the middle of setting up the charitable arm of Constantine Worldwide. In every country where we have a hotel, your father wanted to fund an orphanage. It was his brainchild, his baby, and his unfinished dream."

"My father wanted to start a charitable organization?"

"He did. Set it up, but it's not running. And now it's funded with millions of euros, sitting there, waiting for the right person with the right priorities to distribute it." Donovan met his eyes. "It's time for you to go out and do what you were destined to do."

Roark had no words. But he turned away before the rush of emotions could catch up with him. "Would you like to meet Amelia?"

"I'm not leaving until I do. I have to meet this woman who so captured my nephew's heart."

Roark put his arm around Donovan. "Your son's heart."

Donovan smiled. "Quite right."

Epilogue

"ARE YOU SURE YOU'RE READY? Absolutely sure?"

Her mother couldn't help it—Amelia knew that, so she tempered her response to something soft, gentle. Outside, leaves tumbled across the parking lot of the Duluth airport, people rushing in with carry-ons and roller bags.

"More than ready, Mom. I'll be fine. My ankle and wrist are healed; my ribs are golden. I'm 100 percent." And that was mostly true, except for the occasional ache when she stepped wrong or reached out too fast.

"I'm not talking about your health, honey," Ingrid said, holding Amelia's boarding pass, her passport. "I'm talking about in here—" she touched her heart—"and here." She pointed to her head. "I don't want your nightmares to follow you to Uganda."

"I'm not sure that can be helped, but yeah, I'm fine, Mom." She still woke sometimes in a cold sweat, the night sinking into her pores like it had in the ravine. But every time, she countered it with the song, the one that refused to leave. And the voice in her head, softly singing.

"And Roark?"

Probably that was the heart part Ingrid worried about. For a second, yes, his absence could dig a spear into Amelia's chest. But she managed a smile. "I'll be fine. I don't need Roark for this trip." Or any trip. Not if she kept her focus on her true Savior.

Ingrid gave her a small, sad smile and reached out, pulled her close. "I'll miss you so much it takes my breath away."

Amelia curled her arms around her mother's shoulders, breathing in the soft flannel of her jacket, the warmth of home. "It's only for three months. I'll be back before Christmas."

"You'd better." This from Darek, who walked up behind them, Tiger skipping alongside. "Sorry I'm late—we had a McDonald's stop."

The evidence dribbled down Tiger's jacket in splotches of creamy-white ice cream. Yulia followed, still working on her cone, Grace holding her hand.

Amelia greeted her sister with a one-armed hug. "How's Max?"

"Training camp with Jace, and Eden says hi by the way."

"You all didn't even have to come—I'm perfectly able to get on an airplane without the entire contingent of Christiansens showing up."

Except the entire contingent *couldn't* quite show up, and her words obviously left a mark on Ingrid, who swallowed, looked away. Casper had called only a week ago, on his way to Seattle to check in with a former teammate of Owen's, having had no luck so far in locating their missing brother.

Amelia shot a glance at her father, on the phone over by the Charles Lindbergh statue in the lobby. She didn't want to go through security without a last hug.

"The Gundersons do have e-mail. And Skype. I promise to check in." Amelia picked up her carry-on, tugged it over her shoulder. A key chain imprinted with the Deep Haven city logo dangled from the side.

"That's a nice memento," Grace said. "Taking something from home."

"Seth gave it to me when he stopped by last night," Amelia said, shaking her head at Grace's raised eyebrow. "It's not like that. He knows it's over. He's just . . . Well, this distance will be good for him. He might be able to move on."

Poor man had initially taken her choice like a prizefighter, refusing to go down for the count despite the fact that Roark had practically set up camp beside her hospital bed for two weeks, and then rented a cabin at Evergreen for the summer, helping her recuperate. Or maybe just reassuring himself that she'd live.

A month ago he'd kissed her, promised to return, and flown back to Brussels.

She tried not to let it bother her, the fact that he'd dipped out of her life again. Yes, she received e-mails from him—chitchat about life in Brussels as he set up the charity organization his father had started, but . . . nothing about their future. And when Barb had reached out to her with an invitation to visit, take promotional pictures of their orphanage, he'd turned suddenly silent.

Which, of course, told her everything. But she didn't need Roark to hold her hand, to make her feel brave.

She could have an adventure all on her own, her hand gripped in the Lord's.

Seth had noted Roark's absence, but Amelia had closed the book on the past, and his visit yesterday, while she was packing, seemed to resonate with good-bye.

"I can't wait for you anymore, Red," he'd said, sitting on the picnic table on the deck, holding an amber maple leaf between his fingers.

"I know." She also knew his words, solemn and sad, were spoken more for himself than for her. "And you shouldn't. I'm not coming back to stay." Or for as far ahead as she could see.

He nodded, looked out over the lake. Ran the

meat of his hand across his cheek. Then gave a small smile.

His smiles had always had the power to sweep the common sense from her brain, lure her into his arms. But not today. She wrapped her arms around her waist, leaned against the railing, a good distance between them.

"We had fun, didn't we?" he said.

She nodded, her throat just a little tight. "Too much fun."

That brought a chuckle from him, probably flipping through the memories. Then he got up, walked over, and kissed her forehead. "You'll always be my girl."

"I know."

He caught her hand and squeezed. "Watch out for the snakes." He left the key chain in her hand and walked away.

Leaving her alone with the wind in the pines, the rustle of the autumn leaves, the loons calling over the water.

She shot another glance at her father, then at the airport clock.

"How long is your layover in Amsterdam?" Ingrid asked.

"A couple hours. Not long enough to see the city, sadly."

To her great relief, her father hung up, headed over. But his expression silenced them.

"That was Kyle Hueston," John said, putting a

470

hand on Ingrid's shoulder. "Amelia, the Deep Haven sheriff's office has finally identified the body you found in the ravine."

She hadn't exactly found it but—

"It's Monte Riggs. Monte's grandfather reported him missing a few months ago, but they had to send the body down to Minneapolis, and it took them this long to confirm the remains."

The silence continued as Ingrid's eyes widened, as Darek stared at his father.

Monte . . . "Wait, wasn't that the guy Raina was dating before she and Casper got back together? Didn't he and Casper have a fistfight?" Amelia said.

"Yeah," John said. "And not just once; apparently they had words at the VFW right before he went missing. There are eyewitnesses who claim Casper threatened the guy, that they exchanged blows."

"He was a jerk," Darek said.

"Darek!"

"Sorry, Mom, but it's true. Whatever Casper said to him, he had it coming."

"What was the cause of death?" Grace said, glancing at Yulia, then at Tiger, who was walking in a circle, putting his feet exactly in the tile squares.

"Not sure. Kyle says there is evidence of head trauma. But it could be exposure. There wasn't much left of him."

"How'd he get in the ravine?" Darek asked.

John blew out a breath. "Well, that's the problem. The police seem to think Casper might have had something to do with it."

A beat; then, from Ingrid, "Are they saying . . . that Monte was *murdered?*"

"And Casper is the prime suspect," John said.

"Oh, that's ludicrous," Grace said. "Casper wouldn't hurt . . . anyone . . ."

Except, landing in Amelia's brain was the very vivid scene of Casper tackling Owen only a year ago at Jace and Eden's wedding. And then the story of his brawl with Monte seven months later.

She read the same memories on the faces of her family in the silence that followed.

"I'm sure there's a perfectly reasonable explanation," Ingrid said. "And when Casper gets back, he'll clear it up."

John nodded, his mouth a grim line. "In the meantime, Amelia is off to Uganda."

Smiles, although forced. She hated to leave this way. "Maybe I shouldn't go—"

"Are you kidding me?" John stepped up, lifted her chin. "You can't say no to this opportunity. The Gundersons are thrilled to have you come and help with the orphanage. It's the perfect way to spend your prize money, and frankly, it's time. I'm tired of you watching *Doctor Who* reruns." He winked at her, then drew her into a hug. Kissed the top of her head. "As long as you don't run off any ravines or get lost in any dark alleys."

Because, well, Roark wasn't around to find her, was he? But she pushed that thought away. "I'll leave the dark alleys to Vivie. She's the one in New York." Amelia had gifted her trip to New York to Vivie, a one-way ticket back to her dreams. "But I promise to be careful, Daddy," Amelia said, kissing his leathery cheek.

Her family waited until she passed through security and gave them one last wave on the other side.

Uganda. The word held mystery and promise, a realization of the awakening she'd discovered that night in the ravine. Yes, it was only a three-month trip to start, but she'd had to leave while she still had a firm grip on her courage.

She hunkered down in her seat, watched a movie on her iPad, then slept as the plane traveled over the ocean. When they touched down in Amsterdam, she unfolded herself from the seat, stretched.

By the time she made it through passport control into the airport, she'd woken fully. She found a bathroom, freshened up, and gave herself a good once-over. Amelia Christiansen, world traveler. Missionary. Adventurer. Brave, or trying to be. Barely a scar remained from where she'd hit her head in the ravine, and her hair had grown out, almost to the middle of her back. She let it hang loose, tightened the belt on her black trench coat, and slung her backpack over her shoulder before heading into the concourse.

She snapped a few pictures of the airport hustle, bought a latte, wishing Roark had made it for her, and found her gate as her section was boarding.

Next stop, Entebbe International Airport.

She had just pulled out her neck pillow, earbuds, and iPad when a flight attendant leaned over to her seat. "Ma'am, I'm sorry; there's been a mistake."

What? No mistake—she was supposed to be here—

"You're in the wrong seat."

Amelia pulled out her boarding pass, checked it. "It says 23A."

The flight attendant nodded. "You've been moved."

Shoot. She'd wanted the window seat, had picked the exit row so she could stretch out. But she tucked her earbuds and iPad away, grabbed her carry-on and neck pillow, and eased out of the row. "Excuse me," she said to her former row-mate.

The flight attendant headed to the front of the section, then, surprisingly, into first class. She indicated a window seat.

"Here?"

"Yes, ma'am."

"Are you sure?"

"Yes, ma'am." The woman smiled, her teeth

bright against her dark face, nothing of guile in her expression.

"All right." Amelia slid into her spot.

"Would you like a beverage?"

"Uh, sure. Water."

The woman left, and Amelia tucked her bag under the seat, pulled out her accessories.

A hand reached over, holding a bottled water, and she took it, looked up to thank—

She stilled, her heart coming to a full stop in her chest as Roark St. John smiled down at her. He was dressed like a billionaire, in a crisp blue suit, white shirt, teal tie. A silver watch glinted on his wrist. Clean shaven, he'd also gotten a haircut, his curls shorter but still tempting.

And his eyes. The richest blue, twinkling, a warmth in them that slid over her, through her. Those eyes she recognized. The mischief of her playboy from Europe, the strength of the lumberjack from Deep Haven.

"Is this seat taken?"

She lifted a shoulder. "I don't—"

"It is now." He slid in next to her, still smiling. And oh, he smelled good, a hint of cherrywood and spice. He motioned to the flight attendant.

"Mr. St. John?"

"A Coke, please?"

"Right away."

"What are you doing here?" Amelia said.

"Aren't you glad to see me?" He turned to

her, the full-wattage grin burning away her shock.

Really, what could she say? "Over the moon."

"That's my girl." He leaned forward, caught her chin with his smooth fingers, and kissed her. Sweetly, just enough to restart her heart. "Wow, I missed you," he said as he backed away. "I'm so sorry I haven't written these past few weeks. I've been working nearly every moment getting Compassion Constantine up and running before I left."

"Your father's project."

"My project now. And as it works out, we have a new hotel opening in Entebbe."

"So you're . . . working on the hotel." She couldn't help the slightest deflation. She'd hoped . . . But no, she could do this without Roark.

"Not exactly." He loosened his tie as the flight attendant returned with his Coke. "We're helping fund an orphanage there, and I'm going to lend a hand. I'm teaching some classes, adding a roof to a building. Might even play some football."

"Soccer." But her heart tharrumphed. An orphanage?

"Only to you Americans." He pulled the tie off. Folded it and stuck it in his jacket pocket. Then he worked off his jacket, turned the lining to the outside, folded it, and handed it to the flight attendant. She tucked it in the overhead bin as he began to unbutton his shirt cuffs.

"Roark, you're killing me."

He laughed, and the sound of it could make her sing. "Maybe you've heard of it—Hope Children's Village?"

She couldn't suppress a smile. "Really?"

He rolled up one sleeve, then the other, over tanned, strong forearms. "Indeed."

Finally he turned to her, his expression soft. "Do you mind terribly that I'm following you across the world again? Because I can't seem to stop. You have eclipsed my world with the wonder of you, and I can't seem to break free."

The wonder of her. The warmth of his words ran through her. "It is becoming quite a habit," she said, still trying to embrace the idea of Roark in Uganda with her. Roark, returning to surprise her, flesh and blood, sitting beside her. "You moved me to first class."

"Of course I did," he said.

"You should know I'm paying my own way. I have my own resources."

"I know," he said. Then he reached out, took her hand. Opened it. "But you will indulge me sometimes, right? Perhaps a trinket here or there?" He pressed a black velvet bag into her hand.

Her breath caught as she opened it. Then wasn't sure if she should be relieved or not.

A silver bracelet and on it, charms. The Eiffel Tower, Týn Church. A pine tree. A camera.

"It's beautiful."

"It has room for more," he said. He picked it up, unlatched it, and she held out her wrist. "The question is, do you have room for me? Would you let me join you as we follow God wherever He takes us?"

She looked up, and tenderness for this amazing, brave, gentle man swept over her at the vulnerability on his handsome face, the question in his eyes.

"You do have a way of invading my world," she said, her eyes filling. "Yes, Roark. Wherever. And together." She lifted her face, and he slipped his hand around her neck. Kissed her, this time lingering, his touch hinting at every vista that awaited them.

His eyes shone as he backed away. "Good. Then you should also have this." He pulled a velvet box from his pants pocket. Opened it.

Oh. My. A silver diamond solitaire, probably too large for her finger but . . .

"Marry me? I don't care where, but please, let it be soon because I can't go another day fearing you will trundle off on some adventure without me."

She ran a finger over the diamond, then met his eyes. "I don't think I could escape you."

He touched his forehead to hers. "Is that a yes?"

"Quite right," she said.

He laughed. "Smashing." He worked out the ring and put it on her finger. "The first of many souvenirs."

As the airplane doors closed, he took her hand and wove his fingers through hers, holding tight.

As if he planned on never letting her go.

A Note from the Author

I'M NOT SURE what is harder to recover from: failing ourselves or failing God.

When we fail God, we are brought back to verses like Lamentations 3:23, which says God's mercies are new every morning. Or Romans 8:1: "There is now no condemnation for those who are in Christ Jesus." Rich, almost-unbelievable truths that saturate our broken hearts and remind us we are loved.

But when we fail ourselves, there is no love waiting to forgive us. To tell us that we are okay, that we can start over. Because, well, we are often our hardest judges, our worst critics, and short of having a second voice inside us to speak truth, we are stuck with the dark voice of our failures resounding over and over in our heads.

The worst part about truly failing ourselves is the self-doubt that lingers. When we fail ourselves, it rocks us to our foundation because we realize we aren't the people we thought we were. Maybe we've been lying to ourselves all this time.

It's this kind of failure that stops us from reaching for dreams, traps us in disastrous habits and relationships, and keeps us from ever finding our true destiny.

This is the failure that stalks both Amelia and Roark in *The Wonder of You*. I wanted to explore the different sides of self-failure—first, the kind that surprises us, teaches us about ourselves, makes us reevaluate who we are. This is the best kind of failure because if we can get back up, it makes us truer, more passionate people. It shows us who we can be when we hang on to God. This is Amelia's failure, and the choice between Seth and Roark epitomizes the two options for her future: should she stay safe or launch again?

The other side of failure is more insidious, coming from a deep-seated belief that we don't deserve happiness, that whatever we do is doomed, and should we be called to do something great, it will only end in destruction. This failure paralyzes. This failure keeps us running.

This is Roark's failure. He carries the certainty that because of his childhood choices, he will never truly live in victory. And should he let God down again, there will be no redemption for him. In short, Roark believes he is flawed, broken, and not worth saving—and we too often believe this as well.

Oh, we treat ourselves with such little grace! Such meager mercy. Left to our own devices, we would punish ourselves, retreating from the flame of God's love because we believe we don't deserve it.

Thankfully, God does not let us alone. He sees

our wretched state and sends a Pursuer to wrestle us away from our lies. To help us glimpse His great love for us, saving us out of every single failure, bringing us over and over to healing, to joy. Because that is the nature of God—He is not content to watch the ones He loves hide from all He has for them. His glory is most revealed when we drink it all in and are changed.

When we experience the wonder of His love.

See, our worth, our victory has nothing to do with us. With our failures or our efforts. It has only to do with the fact that we belong to the Father. And thus, we are forgiven. Empowered. Loved.

It's time to forgive yourself. To turn to the God who wants to save you. To be set free.

To wonder at the love of your heavenly Father and let it give you victory.

Thank you for reading the Christiansen Family series. I hope you'll stick around for Owen's story. Can a prodigal ever really come home? We'll see!

In His grace,
Susan May Warren

About the Author

SUSAN MAY WARREN is the bestselling, Christy and RITA Award–winning author of more than forty novels whose compelling plots and unforgettable characters have won acclaim with readers and reviewers alike. She served with her husband and four children as a missionary in Russia for eight years before she and her family returned home to the States. She now writes full-time as her husband runs a resort on Lake Superior in northern Minnesota, where many of her books are set.

Susan holds a BA in mass communications from the University of Minnesota. Several of her critically acclaimed novels have been ECPA and CBA bestsellers, were chosen as Top Picks by *Romantic Times*, and have won the RWA's Inspirational Reader's Choice contest and the American Christian Fiction Writers' prestigious Carol Award. Her novels *You Don't Know Me* and *Take a Chance on Me* were Christy Award winners, and five of her other books have also been finalists. In addition to her writing, Susan loves to teach and speak at women's events about God's amazing grace in our lives.

For exciting updates on her new releases, previous books, and more, visit her website at www.susanmaywarren.com.

Discussion Questions

1. In her letter, Ingrid tells Amelia, "Your challenge is to look past the view others choose for you, look past even your own limited perspective, and see the view your heavenly Father has chosen for you." What does she mean by this? In what ways is Amelia's perspective limited and short-sighted at the beginning of this book? How does her view widen over the course of the story?

2. In chapter 1, Amelia reflects, "It wasn't just her colossal embarrassment with Roark. It was that she no longer trusted her own instincts." What about her experience in Prague and her relationship with Roark undermined Amelia's trust in her own instincts? Have you ever gone through a trial that caused you to deeply question yourself and your abilities? What was the outcome? What would you say to someone who's in the middle of self-doubt?

3. After returning to Deep Haven, Amelia feels like a failure in comparison with her friends from high school, whose careers and lives

seem more successful than her own. What advice would you give her? Can you think of a time when you were tempted to compare yourself to someone else? What were the results?

4. Max and Grace are drawn to Yulia from the first time they meet her, but Max resists the idea of adopting her. Why does he feel unfit to be a father? Do you agree with his reasoning? What causes him and Grace to eventually decide to make her part of their family?

5. Is Roark at all justified in hiding his wealthy status from Amelia? Should he have told her earlier? Why doesn't he? Why does she react the way she does when she finds out? Would you have done the same?

6. In chapter 17, Ingrid tells Roark, "[God] loves us simply because He finds joy in loving us. And no amount of our running, our disobedience, our mistakes will keep that love from us. God requires nothing from us but to turn and embrace Him." Why does Roark need to hear this truth about God's love? What does he do in response? What would it look like for you to stop running and to embrace God, to accept His love and forgiveness?

7. Ingrid also says, "God's blessings fall on the wicked and the righteous alike. It's our response—our embrace or our rejection of those blessings—that determines whether they bear fruit in our lives." Was there a time in your life when you rejected a potential blessing from God? What about a time when you embraced one of God's blessings? What happened?

8. For much of the book, Amelia goes back and forth between Roark and Seth. Why is it so difficult for her to choose? What does each man represent to her? Do you think she makes the right decision in the end? Why or why not?

9. Amelia comes to a realization when she's lying injured in the ravine: "Maybe she no longer had Seth. Or Roark. But she didn't need them to be brave. She simply had to look at Jesus. Who would show up. Who had always shown up. Who, really, had never been away from her." What does it mean to "look at Jesus"? Why does it sometimes feel that God is most present with us when we are at our most helpless and vulnerable points?

10. Both Amelia and Roark are moved by the lyrics of "Be Thou My Vision." What about

this hymn connects to their personal circumstances? Why is it such a comfort to them? Can you think of a song that's been particularly meaningful to you in some season of life?

11. Several characters in this story have a connection to overseas missionary work: Roark grew up as a missionary kid; a missionary family speaks at the Christiansens' church; Amelia herself senses a call to missions in Uganda. Do you know any missionaries, or have you yourself ever considered short- or long-term missions? For you, what would be the most difficult cost of overseas missions? The greatest reward?

12. Casper feels the need to track down Owen before he can marry Raina and adopt Layla. Is this a wise decision? Why or why not? What do you think will happen if he finds Owen?

Center Point Large Print
600 Brooks Road / PO Box 1
Thorndike, ME 04986-0001 USA

(207) 568-3717

US & Canada:
1 800 929-9108
www.centerpointlargeprint.com

D